The Fortune's Folly Social Bulletin for January 1810

**Issued by Mr. Argyle, Master of Ceremonies,
The Pump Rooms, Granby Hotel,
Fortune's Folly, Yorkshire.**

The winter season has seen relatively few new visitors come to town, a relief for those ladies who have complained that Sir Montague Fortune's revival of The Dames' Tax has turned Fortune's Folly into the marriage mart of England and attracted all manner of penniless rakes and adventurers. Perhaps the ardor of these gentlemen has been dampened by the harsh weather in the north of England. If so, they are evidently too feeble to be worthy of our ladies anyway.

Amongst those who *have* returned after Christmas are Stephen, Lord Armitage, who is to wed Miss Mary Wheeler in a few weeks' time, and Miles, Lord Vickery, who has unexpectedly inherited the title of Marquis of Drummond on the untimely death of his cousin. We wish his lordship every felicitation in his new role despite the family curse that is said to afflict all the Marquises of Drummond and lead them to an early grave.

We hear that Mr. and Mrs. Dexter Anstruther are already anticipating an addition to their family and extend our congratulations to them. Mr. and Mrs. Anstruther have been wed *a very short time indeed,* but the clear air of Fortune's Folly is said to be most intoxicating and can go to the head with marvelous effects.

Sir Montague Fortune has departed Fortune's Folly for a few months' sojourn in London. He will not be missed.

There will be a ball every second Tuesday at the Granby Hotel. I look forward to welcoming you there.

NICOLA CORNICK

**is an international bestselling author and a
RITA® Award finalist. Her sensational and sexy
novels have received acclaim the world over**

"A rising star of the Regency arena."
—*Publishers Weekly*

"Nicola Cornick creates a glittering, sensual world of
historical romance that I never want to leave."
—Anna Campbell, author of *Untouched*

"Ms. Cornick has a brilliant talent for bringing
her characters to life, and embracing the reader
into her stories."
—*Romance Junkies*

Praise for Nicola's previous HQN titles

"A powerful story, rich, witty and sensual—
a divinely delicious treat."
—Marilyn Rondeau, Reviewers International Organization,
on *Deceived*

"Cornick masterfully blends misconceptions, vengeance,
powerful emotions and the realization of great love into a
touching story."
—*Romantic Times BOOKreviews,* 4 1/2 stars, on *Deceived*

"If you've liked Nicola Cornick's other books, you are sure
to like this one as well. If you've never read one—what are
you waiting for?"
—Lynn Lamy, *Rakehell,* on *Lord of Scandal*

"RITA® Award-nominated Cornick deftly steeps her latest
intriguingly complex Regency historical in a beguiling
blend of danger and desire."
—John Charles, *Booklist,* on *Unmasked*

NICOLA CORNICK

❦ THE BRIDES OF FORTUNE ❧

THE SCANDALS *of an* INNOCENT

HQN™

Recycling programs
for this product may
not exist in your area.

ISBN-13: 978-0-373-77389-3

THE SCANDALS OF AN INNOCENT

www.HQNBooks.com

Printed in U.S.A.

To the memory of William Craven, man of action, soldier of great fortune.

THE
SCANDALS
of an
INNOCENT

CHAPTER ONE

"Love, like other arts, requires experience…"
—Lady Caroline Lamb

The Village of Fortune's Folly
Yorkshire, February 1810

ALICE LISTER WAS NOT CUT OUT for a life of crime.

She had not even committed the robbery yet and already her palms were damp with anxiety and her heart was beating light and fast.

This, Alice thought, as she tried to calm her breath, *is a very big mistake.*

There was no going back. That was the coward's way. Bravely she raised her lantern to illuminate the interior of the darkened gown shop. She had broken into the workroom at the back of the premises. There was a long table with piles of fabric heaped up on one end. A half-finished gown was draped across a stool, the pale silk glimmering in the light. Paper patterns rustled and fluttered in the draft from the open window. Ribbons uncurled on the floor. Sprays of artificial flowers wilted in a corner. Lace trimmings wafted their ghostly fingers against Alice's cheek, making her jump. The whole place with its unnatural silence and its darkness made her think of a sinister fairy story in which the gowns would come to life and dance in front of her—and she would run screaming from the shop straight into the arms of the night watch. Yes indeed, burgling Madame Claudine's gown shop was not for the fainthearted.

Not that this was theft, precisely. Alice reminded herself that the wedding gown she was hunting had been bought and paid for. It would have been delivered in the normal manner had Madame Claudine not gone out of business so abruptly and shut up her shop in the face of all inquiries from her anxious clientele. The modiste had disappeared one night, leaving nothing but a pile of debts and bitter words for those of her aristocratic customers who lived on credit. The contents of Madame Claudine's gown shop had been declared the property of the moneylenders, and all the stock impounded. This was particularly unfair to Alice's friend Mary Wheeler, for Mary's father had paid the bill already with the same promptness he had paid a gentleman to marry Mary. Sir James Wheeler had been one of many to take advantage of the Dames' Tax, the wholly outrageous edict leveled the previous year by the squire of Fortune's Folly, Sir Montague Fortune. Sir Monty had discovered an ancient tax that had entitled him to half the dowry of every unmarried woman who lived in the village of Fortune's Folly—unless they wed within a twelvemonth. Sir James Wheeler had been only one of many fathers who had seen this as an opportunity to get his daughter off the shelf and off his hands, parceled away to the first fortune hunter who asked.

Mary Wheeler had been distraught to hear of the

gown shop's closure. In the months of her betrothal she had managed to persuade herself that hers was a love match despite the fact that her ghastly fiancé, Lord Armitage, had returned to London and was carousing in much the same way as he had before their betrothal. With the wedding date only a matter of weeks away, Mary had taken the whole thing as a bad omen. And to be fair, Alice thought, marrying Lord Armitage was a poor enough proposition without getting off on the wrong foot....

"Alice? Have you found it yet?" The urgent whisper brought Alice back to the present and she raised the lantern again, scanning the piles of clothing hopelessly, for there were so many gowns and they were as tumbled as though a wintry gale had blown through the shop.

"Not yet, Lizzie." Alice tiptoed across to the open window where her coconspirator, Lady Elizabeth Scarlet, was keeping watch in the passage at the side of the shop. This whole venture had been Elizabeth's idea, of course. It was she who had thought it the most marvelous scheme to go to Madame Claudine's shop and simply *take* Mary's wedding gown. After all, Lizzie had reasoned, the gown belonged to Mary and she had set her heart on wearing it at the wedding, and even if they had to break in to take it, no one would know and right was on their side.

It had been another of Lady Elizabeth's astoundingly bad ideas. Alice shook her head to have been so easily led. Naturally, once they had reached the shop it became apparent that Lizzie was too tall to squeeze through the window and it was Alice who was the one who had to break in.

"What is keeping you?" Lizzie sounded decidedly testy, and Alice felt her temper prick in response.

"I'm doing my best," she whispered crossly. "There is a mountain of gowns in here."

"You are looking for one in white silk with silver lace and silver ribbons," Lizzie reminded her. "Surely it cannot be so hard to find? How many gowns are there, anyway?"

"Only about two hundred. This is a *gown* shop, Lizzie. The clue is in the name.…"

Sighing, Alice grabbed the next pile of dresses and hurriedly sorted through them. Silver with pink trimmings. White with green embroidery…golden gauze… that was pretty…white and silver with silver ribbons— Alice snatched up the wedding gown even as Lizzie's agonized whisper floated up to her.

"Alice! Quick! Someone is coming!"

With a muttered and very unladylike curse, Alice ran for the window, squeezed through the gap at the bottom of the sash and struggled to climb out and down into the street. It was only a drop of about four feet, and she was wearing boy's britches, borrowed from the wardrobe of her brother, Lowell, which made movement a great deal freer and easier. But as she tried to ease her leg over the sill the britches caught on something and stuck fast.

"*Alice!*" Lizzie's hissing held a note of panic now. "Come on! Someone is almost upon us!" She caught Alice's arms and tugged hard. Alice heard the material of the britches rip. She wriggled free for a few painful inches and then stuck fast again. She was not a slender girl and every one of her curves currently felt as though it was squashed into too small a space. The edge of the windowsill dug painfully into her hip. She dangled there helplessly, one leg out of the window, the other on the sill. She could hear footsteps coming ever closer, their measured tread loud on the cobbles of the road.

"He will see us," Lizzie groaned.

"He will certainly *hear* you," Alice said crossly. Lizzie's idea of being quiet seemed to equate to behaving like a bull in a china shop. "If you will cease that pulling and pushing and keep still and quiet for a moment, he will pass by the end of the alley. And put the lantern out!" she added fiercely.

It was too late.

She heard the footsteps stop. There was quiet for a moment; quiet in which Alice's breathing seemed loud in her own ears and the window ledge creaked in protest beneath her weight. She lay still like a hunted animal. Instinct told her that the man, too, was watching and waiting....

"Run, Lizzie!" Alice gasped. "I am right behind you!" She gave her friend a shove that sent Lady Elizabeth stumbling off down the passage even as everything seemed to explode into noise and movement around her. A man came running out of the darkness, and Alice wrenched herself free of the ledge and tumbled headlong on top of him, wrapping them both in the silky, voluminous folds of the wedding gown as they fell to the ground. As an ambush it could scarcely have been more effective had she tried.

Alice scrambled up, lost her footing on the slippery folds of material and fell to her knees. The man was quicker. His arms went about her, scooping her up and then holding her fast against him, so that all her kicking and pummeling was quite in vain. His grip was too tight to break, as taut as steel bands about her waist and back. Her struggles were embarrassingly puny against such quiet, almost casual, strength.

"Hold still, urchin," he said. His voice was mellow and deep, and he sounded carelessly amused, but there was nothing careless in the way that he held her. Alice could tell she was not going to be able to break his grip. She also sensed by instinct that this was no drunken lord returning home after a night's entertainment at the Morris Clown Inn. There was something too powerful and purposeful about him—something too dangerous to dismiss easily.

She was in deep trouble.

Fear clawed at her chest as she frantically tried to think of a way to escape him. Her whole body was shaking with fear and panic and a desperate need to flee. She stopped struggling and went limp in his arms in an attempt to trick him into loosening his grip, but he was evidently too old a hand to fall for the ruse, for he simply laughed.

"So docile all of a sudden? Listen, boy—" He stopped.

Held so close to him, Alice could feel the hard muscles of his body tense against her own and she recognized the precise moment that he realized, despite the evidence of her attire, that she was not a boy at all.

"Well, well…" The amusement was still in his voice, but it had a different quality to it now. He shifted, his chest unyielding against the betraying softness of her breasts, his hand moving intimately over the curve of her bottom where the rip in her britches exposed rather more bare skin than she would have wanted. His grip on her slackened, not much, but enough for Alice to wrench herself from his arms and turn to run.

It was the treacherous wedding dress that foiled her again. Wrapping itself about her ankles, it tripped her so that she staggered and almost fell. The man caught her arm in a savage grip, spinning her around so that her back was against the rough brick wall of the alley. Alice gasped as the pain jolted through her, and gasped again as he deliberately brought his body into closer contact with hers, holding her pinned against the wall with his hips, his hands braced on either side of her head. She was trapped, caged. A long shiver went down her spine that was neither fear nor cold.

The man took her chin in his hand and turned her toward the pale light of the lantern. His face was only inches away from hers, the harsh lines and planes shadowed in the darkness. She could feel the beat of his heart against her breast, feel his breath against her skin and the press of his lower body, lean and hard, against hers. It filled her with a strange, unfamiliar kind of ache and a weakness she did not much care for. Alice hated to feel out of control. She had never experienced such waywardness from her body before.

The man pushed the hat roughly back from her brow, and her hair escaped its confinement and fell down about her shoulders. He brushed the tangles away from her face. Then his fingers stilled. She felt the shock rip through his body.

"Miss Lister?" There was flat disbelief in his tone.

Oh, dear. So much for her desperate hope that whoever he was, he would not be able to identify her. And she recognized him, too. Miles Vickery. She knew his voice now. She had *loved* his voice. It was so smooth and mellow Alice had sometimes thought that he could have seduced her with his words alone. He almost had.

She had been such a fool to believe even for a moment that his attentions to her had been sincere....

Even as her treacherous body responded to the touch of his hand against her cheek, the knife twisted within her as she remembered that she did not like Miles Vickery very much at all. In fact, she absolutely detested him.

Nevertheless, they stood staring at each other for what felt like a very long moment while Alice's heart beat in her throat and the heat washed through her body and left her trembling. She could not move. She could not even tear her gaze from his. She was captured in the moment by the fierce, intent look in his eyes and in the strange, aching demand of her body where it touched his.

Then a carriage rumbled across the cobbled road at the end of the passageway, and the sudden noise made them both jump. Alice took advantage of the moment to raise her elbow in a sharp and persuasive jab into Miles's ribs, and as he doubled up in pain she ducked away and ran, leaving him standing staring after her, the wedding dress still in his hand.

TWENTY MINUTES LATER, tucked up in her bed, Alice lay and watched the patterns made by the moon on the ceiling as her curtains shifted a little in the cold night breeze from the open sash window.

Lizzie had been waiting for her, full of questions. In typical melodramatic fashion she had told Alice that she had run all the way back to Alice's home, Spring House, without pausing even to draw breath and then had fretted and fidgeted for a full ten minutes before Alice had appeared for fear that her friend was lying in the street, raped, murdered or worse, whatever worse might be.

"I thought you were behind me!" Lizzie had said, nursing the cup of hot chocolate that Alice had rustled up for both of them on the kitchen hob. "You *said* you were! And then when I realized you were nowhere to be seen I did not know whether to wait or go back for you, or *what* to do!"

Alice had made some excuse about twisting her ankle and having to hop home, and that had satisfied Lizzie, who had spotted that Alice no longer had the wedding dress and was berating her for dropping it in the street. The girls had taken their cups of chocolate upstairs, tiptoeing through the quiet house so as not to wake its sleeping occupants, and Lizzie had completely failed to notice that Alice no longer appeared to be limping.

And now, lying in her bed, Alice could not really understand why she had not told her friend about Miles Vickery catching her. Perhaps it was because she did not wish to think about Miles, let alone speak about him. She had never told anyone what had happened between her and Miles the previous autumn, probably, she thought, rolling over in bed in a vain attempt to relax, because nothing *had* happened. There was nothing to think about and nothing to remember. Miles was a penniless adventurer who had set out with calculated intent to seduce her. He had failed. That was all there was to it.

Actually, that was *not* all that there was to it. Alice winced as she felt pain like an echo in the recesses of her body. She had fallen in love with Miles Vickery, with a naive, hopeless and very innocent passion. She had admired him for the honorable man that she had believed him to be, the army hero who had become a warrior for justice, working for the Home Secretary to keep the country safe. She had thought him all that was courageous and principled and daring. She had been a complete fool, for, after a couple of months of courtship, he had shown his true colors when he'd abandoned her to pursue a richer heiress.

Now that she was so thoroughly disillusioned with him, Alice could see that she had imagined Miles to be the man she wanted him to be. She had invented a hero, who was very different from the reality. For in reality Miles Vickery had been a callous philanderer who had only been interested in her money. She still felt physically sick when she thought about the wager he had made. Thirty guineas against her virtue.

Alice punched her pillow rather violently. Miles had deserved that jab in the ribs. She wished she had stabbed him all the harder. There were several tricks she had learned when she was a housemaid to enable her to deter amorous gentlemen. Miles deserved to experience every one of them, especially the knee in the groin.

She rolled onto her back and stared up at the shadowy canopy of the bed.

Fortune hunter, rake, unscrupulous deceiver… Miles's strength and apparent sincerity had almost been her undoing the previous year. Alice had had to fend for herself from an early age, and to have someone strong and steadfast to rely on had felt ridiculously seductive. But that had been the point of Miles's actions, of course. He had been set on seducing her into marriage for her fortune and she, silly girl that she was, had almost fallen for it. Strange that in some ways she could be so wise in the ways of the world—what servant girl could fail to see the less salubrious side of life—and yet when it had come to her own heart she had been so utterly naive.

She turned her cheek against the cool linen of the pillow. She could not sleep. Her mind was too full of Miles—of the sensation of his hands on her and his body hard against hers and the heat and the power and the strength in him. It did not seem to help that she told herself Miles was an experienced man who had deliberately used his amatory skill to lead her astray. Her wanton body responded to him regardless. It betrayed her at every turn. It did not care that Miles was a scoundrel. Her body wanted him even as she told herself that she hated him.

Alice knew all about physical passion even though she had never experienced it herself. She had been brought up on a farm and had gone into service early. She had not been a cosseted, protected debutante, and as a servant she had seen enough licentious behavior to leave her with few illusions about lust. She understood her own nature and knew full well that it was within her to behave with absolute passionate abandonment if she chose to give herself to a man. There would be no shame in it—not with the right man. But that man would be honest, truthful, respectful and trustworthy. All of which ruled out Miles Vickery. In fact, any one of those ruled out Miles Vickery.

Alice rolled over again, seeking to quell the flame that burned in the deepest part of her. Miles had proved himself dishonest and untrustworthy, and she would do well to remember that fact. She must ignore her physical response to him. It meant nothing and it was dangerous.

Alice shivered a little beneath the covers. She had not expected to see Miles again. Although she had heard a rumor that he was back in Yorkshire on some business connected with his work for the government, she had imagined it would be a fleeting visit and that he would soon return to London. Evidently it was the place that suited him best. After he had failed to secure Miss Bell, the nabob's heiress, in marriage, he had cut a swathe through the bawdy houses of the capital and had set up one of the most famous courtesans in the city as his *inamorata*. Lizzie Scarlet had told her all about it, and Alice had pretended that she had not cared. But she had cared. She had cared dreadfully. It had hurt her so much to think of Miles's profligate ways when once she had naively imagined he had some feelings for her. It had been a salutary lesson in the pitfalls of imagining herself in love. She was never going to make that mistake again.

Alice thumped her pillow into final submission and rolled over onto her side in a vain attempt to sleep. It was a great pity that Miles had recognized her tonight. She wondered what he would do. When she had heard the gossip about his despicable wager, she had written to him to demand that he never approach her again. Her pride had prompted her to tell him what she thought of him and she had confidently expected never to hear from him again. Now, though, she had a suspicion that he might seek her out to ask her what on earth she had been doing robbing a gown shop in the middle of the night. He was, despite his shameful behavior, still an officer of the Crown, with certain responsibilities. And she was, indubitably, a criminal.

Alice wriggled uncomfortably. She was well aware

that she was now in Miles's power, and the ways in which he might choose to exert that power made her shiver. Yes indeed, robbing the gown shop had been a dangerous mistake and now she knew she was going to have to pay.

CHAPTER TWO

"WHERE ON EARTH did you get to?" Dexter Anstruther
and Nat Waterhouse looked up curiously as Miles
Vickery reentered the salon of the Granby, the most respectable hotel in Fortune's Folly. Miles and his colleagues had been talking business late into the night
and had chosen the Granby over the rather more
dubious pleasures of the Morris Clown Inn because,
as Nat said, if they had met at the Morris Clown then
every criminal in Yorkshire would have known their
business within the hour. In contrast, the staff at the
Granby were discreet, even if they were glancing ostentatiously at the clock and barely stifling their yawns.
The other guests, a couple of half-pay officers and a
respectable, gentrified couple, had retired to bed long
since. Fortune's Folly out of the spa season was as in-
hospitable as the grave. Not even hardened fortune
hunters had chosen to spend the winter in the snow-
bound Yorkshire dales, though no doubt they would
flock back in spring when the weather improved in
order to take advantage of Sir Montague Fortune's
Dames' Tax and find a local heiress to wed.

By then, Miles thought, he would have stolen a
march on all the others and carried off the richest prize
in the Fortune's Folly marriage mart. His recent, un-

expected and wholly unwelcome inheritance of the Marquisate of Drum had left him with a monstrous pile of debt—twice his original commitment—and so once again he intended to pay court to Miss Alice Lister, a former housemaid whose eccentric employer had left her the magnificent sum of eighty thousand pounds when she had died the previous year.

Alice's inheritance had caused a sensation among Yorkshire society who could not decide whether to cut her dead for her humble birth or embrace her for her money. Miles had not suffered from any such dilemma. A fortune like Alice's was there for the taking, and since Alice herself was so pretty, taking *her* into the bargain would be a positive pleasure. He had set out to seduce her with a single-minded intent and had very nearly succeeded. But then he had made a strategic error—he had heard of an even greater prize, a London heiress with one hundred thousand pounds to her name, and he had abandoned Alice's conquest for the greater reward. He had thought about it for all of five minutes, ruthlessly weighing his lust for Alice and the work he had already done to win her against the prospect of claiming Miss Bell's one hundred thousand pounds. Miss Bell's money had won, of course. And he had quenched his lust elsewhere.

Except that holding Alice in his arms tonight had reminded him of just how much he had wanted her. There was something about her that aroused some very basic instincts in him, instincts other than greed for her money, of course. Tonight she had smelled heavenly, of roses and honey, rather than the heavy, manufactured perfumes preferred by the courtesans he had known. The scent had clung to her hair, which, once he had dispensed with her hat, had glowed a glorious pale silver color in the moonlight. Alice was small in terms of height, but she was rounded rather than slender, and her body had been curved, soft and yielding against the hardness of his. Some people might consider Alice plump—in fact some society matrons, looking for things to disparage about the housemaid-turned-heiress, had criticized Alice's robust peasant build and commented on how useful such sturdiness must have been when she was turning mattresses and beating carpets. Miles had no criticisms to make at all when it came to Alice's figure. She might not be convention-ally beautiful but she was strikingly pretty with the promise of something sensual within. The fact that her sensuality was deliciously unawakened only made her more of a temptation to him. He had a primitive urge to be the one to waken all that promise.

He shifted in his chair as he remembered the gentle curves of Alice's body molding themselves so confid-ingly to his. He had been instantly aroused, trapped by a sensuality so hot and fierce he had wanted to strip those boy's clothes off her there and then, and take her against the wall.

His ribs gave a painful twinge, dampening his ardor most effectively. In order to get away from him, the little minx had pulled a trick that would not have dis-graced a pickpocket from the stews of London. He supposed that as a servant, Alice would need to know such ruses to defend her virtue. He would do well to remember that in future before he was felled with a painful knee in the groin.

"I was merely taking the air," he said, to looks of patent disbelief from his friends. "Too much claret."

"You were so long we thought you had been taking the maidservant at the Morris Crown, never mind the air," Dexter observed.

"And what is that?" Nat followed up on Dexter's comment, pointing at the rather grubby wedding gown in Miles's hands. "Miles, old fellow, I think the inheritance of another fifty thousand of debt along with the Drum title is turning your mind."

"I found it in the street," Miles said, looking at the dress and deliberately neglecting to add that he had found one of the Fortune's Folly heiresses attached to it. "It is a wedding gown," he added. He cast it over the arm of the chair and reached for the brandy bottle. He would reunite Alice with the gown in the morning, and ask her what the devil she had been doing. She had given him the perfect excuse to call—and the perfect weapon to use against her in his negotiations to persuade her into marriage. His previous abandonment of her was a rather large stumbling block to his plans, for he doubted that she would be very susceptible to his suit as a result, and her recent discovery of the wager he had made against her virtue was even more unfortunate. The letter she had sent him had spelled out her feelings most precisely:

I never had the remotest inclination to fall prey to your somewhat tarnished charm, Lord Vickery, and when I heard about your sordid wager I could only congratulate myself on seeing you from the first as nothing more than a squalid fortune hunter with no saving graces whatsoever.

Miss Lister, Miles thought, had quite a way with words, far more so than any other servant girl he had ever come across. Not that talking had been what he was interested in when he had dallied with maidservants in the past....

At least he had leverage now. He would stoop to blackmail if he had to do so. Alice's fortune would be sufficient to wipe out the majority of his debt and stave off the most pressing of his creditors for a little while. And if it meant that a former housemaid became Marchioness of Drummond, well, her money for his title was a fair bargain.

"I'm surprised you recognize such a thing as a wedding gown," Dexter said with a grin. "Marriage isn't exactly your forte, is it, old fellow?"

Miles shot him an unfriendly look. Dexter was so hopelessly in love with Miles's cousin Laura that he never ceased to extol the virtues of wedlock in what Miles considered to be a deeply boring manner. To Miles's mind it was ridiculous even to consider that Dexter and Laura had something valuable. When he wed he fully intended to spend as little time as possible with his wife. That was his idea of a happy marriage. Love for a woman was a weakness in his opinion, the most pointless emotion that existed. It made a man too vulnerable. He had no use for or interest in love at all and had cut it out of his life when he had quarreled with his father and walked away from his family at the age of eighteen to join the army. If once he had had a heart, it was long gone.

"Just because you cannot help but preach the merits of a happy alliance, Dexter—" he began.

"Gentlemen," Nat intervened, "we are here to discuss what we are to do about Tom Fortune's escape from Newcastle jail, not to argue the toss about the benefits of marriage. We need to recapture Fortune as quickly as possible, and since you were both instrumental in arresting him in the first place, we also need to consider the possibility that he may bear a grudge against you and come seeking revenge."

"Thank you for the warning, Nathaniel," Miles said, downing a glass of brandy and savoring the taste. "I imagine there are any number of men who would not mourn if something terminal happened to me."

"Cuckolded husbands," Dexter murmured, "outraged fathers. Does not your inheritance of the Marquisate of Drum bring with it a family curse, Miles? I seem to remember hearing some stories. This could be the moment it carries you off—"

"I don't believe in family curses," Miles said.

"Your mother does," Nat pointed out. "I remember thinking it most unusual for a bishop's wife to be so superstitious. I am surprised that she has not yet arrived in Yorkshire to warn you of the dangers of the Curse of Drum."

"God forbid," Miles said. He had been virtually estranged from his family since he had left eleven years before, and he had no intention of letting his mother interfere in his life now. "She is safely in Kent," he added. "I doubt she will ever venture this far north. She considers Yorkshire to be a foreign country."

"Strange about the Curse of Drum, though," Dexter said. "So many of the previous marquises died young and in horrible circumstances."

"Coincidence," Miles said shortly.

"The twelfth marquis was struck down by the sweating sickness," Nat mused.

"There was a lot of it about that year."

"The thirteenth marquis was run over by a carriage…." Dexter murmured.

"He was always very careless when crossing the street," Miles countered.

"And your predecessor, Freddie, burned to death in that brothel."

"Freddie was such a roué that he was destined to die in bed one way or another," Miles snapped. He had no time for superstition, but a rehearsal of the deaths of all sixteen previous marquises of Drum was not a happy event. "Can we please get back to business?"

"Very well." Dexter settled back in his chair and accepted the change of subject Miles so clearly wanted. "Extraordinary that we all thought it was Warren Sampson who pulled the strings around here when all indications now seem to point to the fact that it was Tom Fortune who was the master criminal. And now that Fortune is free, it will be the devil of a job to capture him again."

"He bribed the prison guard, I suppose?" Miles said. When he and Dexter had arrested Tom Fortune for murder the previous autumn it had been on the grounds that he had killed Warren Sampson, a local industrialist with a very murky reputation whom the Home Secretary had suspected of being involved in all sorts of criminal dealings. Further investigation had suggested, however, that it was Tom Fortune who had been the leader of Sampson's men, and that he had used Sampson as a decoy.

"Either bribed him or threatened him," Nat agreed. "And since then there has been no word of him. He has gone to ground."

"He will be biding his time," Miles said. "Is there anyone who might have heard from him?"

"Sir Montague certainly wouldn't give his brother the time of day," Dexter said, "so I doubt Tom will have looked to him for help." He looked at Nat. "I doubt that Lady Elizabeth would have any sympathy for him, either—not after his treatment of her friend Miss Cole."

"Certainly not," Nat agreed.

"Miss Cole…" Miles said thoughtfully. "Since Tom Fortune seduced her and she carries his child, he might try to get in touch with her. Where is she now?"

A frown settled on Dexter's brow. "The Duke and Duchess of Cole threw her from the house when it became apparent that she was increasing. They wanted her to go abroad and have the child in secret but Lydia refused. There was the most appalling scandal. You missed most of this, Miles, being in London, but it was the *on dit* of Fortune's Folly all winter."

Miles grimaced. He could well imagine the outrage and horror with which the ghastly Duchess of Cole would have greeted the news of her daughter's disgrace. There would have been no kindness or sympathy for Lydia at Cole Court. Her fall from virtue would have been roundly condemned.

"Laura offered her a home with us," Dexter continued, "but she has found her own pregnancy difficult this time, and Lydia did not wish to be an added burden, nor to add to our financial problems."

He looked at Nat. "I believe that Lady Elizabeth also offered Miss Cole a home at Fortune Hall, did she not?"

"She did," Nat confirmed, "but Sir Monty refused to countenance it. He said that since Miss Cole had not seen fit to give herself and her dowry in respectable wedlock, she must live with the consequences of her immoral actions."

"Monty is a narrow-minded fool," Miles said dispassionately. "It was his brother who seduced an innocent girl in the first place."

"True," Nat said, "but there are always plenty of hypocrites in situations like this."

"Poor girl," Dexter said. "It is hardly as though she flaunts herself! No one has seen or heard a word from her since she went to stay with Miss Lister."

"Miss Lister?" Miles said, startled. He put his glass down with a jerk. "Lydia Cole is staying with Alice Lister?"

"Both Miss Cole and Lady Elizabeth are staying with Miss Lister at Spring House," Nat said. "Monty is up in London at present, so Mrs. Lister chaperones both the girls around."

"It was brave of Miss Lister to give Miss Cole shelter when there are people who already cut her dead because of her own background," Miles said. He had noticed the previous autumn the way in which snobs like Faye Cole had drawn aside to avoid speaking to Alice because of her humble origins. No doubt her daily life was full of these little pinpricks of spite and disapproval. "We should speak to Miss Cole," he added. "She may be the only one who can lead us to Tom Fortune."

Nat shook his head. "I doubt she would agree to see any of us. She refuses all company."

"Then we need to speak with Miss Lister instead," Miles said. "Apart from anything else, Miss Cole might be in danger."

Dexter gave him a searching look. "Does that trouble

you, Miles?" he said dryly. "You are not known for your sympathetic qualities."

"No, it doesn't trouble me personally," Miles said, "but it is likely to be influential in persuading Miss Lister to convince her friend to speak with us. If we impress upon her that Tom might be a threat to Lydia—"

"We can frighten both girls and use them to get to Tom Fortune," Nat finished. "Nice work, Miles."

"We cannot afford to be scrupulous," Miles pointed out.

"Miles is right," Dexter said, "much as I deplore his methods, he is, as usual, correct."

"Thank you, Dexter," Miles said acerbically. "Nat, will you prepare the ground with Lady Elizabeth? I will speak to Miss Lister. I think we need to make a few discreet enquiries first before we tell them that Fortune has escaped."

"Agreed," Nat said. "The perfect opportunity for you, Miles."

Miles raised a sardonic eyebrow. "Construe?"

"To renew your attentions to Miss Lister," Nat said, with a mocking smile. "Now that you are so utterly sunk in debt, you will be needing a rich heiress more than ever."

"That," Miles said, "is exactly what I thought, too."

Dexter almost choked on his brandy. "I'm sorry," he said, when he had recovered his breath, "but which part of Miss Lister's scathing rejection of your suit did you not understand, Miles?"

Miles shrugged. "It is unfortunate that I was obliged to abandon my previous pursuit of Miss Lister—"

"Unfortunate?" Dexter's brows almost disappeared into his fair hair. "You dropped her for a richer heiress!"

"And even more inopportune that my courtship of Miss Bell did not come to fruition—"

"She threw you over for an earl."

"And likewise extremely annoying that Sir Montague chose to tell Miss Lister of my ill-advised wager on her virtue," Miles continued smoothly, "but I am certain that I can persuade her to accept me all the same."

"If I were a betting man," Nat said, lips twitching, "which I am not, as I have seen the predicament it has got you into, Miles, I would make a wager that you have not a hope in hell of pulling this off. Miss Lister is no fool and she knows now that she cannot trust you an inch."

Miles shrugged again. He drained his glass and picked up the wedding dress. It felt cool and silky soft against his fingers. The perfume of honey and roses seemed to cling to it, reminding him of Alice and the softness of her hair against his fingers and the scent of her skin. It raised an echo of primitive arousal in him. He wanted Alice Lister. It was a simple matter of physical attraction. And he wanted her money. That was a simple matter of economics.

"We shall see," he said. "I have an ace or two up my sleeve."

CHAPTER THREE

"THERE IS A GENTLEMAN to see you, ma'am." Marigold, the youthful housemaid, dropped Alice a respectful curtsy. "Shall I show him in, ma'am?"

"Who is it, Marigold?" Alice asked. Having once been a servant herself, she absolutely hated employing other people to wait on her and would frequently do their work herself. If she was near the front door when a caller arrived, she would answer it. If she saw dust on the mantelpiece, she would clean it. Her mother was forever chiding her that she did not behave as a lady should.

"I don't know, ma'am." Marigold looked suddenly apprehensive, caught out failing in the execution of her duty. "He did not say."

"Always ask a caller to give their name," Alice said, smiling reassuringly at the girl at the same time so that Marigold would know she was not angry with her. "You may show him in anyway, but please remember for next time."

"I do wish you would permit me to change that girl's name," Mrs. Lister said as the maid sped away. "Marigold is a wildly unsuitable appellation for a housemaid. It is far too pretty and will give the girl ideas above her station. Mary would be more acceptable."

"Mama!" Alice said sharply. "We have had this discussion before. Marigold's name is Marigold and that is how it stays. It is not our place to change someone's given name and call them something entirely different."

"Why not?" Mrs. Lister countered. "Lady Membury called you Rose when you were in service."

"Precisely," Alice said. "I hated it. My name is Alice."

"Rose is a delightful name." Mrs. Lister said.

Her mama was missing the point as usual, Alice thought. It seemed strange to her that the unexpected inheritance of a large fortune had changed her character not at all—at least, she thought it had not—but that it had changed her mother almost out of recognition. Margaret Lister had once been a tenant farmer's widow who struggled to make ends meet and feed her family. Alice's legacy from her employer Lady Membury had changed all that. Alice's younger brother, Lowell, now ran the tenant farm whilst Mrs. Lister lived in this smart villa in Fortune's Folly. There had been elocution lessons that had almost succeeded in smoothing out Mrs. Lister's broad Yorkshire vowels; there had been visits to the dressmaker and the purchase of gowns with copious frills and furbelows, so different from the plain, serviceable work clothes Mrs. Lister had worn before. Most of all there had been the endless nagging of Alice to ensure that she made a marriage to a titled gentleman. Mrs. Lister had been cock-a-hoop that so many aristocratic fortune hunters had courted her daughter and furious when Alice had rejected each and every one of them. And then she had been desolated that the stream of aristocratic callers had ceased. Very few people came to call now, demonstrating to Alice more effectively than any cruel words that she had only been welcomed in Fortune's Folly society because of her money, and now that it was clear she was not going to bestow it on some greedy, penurious nobleman she was not welcome at all.

"I expect that this will be another marriage proposal," Mrs. Lister said now. "Oh, Alice, you must take this one, no matter who it is! Please! Sir Montague will take half your fortune under the Dames' Tax in six months' time if you do not wed! Besides, unless you marry a lord no one in Fortune's Folly will ever speak to us again! As it is, no one calls on us—"

"Mrs. Anstruther calls," Alice pointed out. "She used to be a duchess. And Lady Elizabeth is living here with us. She is an earl's daughter and half sister to a baronet." She sighed at her mother's obstinate expression. "We cannot force people to accept us, Mama," she said. "You should know by now that money cannot buy everything."

"But why not?" Mrs. Lister wailed. She patted the enormous diamond necklace that she was wearing like an armored chest plate. "I have all *this!* I am *at least* as rich as the Duchess of Cole, so why does she not acknowledge me?"

Alice shook her head gently. Mrs. Lister seemed incapable of accepting that she could buy as many diamonds as she liked, she could order a dozen sets of china, she could paint the ceiling of the dining room with gold leaf—which she had done—she could even have her bedroom decorated with Chinese wallpaper featuring painted dragons, and still no one would see her as anything other than a *nouveau riche* arriviste to be looked upon by old money and old titles.

"Mama," Alice said gently, "you are worth more than ten of the Duchess of Cole, and I do not mean in monetary terms—" She broke off, for Mrs. Lister was not listening. She was wearing the same puzzled and hurt expression that Alice had seen on her face before. She had lost the society of her own friends when she had gone up in the world, but now she had nothing to replace it. All the invitations from high society that she had anticipated had never materialized. Alice's heart ached for her because, for all her snobbery, Mrs. Lister was lonely and unhappy.

Mrs. Lister grabbed Alice's teacup. "Now, let me see…"

"Oh, Mama," Alice said. Her mother had read tea leaves all her life, a skill she learned from *her* mother who had learned it from her mother before her and so on back into the mists of family history. Mrs. Lister took the cup in her left hand and swirled the dregs around three times in a clockwise direction before overturning the cup in the saucer. She held it down for a few seconds before righting it again and setting the handle toward herself as she peered into the depths.

"A parasol!" she declared triumphantly. "A new lover."

"It looks like a mushroom to me," Alice said, peering at the splodge of tea leaves in the bottom of her cup. "An upside-down mushroom, signifying frustration— at yet another man courting me for my money." She had fended off nineteen marriage proposals in the past six months, all from the fortune hunters who had flocked to Fortune's Folly after Sir Montague Fortune had revived the ancient Dames' Tax, requiring that all the village spinsters should marry within a twelve-month or forfeit half their fortune to him.

"The Marquis of Drummond, ma'am," Marigold said, from the doorway.

Alice heard her mother give a little hiss of satisfaction at the news that the visitor was no less than a marquis. No one of a rank higher than an earl had previously come to pay court.

"It is Lord Vickery," Mrs. Lister whispered loudly in Alice's ear, "come to renew his addresses to you. I had heard that he had inherited the Drummond title. I knew he would not be able to keep away from you, now he has returned to Yorkshire."

Alice turned to see Miles Vickery enter the room. Her heart was racing in a most unfamiliar fashion, her breathing was constricted and butterflies fluttered frantically in her stomach. She fought a desperate urge to run away. This, she told herself sternly, was entirely due to the uncomfortable mixture of guilt and anxiety that her escapade at the gown shop had roused in her. It certainly had nothing to do with Miles himself.

For a moment she found herself wondering if Miles did indeed possess the audacity to renew his attentions to her, for rumor had it that his finances were now in an even more parlous state than they had been in the autumn. In fact, he probably needed to marry at least two heiresses, let alone one, since he had inherited the Drummond debts to add to his own. She thought that he would need to have the hide of a bull elephant even to consider making his addresses to her, but perhaps he was impertinent enough to think that having almost succumbed to his charm once, she would be an easy mark. She drew herself up a little straighter. She would soon remind him that she despised him for his utter lack of respect for her.

Miles came forward and bowed first to Mrs. Lister and then to Alice. He was impeccably dressed with a casual elegance that Alice knew could only be achieved with a great deal of time, and with money he did not have. His coat of blue superfine fitted his broad shoulders to perfection. His brown hair was faultlessly disordered in the windswept style. His linen was an immaculate white, a striking contrast to the golden tan of his skin. His boots had a high polish. And in his hazel eyes was the same wicked, devil-may-care spark that had almost stolen her foolish, susceptible heart back in the autumn.

He smiled at her and Alice felt that traitorous heart skip a beat. She quickly averted her gaze from Miles's face, and her eye fell on the rather grubby wedding gown he was carrying. It was folded neatly but looked rather the worse for wear. Alice hastily averted her gaze again, desperately searching for somewhere safe to look. She could not look at Miles—he was too disturbing—and she did not wish to display any interest whatsoever in the wedding gown. She fixed her eyes very firmly on the clock on the mantelpiece.

"My lord!" Mrs. Lister was making up in effusiveness for everything that Alice was failing to say. "What a very great pleasure to see you again! You will take refreshment? A pot of tea?"

"Lord Vickery will not be staying, Mama," Alice said quickly, forestalling any answer that Miles might otherwise have given. She turned back to Miles with a quick swish of her skirts and met the look of quizzical amusement on his face. Many men of rank would have been horribly affronted by her ungracious words, she knew. It was one of the disconcerting things about Miles that it seemed almost impossible to offend him.

"You did not receive my letter, Lord Vickery?" she said coldly.

A delicious smile crept into Miles's hazel eyes. Alice could feel the color rising in her cheeks. It sprang from sheer annoyance, or so she assured herself. Annoyance was a very heated emotion.

"I did," he said, his lazy, masculine drawl very much in evidence.

"Then it seems unaccountable bad manners that you would approach me again when I had expressly asked you not to!" Alice snapped. "I never wanted to set eyes on you again."

"Oh, but you were angry with Lord Vickery when he was only a baron," Mrs. Lister interposed helpfully. "Now that he is a marquis all is forgiven."

"Now he is a marquis I daresay he is no more a gentleman than he was before," Alice said crossly. "Please, Mama, leave this to me. Lord Vickery—"

"I came to bring you this," Miles said, holding out the wedding gown, "and to beg a few words in private, if I may."

"That is out of the question," Alice began, but in the same moment her mother, that most compliant of chaperones, beamed and hurried toward the door.

"Of course!" Mrs. Lister said. "I am sure you have something very particular to say to Alice. I shall be in the parlor if you wish to speak with me afterward, Lord Vickery. A marchioness!" Alice heard her add, as she whisked out of the room. "Eight strawberry leaves in the coronet!"

"It is *four* strawberry leaves for a marquis, Mama!" Alice called after her. "Eight for a duke."

She saw Miles laughing and despite herself could

not prevent a small, embarrassed smile in return. "Oh, dear. I do apologize. Mama seems to exist on a different plane where every titled gentleman is embraced as the perfect prospective son-in-law."

"She is very anxious to see you wed," Miles said. "Why would that be?"

Alice moved away, avoiding his surprisingly perspicacious gaze. "She imagines that marriage into the aristocracy would provide security for all of us," she said carefully. Some of Mrs. Lister's aspirations were based on snobbery, but at their core was an unshakable fear that she and Alice might once again be plunged into penury.

"I suppose she wants you to have the type of security that your family has never had before," Miles hazarded. "Based on inherited rights and privileges—"

"Rather than the endless need to work one's fingers to the bone for a pittance on a farm, or in domestic service," Alice finished for him. "Precisely. Poor Mama, she so longs to be accepted in society and cannot understand why we are not. She thinks that marriage to a man of rank will solve all problems."

"You must have had many offers," Miles said. "Why have you not taken one?"

"I do not care to be wed for my money by a man who otherwise deplores having a one-time housemaid as a wife," Alice said coldly. She took a seat, realizing a second too late, as Miles sat down, as well, that by her actions she had tacitly encouraged him to stay. "But that cannot be of any interest to you, Lord Vickery," she said. She looked at the wedding gown, which was now drooping rather forlornly over the arm of Miles's chair. "I thank you for returning the gown to me. Now you may go."

Miles sat back in the chair and stretched out his legs, showing every sign of settling in for a long chat in direct contradiction of her words. "Not so fast, Miss Lister," he murmured. A rather disquieting smile curved his lips. "I am not at all sure that as an officer of the law I should be returning stolen property to you."

Alice felt ruffled. It was not a sensation she was accustomed to feeling. As the elder child, she had always been the sensible one. She never got into trouble.

"The gown was bought and paid for," she said defiantly. She knew she was blushing.

"It may well have been," Miles said, "but then it was removed from the shop by theft."

"The shop had gone out of business without honoring its customers' purchases! Madame Claudine is the one who has cheated her customers!"

"Your case would not hold water for a moment in a court of law, I fear," Miles drawled. "Would you like me to be a character witness for you, Miss Lister, and protest that you were suffering from a moment of madness?"

"No, thank you," Alice said crossly. "All I require is for you to hand it over, promise to keep quiet and go away."

"You ask a great deal," Miles said. "The very least you owe me is an explanation. Is the wedding gown for Miss Cole?"

Alice was startled. "For Lydia? No, of course not! How could it be when Tom Fortune is in prison?" She sighed. "It is Mary Wheeler's wedding gown. If you must know, Mary was inconsolable when Madame Claudine's business closed, and she took it as an omen that her marriage was doomed from the start."

"It probably is," Miles murmured. "Stephen Armitage is a scoundrel."

"Well," Alice said, "Lizzie and I tried to make her see that he is a blackguard but it did no good, for the foolish girl is in love with him. So what could we do—" She stopped, realizing that she had somehow managed to implicate Lady Elizabeth Scarlet in the conspiracy as well now.

"It's all right," Miles said reassuringly. "I know Lady Elizabeth was party to your housebreaking last night. I heard you address her. I hope that you both arrived home safely?"

"Perfectly, I thank you." Alice shifted in her seat. This conversation was not going in the direction she had intended and she appeared to have no control over it at all. The clock chimed the quarter hour, reminding her of the fact that Miles had been there quite a while already. She really had to be rid of him soon. Even her mother, with her rather idiosyncratic views on chaperonage, would not tolerate a prolonged private interview. Everyone would be imagining that they were *consummating* a marriage in here, never mind arranging one.

"I wish you would not call it housebreaking and… and theft!" she said, knowing she sounded guilty. "We were merely trying to help Mary."

"And very laudable, too," Miles approved. "But still illegal."

"Then pray give the gown back," Alice said, "and I will undertake never to come up with such a foolish plan ever again."

"I don't suppose you *did* come up with it," Miles said, once again showing a flash of perception that disturbed Alice. "This has all the hallmarks of Lady

Elizabeth's rather wayward planning. She never was one to think matters through. Where is she this morning? I understand that she is staying here at Spring House with you?"

"She has gone riding with Lord Waterhouse," Alice said. "Now that Tom is imprisoned and she has fallen out with Sir Montague, Lizzie says the earl is the closest thing to a brother that she has."

She saw Miles's firm mouth twitch into a cynical smile. "One hopes that she will wake up to the falseness of that notion before too long," he said. "It is plain to everyone that she is in love with him."

There was an awkward pause. The sun had crept around the room now and was falling directly on Alice's chair. The fire crackled and hissed in the grate. Alice felt very hot and bothered. She could not for the life of her see why Miles's casual reference to Lizzie being in love with Nat Waterhouse should make her feel so uncomfortable. Nor could she see why it should remind her of Miles holding her fast against the wall the previous night with the shocking, intimate press of his lower body against hers. A sensation that was sweet and warm pooled deep inside her, making her want to squirm in her chair. The sweat prickled at her hair. She knew her face would be all red and shiny. It really should not be this hot in February. There was something quite disturbingly unseasonable about it.

"I believe that Miss Cole is living here with you, too?" Miles asked, breaking the silence. He looked very cool and unrumpled, lounging in his chair. The sunlight struck along the clean, hard line of his jaw and lit his hazel eyes. It was strange, Alice thought, that for all his elegance he still looked virile and tough; the perfection of his tailoring seemed to emphasize rather than detract from that dangerous masculinity. For some reason, looking at him made Alice feel hotter still. She, in contrast to his coolness, felt like a crumpled rag and thought that she might spontaneously combust at any moment.

"Yes, yes, she is." Alice jumped to her feet. "It is very warm in here, isn't it?"

"I had not noticed it," Miles said. "Miss Cole is well?"

"As well as can be expected under the circumstances," Alice said. "She prefers not to go into company."

"So she never sees anyone?"

Alice shook her head. "Never."

She was always extremely careful of discussing Lydia's situation. When Lydia had first come to live with her at Spring House the place had been besieged by scandal seekers come to gawk and gossip. Poor Lydia had hidden away in terror and Alice had been appalled by the visitors' capacity for cruelty. It had been like a freak show with people lining up in the hope of seeing the disgraced, pregnant daughter of the Duke of Cole. These days Lydia seldom went beyond the garden and would sit reading for hours on end, or gazing raptly into space in a way that made Alice feel worried for her sanity. She and Lizzie tried to draw her friend out but sometimes it was as though Lydia inhabited a different world.

Alice threw up the sash on the window and a blast of cold air, directly from the moors, whistled into the room and almost extinguished the fire. "That is much better," she said with relief, shivering.

Miles raised his brows. "Perhaps you require a drink, Miss Lister. A restorative cup of tea? You will not feel so mortified over your criminal activities once you have had a cup, of that I am sure."

"I am *not* a criminal," Alice said. She slammed the sash closed and spun around. "The only thing that pains me is your presence, Lord Vickery, but if we have resolved the situation with regard to the wedding gown you may be on your way."

"Of course," Miles said. He stood up, too, but rather than moving toward the door he walked purposefully toward her instead. Alice's throat dried. How was it possible to dislike Miles so intensely and yet find his physical presence so overwhelmingly attractive? she wondered desperately. Whatever the reason, it was most uncomfortable.

"There was one other thing," Miles said softly, when he was close enough to her to revive all the hot shivery feelings that Alice had just banished with a blast of cold winter air. "It concerns my proposal of marriage to you."

Alice's heart did another breathless little flip. She felt shocked and dizzy. Then she felt furious, more incensed than she could remember feeling in a very long time. She looked at him. He met her gaze with complete equanimity. So it was true, Alice thought. Miles Vickery *did* possess the extraordinary arrogance to think he could simply walk in here and resume his courtship where he had left off. He thought he could consign the wager on her virtue, his pursuit of a richer heiress and his *affaire* with a notorious courtesan to the past, and simply make her an offer.

"You are deluded, my lord," she said politely, "and your conceit knows no bounds. There is no proposal, nor ever will be. Our previous relationship makes a mockery of such an idea."

"You concede that we had a relationship, then?" Miles said, brows raised.

Alice made an irritable gesture. She did not understand why he was persisting with this unless it was out of a desire to provoke her. In that he was succeeding admirably.

"We knew each other," she snapped. "Our... acquaintance...was at an end when you left Yorkshire last time, and I have no desire to revive it." The anger she had tried so hard to suppress suddenly jetted up. Be damned to restraint and good manners. She was a servant girl not a lady and he deserved a piece of her mind.

"Truly, Lord Vickery," she said, "do you think I am so poor a creature with so little self-respect as to give myself and my fortune to a man who courted me for my money alone, who made a wager to seduce me into marriage and who subsequently departed for London without so much as a word in order to woo a richer prize? I would rather wed a...a *snake* than marry you! There is not one honest bone in your body. You will be telling me next that your time in London in the arms of some *harlot* made you realize just how much you had come to esteem me, and so you hurried back here hotfoot to profess your undying love."

She stopped, wishing she had not mentioned the episode with the courtesan. She would hate Miles to think that she actually cared about his rakish ways when in fact she detested him.

"I would have told you that," Miles said, "if I thought for a moment that you would believe me."

Alice's feelings felt surprisingly raw to hear him admit it. "I know you would!" she said. "You are ruthlessly manipulative." She glared at him. "You will say or do whatever is necessary to get you what you want."

"That is pragmatism," Miles said.

"It is dishonesty," Alice said. "You could not tell the truth to save your life!"

There was a brief silence.

"Miss Lister," Miles said, "you have my measure exactly. So in the spirit of saying—or doing—whatever I have to, in order to get what I want, I am telling you unless you agree to marry me I will tell everyone about your career as a thief."

Alice's gaze locked with his. His expression was completely serious. There was a cool, intent look in his eyes, as though he were measuring the odds on a wager. Alice felt her heart start to race. In the early days of their acquaintance she had observed that Miles's detachment, his air of withdrawal, was part of his attraction. He seemed so cool and aloof. To be able to reach him, to kindle something in him that was more than physical passion, would be the dream of some woman with less common sense than she had now.

"You are seeking to blackmail me into marriage," she said, trying to match his calmness while her blood thundered in her veins and a part of her mind protested that he simply could not mean to do it, while another part was damned sure that he did.

Miles shrugged easily. "*Blackmail* is such an ugly word, Miss Lister. I desire to marry you. In fact, it is essential to me that I do marry you. So let us call it a bargain."

"Why prettify something that is fundamentally unpleasant?" Alice asked steadily. She pressed her hands together. "You propose. I refuse." Her voice lit with anger. "You are despicable, Lord Vickery." She examined her feelings and added with some surprise, "In fact, you are even more ruthless and less likable than I had thought you were."

Miles's dark brows lifted in mocking amusement. He seemed unmoved by her disapproval, which, Alice thought, was surely further proof of his detestability. "Do you want me to tell everyone that you are a thief?" he asked gently.

"Of course I do not want that," Alice said. She held his gaze and tried to hold her nerve. "I know you would not really do it."

Miles laughed. "My dear, you underestimate me. If that is what it takes to gain your hand in marriage—"

"But it will not gain you that." Alice turned away from him and took a few agitated steps across the room then turned to meet his gaze with unflinching directness. "No one would believe you, my lord. You must be able to see the weaknesses of your position. I could conjure up half a dozen people to say that I was blamelessly at home in bed last night and that you must have made a mistake."

She saw the flash of calculation in his eyes as he realized that she was not going to surrender easily. The conflict between them tightened a notch, sending the blood buzzing through her veins.

"You would add perjury to your offenses?" Miles asked softly.

"Yes," Alice said. "If I had to."

"Even though I have the gown as proof of your theft?"

Alice made a grab for the wedding dress but Miles was too quick for her, holding it up out of her reach.

"I will tell the authorities that I caught you red-handed with this," Miles said. "You know that the penalty for theft on this scale is death? Even if the courts showed you leniency you would be transported or imprisoned. Are you really prepared to take the risk of being found guilty, Miss Lister? How do you think your mother would feel about that?"

For a moment the black shadows threatened to close in on Alice's mind and she was afraid she would faint.

Death. Transportation. Imprisonment.

She grabbed the edge of the table to steady herself.

"And then there is Miss Cole," Miles continued. "What would happen to her if you were sent to jail? Her lover betrayed her, her family has cast her out and she is pregnant and destitute." His gaze, cool and mocking, rested on Alice's face. "She would be utterly without protection."

Alice pressed a hand to her forehead. "You are despicable!"

Miles laughed. "So you have already told me. It is not in dispute."

Alice tried to rally herself. Surely he would not, *could* not, do such a thing. These were only empty threats. All she had to do was to hold her nerve.

"My lord, there is not the remotest chance that I will wed you," she said, raising her chin stubbornly. "Do not seek to frighten me. The only way in which you are like to succeed in your aim would be for you to abduct me."

Miles grinned. "My dear Miss Lister, do you know, I had not even thought of that? But now that you have suggested it I think it is an excellent plan."

Alice chewed her lush lower lip hard. She was furious with herself for making the suggestion. She could feel her temper almost getting the better of her. "Even *you* would not stoop to that," she bit out.

Miles laughed. "You know that I would," he said. "In fact, you seem to understand my character very well. That could be an excellent basis for marriage."

Alice made a sound like an enraged kitten and flounced away. "If you kidnapped me I would still refuse you," she said. "You would need to pay a crooked clergyman to ignore my protestations."

"Another excellent idea," Miles said. "I will if I must." He sighed. "But to be quite honest with you, Miss Lister, it is a vast amount of trouble to go to when blackmail is available as an option instead." He moved a little closer to her. "Think about it," he said. "Transportation…imprisonment… These are harsh options, Miss Lister. They really would not suit you. You have already scrambled out of poverty once. I am sure that you do not wish to return. And being married to me has its benefits. Your situation in life would improve immeasurably. You would have the title of marchioness—and four strawberry leaves in the coronet, for a start."

"If you are looking for a woman who wishes for nothing more than to marry a marquis then you should wed my mama rather than me," Alice snapped. "You are lower than a louse to seek to force me like this." She gritted her teeth. "You are a worm and a weasel—"

Miles laughed again. "Is a weasel lower than a louse?" He spread his hands wide in a gesture of appeal. "Shall we take your poor opinion of me as read, Miss Lister, and get down to business? Think of your mother. She will be delighted if you accept my proposal. Remember that she wishes you to marry into the aristocracy—not be clapped in Fortune's Folly jail or dispatched to Australia."

Alice could feel a headache building behind her eyes. She rubbed her forehead. Think of your mother, Miles had said. She thought of her family and the fragile security that they had achieved since her inheritance. Could she risk losing all that? Her brother, Lowell, had the modern machinery he needed to make the farm profitable now. He was working hard to secure his future but it was not easy for him. Her mother felt safe if not happy as a wealthy matron in country society, but her confidence was so brittle. Any scandal involving Alice would devastate her. Then there was Lydia, pregnant, abandoned and alone, who would lose the roof over her head if anything happened to Alice. She could turn to her cousin, Laura Anstruther, but Laura and Dexter were poor as church mice themselves.

Miles was threatening to take everything away that Alice had worked to build. He was an officer of the Crown, working for Richard Ryder, the Home Secretary, and as such, one word from him could ruin her forever. It would break her mother's heart, and leave Lydia defenceless. As for a court actually convicting her…her mind reeled in horror at the prospect. For she was guilty as charged. She was totally in his power.

She pressed her fingers to her temples. If only she could negotiate with Miles, make some sort of compromise. That might suffice.

"I will make a bargain with you, my lord," she said. "I understand that you are deeply in debt and that you must want my fortune, and so, if you do not speak of what happened last night, I will consent to the pretence of a betrothal between us to help you stave off your creditors for a little while—" She stopped, shocked. For a moment there was such a bleak and desolate look in Miles's eyes that it took her breath away. She had never, ever thought to see an expression like that on his face. And then it was gone, as swiftly as it had come, and she wondered if she had imagined it.

"It is far too late for half measures, Miss Lister," he said. "The sale of the Drum estate and all the castle contents starts in a couple of weeks." He smiled faintly. "I am in far deeper debt than you can ever imagine. I have already sold everything I can, and if I do not wed an heiress, and soon, I will be thrown in the Fleet—or be forced to flee the country." He shifted a little. "That is why I am prepared to do *anything* to oblige you to marry me, Miss Lister. There will be no compromises. You wed me or you go to jail."

CHAPTER FOUR

MILES WATCHED as Alice wrestled with his not in the least romantic proposal. Every expression was written clearly on her face. He could read that she wanted to tell him to go to hell. It was in every defiant line of her body and in the jut of her chin as she stood, hands on hips, staring him down. Miles was accustomed to calculating each cynical risk he took in his life and this was one he knew was a racing certainty. No matter how much she hated him, Alice had too much to lose to refuse him. She would succumb to his blackmail, wed him, and he would have the fortune he craved.

He would have Alice in his bed, as well, and that was beginning to matter as much as the money. Well, not quite. But their sparring had only sharpened his hunger for her. For a moment Miles allowed himself to imagine Alice naked in his arms, the curves and hollows of her skin exposed to his questing hands, the scent of her wrapped about him as it had been the night before.

The arousal ripped through him, startling him in its intensity.

Miles clamped down on his excessive lust. This was not going to help him think straight and he was too calculating to be led astray by his desire. He looked at

Alice again and almost forgot the resolution he had just made. She looked slightly flustered, completely defiant and totally irresistible. He wanted to kiss her. He wanted it very much.

Something flickered in Alice's blue eyes—fury and despair in equal mixture. She was trapped and she knew it but she was not going to break down. Miles felt a sudden admiration for her. Most women would have given in to the vapors by now, or have withdrawn into a strategic swoon. Alice, it seemed, had nerves of steel and a fundamental strength of character he had seldom encountered in a female before, the only other exception being his cousin Laura Anstruther. Miles was not conventional enough to believe that women were the weaker sex—he had seen enough of their strength and courage under duress to know that they had a hardiness that many of his peers would deplore as unfeminine and unbecoming. But Alice had something in addition. She had enormous resolution.

He watched her narrowly as she paced the room. He was accustomed to weighing up his adversaries, assessing their strengths and weaknesses. Before he had gone to work for the Home Secretary he had been in the army and his work had taken him into dark places where he bartered for the lives of prisoners or hostages held by the other side, where he made bargains with men's lives and futures as though they were no more than pieces on a chessboard, where he had always to consider the greater good and be prepared to sacrifice the individual. Over the years he had abandoned people whose only hope was that he could secure their safety. Always he reminded himself that a few had to suffer for the benefit of the majority. And gradually the choices had become less painful, more calculated, and with each decision another piece of his soul had been lost. He knew this was why he could look at Alice now and feel nothing but a tightening hunger for her and for her money, and a triumph that the game was almost won. He doubted that there was a man alive who was more unfeeling or cynical than he was now, so he felt no compunction about forcing Alice into marriage. She had something that he wanted. He had the means to compel her to his point of view. It was as simple as that.

"Even if I agreed—" Alice began and Miles's heart leaped to know that what he desired was so close to being within his grasp "—and I have not said that I will—there is a difficulty."

"I am sure," Miles said, "that it is nothing we cannot overcome."

Alice's eyes flashed with disdain. "I think it most unlikely you will be able to overcome this particular problem, my lord." She turned on her heel sharply and walked away from him, the lemon silk skirts of her gown making a soft swishing sound.

"Try me," Miles said. Now that he was within an ace of winning Alice's consent he was absolutely determined that nothing would stand in his way. He was aware of tension rippling through all the muscles in his body, and the hairs of the back of his neck standing on end. He only just managed to suppress a shiver.

Alice gestured him to a seat and sat down opposite him. All her movements were very precise, as though she had herself under tight control. She was remarkably self-contained but he could see how much it was costing her in the tense way that she held herself together. Her strain showed in the tight grip of her hands in her lap and in the taut line of her shoulders as she sat up very straight.

"The inheritance of my fortune is not without conditions," Alice said, breaking the silence between them. She looked at him, her blue eyes fierce, as though she were daring him to challenge her. "My lawyer, Mr. Gaines, will confirm what I am about to tell you, my lord, lest you think this no more than an excuse on my part." She swallowed hard and took a deliberate breath, meeting his gaze directly.

"The fact is that when she left me her fortune, Lady Membury also laid down a stipulation relating to the man I would marry," Alice said. "It has to be fulfilled or all my remaining fortune reverts to the charity for the welfare and upkeep of the stray animals of the parish. Lady Membury," she added sweetly, "was very fond of animals."

"I can imagine," Miles said. He had heard a little of the elderly widow who had left her housemaid a vast fortune. It was said she had been completely mad.

Alice's blue gaze flickered over Miles again. "When she made this stipulation, Lady Membury was seeking to protect me from fortune hunters and to ensure that I chose to marry a man who loved and respected me for myself alone," she said. Her tone was ironic.

"That was very laudable of her," Miles said, "but probably a little optimistic."

"So it seems," Alice said coldly, "given the nature of your marriage proposal. Lady Membury's wishes are quite clear, however. She stated that as she would not be present to scrutinize my suitors herself, she requires that the man I marry fulfill certain criteria.

Specifically he has to be proven to be an upright and worthy gentleman." She let the words drop into the silence of the room. "Perhaps if she had required that I should marry an out-and-out scoundrel, you would have a better chance, my lord."

Miles laughed. "You do not feel that I meet her conditions, Miss Lister?"

"In no particular," Alice said. "More to the point, my lord, Mr. Gaines, and my other trustee, Mr. Churchward, who was Lady Membury's London lawyer, both surely know of your poor character and know that whatever else you may be, you are neither upright nor worthy. So I fear that your suit is doomed, my lord, blackmail notwithstanding."

It was a setback, Miles allowed, but he could not accept that it was insuperable. He had not come this far in order to give up now.

"Churchward is my family lawyer, too," he said thoughtfully. "Perhaps he could be…persuaded…to my cause."

"I have met Mr. Churchward and I doubt that he is corruptible," Alice said sharply, "family lawyer or not."

"I am afraid you are probably right," Miles conceded wryly. "Which is how it should be, I suppose. I do not really want a dishonest solicitor working for me."

"Only when it suits you," Alice said. "There is more, my lord."

"Of course there is," Miles said ironically.

"In order to *prove* his worthiness to Lady Membury's satisfaction—and to that of my trustees," Alice said, "my future husband has to fulfill a certain requirement."

Miles sighed. He was starting to dislike the deceased

Lady Membury quite intensely. He had no doubt that Alice was telling him the truth about the codicil to her inheritance—and that she was taking great pleasure in doing so. He supposed that it was the least he deserved for forcing her hand.

He sat forward. "Name Lady Membury's stipulations," he said.

"Her terms are that for three months you must be proven to be utterly and completely honest in your dealings, not only with me, your future wife, but with everyone else, too," Alice said very clearly. "You must speak the truth on all occasions. You must be honest in all your transactions." Her gaze held a hint of mockery as it rested on him. "You are a ruthless, deceitful manipulator, my lord. Never in a thousand years could you achieve such a thing as total honesty, though I do believe it would be the most painful punishment for you to try. I feel sure you would fall at the first hurdle."

Miles stared at her. For a moment he thought— hoped—he had misheard her.

Utter and total honesty in his words and his dealings?

What had that mad old fool Lady Membury been thinking?

Utter and total honesty *for three whole months?*

He was not sure what was showing on his face. Alice was watching him with interest and a certain degree of amusement.

"I knew you could not do it," she said with satisfaction.

"Miss Lister," Miles said, "there are very good social reasons for not being honest all the time."

Alice smiled slightly. "You need not tell me that," she said. "I was not the one who set the condition. And

I would not be expecting you to be honest if I ask you whether I look plump in a particular gown," she added. "We are talking here about fundamental honesty of character, Lord Vickery. We are talking about you being at heart a sincere and worthy man." Her smile grew. "Oh dear, you look appalled. I do realize that the concept of honor is completely foreign to you." She raised a brow. "I take it, then, that you are withdrawing your attempt at blackmail and that we need not trouble Mr. Churchward and Mr. Gaines? I know you would not be able to meet the terms, anyway."

"Oh, I can meet the terms," Miles said. He got to his feet and turned away from Alice for a moment so that she could not see his expression and know he lied. It was impossible to open his heart and reveal the unvarnished truth about his thoughts, feelings and behavior. He had not done such a thing since he was a youth, in the last, appalling, disillusioning interview he'd had with his father before he'd left to join the army. Telling the absolute truth was to reveal one's weaknesses and vulnerabilities. It was to lay oneself open to pain and hurt. Being honest never paid. It was not a course of action that he would ever take voluntarily.

And yet that did not mean he could not meet Lady Membury's ridiculous conditions and win Alice's fortune. Over the past ten years Miles had become so accomplished at disguising the truth, bending it, using it, molding it to his will that he was completely sure he could do the same now. Alice and her trustees would never know the difference between his carefully constructed pretence and total honesty.

He turned back to her. She was waiting with nothing but the most polite interest showing on her face. Miles took her hand in his and rubbed his thumb gently over the back of it. Her skin felt warm and deliciously soft. He felt a tiny tremble rack her. Her lips parted and he heard her catch her breath. The hunger for her that was within him sharpened like a knife. He had to have Alice Lister. One way or another he would achieve it.

"I will do it," he said.

"Money is a truly remarkable inspiration," Alice said, "if it can persuade even you to reform." Her voice was slightly husky. Miles felt his body stir. Once again he had a sudden, shocking urge to kiss her, to take that soft red mouth with his and dip deep within her. He pulled her to her feet, drawing her closer to him until her hands were resting against the smooth blue superfine of his jacket.

"It is only for three months," he whispered against the golden curls that had escaped from her neat little yellow bandeau and were tickling his lips. "I do not intend to reform for good. Only until I have you—and your money."

He watched the color spill up under her skin, pink as an opening rose. "Of course," Alice said. "How foolish of me. You cannot change."

"Why would you seek to change me?" Miles asked. "I am far more amusing unreformed."

He saw a flash of something in her eyes that looked almost like pain. "You are dangerous and ruthless and arrogant unreformed," Alice said. Her voice was husky.

"Precisely," Miles agreed. He leaned closer until his lips were barely an inch from hers, tantalizingly close. "Much more amusing."

Alice shook her head a little. He saw the deep blue of her eyes darken to the color of twilight. He could sense the resistance in her, but it was overwhelmed by the attraction she had to him. He doubted that she even understood what was happening between them. She was so transparently innocent that it felt unfair to be taking advantage. Except that Miles never let such scruples weigh with him.

"Do we have a deal, Miss Lister?" he murmured. His lips brushed hers. "I will contact Churchward and Gaines to confirm that I will fulfill Lady Membury's requirements as your affianced husband. By good fortune I am expecting Mr. Churchward to arrive from London any day to discuss my inheritance of Drum…."

He saw Alice blink and pull herself back from the brink of sensual awareness. A shade of disquiet touched her face. She took a step back from him as though she had belatedly become aware of how far she had let him take control and how far he had affected her senses.

"You go too fast, my lord," she said. "I have not given my consent yet."

"But you will," Miles said. "Think of your mother. Think of Miss Cole. You have no choice."

A flicker of temper flashed in Alice's eyes. "I understand that there is a family curse associated with your inheritance of Drum, my lord," she said. "Can I rely upon it to carry you off before the knot is tied?"

Miles laughed. "It certainly won't happen before our wedding night, sweetheart."

Alice pulled a face. "A pity. But perhaps I could hasten it along." She swished away from him. "Let us be clear, Lord Vickery. I detest you. You are the last man on earth I would wish to wed and if I am forced into this then—" she paused and then met his eyes defiantly "—ours will never be more than a marriage in name only."

Miles burst out laughing. "You are in no position to be negotiating terms, Miss Lister. A marriage in name only? I don't think so." He crooked a finger under her chin and brushed his lips to hers again. They were soft and yielding and he wanted to deepen the kiss and taste her and take her. Desire twisted in him.

"Surrender to me now," he said, against her mouth. "Accept my proposal. You know you have no choice."

"No!" Alice jerked back from him, pressing her fingers against her lips. "I need time to think," she said.

"No, you don't," Miles said. "There is nothing to think about." He did not want to give her even a second to think of a way out—not that there was one for her.

Alice stared at him for a long moment and then she nodded slightly, and Miles's heart leaped with relief and triumph.

"Very well," she said, very low. "You have my consent to an engagement. I realize that if I do not accept, others will suffer, and that I cannot allow." She swallowed hard. "But I do not believe that it will ever come to marriage between us. You will fail to meet the terms of the will. You will fall at the first hurdle."

"You mean that you hope I will," Miles corrected gently.

Alice glared at him. "We cannot announce our betrothal immediately," she said. "I need time—a few days—to explain to my family and friends." She made a slight gesture. "They will be…puzzled…that I have changed my mind and that I am willing to accept you when they know I hold you in such strong dislike."

"I am sure that your mama will be delighted and

will ask no questions," Miles said. "I foresee no problems there."

"No," Alice said. She turned away from him slightly so that he could see her face only in profile. "But my brother, Lowell, will be a different matter. He hates you and would very likely call you out if he guessed the truth, and then you would probably kill him, which will make matters a great deal worse. So I have to come up with a reason that will convince him... And then there is Lizzie." Miles saw her lips curve into a faint smile. "I imagine she, too, might do you some physical damage if she ever discovers that you are blackmailing me."

"I do not intend to bring Lady Elizabeth into this at all," Miles said. "And I expect you to keep her out of it, as well."

"Of course." Alice's tone was scornful. "I appreciate that you do not wish to risk Lord Waterhouse's wrath by dragging Lizzie into this mess." She sighed. "And Lizzie is my friend and I love her and I do not want her involved, so for that reason I will not tell her the truth, but—" she shrugged "—as I said, I need time to think of a convincing reason why I might wish to wed you." She looked disdainful. "The benefits are not obvious to anyone who knows me."

"I will give you two days," Miles said. "You may tell your family whatever you please, as long as it is not the truth. That will also give me time to speak to your lawyers. Then we will make the formal announcement of our betrothal." He saw a shiver rack her, but then she squared her shoulders and met his gaze.

"No," she said, "I consent to the betrothal being known within my family and friends but *not* to a formal announcement. Not until the three months' courtship is up—and you have fulfilled the conditions of Lady Membury's will. I absolutely *will not* compromise on that, my lord. I do not wish to emerge from this with my reputation any more tarnished than it will be already."

Once again the frustration gripped Miles. Devil take it but she was strong, and he did not know whether he admired her for it or wanted to shake the resistance out of her. "Forgive me, Miss Lister," he said, "but once again I must remind you that you are in no position to negotiate."

She held his gaze fearlessly. "And I would advise you not to push me too far, my lord, or I will call off the entire deal and tell you to go to hell, blackmail or no blackmail."

They faced each other like fencers and then Miles nodded. "Very well," he said.

He heard her give a tiny sigh of relief. "I should also warn you, my lord," she said, "that should you miraculously manage to convince the lawyers of your upright character and respectability—" she made an exasperated gesture "—then I will do my utmost to make you the devil of a wife."

Miles smiled. "And I shall be the devil of a husband, so we shall deal extremely well together." He bowed to her. "I will see you at the Granby Ball tomorrow night, Miss Lister. You will save a dance for me."

He saw Alice's eyes narrow at the fact that his words were a statement not a request. "Dance with you?" she said. She quoted his own words back to him. "I don't think so."

"Yes, you will." Miles smiled. "It is the beginning

of our three-month courtship during which I shall prove myself the most honorable, worthy and upstanding of suitors." He held her eyes, and she dropped her gaze first, the rose color deepening in her cheeks. "I assure you, Miss Lister," he added, "that we shall be in each other's company a great deal from now onward."

"That is ridiculous," Alice snapped. "There is no need for us to spend more than the minimal amount of time together. No one is suggesting that this is a love match. It is a business arrangement!"

"That may be so," Miles said smoothly, "but I am not giving the lawyers any opportunity to suspect me. You will find me the devoted suitor, I assure you."

"I do not want you paying court to me," Alice said. She was flushed with indignation now. "I loathe the idea. It…it makes a mockery of the whole concept of love and marriage."

Miles laughed. "Miss Lister, you are so charmingly naive. Accept it."

Once again he watched her struggle with her temper. "I suppose I have no choice," she said angrily. She took a deep breath, recovered herself. "Mama will, of course, be present on all occasions to chaperone me, so that will at least ensure that you cannot try to circumvent the conditions and seduce me into marriage."

"Excellent," Miles said cheerfully. "I cannot help but feel that Mrs. Lister will support my suit."

"Pray do not take that as personal approval," Alice said sweetly. "If a duke comes along Mama will no doubt change her allegiance."

Miles laughed. "I have no illusions, Miss Lister."

"Nor indeed any principles," Alice said.

"Naturally not," Miles said. "But I can adopt some

on a temporary basis." He bowed again. "Good day, Miss Lister. Until tomorrow night." He kissed the back of Alice's hand and let her go, noting with satisfaction that she clasped one hand in the other, unconsciously running her fingers over the place his lips had touched her skin. She might detest him, he thought, but she was far from indifferent to his touch. This was going to be the perfect arrangement. He would have Alice in his bed, and her money would save him from the debtor's prison. Everything was within his grasp.

Three months.

Total honesty.

The words echoed ominously in Miles's head as he went out, down the steps of the house and onto the gravel sweep, but he told himself that he could do it to save himself from ruin. It would be easy.

CHAPTER FIVE

ALICE STOOD BY THE WINDOW and watched as Miles walked away up the drive. There was a casual assurance in his gait that spoke of utter confidence. He turned to look back and raised a hand in farewell, and she chided herself fiercely at having been caught watching him. Miles Vickery was the sort of man that women watched all the time and he knew it. She wished she had not been the one to confirm it.

With a sigh she dropped into the armchair that she had only recently vacated. She felt exhausted from the pressure of withstanding Miles's blackmail and drained by an anger so deep and intense that she had thought it would consume her alive.

Miles Vickery. He was despicable.

He was just like all the rest. Men like Miles took what they wanted with a coldhearted disregard for the feelings of others.

She thought of Miles, and of Tom Fortune, who had ruined Lydia and callously abandoned her, and of all those nameless, faceless, *careless* sons of the nobility who saw any woman as fair game and who believed that a servant girl in particular was placed on earth to clean *their* boots and tend to *their* pleasure, to be picked up, used and discarded at whim, and she felt the fury well up in her again. She remembered Jenny, the sixteen-year-old scullery maid at the house next to Lady Membury's in Skipton, whom she had found crying on the area steps, having been turned out for being pregnant.

Jenny had sworn the master of the house had forced himself on her and that the mistress had turned her out in a jealous fury. Alice often wondered what had happened to Jenny. She had tried to find her when she had come into her money, but like so many other disgraced servant girls, Jenny had vanished without a trace. Then there was Jane, who had worked for the Cole family. Alice's brother, Lowell, had found Jane lying in a ditch near Cole Court, raped, bleeding and bruised. He had taken her to the farm at High Top and Alice had sent for the doctor, but it had been too late to save Jane. No charges had even been brought against anyone for Jane's assault. Alice had known the constable did not really care. It was as though because Jane had served others she did not count as a person. She did not matter. She had died and no one had paid any heed....

Restless with anger, Alice got to her feet and walked across to the window again, where she stood tapping her fingers on the sill. It was blindingly obvious, she thought bitterly, staring blankly out at the bright, sunny day, that had she still been a maidservant, Miles would only ever have looked at her with seduction in mind if he had noticed her at all.

Seduction, conquest, desertion...

The man was beyond despicable. He was unforgivably selfish and callous. Now that she was rich, he wanted both her money and her body, but his lack of respect for her was exactly the same as if she were still the housemaid she had been two years before. He wanted her only for what she could give him.

She was in the devil of a coil now, blackmailed into an engagement to a man she detested in order to protect those she loved. She could only hope that Miles would fail utterly to meet the requirements of Lady Membury's will. He *ought* to fail, since he was congenitally incapable of honesty. He had proved it time and again. And yet... She shivered. There was something utterly single-minded about Miles and she had the dreadful conviction he was going to succeed.

He wanted her money.

He wanted her.

Alice wrapped her arms about her, cold now even with the fire burning hot in the grate. She didn't understand the way Miles made her feel but she didn't like it. How could she be so drawn to a man she despised, how could she tremble when he kissed her, how could she feel his touch echo through her whole body, when she hated him? Miles's behavior only served to prove the arrogant disregard with which he went about taking whatever it was that he wanted. She was not going to succumb to this insidious desire, fall into his arms and give herself to him when he deserved nothing from her other than that she should tell him to go to hell.

For a moment she considered going to the authorities and telling them the truth about the theft and begging for clemency, but before the thought was even formed she realized that it would not serve. She could never take the risk of leaving her family ruined, and of leaving Lydia unprotected and alone for a second time.

Her skin flushed with heat as she thought about her encounter with Miles. He was so dangerous, predatory and utterly merciless in taking what he wanted, and she was so ridiculously naive and inexperienced. It was richly ironic that she was such an innocent, for she was no pampered heiress who had grown up cosseted and protected by wealth and privilege. She had gone out into the world and worked until her bones ached and her head had spun with tiredness. She had seen much of life, but she had never before had to deal with a man like Miles Vickery and she knew now that she was far, far out of her depth.

The door opened and Lydia Cole stuck her head around. "Has Lord Vickery left? Your mama tells me that you are going to marry him."

"Mama is imagining things, as usual," Alice said quickly. She did not want to have to tell anyone about the agreement between herself and Miles yet. They all knew her so well that none of them would believe she had agreed to marry him voluntarily. She had to think of a convincing excuse. Madness sprang to mind.

"You know that Mama wants me to marry a lord," she said. "Which one is immaterial—and so she imagines that every man who calls is a potential husband."

"Well, to be fair, most of them have called to press their suit," Lydia said, "and you know how desperately she wishes you to be settled." She came into the room and eased herself into the other armchair, sighing heavily as she sat down. "Oh, I am so tired these days! I swear I could sleep the whole day away."

"At least you have a better color today," Alice said approvingly. "I was very worried about you yesterday. Has your sickness improved?"

"No," Lydia said. "I feel wretchedly ill morning, noon and night!"

Alice privately thought that a part of Lydia's suffering might well be caused by the mental anguish of having loved Tom Fortune so dearly and having been so horribly disillusioned in him. He was another reckless gambler like Miles Vickery, an out-and-out rake and philanderer who had taken Lydia's love and smashed it to pieces. He had seduced her, made her pregnant, abandoned her and wound up in prison for his criminal activities. Lydia never spoke of her feelings for Tom, and Alice did not push her into it. She knew that Lizzie sometimes tried to get Lydia to open up, but Lydia remained adamantly silent.

The other matter they never discussed was what would happen when the baby was born. Alice had every intention of making over to Lydia the house in Skipton that Lady Membury had left her, so that Lydia and the baby could have a secure future. She had already instructed her lawyer to draw up the papers and she hoped desperately that her betrothal to Miles could not alter the arrangement. Lydia had once been an heiress herself but it seemed unlikely that her parents, the current Duke and Duchess of Cole, would settle any money on their disgraced daughter now, so Alice thought it imperative that she should protect her friend.

Lydia lay back in her chair with a heartfelt sigh and closed her eyes. She was now well advanced into her fourth month of pregnancy, and her slight body looked swollen and a little ungainly already. Mrs. Lister had commented that Lydia was increasing at so great a rate that she might be carrying twins.

"I will go and make you some dry toast," Alice said, getting up. "Lady Membury told me that when she was increasing she found it was the only thing she could manage to eat."

Lydia waved a hand to stop her. "That would be kind—in a moment. I did not realize that Lady Membury had had any children," she added. She looked at Alice, hesitation reflected in her eyes. "If she had children of her own, why did she leave her fortune to you, Alice?"

"Her daughter died and she had no other relatives," Alice said. Her former employer's eccentric decision to leave her vast fortune to her housemaid had caused uproar in the tight-knit local society. It had been a shock to Alice, too, but it was also understandable and deeply poignant for her. "You know that she had been a recluse for many years," she said. "She had no family or friends and she had turned against the local vicar years ago, so there was no way in which she would choose to leave her money to the church."

"I can see myself ending like that," Lydia said, with a flash of bitterness. "Alone and with no one in the world…"

"No, you will not," Alice said fiercely, grabbing her hand. "You have friends about you, and anyway, this baby of yours thrives and is strong. Perhaps when he or she is born your parents will relent—"

"God forbid," Lydia said involuntarily, and they both burst out laughing. "Lady Membury must have loved you," Lydia added. "You would have been a great comfort to her, Alice. I imagine she was very lonely and saw you as the daughter she had lost."

"Perhaps she did," Alice said. There was a lump in her throat. "We used to talk about all manner of things," she said, thinking back, "and go driving together, and drink bohea tea and gin, and play cards together."

"And I suppose you let her win," Lydia said.

"Well, of course," Alice said. "She was my employer—and she had a fortune of eighty thousand pounds!"

They both burst out laughing again but then Alice sobered. "All the same, Lydia," she said, "I sometimes wish that she had never left me her money. It can be a curse as well as a blessing." She stopped, finding that she was on the verge of blurting out the truth of Miles's blackmail to her friend. "I'm sorry," she said, with a little constraint. "That sounds most appallingly ungrateful when my life is materially so much easier now than it was a few years ago."

"Being an heiress is not always a fortunate thing," Lydia said bitterly. "Look at the depths of greed it has driven Sir Montague to, with his ghastly plans to fleece us all with the Dames' Tax and all his other medieval laws! And then there is Tom…" Her voice faltered a little, and Alice saw her knuckles whiten as she pressed her hands together in her lap. "I do not think he would have paid me the slightest attention had I been penniless. I think he knew that as he is a rackety younger son, Mama and Papa would never countenance his attentions to me. He deliberately sought to get me pregnant so that I would be obliged to marry him. The plan only went wrong when his criminal actions were exposed and he was arrested."

"Oh, Lydia!" Alice was appalled at the heartless tale her friend was outlining. The same thoughts had occurred to her but she had hoped that Lydia had kept at least a few of her illusions. "I am sure that Tom cared for you—" she began, knowing that she did not believe it but wanting only to give comfort.

"Oh, pish!" Lydia said. "Tom cared for no one but himself. Which is why you should be careful of Miles Vickery, Alice." Her gaze sought Alice's and there was anxiety in the depths. "I know he is different in that he is a marquis, even if an impoverished one, and so has a title to trade for your money, but in terms of character I think him even more of a rake than Tom, more ruthless, more dangerous."

"How right you are," Alice said with feeling.

Both girls looked around as there was a clatter in the hall outside. Lizzie had evidently arrived back from her ride with Nat Waterhouse, for she could be heard chattering and laughing with Marigold, and then Alice heard her mother's voice rising with excitement as she gave Lizzie the news.

"And the Marquis of Drummond called and I have every expectation of an engagement being announced shortly between him and Alice..."

The drawing room door crashed open. "Your mama tells me that you are going to marry Miles Vickery, Alice," Lizzie announced as she rushed in. She pulled off her riding gloves and dropped them carelessly on the table. "Am I to congratulate you?"

"That would be premature," Alice said.

"Ha! I thought so!" Lizzie said, flinging herself down on the window seat. "I told her you should be clapped in Bedlam if you were even considering it!"

"Well," Alice began weakly, thinking that perhaps she should take the opportunity to start preparing the ground, but then she realized that Lizzie was not attending, anyway.

"You will not believe what has happened!" Lizzie said, sitting bolt upright and fixing her friends with a furious glare. "Nat Waterhouse is to marry that pea brain Flora Minchin!"

"Good gracious!" Alice said, startled. She remembered Miles's lazy observation that Lizzie was in love with Nat even though she had known him forever and treated him like a brother. Miles had not, she realized now, said that Nat felt the same way. And everyone knew that Lord Waterhouse was yet another impecunious fortune hunter out to snap up a rich prize.

"How do you feel about that, Lizzie?" she asked.

"Oh, it is none of my affair if Nat chooses to throw himself away on a featherbrained heiress who will bore him silly within a se'nnight!" Lizzie said crossly. "I could not care one iota!"

Alice exchanged a look with Lydia. "I expect you told him that, too," Lydia said.

"Of course!" Lizzie wriggled impatiently. "But I need not concern myself because it will never happen. Nat could not be so stupid as to marry that henwit. He will see sense before the knot is tied."

Once again Alice's eyes met Lydia's. Lydia raised her brows slightly and Alice shook her head. Both of them knew that Nat Waterhouse was eminently capable of going through with such a marriage for money and that if he had already made Miss Minchin an offer he could not now, in honor, back out. There was no point in telling Lizzie that, of course, for she was in no mood to listen.

"Flora Minchin is a sweet-natured girl," Alice said.

"Only because she is too stupid to be anything other than agreeable," Lizzie snapped.

"I don't think she is anywhere near as stupid as you think, Lizzie," Lydia said surprisingly. "I think you misjudge her."

"I don't care about Flora," Lizzie said impatiently. "The problem is that now I do not even have Nat's escort to the ball at the Granby tomorrow, for he is to accompany Flora and her family!"

"How thoughtless of him," Alice murmured. "Well, we shall both have to make do with my brother, Lowell. He has promised to escort me and I am sure he will be happy to do the same for you, Lizzie. Besides, you are seldom short of admirers."

"I like Lowell," Lizzie said, brightening. "That will be delightful."

"He likes you, too," Alice said dryly, "but he is wasting his time. You would make a terrible farmer's wife."

Lizzie laughed, her good humor restored. "With my fortune he could be a gentleman of leisure. It is worth a thought…."

"No, it is not," Alice said quickly. The idea of Lizzie and Lowell making a runaway match was, she thought, the worst scheme since Lizzie's last bad idea about robbing the gown shop. Lizzie would run rings around Lowell. She needed a firm hand and Lowell was far too easygoing. "Lowell likes working for a living," she said. "I know that may seem strange but some of us require occupation."

"Oh, do not worry." Lizzie yawned. "I know Lowell prefers to work morning, noon and night. We would see a great deal more of him here at Spring House if it were not so. Last time we met I told him how very tedious and *bourgeois* it was of him!" She slewed around in her seat so she could look at Alice properly.

"And do not think that I have not noticed how restless *you* become when you feel you have little to do, Alice. You are the same."

"Bourgeois," Alice said. "I know."

Lizzie had the grace to look a little ashamed. "I did not mean that. It is merely that you prefer to keep occupied."

This, Alice thought, was true and well observed of Lizzie, who could sometimes surprise with her insights. "Leading the life of an heiress bores me dreadfully," she admitted. "I need to be active. It is a pity that Mama does not feel the same. She sits here each day waiting for genteel callers who never arrive and then she feels most dreadfully snubbed."

"Now that you plan to start a charity for destitute servants, you will be very busy indeed," Lizzie said. "I am surprised that Mr. Churchward agreed to advance you the money for it. I hear he is very proper and some of those girls are fallen women."

"Most of them have done nothing more than make a mistake," Alice said carefully, wishing that Lizzie were not quite so tactless with Lydia sitting there, pregnant and unmarried, in front of her. "It is wrong to judge. Besides," she added, to turn the subject, "I can only use my interest, not my capital, so neither of my trustees need worry that I am spending profligate sums."

Mrs. Lister entered the room followed by Marigold with the luncheon tray. This was set out on a cloth with the Lister coat of arms embroidered on it. In vain had Alice explained to her mother that they were not entitled to use the arms because they had never been awarded to their branch of the family. Mrs. Lister had tossed her head and claimed that since the Duchess of

Cole had a coat of arms, she would have one, too. She had then proceeded to embroider or net them onto anything and everything: chair backs, tablecloths and even the knitted coat worn by her pet dog.

"Oh, delicious!" Lizzie exclaimed as she saw the luncheon. "Jellied chicken and ham pies!"

Lydia had paled at the sight of the chicken and now she got hastily to her feet. "I think I will take a rest in my room," she murmured. "No, dear ma'am—" She fended off Mrs. Lister's inquiry as to whether she would take any food, "I have no appetite today."

"Oh, dear," Alice said as the door closed behind her, "she seemed so much better today. I'm afraid she will starve herself into a sickness at this rate."

"Nat was asking after Lydia's health," Lizzie said, munching through one of the little pork pies.

"So was Lord Vickery," Alice said, accepting the cup of tea that Marigold proffered.

"Nat asked if she ever received any letters," Lizzie added. "I thought it an odd question, for why should he be interested? And who would write to her? Her cousin Laura is close by so need not send letters, and the rest of her family have cut her off and it is not as though she will ever hear from Tom…."

Alice paused, remembering that Miles had asked if the wedding dress had been for Lydia. She had been startled, because the only person Lydia was likely to marry was Tom Fortune and he was locked up in jail. And then Miles had also asked if Lydia ever saw anyone, and Nat had asked if she received any letters… A nasty suspicion formed in Alice's mind and she looked sharply at Lizzie to see if the same doubts had also occurred to her, but Lizzie was digging her spoon into the dish of jellied chicken and chattering to Mrs. Lister about what she could see in the tea leaves.

"The raven," Mrs. Lister said, peering into the depths of her cup. "That means bad news or a reversal of fortune."

"That will be for Lord Vickery then," Lizzie said. "Nat told me that he was planning to auction off the contents of Drum Castle next week because he is so debt-ridden that he will be clapped in the Fleet before long."

Alice remembered the bleak look in Miles's eyes when he had told her he stood to lose everything. No wonder he had pressed her so hard to accept him. He had not lied when he said that he would be ruined by debt. She struggled against a sudden and treacherous feeling of sympathy for Miles having to endure the humiliation of losing his entire birthright in so public a manner. Then she felt angry at her own weakness. Miles deserved no pity from her.

"Truly?" she said. "Lord Vickery's situation is genuinely that bad?"

"Worse than bad," Lizzie said cheerfully. "That is why the sale is happening so soon. The lawyers pressed Lord Vickery to it as soon as he inherited as the only way to save himself. They are to sell off the farmland and other parts of the estate, and the entire contents of the castle. The only thing that cannot be sold is the castle itself, for it is entailed." She turned back to Mrs. Lister. "I thought that we might take the carriage out to Drum next week, ma'am, and see how the sale goes? We could buy ourselves a few souvenirs—"

"Lizzie, no!" Alice said, revolted. "That is like vultures picking over a carcass!"

"Well someone has to buy the goods," Lizzie said, unmoved, "and it might as well be us! I hear that the late marquis had some delightful porcelain figures—though not all of them are quite respectable—but I know that your mama would like to increase her collection by buying some of the more tasteful ones."

This decided the matter. Mrs. Lister was most enthusiastic, and Alice found herself overruled. "For, my dear," Mrs. Lister said reasonably, "our money is as good as anyone else's and I think we should make a show."

It went much against the grain with Alice, but then she thought of Miles's ruthless attempt to blackmail her into marriage and she felt cold and sick. Why was she wasting her sympathy on a man who did not understand the meaning of the word *compassion?* He deserved nothing from her other than her absolute disdain. Her money was her own to do with as she chose until she wed, provided that her trustees approved. If she embarrassed Miles by making a vulgar show of her fortune only a week after being blackmailed into accepting his hand in marriage, then he had no one to blame but himself.

"By all means let us go to Drum," she said, "and buy up the marquis's entire estate if we wish. The more I think about it, the more the idea appeals to me."

CHAPTER SIX

"OH, DARLING, I cannot believe that such an *appalling* thing could have happened!" Dorothea, the Dowager Lady Vickery, rushed into the drawing room of Drum Castle, enfolded her elder son in a scented embrace, then released him to stand back and dab artistically at her eyes with her inadequate and lacy handkerchief. "I am so sorry for you, Miles, darling! To have inherited the Marquisate of Drum is... Well, it is quite..." Words seemed to fail her and she took refuge once more in wiping the tears from her eyes.

"It's a damned disaster," Miles finished for her, "begging your pardon, Mama." He had been working on the estate finances in preparation for Churchward's visit, and the grim columns of figures had not improved his mood. Drum had been badly run for years and had brought in very little income. His cousins had suffered from a congenital failure to understand that they had no money to spend. The combination of the two was disastrous and meant that he was more deeply in debt than he had realized. Alice's eighty thousand pounds would clear most of the debt, and selling off those parts of the estate that were not entailed would ease the situation a little, but once he and Alice were married and her money spent the two of them would have nothing other than his Home Office salary—which was barely enough for one to live on, not two—and this ruined monstrosity of a castle. They would be surviving on credit for the rest of their lives unless he could think of a way to make a fortune.

Under the circumstances the arrival of his mother was about as welcome as one of the plagues of Egypt. He looked at her with ill-concealed impatience. "Might I ask what you are doing here, ma'am?" he said. "I really did not expect this."

The dowager opened her hazel eyes plaintively wide. "We came to support you in your hour of need, darling," she said. She gestured airily toward the door. "Celia is here, and Philip, too. When I realized that dear Mr. Churchward was coming to consult with you on matters of business—" she waved a hand at the lawyer, who was struggling into the room weighed down with what looked like a monstrous amount of the dowager's luggage "—I prevailed upon him to allow us to accompany him. We knew that you would need us by your side at this difficult time."

"How perceptive of you, Mama," Miles said grimly. He nodded to the lawyer. "Churchward, you have my sympathies. I wish you had not bothered to come, Mama," he added brutally, turning back to his mother. "This place is utterly uninhabitable, there are no servants and I will be selling off all the contents next week. There is nowhere for you to stay and you know you hate the north of England."

The dowager's expression set into lines that were surprisingly mulish. "Well, we shall all manage somehow," she said briskly. "And you need not fear that we will have to stay in this ghastly *ruin*—" she cast the baronial room a look of profound dislike "—for we have arranged to visit your cousin Laura Anstruther at the Old Palace in Fortune's Folly. I only had the luggage brought in because the carriage is so ancient that it *leaks* and the weather in the North is so *appalling.*"

"You are staying with Laura?" Miles asked. That was bad news, he thought, for it meant that Lady Vickery would be established in Fortune's Folly for at least a month, possibly longer. He groaned inwardly. That would give her ample time to interfere in his courtship of Alice and cause all sorts of problems.

"I am so looking forward to getting to know Laura's new husband better," his mother was saying. "The Home Secretary speaks most highly of him. I hear he is one of the Hertfordshire Anstruthers. He is *vastly* handsome, is he not?"

"Dexter isn't my type," Miles said grimly, making a mental note to ask his friend what the hell he was playing at to allow Laura to invite his entire family to stay.

Celia Vickery came up to him and offered a cool cheek for him to kiss. "How are you, Miles?" she said, appraising him with her sharp hazel gaze. "Still alive, I see. The Curse of Drum has not yet carried you off."

"Give it time," Miles said. "Could you not have dissuaded Mama from coming, Celia?" he added, scarcely bothering to lower his voice. "You know I don't want any of you here."

His sister, the eldest of the family and unmarried at thirty-three, gave him an old-fashioned look. In appearance Celia was like their mother, with the same oval face, dark brown hair and winged eyebrows that had once proclaimed Lady Vickery a beauty. Yet it was odd, Miles thought, that the looks that had made

Dorothea Vickery a diamond of the first water were somehow muted in her daughter. Celia could probably be described as well to a pass but she was no incomparable. Nor was she remotely like their mother in temperament but more like Miles himself, cool, cynical and direct.

"Of course I could not put her off," Celia said. "You know mother is as persuadable as a Nile crocodile! Do you think I wanted to traipse all the way up here to see you, Miles?" she added. "It is the most damnable nuisance." Her expression softened slightly as she looked at Philip, who was admiring a huge, dusty suit of armor that stood in a dark corner. "Actually I think Philip wanted to come. He enjoyed the travel and the new scenes, and he wanted to see you, Miles—"

Miles turned away from the appeal in her eyes. Philip, a late child and the apple of his mother's eye, had been five years old when Miles had quarreled so dreadfully with their father and had left home to join the army. The boy was a stranger to him and that was the way Miles intended to leave it. It was far, far too late for him to establish a relationship with his family and he did not even want to try.

"There are no servants to make any refreshments, I fear," he said pointedly as his mother sat down on an ancient chaise longue and raised a cloud of dust that almost choked them. "Why do you not repair to Fortune's Folly now whilst Mr. Churchward and I conduct our business, Mama? I could join you all later for dinner."

The dowager turned her expressive hazel eyes on him. "But, Miles, darling, we have only just arrived," she protested. She settled back more comfortably, gestured Philip to sit beside her, and it was clear that she was going absolutely nowhere.

Miles sighed. He drove his hands into the pockets of his well-cut jacket of green superfine—fourteen pounds from Mr. Welbeck, the premier men's outfitter in York, who was never likely to see the cash for it—and strolled over to the window. Outside, the early February day was already closing in; a gray mist hung over the Yorkshire fells, and the sleet spattered the window. The wind whistled in the chimneys and sent the cobwebs scurrying across the floor. The last thing that Miles wanted was his family with him in Yorkshire at such a time. They had already been obliged to sit by when he had sold Vickery House out from under them two years before, and before that Vickery Place, the sprawling country house in Berkshire where Miles and his brother and sisters had grown up. Now he would be selling Drum, as well, or at least the bits of the estate that were not entailed, plus all furnishings, fixtures and fittings. The *Ton* would soon be calling him the Merchant Marquis, or some such cutting sobriquet, for he was the man who had put his entire birthright on the market. He did not care, but he knew his mother would. The financial ruin of the Vickery barony and her consequent loss of status had hit her hard.

"I appreciate your concern for me, Mama," Miles said carefully, without turning back to look at his mother, "and I realize that it is distressing for you to know that I am even more deeply in debt now than I was before I inherited Drum—"

"Oh, I am not worried about the debt!" Lady Vickery declared. She had always had a rather tenuous grasp of finance. "You can always find an heiress to wed, Miles! No, I am here because of the Curse of Drum! It is the most lamentable piece of bad luck to befall our family in years! You are doomed, Miles, positively doomed!"

Miles remembered Nat Waterhouse commenting on his mother's superstitious nature and tried to smother his annoyance. "The only doom that is waiting for me, Mama," he said, "is a sojourn in the Fleet if I cannot find myself an heiress in short order. You know I don't believe in all that superstitious twaddle about the Curse of Drum."

"You should do," the dowager said crossly. "Look at your cousin Freddie! Dead in a bawdy house fire and he had only been Marquis of Drummond for a twelvemonth!"

"Miles is more likely to die worn out by one of his mistresses, like Cousin William," Celia put in waspishly.

"Thank you, Celia," Miles said as Lady Vickery covered Philip's ears. "I am duly warned and can only hope that I have more stamina or perhaps more discrimination in my amorous adventures than Cousin Billy had." He sighed irritably. The family curse was something that he treated with absolute contempt. He had not been a soldier for eleven years in order to develop a superstitious fear of death. As far as he was concerned the Curse of Drum only related to the fact that his cousins had been profligate to a man and had left thousands of pounds owing to the moneylenders.

"Miles, you are a disgrace," his mother said reproachfully. "I am sure that your poor papa would be turning in his grave to hear you speak thus."

"Papa did not have to be dead to disapprove of me," Miles said evenly. "He would probably feel that the inheritance of Drum was my just deserts for a misspent life. No doubt he would say it was a judgment on me."

Lady Celia stifled a laugh. "Papa was very keen on hellfire and damnation," she said.

"As was appropriate for so eminent a man of the cloth," Lady Vickery pointed out, smoothing the widow's weeds she had worn for the past five years, since her husband had died. In the pale winter light she looked delicate and artfully pale, the epitome of the grieving widow. Miles's father had been a younger son who had gone into the church, had unexpectedly inherited his brother's barony and had risen to become Bishop of Rochester. The presence of the beautiful, high-born, gracious Dorothea at his side had done much to ensure his preferment and it was frequently said that His Grace would have reached the dizzy heights of the See of York or even Canterbury if only he had not died relatively young.

"Oh, we all know that Papa was all that was appropriate for a bishop," Lady Celia said, with an edge to her voice that made Miles look at her closely. She did not meet his eyes but fidgeted with the stitching on her cuff. "He was an example to us all."

"Celia, a little respect, if you please," Lady Vickery said in a fading voice. "I know that you and your father had your differences, but Aloysius is *dead*."

Celia made a small sound of disgust. Looking at her, Miles could see pity as well as impatience in her eyes as they dwelled on their mother's tragic, piquant face.

"Mama," Celia said, "it is Papa's fault that Miles is in such desperate financial straits. Had he not been so extravagant, Miles would not have *two* cursed inheritances to contend with rather than one—"

Lady Vickery gave a little cry of distress and her

daughter fell silent as the lacy handkerchief was applied again.

"Your papa was a good man." Lady Vickery sniffed. "I will not hear another word against him, Celia! Do you hear me? He did his best for us all."

There was an awkward little silence in the room. It was generally known within the *Ton* as well as within the Vickery family that the late bishop had been a deplorable spendthrift, just as Celia had said. He had entertained on a lavish scale and had not understood the meaning of the word *retrench* even when the bailiffs were at his door. Lady Vickery, Miles knew, tried to forget this regrettable aspect of her late husband's character and had unofficially canonized him. As for the rest of the late Lord Vickery's sins, they had been hidden so deep that no one would ever uncover them. Miles was aware that he was the only person who knew of his father's transgressions.

He knew because he was the one who had taken the blame.

The anger stirred in him again, dark, painful and poisonous. He had worked so hard to lay those memories to rest along with his father. He would not allow them to be exposed now. It was ancient history, dead and buried. There was nothing that could be done to right old wrongs.

Mr. Churchward cleared his throat very loudly. The tips of his ears glowed bright red, a sign of his extreme discomfort on hearing family squabbles rehearsed before him.

"Returning to the Curse of Drum, my lord," he said.

"I do believe that you should treat the tales with a little more circumspection."

Miles raised his brows. "I would not have expected you to indulge a belief in superstition, Churchward," he drawled. "You are a man of the law, a believer in evidence and reason."

Churchward blushed rather endearingly. He removed his spectacles and polished them agitatedly. "The empirical proof is too strong to ignore, my lord," he said. "Sixteen marquises dead in less than one hundred years—"

"All dying in violent and horrible ways." Lady Vickery shuddered, whilst Philip looked rather excited, as though he wanted the details.

"The result of no more than excessive carelessness," Miles said. "You know our cousins were the most reckless, foolish and generally decadent of men."

"But once the curse has taken you…" Churchward said unhappily.

"Philip will be next in line for the marquisate," Celia Vickery finished, her words dropping into the room like pebbles down a well.

This aspect of the situation had already occurred to Miles although he wished that his sister had not made it quite so explicit. The Dowager Lady Vickery was looking stricken now, and Miles felt impatient to see his mama's distress. She cared too much, that was the problem. She cared about their father's reputation, she cared desperately about Philip's future, she cared about the loss of Drum, and she even cared about *him* with a fondness Miles found inexplicable and utterly unwelcome. Looking at Philip's youthful, clear-cut profile, Miles felt some emotion stir within him and dismissed it abruptly. It was too late for him to have any feelings of love or affection or even obligation toward his family. Old memories and emotions rose in him and he slammed the door on them, trapping them in the dark recesses of his mind. He wanted no love from his family now. He had lost them all when he had been eighteen, and it was too late to heal the breach. He would pack his mother and siblings off back to the South as soon as he could. They had, at least, been offered the sanctuary of a grace-and-favor cottage on a cousin's estate in Kent so he need not worry that they would starve. They lived in vastly reduced circumstances, they were poor relations, but at least they were not begging on the streets.

"Mr. Appleby," Philip said importantly, "is of the opinion that a belief in superstition is no more than a demonstration of an ill-educated mind."

"Your tutor is a man of great wisdom," Miles said. "I am glad to think that you are not in the care of a superstitious fool."

"But we must make *sure*," Lady Vickery protested. "We cannot afford to take any risks!" She sat forward in her seat and grabbed hold of Philip's hand in what she clearly thought was a reassuring grip. "The only solution is for you to marry at once, Miles. I know that you have always been most resistant to the idea of matrimony, but it is your duty to provide an heir immediately in order to save your brother!"

"A charming thought, Mama," Lady Celia murmured. "Miles can ensure the succession of another hapless sacrifice to the Curse of Drum."

Miles smiled at her. "On past experience I do not think that one son will be enough, Mama," he said.

"Drummond needs an heir and several spares before Philip is safe. Look how many of our cousins have been cut down in the past."

"Pray do not joke about it, Miles," his mother said, her lip quivering piteously. "You always had a most lamentably odd sense of humor."

"Your mama does have a point, my lord," Mr. Churchward said. "It would be extremely advantageous for you to marry, and preferably to an heiress. Leaving aside the so-called curse, that would at least buy you time and stave off the most pressing of the moneylenders—"

He broke off as there was a loud ping from one of the springs in his wing chair. "I do beg your pardon," he added. "This chair is particularly uncomfortable."

"The furnishings here are all ghastly," Lady Celia agreed, looking around the high-ceilinged room with deep disapproval. "The first thing that Miles should do is to have a bonfire."

"Can't do that," Miles said. "When I say we have to sell everything, Celia, I mean everything, down to the last stick of firewood and the last chamber pot."

Once again there was a silence. Lady Vickery fidgeted with her gloves. She looked pained, as though she had swallowed a fish bone. Celia's firm expression softened slightly.

"I am sorry, Miles," she said. "First Vickery Place, then Vickery House and now this! You must feel dreadful—"

"It can't be helped," Miles said briskly. Celia's sympathy was the last thing he wanted. He did not need her pity. He looked at his mother's pinched, white face. She was aware that he would forever be remembered as the man who had sold Vickery and sold Drum, too, the reckless, extravagant marquis who had brought the family fortunes so low that they were in the dust. It was unfair that he would take the blame for the extravagance of others but Miles was blisteringly aware that life was never fair. He had learned that lesson at eighteen when he was banished by his father for bringing the family honor low. Since then he had taught himself to care for nothing.

A knock resounded through the castle, the sound echoing off the stone of the walls and bouncing back to assault the eardrums. Lady Vickery winced.

"I believe that will be Frank Gaines, of Gaines and Partridge, the Skipton law firm," Miles said. He looked at Mr. Churchward. "I asked him to join us to discuss the very matter you touched upon, Churchward—the business of my marriage."

Lady Vickery gave a squeak of excitement. "Oh, Miles, you good, good boy! I knew you would not stand by and see your brother taken by the family curse!"

"This has nothing to do with the curse, Mama," Miles said harshly, "and everything to do with my need to marry money very quickly indeed."

"I will answer the door," Lady Celia said practically, rising to her feet, as the knocker thudded again.

"Celia, no." Lady Vickery was appalled. "That is what the servants are for."

"Miles has no servants, Mama," Celia said. "Have you not been attending? He is ruined, in Queer Street." The knocker sounded a third time and she frowned. "Good gracious but Mr. Gaines is an impatient man."

"Thank you, Celia," Miles said as she headed for the door.

His sister dropped him a curtsy laced with irony and left the room. Whilst she was gone, Miles leaned an arm along the top of the stone mantelpiece—which needed a good clean and left a line of dust on the sleeve of his jacket—and reflected how uncomfortable the other occupants of the room looked. Philip was fidgeting and looked thoroughly bored to be so confined. Miles wished his mother had left Philip in London with his tutor. The boy should really be at school, but Miles could no longer afford to pay for his brother's education and had only been able to afford the services of Mr. Appleby because he was a distant connection of the dowager and had grudgingly offered to reduce his fees out of family feeling. It was something, Miles thought, when even the tutor was patronizing his poor relations.

Lady Vickery, meanwhile, looked as though she was sitting on a bed of nettles. Clearly the news of Miles's imminent betrothal had excited her considerably and she could not wait to hear the details. She huddled on the sofa in her winter pelisse, holding her hands out toward the fireplace in a vain attempt to get warm. In this drafty medieval castle it seemed almost impossible to build up any heat at all. The stone fireplaces were all broad enough to house an army, and the fire that Miles had coaxed into life in the red drawing room today could not be felt beyond a radius of three feet.

Mr. Churchward shuffled his papers again for no particular reason and cleared his throat simply to break the silence. He looked as though he would be happier taking refuge behind a desk and preferably one a long way away from this shabby castle with its uneasy atmosphere. He, too, was a man who preferred the bustle of city life, and Miles knew that the isolation and harsh beauty of these Yorkshire hills was not to everyone's taste, particularly in winter. And then there was Drum Castle itself, which seemed so different from Miles's childhood memories. He had spent a great deal of time here in his holidays from Eton, for his cousin Anthony had been an almost exact contemporary of his and the castle had rung with sounds of their martial games. Miles was not remotely superstitious, but even he was forced to admit that there was something strangely oppressive about these dark rooms now, crisscrossed as they were with spiders' webs and trails of dust. Drum Castle seemed positively Gothic now, weighed down by its heavy furnishings and by the dark curtains that closed off the dusty windows. Today, with the wind lifting the hangings from the old stone of the walls and making the building creak and groan, it felt like a castle in a nightmare. Really, Miles thought, one would hardly need a family curse to send one demented in a very short space of time.

Miles thought of the so-called Curse of Drum and of the deaths of his two predecessors. His cousin Freddie's death had been unpleasant, but it could have happened to anyone, Miles thought ruefully, or at least to anyone who had the sensual appetite of his cousin and the lack of discretion to match.

Anthony, the fifteenth marquis, had been a different matter. He had been cut down at Vimiero, a member of the 20th Light Dragoons who had suffered shocking losses during a cavalry charge. Miles, who had seen the action himself, shuddered inwardly. He had liked Anthony very much and still felt his loss keenly. Their childhood friendship had matured into an easy adult comradeship. His cousin was one of the few people he had been able to talk to of their shared experiences in the Peninsular Wars. Coming back to civilian society had been a strange and isolating experience after the carnage of the battlefield. No one who had not been there could understand what it had been like, and the well-meaning attempts of some of Miles's relatives and friends to assure him that they understood his dark moods simply made him feel more alone.

The door opened and Celia reentered the room, followed by a man in well-cut clothes who looked to Miles's eyes more like a sportsman than a lawyer. Frank Gaines was a big man, tall, broad shouldered and with the durable air of someone who would wear well in adversity. He had brown hair peppered with gray and a humorous but observant glint in his gray eyes. His face was lined and burned dark from the sun, and his nose looked like a bent bow. Miles liked him on sight, although he was fairly certain that any cordiality between them was unlikely to last through the discussions of his proposal of marriage to Alice Lister. As one of Alice's trustees, Gaines would be a difficult man to win over.

Miles was also amused to see that Celia, whose chilly composure in the presence of the opposite sex was legendary, was looking ever so slightly flustered. He wondered what on earth had occurred between Frank Gaines and his sister in the hall.

Gaines set a chair for Celia, who thanked him in arctic tones. He gave her a look that made her blush, faintly but distinctly, and set her lips in a very straight line. Mentally raising his brows, Miles held out a hand to Gaines and was not surprised to discover that the other man had a very firm handshake.

"Glad you were able to join us, Gaines," he said.

"How do you do, my lord," Gaines responded. "It is a pleasure to see you in such good health."

Miles's lips twitched. "Thank you, Gaines. Give me time. I have only been Marquis of Drummond for a very short while. My relatives are doing their best to convince me that the family curse will carry me off in the fullness of time."

"Indeed, my lord," Gaines said, smiling.

"May I introduce my mother, the Dowager Lady Vickery, and my brother, Philip," Miles said. "My sister you have just met, of course, and Mr. Churchward must be well-known to you, I imagine."

Gaines bowed to Lady Vickery and to Philip with aplomb, gave Lady Celia a look that made her raise her chin with hauteur and nodded to Churchward. He took the chair Miles indicated and sat down, uncoiling his long length with a sigh.

"Would you care for refreshment, Mr. Gaines?" the dowager asked hospitably.

"Because if so," Celia put in, "you will have to make it yourself. My brother has no servants, having no money with which to pay them."

"At the least we are spared that shocking stew that passes for tea in these parts," the dowager said with a shudder. "You can stand a spoon up in it!"

"That is how we drink tea in Yorkshire," Miles said. "Churchward, Gaines and I are going to get down to business now, Mama," he added. "Might I try to persuade you once again to repair to Fortune's Folly where, one hopes, Laura's servants will be able to serve you tea to your satisfaction?"

"I would not dream of it!" the dowager declared. "If

you are to discuss your marriage plans, Miles, then I wish to be here!"

"And so do I," Celia added, unexpectedly, "to hear which deluded woman is actually prepared to accept your suit, Miles."

"As to that," Miles said, "I yesterday made a proposal of marriage to Miss Alice Lister of Fortune's Folly." He turned courteously to Churchward. "I apologize that I have not had the opportunity to apprise you of my plans in advance, Mr. Churchward. I understand that you are one of Miss Lister's trustees, with Mr. Gaines here as the other, which was why I asked to speak with both of you today."

"Indeed I am Miss Lister's trustee, my lord," Churchward said, surprise registering in his voice. He exchanged a look with Frank Gaines, who raised his brows expressively.

"Has…has Miss Lister accepted your suit, my lord?" Churchward continued, in tones that did not fall far short of incredulity.

Miles nodded. "She has."

He saw Frank Gaines stiffen at the news and his brows snap down in intimidating fashion. "Indeed, my lord," he said. "You do surprise me. I was under the impression that Miss Lister held you in strong dislike."

"I managed to find a way to persuade her," Miles said smoothly. He knew the lawyer was suspicious but told himself that Gaines could not prove anything—not if Alice kept quiet about the blackmail, which she surely would having so much to lose.

"Oh, Miles could persuade any woman to marry him if he tried hard enough," Lady Vickery put in helpfully, "and what young lady would not wish to be Marchioness of Drummond?" She leaned forward. "How big is Miss Lister's fortune?"

Mr. Gaines and Mr. Churchward exchanged another look. "Miss Lister inherited a sum in the region of eighty thousand pounds, madam," Gaines said carefully, "and in addition she has properties in London and Skipton. There are, however, conditions attached to the inheritance when Miss Lister comes to wed."

"So I understand," Miles said.

"How tiresome," the dowager proclaimed. "Why must people always make these matters so complicated?"

"In order to protect the heiress from unscrupulous fortune hunters, madam," Gaines said, looking straight at Miles. Miles smothered a grin. The lawyer had his measure, no doubt of it, but there was little that he could do.

"Since you are insisting on being party to this discussion, Mama," Miles said, "I suppose I should inform you of the background. Miss Lister is a former maidservant who last year inherited the fortune of her late employer—"

Lady Vickery's face registered an appalled expression. "Miles, darling," she said, "surely you cannot be considering an alliance with the *servant classes?*"

"Better Miles wed a servant girl with money than be clapped up in the Fleet prison for debt, Mama," Celia said bracingly.

Lady Vickery sighed melodramatically. "Do you think so? I suppose it might be. At least we can use her money to pay off the debts and we can all move into her house in London. It does not matter if she is not presentable. Well, it matters a little, for people *will* talk scandal about you marrying beneath you, Miles, but we shall just have to manage. We can make up some excuse as to why your wife cannot go into society. She could be delicate, perhaps. Everyone will know that we are lying, but at least she need not be seen in public—"

"Mama," Miles interjected, holding up a hand to stop the flow of words, "Miss Lister has perfect manners and is entirely presentable."

"Then I suppose she must be as ugly as sin," Lady Vickery mourned, "for there is bound to be something wrong with her. A servant! Hands the size of hams to do so much manual labor, I suppose—"

"Miss Lister is accounted uncommonly pretty, my lady," Frank Gaines interposed, steel underlying his tone. "She would grace the name of Vickery." *More than your family deserves,* his tone implied.

"A pretty servant girl," Celia snapped. She sounded put out at Gaines's words. "Why, that is right up your street, Miles. What are we waiting for? Call the banns!"

Miles looked at the lawyers, who both looked back at him with very straight faces. "There is, as Mr. Gaines mentioned, a small difficulty," he murmured.

"The conditions attached to the match?" Celia asked.

"Quite so," Miles said. "Miss Lister's trustees—" he inclined his head toward the lawyers "—have to agree that I am a worthy suitor. In fact, I believe I have to prove it to them over a period of three months." He raised his brows interrogatively. "Gaines? Churchward? Do you think I stand the remotest chance?"

"You put me in a very difficult position, my lord," Mr. Churchward said unhappily. "Very tricky indeed." He shook his head. "Oh dear, oh dear. I hope you will not take offense when I say I wish that your choice had *not* alighted on Miss Lister, of all people."

"I told you there was something wrong with the gel!" Lady Vickery said triumphantly.

"On the contrary, madam," Churchward said, looking chagrined, "I am of the same mind as Mr. Gaines that Miss Lister is an utterly charming young woman." He turned to Miles. "As your family lawyer I have to advise you to marry an heiress, my lord, but as Miss Lister's trustee I have to say that you are an entirely inappropriate and unworthy suitor, and I would be very remiss in my duty to give my permission to the match."

"Not an overwhelming endorsement, then," Miles said. "Gaines." He turned to the other man. "Are you of the same mind?"

"No, my lord," the lawyer said. He met Miles's gaze very squarely. "I would put the matter more starkly than Mr. Churchward has. I am of the mind that it would be well nigh impossible for you to convince me of your worth. You are a rake, a gamester and a blatant fortune hunter—"

"Oh, that is nonsense!" Lady Vickery interposed. "Miles does not gamble!"

"Lord Vickery has never made any secret of his *affaires,* madam," Gaines said sharply. "He set up a notorious courtesan as his mistress—"

"Not in front of the boy!" Lady Vickery said, covering Philip's ears again.

"The relationship between myself and Miss Caton is over," Miles said. "I am quite reformed."

Celia smothered a snort of disbelief and Gaines gave Miles a wintry smile. "That remains to be seen," he murmured. "Then there was the matter of Miss Bell, the nabob's daughter."

"That was most unfortunate," the dowager put in. "Unfortunate in that she jilted Miles, I mean. She was the biggest heiress in London. Ghastly parents, of course, but one must simply concentrate on the money."

"I am aware of the circumstances, madam," Mr. Gaines said, with cold courtesy. "Lord Vickery abandoned his earlier pursuit of Miss Lister in order to win the larger financial prize—"

"And then lost his gamble because at the time he was only a baron and Miss Bell preferred an earl," Celia said, smiling. "She will be kicking herself now that Miles has inherited a marquisate."

"Such accidents of fate overset even the most careful planning," Lady Vickery said. "All the same, it serves the chit right."

"I accept," Miles said, "that the episode does not reflect well on me." Under Frank Gaines's chilly scrutiny he was starting to feel like a schoolboy hauled up in front of the headmaster at Eton.

"You are a cad," Celia pointed out.

"Thank you, Celia," Miles said. "Your help in this matter is much appreciated."

"I believe your sister has summed up the situation very succinctly," Gaines said.

"So," Celia said, eyebrows raised, "no lawyerly approval, then?"

Churchward shuffled his papers again and avoided Miles's gaze. Gaines met it head-on in a moment of tension.

"Mr. Gaines and Mr. Churchward cannot actually refuse me at this point," Miles said softly. "If I fulfill

Lady Membury's conditions, which are that I prove myself an honest and worthy gentleman over a period of three months, then they must accede to Miss Lister's wishes and agree to the match."

"Three months!" the dowager said. "That might be a little ambitious for you, darling."

"Well nigh impossible, as Mr. Gaines has said," Celia opined.

"Not at all," Miles said. "I have reformed in order to win Miss Lister's hand."

He saw Frank Gaines's lips set in a line of grim disapproval. "Why Miss Lister would even consider you as a suitable husband is beyond me, my lord," he said.

Miles smiled blandly. "Perhaps Miss Lister pities me, being doubly burdened with both a family debt and a family curse. Or perhaps she feels that I need to change my ways and she thinks she is the woman to reform me," he said.

Churchward looked at Gaines, who shook his head in a gesture of exasperation.

"It is true that Miss Lister devotes herself to a variety of lost causes," Mr. Churchward said with resignation, "but in this case…"

"You feel that she has overreached herself?" Miles murmured.

"I think, my lord," Churchward said with asperity, "that Miss Lister is most misguided. Reform you indeed! A desperately unlikely state of affairs!"

"I can barely wait to meet her, Miles," Celia said. "A devotee of lost causes, eh? She might be just the woman for you."

"So I think," Miles said smoothly. He turned back to the lawyers. "If I do somehow manage to meet the requirements of Lady Membury's will and behave as an upright and worthy gentleman for three months," he said, "you cannot refuse consent, can you, gentlemen?"

Once again Gaines and Churchward exchanged a look. "No, my lord," Gaines admitted reluctantly, "we cannot. Not if you fulfill Lady Membury's stipulations." He gave Miles a particularly piercing look. "I take it that Miss Lister has at least had the sense to refuse an official announcement until you have fulfilled the conditions?"

"Sadly," Miles said, "she has. And I have agreed."

He saw Gaines relax infinitesimally. "Then perhaps she has not completely lost all sense," he said grimly.

"I assure you that Miss Lister made her decision in full possession of her faculties," Miles said. "She is an admirably strong and resolute woman." He nodded politely to the lawyers. "I look forward to fulfilling the terms of Lady Membury's will and making the official announcement in due course." He smiled. "You will see, gentlemen, just how worthy I can be when there is a fortune at stake."

CHAPTER SEVEN

"IF THIS IS THE CREAM of Fortune's Folly society," Lizzie Scarlet said, flicking her fan crossly as she and Alice stood viewing the sparsely populated ballroom at the Granby Hotel that evening, "then I may as well resign myself to remaining a spinster. Fortune's Folly in the winter is so dull! There is not a single gentleman here that pleases me, Alice, except for your brother, Lowell, and you will not let me flirt with him, so where is the fun?"

"You are only cross because Lord Waterhouse is dancing attendance on Miss Minchin," Alice responded. It had been hard to ignore the fact that Lizzie had been in a foul temper all evening. If it came to that, Alice was in a foul temper, too, and was out of patience with herself because of it. She felt edgy and anxious. She had expected to see Miles and had found herself looking for him as soon as they entered the ballroom. When she had realized he was not present she had felt angry and slighted. It was typical of Miles's breathtaking conceit to demand that she be there and that she save a dance for him, and then to be absent. She slapped her fan into the palm of her glove in a gesture of irritation.

Lizzie was still grumbling about Nat Waterhouse.

"You are quite unreasonable, you know, Lizzie," Alice said, cutting her off, "for poor Lord Waterhouse must devote a *little* time to his affianced bride. You know he will come back to you in the end, for he enjoys your company too much to give you up."

She did not miss the small, self-satisfied smile on Lizzie's face as her friend contemplated her eventual triumph over poor Flora Minchin. No doubt Lizzie had not even spared one second's thought for how Miss Minchin might feel to have a suitor who spent much of his time with another woman. Lady Elizabeth Scarlet was very sure of her power, Alice thought, and why should she not be confident when she was beautiful and rich and titled, and had all the self-assurance that came with inherited privilege? In her beautiful sea-green silk and lace gown Lizzie looked poised and elegant with an innate style that bespoke birthright. She looked glossy, Alice thought, in the same way that Miles Vickery also looked expensive and self-assured even though he was a pauper.

Alice shifted a little, sighing. In contrast to Lizzie she still felt a little unsure of herself whenever she went out into society. She had had the dancing lessons and she could converse and play cards and do all the things that a real debutante heiress could do, but every day she was conscious of the sideways looks and the whispered comments. She thought that she always would be. Even her gown of rose pink, which both Lizzie and Lydia had admired extremely, could not give her the inner confidence she lacked.

One of Lizzie's admirers, a young army captain called John Jerrold, came over to carry her off for a cotillion, and Lowell arrived with two glasses of lemonade, one of which he handed his sister.

"I see I have missed my chance with Lady Elizabeth," he said in his lazy country drawl, putting the second glass down on a ledge beside them, next to one of the carved marble busts of Grecian goddesses that adorned the alcoves in the ballroom. "Can't drink this ghastly stuff myself and the Granby never serves beer on evenings like this."

Alice smothered a snort to think of her brother bringing a tankard in from the taproom.

"I'd give a great deal to see you drinking beer in the ballroom in front of the Duchess of Cole," she said, nodding toward Lydia's mama, who was holding court in the chaperones' corner, surrounded by her cronies. Faye Cole had managed to ride out the scandal of her daughter's pregnancy by virtue of being the first and loudest to condemn Lydia, and she remained an arbiter of county society. Alice could not abide her. Neither could Mrs. Lister, who quite rightly blamed the duchess for being the architect of her social exclusion. Every so often the two of them would eye each other like prizefighters.

"The duchess will be distraught that Mama's feathers are higher than hers tonight," Lowell continued. "Could you not prevent her from buying such a monstrous headpiece, Allie? She looks like a cockatoo with such a high crest!"

Alice gave him a speaking look. "I would not dream of spoiling Mama's fun, Lowell. If she wishes to wear pearls and feathers and artificial roses, that is her choice."

"She's wearing them all together tonight," Lowell said gloomily. "Looks like an accident in a flower cart."

"I did not think you would care about it," Alice

said, slipping her hand through her brother's arm. "You never bother about what people say."

Lowell shrugged moodily. The morose expression sat oddly on his fair, open features. Normally he was the most equable of characters but Alice sensed there was something troubling him tonight.

"Lowell?" she prompted. "You do not really have a *tendre* for Lady Elizabeth, do you?"

Lowell's grim expression was banished as he gave her his flashing smile. "Good God, no! Did you think I was sulking because she prefers some sprig of the nobility to me? Lady Elizabeth is far above my touch. Besides, we would not suit."

"No," Alice agreed. "She needs someone less tolerant than you are."

"She needs to grow up," Lowell said brutally. "She's spoiled."

"She's been a good friend to me," Alice said, whilst not exactly contradicting him.

"I appreciate that," her brother said. He shot her a look. "You're not happy though, are you, Allie?"

Alice was startled at his perspicacity. "What do you mean? Of course I am—"

"No, you are not. Neither am I, and Mama is the unhappiest of all. She hates to be slighted like this." Lowell's gesture encompassed the ballroom with its neat rows of dancers, their reflections repeated endlessly in the long series of mirrors that adorned the walls. "Strange, is it not, that when you are hungry and exhausted from working all the hours there are, you think that to have money will cure all your woes?"

"It cures a great many of them," Alice said feelingly.

"But not the sense that somehow you have wandered

into the wrong party," Lowell said, his eyes still on the shifting patterns of the dance. "I am coming to detest the way in which we are patronized. This isn't our world, is it, Allie? If it was, you would be dancing rather than standing here like a wallflower."

"The only reason I am not dancing," Alice said, "is that I have refused proposals of marriage from so many of these gentlemen that there is no one left to stand up with me. No one except you, that is," she added. "If we do not fit in, then the least we can do is stand out with style."

Lowell grinned and let the matter go as he led her into the set of country dances that was forming.

"He dances well enough for a farm boy, I suppose," Alice heard the Duchess of Cole say as the movement of the dance took them past her coven, "but I never thought to see the day a *laborer* would be dancing in the Granby!"

Lowell laughed, executed a particularly ostentatious turn under the duchess's disapproving eye and bowed to Alice as the dance came to an end. "Better be getting back to the byre, I suppose," he drawled in his best rural accent. "Time's moving on and the cows will need milking early. Dashed slow business squiring my own sister about, anyway, when I would rather be tumbling a milkmaid in a haystack."

"Lowell, will you be quiet!" Alice grumbled, dragging her brother away as Faye Cole squawked like an outraged hen. "People will believe you!"

"Who says I am lying?" Lowell said unrepentantly. He glanced over her shoulder and his expression changed abruptly. "Alice—"

"Good evening, Miss Lister."

Alice spun around. Miles Vickery was standing just behind her, immaculate in his evening dress. Her stomach tumbled as she looked at him. Her breathing constricted. Miles took her hand. Determined not to show him how much his appearance had affected her, Alice gave him a cool smile.

"Lord Vickery," she said. "You are well?"

She saw Miles smile in return as he took her meaning.

"In the best of health, Miss Lister, I thank you," he said. "The Curse of Drum has yet to carry me off."

Alice could feel Lowell shifting impatiently beside her. He seemed incredulous that Miles should even approach her, which, Alice thought, was no great wonder given the nature of their previous acquaintance. She cast a quick look at her brother's face and saw that he was frowning ferociously. "Alice," he began again.

Alice turned to him, gripping his arm tightly in a gesture she hoped conveyed a plea for good behavior. "I am sorry," she said quickly. "Lord Vickery, may I introduce my brother, Lowell Lister? Lowell, this is Miles Vickery, Marquis of Drummond." She squeezed Lowell's arm again and gave him a speaking look into the bargain.

Miles held his hand out to shake Lowell's. "How do you do, Mr. Lister?" he said pleasantly. He did not adopt the patronizing air of superiority that most of the local aristocracy used when greeting the Lister family, the condescension of the great recognizing their inferiors. Alice noticed it and felt surprised.

Lowell, however, ignored both the hand and the greeting. "I know who you are," he said. "You are the… nobleman…who made a wager concerning my sister last year." His tone was steely.

Alice caught her breath. "Lowell—"

"I was," Miles said truthfully, his gaze meeting Alice's very directly. A smile still lurked in the depths of his hazel eyes. "Although," he added, "I now regret it most profoundly."

"Twenty guineas against my sister's virtue, so I heard," Lowell said, the contempt in his voice as cutting as a knife.

"You heard incorrectly," Miles said. "It was thirty guineas."

Alice drew a sharp breath. Why had she not foreseen that this might happen? This was such an inconvenient moment for Miles to start telling the truth on everything. The tension radiating from Lowell was so powerful as to be palpable. He clenched his fists.

"When my mother told me that you wished to renew your addresses to Alice, I thought there was some mistake," Lowell said. His eyes were narrowed pinpricks of fury. "Is it true that you still seek to marry her for her fortune?"

"My interest is not entirely in Miss Lister's fortune," Miles drawled, making his meaning explicitly clear. Alice felt the color rush into her face. She saw Lowell take an involuntary step forward.

"Lowell," she said again, "not here, not *now*."

Lowell turned on her. "I cannot believe that you are prepared to tolerate this man's company for a single moment, Alice!"

"It's complicated," Alice said, avoiding looking at Miles and placing a placatory hand on her brother's arm. "Lord Vickery and I have an understanding. I'll explain later. Please leave this—"

"You're defending me," Miles said. "That's very sweet."

"I am trying to avoid a public scene," Alice said tersely. She gave a sharp sigh as Lowell shook off her hand and stalked away. "Perhaps I should follow him and try to explain," she said.

"Don't," Miles said. "He has gone to the card room. You will only cause more speculation if you follow him in there. The worst that is likely to happen is that he will be so angry he will lose heavily. Inconvenient, I know, when you are paying his bills, but there it is."

Alice gave him an exasperated look. "Did you have to provoke him like that?"

"I was telling the truth," Miles said. "I am obliged to do so under the terms of Lady Membury's will, if you recall." He took her arm and steered her away from the curious gazes of the other guests. "Am I supposed to lie and pretend that I do not want you, Miss Lister?" he added softly.

"Yes! No! I don't know!" Alice looked up, her troubled blue gaze tangling with his hazel one. There was a lazy smile on his lips but it was belied by the glint in his eyes. He looked dangerous. Alice pressed her fingers to her temples. "I did not realize that it would be like this!" she said.

"I appreciate that," Miles said, "but if I am to fulfill the terms of the agreement I must be honest." His fingers tightened on her elbow. "You wanted the truth from me, Miss Lister," he said. "Well, you will have it. And you will have to deal with that."

Alice bit her lip. She shook her head fiercely. "You said that there were good social reasons for not always telling the truth."

"There are. You have just experienced one of them." Miles laughed softly. "Never tell the hotheaded brother of a young lady that you desire her. It is asking for trouble."

"He could have challenged you!"

Miles shrugged. "I had every faith that you would come to my rescue before that happened, my sweet. Which you did."

"It was more than you deserved," Alice said hotly. She wished now that she had not followed her natural instinct to help him. She knew that she had always been far too kind.

Miles smiled. "That is true, as well. I deserve nothing from you."

His matter-of-fact acceptance of it, his utter lack of emotion, made Alice blink, until she remembered that Miles Vickery was renowned for having ice rather than blood in his veins. He did not care whether she was kind to him or not. It was not kindness he wanted from her.

"Very likely Lowell will never speak to me again," Alice said forlornly, suddenly feeling acutely lonely. She felt bereft to have lost her brother's support so swiftly and unexpectedly. She knew that she should have grasped the nettle before now and told her family and friends that she had accepted Miles's proposal, but there had never seemed to be a right time. There never would be, she realized. Her mother would be delighted, of course, and ask no difficult questions, but Lowell and Lizzie and Lydia all knew her too well to accept a feeble explanation and she could not think of any convincing ones.

"Lowell will come round," Miles said. "He'll speak to me, too. I'll think of a way to smooth matters over.

It would not do to be at odds with my future brother-in-law."

Alice glared at him. "This is all an entertainment to you, is it not, my lord!"

Miles shook his head. "On the contrary, Miss Lister, I am deadly serious. You have already seen tonight how determined I am to win your hand by meeting Lady Membury's stipulations. I assure you that I will stop at nothing."

They stood staring at one another whilst the tension seemed to spin out between them and the chatter and hum of the ballroom carried on unnoticed around them. Alice felt trapped and alone, captured by the intensity she could see in his eyes. There was such single-mindedness in Miles, such unwavering intent. When she had surrendered to his blackmail she'd had no idea of what she was unleashing.

"This frightens me," Alice whispered. "I don't like you. I hoped the terms of the will would make matters difficult for you."

Miles did not smile this time. "Oh, they have," he said. He raised a hand to her cheek and she felt his gloved fingers brush her skin in the lightest of touches. His hazel eyes were dark. "Be careful what you wish for, Miss Lister," he said. "The terms of the will have made matters difficult for you, as well, because my honesty now compels me to show you how much I want you."

He stopped and bent closer to her, and despite the crowded ballroom and the press of people about them and the curious glances, Alice had the absolute conviction that he was about to kiss her. His face was so close to hers that she instinctively closed her eyes. Immediately she did so her other senses took over. She could hear Miles's breathing, smell the tang of his cologne and the delicious scent of his body beneath it, a smell that went straight to her head and made it spin. She knew he was so close, only inches away from her, and then she sensed his withdrawal and opened her eyes quickly.

Miles had straightened up, swearing softly beneath his breath, and Alice turned to see a tall, rather gaunt woman bearing down on them with a determined look on her face. She had Miles's hazel eyes and brown hair, and an air of piercing intelligence.

"Celia, I had not forgotten that you and Mama had asked for an introduction to Miss Lister," Miles said. "I was intending to bring her over to you."

"You were such an unconscionably long time about it that Mama sent me instead," Celia Vickery said. She held out a hand to Alice. "How do you do, Miss Lister?"

"This is my sister, Celia," Miles said. "I apologize in advance for her. She is quite terrifying."

Celia Vickery gave her brother a look that would have stripped paint and then turned to smile at Alice. "I have been in a positive fever to make your acquaintance, Miss Lister," she said. "I was desperate to meet a woman brave—or foolish—enough to accept my brother's suit. You know that he is an inveterate fortune hunter, of course, so you can have no illusions about him. He has very little to commend him, I fear, other than the marquisate and his good looks, and you do not strike me as a ninnyhammer who would have her head turned by those. Are you sure you do not wish to reconsider?"

Alice glanced at Miles. His stance betrayed tension. He was watching his sister, not with the sort of acceptance and affection that Alice had for Lowell, for example, but with a definite wariness.

Alice smiled back at the older woman. "It is a pleasure to meet you, Lady Celia," she said. "I am sure you are right that your brother has little to commend him. I am accepting him out of a sense of pity, and in the unwavering belief that the Curse of Drum will carry him off before long, leaving me a widow."

Celia gave a bark of laughter. "Pity! How marvelous!" She gave Miles a malicious look. "I do not believe any woman has ever pitied you before, Miles."

"I am happy to take whatever Miss Lister offers me," Miles said smoothly, with a speaking glance at Alice.

"Hmm, well, I do not believe you for a moment, Miss Lister," Celia Vickery said, "but no doubt you have your reasons and I shall not press you. Oh, there is Mr. Gaines!" she added. "Pray excuse me. I really must go and importune him for a dance. It is rare enough for me to meet a man who is tall enough to partner me, but when he can also hold an intelligent conversation he is to be prized indeed." She smiled at Alice, gave her brother a sharp nod and walked away.

"Pity," Miles said thoughtfully as she walked away. "A neat setdown, Miss Lister."

"I thought so," Alice said. She watched Celia stroll over to Frank Gaines, who was standing with Mr. Churchward at the edge of the ballroom. Mr. Churchward was nursing a glass of lemonade and looking very ill at ease. Mr. Gaines was drinking some hot rum punch and looked entirely at home and entirely oblivious to the glances of disgust that the Duchess of Cole was shooting in his direction.

"I see that my lawyers are here tonight to ensure that

you behave in an upright and worthy manner, my lord," Alice said. She could not help a smile. "How tiresome for you! Do you think they will follow you around everywhere for three months?"

"Very probably," Miles said. "I am sure they will be disappointed by my blameless life. Mr. Gaines in particular is determined to catch me out and protect you from my dangerous ways."

"Well, that is what I pay him for," Alice said. She watched as Gaines handed his glass to Churchward, who looked as though he did not know what to do with it, and offered Celia Vickery his hand for the country dance that was forming.

"I think your sister is marvelous," she said. She looked up into Miles's face. "But tell me, does she really dislike you or is it merely her manner?"

Miles was silent for a long time, a rueful expression on his face. "Honesty compels me to say that I do not know Celia well so cannot answer with any certainty," he said finally.

Alice was startled. "How is it that you do not know her?"

"Not everyone is as close to their siblings as you are to Lowell," Miles said. There was a shade of expression in his voice that Alice could not place. "I have been away from my family a great deal and so have not had the opportunity to build a close relationship with them."

"I did not realize," Alice said. Once again she felt a treacherous stir of sympathy for him. She looked at him but his face was dark and closed, his expression impossible to read. "That must have been difficult for you," she said slowly, thinking of how she had always relied on the love and support provided by her mother and by Lowell in particular.

Miles shrugged. There was tension in the line of his shoulders. "There is no need to commiserate with me," he said. His voice was terse. "I have managed tolerably well to survive without them."

Alice frowned. "But surely it must have hurt you to be estranged from them?"

Miles's hand tightened on her arm. "Miss Lister, pray do not endow me with feelings that I do not possess. I assure you that I am not hurt." Then, as Alice shook her head slightly in disbelief, he added a little roughly, "Do I look vulnerable to you, Miss Lister?"

Alice looked at him and caught her breath at the hard, dangerous look in his eyes. "No," she whispered. "You look…" *Virile? Menacing?*

A man who was prepared to blackmail a woman into marriage for her money was hardly weak and defenseless, she thought, nor did he deserve any sympathy. Alice shivered, and knew that he had felt it.

"Quite," Miles said. "Save your pity for a more deserving cause." His grip on her arm was at the same time a warning and a gesture of possession as he steered her toward the corner where a gaggle of matrons occupied their rout chairs.

"You will allow me to introduce you to my mother, I hope, Miss Lister?" he said formally. "She is aware of our betrothal and as Celia mentioned, she is anxious to make your acquaintance."

"I am sure she is," Alice said. Miles had asked courteously, but she knew she had no choice other than to fall in with his wishes. His politeness was just for show.

Miles slanted a look down at her. "You will oblige me

by showing some enthusiasm for our betrothal this time, Miss Lister," he said, his words echoing Alice's thoughts.

"I shall muster what eagerness I can, my lord," Alice said coldly.

Unlike her daughter, Lady Vickery was tiny, and Alice thought that she must have been a diamond of the first water in her youth. She was still a very beautiful woman, with stunning bone structure, a very slim figure and not a trace of gray in the rich chestnut hair that was exactly the same shade as her son's. Her presence in the Granby's ballroom was provoking some interest and the Duchess of Cole was looking very put out to have a rival for the role of *grande dame* of the neighborhood. Lady Vickery might only be a baron's widow but that baron had also been a bishop, and Lady Vickery was the daughter of a viscount and had family connections to half the blue bloods of England. Faye Cole, on the other hand, might be a duchess now but had once been a mere Miss Bigelow, daughter of a coal magnate.

"My dear!" Lady Vickery grasped Alice's hands tightly as soon as she was within touching distance, drawing her down to sit beside her. "You look like a young woman with a *great deal* of compassion. Can I not *prevail* upon you to marry my son at once and do away with all these tiresome conditions and requirements? For my sake, if no one else's?"

Alice was laughing as she took a seat beside the dowager. "Yours is certainly an unusual approach, ma'am," she commented.

"May I appeal to you as a mother?" the dowager persisted. "I am absolutely *desperate* for you to marry Miles, my dear. Can you not elope and confound the lawyers that way? Three months is a dreadful long time to expect Miles to behave well. I am not at all sure he can do it. Besides, I must be frank and say that we are as poor as church mice, and we *need* you. We need you now! We are all in Queer Street and then there is this wretched family curse that is ruining all our lives and positively driving me to distraction! One cannot trifle with such dangerous things as curses, you know." She looked at her son. "And though we all know that Miles is an out-and-out scoundrel, and it would be foolish to pretend otherwise, I confess I am still too fond of him to wish him to die horribly."

Alice looked up at Miles. His expression was, she thought, particularly wooden. This time he met her gaze with absolutely no emotion at all.

"How interesting to know that your mother cares so deeply for you, my lord," Alice said. "What have you done to deserve her love?"

Miles laughed harshly. "That is a mother's privilege," he said, "regardless of whether or not such affection is justified."

Alice returned the grasp of the dowager's hand. She felt a slight shock as she saw the depth of sincerity in Lady Vickery's eyes. She had assumed that Miles had set his mother up to plead his case, but now she was not so sure. There was anxiety in the dowager's gaze as well as hope and a rather touching appeal that Alice found difficult to resist.

"Dear ma'am," she said gently. "As Lord Vickery's mother you would naturally feel a degree of attachment to him. I imagine that most mothers know something of their sons' faults and love them anyway."

"I *knew* you would understand, Miss Lister!" Lady

Vickery said. "You are a delightful young woman. And you are *excessively* pretty, just as Mr. Gaines said that you were. Yes, really, much prettier than I had imagined." She sat back a little and cast an appreciative look over Alice's rose-pink evening gown. "You have good taste, too, for a provincial."

"And very good manners, Mama," Miles intervened smoothly, "unlike you and Celia, who have been distressingly blunt with Miss Lister."

"What have I said?" Lady Vickery demanded. "Only what everyone else is thinking, I'll wager, since Miss Lister was once a housemaid and could have been impossibly unpresentable—"

"I see my own mama approaching," Alice murmured, entertained against her will by the discovery that the elegant and highborn Dowager Lady Vickery had such an unfortunate penchant for putting her foot in her mouth. "If you will permit, ma'am, I should like to introduce you to her."

"Of course!" Lady Vickery said, beaming. "Of course! I am sure that she will agree with me that a marriage between you and Miles is greatly to be encouraged as soon as possible. We mamas must put our heads together and see if we can come up with a way to persuade Mr. Gaines and Mr. Churchward to overlook the trifling matter of the conditions...." She squeezed Alice's hand. "You should know, Miss Lister," she said, a slight shadow touching her face, "that it is not merely for his own sake that Miles wishes to pay off his debts and to evade the Curse of Drum. He has a young brother, Philip, who will inherit if Miles dies, and it would distress all of us unbearably if he were to be crippled by debt or, even worse, if the Curse of Drum fell on a mere boy."

"Mama!" Miles's voice cut like a lash and Lady Vickery jumped, as did Alice. "You have already importuned Miss Lister quite shamefully," Miles said, moderating his tone. "Pray, say no more."

The dowager drooped like an elegantly cut flower. "But, Miles, darling," she protested, "we all know that you would positively *detest* anything bad happening to your little brother—"

"Mama, I beseech you. You have said *enough*." This time Miles sounded really angry, and Lady Vickery looked hurt and downcast. Alice hurried to smooth matters over. Lady Vickery, she thought, was far too good for her son.

"I understand, ma'am," she said. "Although Lord Vickery has not spoken of his younger brother to me…no doubt not wishing to influence me unduly—" she cast an ironic look at Miles "—it would be unnatural indeed for him not to be moved at the *horrid* thought of the Curse of Drum falling upon him."

Lady Vickery smiled. "I *knew* you would understand," she said again. "My very dear Miss Lister, you are indeed a charming young woman, and so I shall tell your mama.…" She let go of Alice and extended a hand to Mrs. Lister, who had swum up to them, very much like a swan, Alice thought, in her regal purple with white feathered headdress.

"Dearest madam," the dowager said theatrically, "I am so pleased to make your acquaintance. Your daughter is delightful and it is my *greatest* wish that she marry my son!"

"Oh, indeed, it is mine, too!" Mrs. Lister said in heartfelt tones. She cast Alice a look in which hope and incredulity were all too clearly at war. "I can scarce believe that Alice is going to accept Lord Vickery," she said, failing to eradicate the doubt from her tone. "She has been distressingly recalcitrant in even considering her previous nineteen proposals, but then Lord Vickery is a marquis and no one of higher rank than an earl has proposed before...."

Alice sighed. There had never been any point in trying to explain to her mother that neither she nor Lowell shared Mrs. Lister's social-climbing ambitions, and anyway, Alice could see the nervous look in her mother's eyes fading as the dowager encouraged her to take the seat beside her. She knew Mrs. Lister had been half expecting a rebuff, for it was the normal response of most titled ladies to the upstart in their midst. But Lady Vickery was talking animatedly and Mrs. Lister was beaming at her as though they were lifelong friends, and really, Alice thought, it was exactly the happiness she would have wanted for her mother if only the circumstances had been different. The bitterness caught in her throat. It was difficult to see her mother's joy and not resent that it had been bought at the high price of her own freedom and desires. And of course if—*when*—Miles failed to meet Lady Membury's conditions and this sham betrothal was at an end, Lady Vickery would no doubt drop Mrs. Lister like a hot brick and Mrs. Lister would be inconsolable.

"Nineteen suitors?" Miles said to her, claiming her attention. "How sought after you are, Miss Lister."

"You mean how sought after is my money," Alice corrected him. "It would have been twenty refusals," she added, lowering her voice so that only he could hear, "had you not found the means to coerce me, my lord."

"Thank you for the reminder, Miss Lister," Miles

said dryly. "I would not wish to forget that this is no ordinary betrothal."

"At least Mama is happy," Alice said, sighing. "One of us is."

"I adore your gown," Lady Vickery was saying to Mrs. Lister.

"I love your shoes," Mrs. Lister responded.

"And the feathers—so chic!"

"And your diamonds. Are they a family heirloom?"

"Paste," the dowager said briskly. "But with your daughter's money..."

"Oh, quite," Mrs. Lister said. "And in return, your son's title—"

"Absolutely!"

Alice shook her head and turned away. "I can scarce believe that they are bosom bows already," she said.

She saw the smile curve Miles's firm lips, and it made her stomach flip and her toes curl within her slippers. "They are united by a very powerful desire, Miss Lister," he said softly. "They both want to see you as Marchioness of Drummond. We all do."

"For all the wrong reasons," Alice said bitterly. She looked at him. "Tell me about your brother, Lord Vickery," she said. "I was fascinated by what your mother was saying."

Miles laughed harshly. "Is this your revenge for my blackmail, Miss Lister? To ask me awkward questions about my family and oblige me to tell you the truth?"

"If you wish to see it like that," Alice said. "Indulge my curiosity, my lord. How old is Philip?"

There was a pause. Miles's face was blank of expression, but Alice could sense a conflict in him, one she could not understand.

"Philip is sixteen," he said, after a moment.

"Hmm," Alice said. "Your mother swears you are attached to him. It would be a callous man indeed who did not care for the fate of a sixteen-year-old boy."

"It would," Miles said.

Alice moved a little closer to him. "Could you be such a man?" she asked.

"I could quite easily," Miles said. He grabbed Alice's arms so suddenly that she could not prevent the gasp that escaped her lips. Several people standing nearby turned to look at them with mingled curiosity and surprise. "Do not look for gentleness in me, Miss Lister," Miles ground out, his fingers digging into her skin. "You will not find it. I care for no one."

"But your mama—" Alice began.

"She deludes herself." He let her go as swiftly as he had captured her. "It makes her happy to think that I love my family, so—" she saw him shrug "—I let her believe it. The truth is that she is the one who worries about what might happen to Philip, not me."

Alice rubbed her arm where he had gripped her. "But surely you must care, too! They are your family."

"And I have already told you that I barely know them and have no desire to change that." Miles sounded cold, as though she was trespassing on dangerous ground.

Alice knew that she was stubborn. Obstinacy was one of her besetting sins. She knew she was persisting long after it would have been polite and politic to give up, but some tenacious instinct pushed her on to challenge him further.

"You are not as cold and unfeeling as you claim," she said, wanting to make him admit it. "You want to marry money not only for your own sake but to save Philip from inheriting crippling debt and to spare your mother the humiliation of seeing your birthright sold. *That* is the reason you are a fortune hunter—"

Miles laughed. He sounded genuinely amused. "Do not endow me with qualities or motives that I do not possess, Miss Lister," he said. "What you mean is that you *wish* I was not so cold and unfeeling." His hazel eyes were hard as they appraised her face. "You want to find an acceptable reason for my behavior. Sadly there isn't one. I cannot fulfill your faith in me. I *am* as callous as I appear, I have no affection for my family and I wish to marry you solely to save myself from the Fleet and in order to bed you. Is that honest enough for you?" He smiled grimly at Alice's look of shock. "Now—" his voice eased "—would you care to dance? We are, after all, pretending to the perfect courtship."

Alice moved a little away from him. She tried to breathe calmly and steady her erratic pulse. It was true—he had shocked her. She had wanted to make him admit that he cared for something worthwhile. Instead he had confirmed that he cared for nothing— and no one.

I wish to marry you solely to save myself from the Fleet and in order to bed you.

The bluntness of it stole her breath and bruised her feelings.

"I can pretend to a devotion to your title," she said sharply, wanting to retaliate, "or even at a pinch to pity you because of your family curse, but I *will not* pretend that this is a perfect courtship nor that I am in love with you, my lord."

Miles's hand tightened suddenly on her arm. He

drew her out of the heated ballroom and through the doors that led to the conservatory. The cooler air was soothing against Alice's hot skin. Through the glass roof she could see the stars pricking the black, winter sky and she could hear the faint splash of a fountain in the depths of the shadows. Miles led her away from the ballroom door and deep into the darkness. His hold on her was unrelenting and he did not release her until they were well away from all prying eyes. The only light in this dark corner was from one lamp high on the wall, and by its glow Alice could see Miles's expression was harsh and uncompromising.

"Perhaps I did not make myself clear enough yesterday," Miles said. His voice was level but there was a hard undertone to it now. "Privately we are betrothed. I am your official suitor. As such we shall be in each other's company a great deal and I expect you to behave as though you are glad of my attentions."

"There is not the least chance of that, my lord," Alice said. Her feelings were so bruised by now that she was not even prepared to try to be diplomatic.

"That," Miles corrected, ignoring her protests, "is precisely how it will be. If you do not manage to summon at least a modicum of enthusiasm for my presence, I will kiss you in front of anyone who happens to be about until it is quite clear that you are *extremely* happy to be courted by me."

Alice was outraged. "How dare you."

"I also expect you to address me by my given name," Miles continued, as though she had not spoken. "When you call me *my lord* you sound like a servant." He saw her flinch. "I appreciate that you do not like being reminded of your past."

"I am not ashamed of my past!" Alice retorted. The anger she had been suppressing all evening flared up. "What I do object to, however, is the fact that if I were still a housemaid I doubt you would even look at me, whereas now I am an heiress you think to *pay court* to me for my money." She invested the words with all the scorn that was in her heart. "You are a hypocrite, Lord Vickery, amongst other things."

"Oh, you need be in no doubt that I would have looked at you," Miles drawled, infuriating her further. "I would probably have touched you, as well."

"Not with marriage in mind," Alice flashed. "You disgust me."

"No, I do not," Miles said. "That is your difficulty, is it not, Miss Lister?" He took her hand. Even through gloves, his touch scalded her. "You know that I desire you," he said. His voice had softened, and his tone raised shivers along her skin. "Why not be honest and admit that you want me, too, and that there would have been lust between us whether you were a maidservant or an heiress." He moved a little closer to her so that his thigh brushed the silk of her gown. "I may have forced your hand with this marriage, Alice, but you know you will surrender to me in the end because, deep down, you want to."

His words and the slippery glide of his leg against her skirts sent a shiver of awareness sliding along Alice's veins. He was right, of course. Through all her disillusionment and betrayal the one stark fact that she could not deny was that she was deeply, helplessly, *disturbingly* attracted to Miles Vickery. She always had been, right from the moment she had met him. There was no sane and rational reason for it. She might logically expect that her dislike for him would cancel out any attraction she felt. It did not. It infuriated her.

A second later she realized that he had read her thoughts with disconcerting accuracy, for his eyebrows lifted and a smile that was as sensual as it was teasing lifted the corners of his firm mouth.

"Alice," he said again. There was a rough edge to his voice now, like the rub of steel against silk. Alice shivered again. She was so close to him that in the lamplight she could see that his eyelashes were golden at the roots fading to dark at the tips, and that his eyes had the same gold color sprinkled deep in the hazel. She stared at him as though she was trying to commit his face to heart, captured in the moment and by the desire in his eyes, knowing that in a minute he was going to kiss her.

Miles had kissed her before, the previous autumn, and she had been dazzled and overwhelmed. Looking back, she could see that that had been the moment when Miles had undermined her defenses and she had started to surrender her guarded heart to him. Now she felt afraid, as though there was so much more at stake. She did not want to be hurt again. She had been foolish and trusting before, but that had not made the pain any the less. She had no illusions now that Miles would ever love her, so in that respect she was armored against him, but she also knew that her perfidious body responded to him with a need and a desire that was as insatiable and seductive as his own.

She freed herself from his grip and stepped back, escaping before it was too late. "I do not want to talk about this," she said. She sounded breathless even to her own ears. "Don't seek to dictate to me, my lord. I will accept your attentions with as much enthusiasm as I can summon up—until you break the terms of the will and I am free of you."

She walked quickly away, slipping open the catch on the long windows and stepping back inside the ballroom. Miles did not follow her and she felt an immense relief. She wanted to retire from the ball, to go home to the privacy of her room where she could vent her frustration and her anger. She hated being in Miles's power. She could not bear to be coerced, and the insidious attraction Miles held for her confused as well as mocked. And yet what alternative did she have? She was bound to this hollow travesty of a betrothal for as long as Miles was able to fulfill Lady Membury's terms and conditions. God forbid that he should succeed completely and that she should be obliged to wed him.

Her heart bled for the naive young girl she had been the previous year. She had built Miles up into such a hero and all her hopes and beliefs had been blighted. Not only was he like every other last scoundrel who had ever seduced and betrayed an innocent young girl, he was without heart and without feeling. She thought of the Dowager Lady Vickery and of Celia and Philip. Miles was blessed to have a family who cared for him and yet he pushed them away, scorning their affection. There had been a moment when he had been telling her of his feelings for his family, when instinct had made her think that there was some terrible secret there, some hidden truth that had wounded him so badly in the past that he could never recover. Yet when she had pressed him on it he had shown no weakness. He had scorned her sentimentality as much as he seemed to reject his family's love for him. So the truth was that he had no capacity to love and she had better remember that for her own good. She would never make the same mistakes again, thinking that she loved him, risking disillusion. Miles Vickery was not worth it and he never had been.

CHAPTER EIGHT

SHE HAD GOT TOO CLOSE with her artless questions and her damnable persistence. Miles stood by the conservatory window and stared out into the darkened gardens, ignoring the cold that was starting to eat into his bones. Alice Lister was too perceptive, and worse, she was too stubborn to back down. There had been a moment when she had challenged him about his feelings for his little brother when he had felt the same uncontrollable bite of anger that had driven him from his family all those years ago. Anger was as unproductive an emotion as guilt or resentment or love, as far as Miles was concerned. It led to poor judgment and rash decisions. It led to a loss of control. It could hurt too much. And he, renowned for his cool head and lack of sentiment, was the last person on earth who wanted to feel that intensity of emotion for anything or anyone.

He knew that Alice had been shocked by his heartlessness. He had heard it in her voice. She had tried to make him admit that he cared. He felt cynically amused that she was trying to persuade herself that he had some softer feelings when he did not. She had sought the truth from him and then she had not liked what she had found.

Too bad.

Little Miss Lister had to learn that honesty could sometimes be diabolically uncomfortable to confront.

Total honesty. To his surprise he had not lied once that evening, neither to Alice nor to anyone else. He had thought that he might bend the truth sufficiently to allow him to feel comfortable but not enough that Alice would guess he was compromising. Instead he had been blisteringly candid. At times it had been a painful experience but he thought that he might actually be getting a taste for it.

Strange.

It was a disconcerting discovery. Unwelcome, too.

The winter wind skittered across the dark gardens, bringing on its edge a stinging sleet that it threw against the glass, and Miles shivered, seeking out the warmth of the lighted ballroom. He deliberately did not look for Alice even though he felt an almost irresistible urge to rejoin her. The impulse troubled him and he found it inordinately difficult to dismiss it.

He propped himself against a conveniently placed statue of Apollo, which he assumed was intended to add an air of classical culture to the Granby's provincial ballroom. He was amused to see that from the waist down Apollo was swathed in a robe, presumably to preserve his modesty and the sensibilities of the Fortune's Folly matrons.

Across the polished expanse of the ballroom floor Miles could see his sister dancing for a fourth, scandalous time with Frank Gaines whilst the Dowager Lady Vickery watched from the chaperones' corner, her face expressing disapproval tinged with resignation. Miles smothered a grin. He wondered which his mother would consider the lesser of two evils: having a spinster daughter so firmly on the shelf she had taken root, or accepting a lawyer as a potential son-in-law. She had already demonstrated her social prejudices once that evening when she had been introduced to Alice. Not, Miles suspected, that her mother's opinion—or indeed anyone else's—would count for a fig with Celia if she decided she wanted Frank Gaines. And the dowager herself was not without admirers further down the social order. Mr. Pullen, the magistrate, had come over to ask her to join him in an old-fashioned country dance, and after a rather startled response the dowager had agreed.

Lizzie Scarlet caught Miles's eye as she twirled ostentatiously down the set on Lowell Lister's arm. She was flaunting herself under Nat Waterhouse's nose, laughing and chattering animatedly, and Miles knew that Nat was noticing, even as he bent in ever more assiduous attendance on Miss Minchin and her parents. The Waterhouse and Minchin match had been formally announced that morning in both the *Morning Post* and locally in the *Leeds Intelligencer.* This, Miles thought, was Lizzie's response. She was completely eclipsing poor little Flora, who looked like a country mouse in her fussy debutante gown compared to Lizzie, dazzling in turquoise, her flaming red hair held in a diamond clasp.

Miles finally allowed his gaze to move on to Alice. She was not dancing. She was sitting on a rout chair next to Mrs. Lister and, Miles noticed, with a sudden, odd contraction of the heart, she was being quite blatantly ignored. Clearly it took more than Lady Vickery's brief patronage to bring Alice and her mother into style. Miles could see a group of young sprigs of fashion nearby who fancied themselves London dandies.

They had their backs turned to Alice, pointedly excluding her, taking their cue from the haughty matrons who had moved their own chairs a little aside as though to emphasize the gap between the Listers and the rest of polite society. Even as Miles watched he saw one of the ladies pass Mrs. Lister on her way to the refreshment room and draw her skirts aside, as though even to be near her would taint her. It was pointed and discourteous, and Mrs. Lister blushed with mortification until she was almost as dark as her puce gown.

Alice had her chin up and was watching the dance and there was no indication on her face that she found people's attitudes embarrassing, but Miles thought that she must care. Most people would, to be so obviously and so rudely ignored, and Alice had already shown how sensitive she was to the feelings of others. She could scarcely be *insensitive* to snubs to herself.

Miles frowned, remembering that Alice had been inundated with dancing partners when he had first met her the previous autumn in Fortune's Folly. But of course that had been before she had rejected nineteen offers of marriage. Now that most of the fortune hunters had left for the winter, no one else had any interest in her, and she was left high and dry. Nothing could have made it more obvious that Alice had only been tolerated in Yorkshire society because of her money.

He saw Faye, Duchess of Cole, smiling contentedly as she observed the social isolation that Mrs. Lister and her daughter were enduring. She was gossiping to her cronies and whispering behind her fan. And then Miles saw Sir James Wheeler's son George laugh immoderately at some joke his friend was making and in the process spill the remainder of his wine all over Alice's silk skirts. The liquid splashed in bright red pools on the pale pink gown. Mrs. Lister gave a little cry of distress and George Wheeler glanced around and said loudly, "Send for a servant to mop it up, ma'am. Oh, no need—there is one here already." Then he and his friends burst into more gales of amusement. It was true that one of the Granby waiters was already kneeling at Alice's feet and wiping the spillage up with his white napkin, but Miles thought that that was not really what George Wheeler had been meaning. He suspected that Alice had taken the point, too, for she shifted a little on her chair, and then turned her face away as though seeking some protection from the malicious words and the spiteful stares. And then, as though that were not bad enough, the Duke of Cole's affected drawl rose disastrously over the ballroom chatter.

"Fetching little piece, ain't she? I'll find a place for her if she's ever looking to go back into service. In fact she could service me whenever she liked, what!"

Someone tittered sycophantically, and emotion kicked Miles hard and unexpectedly in the gut, a mixture of anger and something feral, deeper and more disturbing. He felt a violent urge to go up to Henry Cole and strangle him with his own neck cloth, or to challenge him to a duel or invite him to meet his maker in any imaginative way he chose. The impulse was so strong that Miles found he had already started across the floor before he had himself back under control and reminded himself that Alice's injured feelings were nothing to him. He might want her in his bed, which was no more than lust, and want her money in his bank, which was desperation, but that was all there was between them. And since Alice had refused a public announcement of their betrothal, he did not even have to defend her good name out of family pride.

Even so, it seemed extraordinarily difficult to leave her unprotected, her reputation bandied about by any ill-bred scoundrel who chose to insult her.

He dismissed his scruples and strolled over to the door where he stood aside with a cynical smile as Nat Waterhouse ushered Miss Minchin and her parents from the ballroom with the immaculate courtesy of the attentive suitor. It was only when the Minchins had vanished through the door that he saw Nat give a shrug as though he was sloughing off an unwanted responsibility. As his friend moved toward the refreshment room Miles stepped forward.

"Perfect son-in-law material," he drawled. "Attentive, deferential, courteous—and titled, of course."

"Well," Nat said, "she is rich and amiable—"

"And witless."

Nat frowned. "Would *you* want to marry an intelligent woman, Miles?"

Miles glanced toward the ballroom again. Alice was talking to Lowell and Lizzie Scarlet now. He felt a sense of relief that she and her brother were back on speaking terms and a stronger one that Lowell had missed Henry Cole's remarks. Had he heard, there would probably have been a brawl in the ballroom by now.

Alice was smiling at something her brother had said, and the curve of her lips sent another kick of something hot and strong through Miles's gut. Devil take it, he wanted her very much. Three months was an impossibly long time to wait.

He cleared his throat. "Yes, I would want an intelligent wife," he said. "I would not spend a great deal of time in her company, but on those occasions when we were thrown together I would rather not be bored senseless."

Nat laughed. "This was precisely why I did not tell you sooner about my betrothal. I knew what you would say."

"And what was that—congratulations?"

"Hardly. Something more along the lines of once the wedding is over and the fortune secured, I will have to live with her for the rest of my life."

Miles shook his head. "You will be living with her money for the rest of your life. That is the material point. You must have me confused with Dexter, old chap. He is the one who is always extolling the virtues of love."

"And yet," Nat said, "Dexter told me once that *you* were the one who counseled him against marrying Laura unless he loved her with all his heart. Your words, not mine."

Miles pulled a face. "I must have been suffering from a fever." He sighed. "Laura wanted true love and I thought that she deserved the best after tolerating Charles for so many years. That is all there was to it." He clapped Nat on the shoulder. "Come and have a drink with me in the taproom. You look as though you could do with it and all this talk of love is making me feel the need for brandy."

"Your own suit does not prosper, then?" Nat asked as they turned in through the door and headed down the stone-flagged corridor away from the gentrified elegance of the ballroom.

"In part it does," Miles said. "Miss Lister has agreed to marry me. That is the good part."

Nat stared at him. "How did you pull that off?"

"I blackmailed her into it," Miles said calmly. He saw the look on his friend's face and nodded. "Yes, I really did."

"Hell and the devil." Nat looked torn between amusement and severe reproof. "First you make a wager to seduce Miss Lister into marriage, then you jilt her for a richer prize and then you blackmail her. You are riding for a huge fall, my friend."

They went into the smoky taproom and took two chairs by the fire. The landlord, working from long experience, came over at once with a bottle of brandy and two glasses.

"I won't inquire as to the terms of your bargain with Miss Lister," Nat said as they sat down. "I'd rather not know. But—" he shook his head "—I hope you know what you are doing, Miles."

"Got it all worked out perfectly, old chap," Miles said cheerfully.

"So if that is the good part," Nat prompted, "what could possibly be the bad?"

"The bad part," Miles said, raising his glass in a toast, "is that the terms of Miss Lister's inheritance are not without condition, and she will not allow me to announce the betrothal formally until I have fulfilled them." He swallowed a mouthful of brandy, relishing the fiery taste. "That mad old trout Lady Membury decreed that Miss Lister's future husband had to prove his worth by behaving honorably for a period of three months and telling nothing but the truth—" He stopped as Nat smothered a snort of laughter in his brandy glass.

"Sorry, old fellow," Nat drawled, failing utterly to wipe the smile from his face, "but I thought you said you were obliged always to tell the truth!"

"I did say that." Miles gave his friend a baleful look.

"But surely you fell at the first hurdle?" Nat inquired.

"Your faith in my ability to be honest is so touching," Miles said. "I have not failed…yet."

Nat rubbed a hand over his hair. "My God, I hope Miss Lister doesn't ask you about your mistresses and expect an honest answer! Did you tell her that there are very good reasons—"

"Why a man does not tell the truth all the time? Of course I did." Miles took another drink. "What can I do? If I break the terms of Lady Membury's will I forfeit the right to marry Miss Lister, blackmail or no blackmail."

Nat raised his glass in ironic toast. "Then there is no more to be said, old fellow, other than to wish you luck and to hope profoundly that you can, against all the odds, behave with honor for the next few months." He shook his head. "All the same," he added, "something is going to go awry. I feel it in my bones."

"You're turning as superstitious as my mother," Miles said. He shifted in his chair. Suddenly he was conscious of a feeling of discomfort prickling between his shoulder blades. He dismissed it, draining his glass and reaching for the brandy bottle again. "What could possibly go wrong?" he said.

LYDIA COLE HAD RECEIVED a letter. It had been delivered by hand late the previous night and it had only been by the remotest chance that she had seen it poking from beneath the mat when she had crept downstairs to heat some milk in an attempt to soothe herself into sleep. She had taken it up to her room and opened it, her hands shaking as she unfolded the paper. When she saw the name at the bottom of the page she trembled so much that the letter fell to the floor.

After a sleepless night and hours of reflection the following day, Lydia had decided to respond to the plea in the letter. She knew she was a fool to do so. She was not even sure what prompted her to go—curiosity, anger or even love. She waited until Alice and Lizzie and Mrs. Lister had gone out to the ball, and the servants were enjoying a quiet evening tucked up in the warm, and then she slipped like a wraith from the garden door of the house and crept out to the stables. There was a light in the window of the little mews house where the coachman lived with his family, but the groom's lodging was in darkness. Lydia suspected that he was probably spending his evening off—and his wages—at the Morris Clown Inn.

It was a cold, damp night, no evening for a young, pregnant girl to be loitering in the dark. Yet Lydia, who had spent so much of the previous few months indoors, turned her face up to the cold, sleety caress of the breeze and felt a spark of life rekindle inside her.

She had her hand on the latch of an empty store-room at the end of the cobbled row when someone stepped from the darkness in front of her and put a gentle hand on her arm. Although she was expecting him, her nerves were stretched so tense she almost screamed. His hand tightened warningly on her elbow and then he had drawn her through the door of the storeroom and bolted it behind them, and in the dim lantern light within, Lydia turned to look at the man who had been her lover.

He looked different. Gone was the dark, devil-may-care Tom Fortune, the adventurer with a twinkle in his eyes and charm enough to burn. She barely recognized the man who stood before her now. His face was thinner. There were deep lines about his eyes. He looked older and harder. It made Lydia realize, with a sudden pang, just how little she knew him. She had been a naive girl who had tumbled into love with a man she had never known at all. Cocooned in the marvelous sensation of being in love, swept away by the discovery of physical passion, she had never questioned Tom's love for her or his commitment to her, and she had paid the price of that misplaced trust in the child she bore now.

He made no move toward her, but stood still just within the door, looking at her with a kind of desperation in his eyes. "I was not sure if you would come," he said. He sounded young and anxious. "I was afraid to contact you, but there was no one else who could help me."

"I am not sure that I can do that," Lydia said. Her voice was cold and hard.

There was no one else who could help me.... That, she thought, the taste of bitterness in her mouth, was exactly like Tom Fortune. He thought only of himself.

"I only came here because I found that I wanted to see you again," she added. "To see the sort of man you really are rather than the man I once imagined you to be."

Tom flinched. "You've changed." His voice fell. "Of course you have. How could you not, with what has happened to you? I am sorry—"

"For what?" Lydia said, still in the same cold voice. "For seducing me for nothing other than sport, like the rake you were, or for running off and leaving me alone and pregnant?" She turned away from him. "Or did you mean that you are sorry you are a murderer twice over and a wanted criminal—" Despite herself, her voice cracked with emotion and she stopped to draw a steadying breath. The pain felt as though it was locked into a tight little box inside her chest. She tried to breathe deeply and to make it melt away, but it was too powerful to be dismissed. The sharp edges of her grief stabbed her, stealing her breath. Suddenly she knew she had to get away from him. This was more difficult and heartbreaking than she had imagined.

"I won't tell anyone that I have seen you," she said, "but I cannot help you, Tom." She shook her head. "That was all you wanted from me, wasn't it?" she said. The tears clogged her throat. "I came here, pregnant with your child, to see if you had ever cared a rush for me, and I find that all you want is my help. You never think of anyone but yourself."

She had turned to leave when he put a hand on her arm, and such was her need to believe that he cared, even a little, that she stopped.

"I do care," he said. His voice was harsh. "Lyddy, I swear I care for you. I want you to marry me."

Lydia almost laughed aloud. "It's too late," she began, but he hushed her, drawing her down to sit beside him on the rough stone floor of the storeroom. He had spread his ragged coat on the stone, but it could not ward off the chill, and even with her thick cloak wrapped about her, Lydia was frozen. *Five months ago,* she thought, *had we met like this, there would have been no words and Tom would have been making love to me by now.* There had never been many words between them.

"Listen," Tom said roughly. "Please." When she

remained silent he seemed surprised, almost as though he could not find the words, now that she had granted him the time he had begged for.

"It is true that I seduced you for sport last year," Tom said, and Lydia could not quite prevent the tiny shudder that went through her at his words. Even now she had hoped in a corner of her mind that it had not been true. "I was bored and spoiled and a scoundrel," Tom said, "and you were pretty and gentle and you loved me. It flattered me to realize that you cared for me. It made me feel good. I am sorry if it hurts you to hear me say this, but I have to tell you the truth now—all of it." He paused and took her cold hands in his. "I am more sorry than I can say, now, that I was so careless and thoughtless and hurtful that I took your trust and I twisted and ruined it."

Lydia said nothing. She felt cold through and through. She could not tell him that it did not matter because it did. It mattered dreadfully.

"It was the same boredom and immaturity that led me to work for Warren Sampson," Tom continued. "I wanted excitement in my life, fool that I was. He paid for my gambling and in return I fed him information. Sometimes I rode out with his men when they were about his illegal business. But I never hurt anyone. I certainly never killed anyone! That magistrate whom I was supposed to have murdered on Sampson's behalf…"

"Sir William Crosby," Lydia said. "You had his ring. You gave it to me as a love token. A secondhand ring taken from a dead man!"

"That was shabby of me," Tom said, "but I swear I did not know it was Crosby's. Sampson gave it to me. He threw it to me carelessly one day and I thought it was pretty and that you might like it."

"I did," Lydia said, "because you had given it to me, and I thought it meant that you loved me."

There was a silence. The wind was rising, catching the edges of the roof and whistling through the gaps in the bricks. Lydia shivered. "Are you staying here?" she asked.

"No," Tom said. "I stay nowhere very long. It's too dangerous."

"You should go to the authorities," Lydia said. "Tell the Guardians. I know they must be looking for you."

"They are," Tom said. "Anstruther and Waterhouse have been tracking down all Sampson's associates, and Miles Vickery has been interviewing the servants at Fortune Hall to see if I have been back there. It will not be long before they pick up my trail. I'm certain of it."

"Then go to them first!" Lydia argued. "Tell Dexter or Miles Vickery what you have told me—" She stopped. Tom was shaking his head.

"I can't, Lyddy," he said. "They would never believe me. I'm a wanted man and I have no proof of any of it. All the evidence is against me." His hands tightened on hers. "But you believe me, don't you, Lyddy? Please say you do."

Lydia was silent for a very long time. She realized with a shock that she had strength now, strength enough to see Tom Fortune without illusion and to judge him objectively.

"I am not sure," she said slowly at last, and heard him sigh.

"You see?" Tom said. "If you do not believe in me, then who will? Certainly my own brother does not. Monty has washed his hands of me."

"Sir Montague was never a very reliable character,"

Lydia said. "He bends with the wind. But, Tom, the question we should be asking is if you did not kill Crosby and Sampson, who did?"

"I did wonder," Tom said, staring at the flickering flame of the lantern, "if it was one of the Guardians themselves. Oh, I know they are sworn to protect and uphold the law, but men have gone to the bad before now, and Sampson could well have been blackmailing them, or Crosby been about to expose them. Any one of them would have the knowledge and the skill to murder."

"No!" Lydia said, recoiling instinctively from the thought. "It cannot be. Not Dexter Anstruther—"

"Probably not Dexter," Tom conceded. "He is too principled, though one never knows. But Miles Vickery now…" Tom laughed. "You cannot tell me that he has not done many a thing that would lay him open to blackmail, and he would be ruthless enough to kill, I am sure of it."

"Lord Vickery has renewed his attentions to Alice," Lydia said, frowning a little. "If he is mixed up in something illegal, he has not profited from it financially, I am sure. He is so poor he is selling everything off."

"Surely Miss Lister has not welcomed his suit," Tom said.

"There is something between them," Lydia said. "I know it." She fidgeted with the seam of her cloak. "I recognize it. For all that she was once in service, Alice is as innocent as I was, and Miles Vickery fascinates her in the way that you used to fascinate me, Tom." She smiled a little sadly. "It is because you are both so very bad, you see. Bad and dangerous and such a temptation to an innocent girl…" She sighed. "But there is one difference between Alice and me. I do not think she will be as foolish as I was. She is very strong and I do not think she will allow herself to be seduced as I was."

"And now you see me as I really am, Lyddy," Tom said, his voice cracking with self-disgust. "Not so attractive now, is it?"

"No," Lydia said, "it is not. But if we are to clear your name and I am to have a father for this baby of ours—"

"Lydia!" Tom crushed her to him so that the rest of her words were lost. "You are too good for me," he said, his breath hot against her hair, "but if we come through this I *swear* I shall be a better man and you will be proud of me."

"Well," Lydia said breathlessly, feeling his arms about her and thinking it heavenly despite the fact that he was dirty and unkempt, "in that case we had better devise a plan. Now, what are we going to do?"

CHAPTER NINE

"THERE IS STILL NO INVITATION to Mary Wheeler's wedding," Mrs. Lister mourned as she and Alice and Lizzie took breakfast the morning after the assembly ball. "I would have thought that now you are betrothed to Lord Vickery, Alice, and I am his mother's *new best friend,* the Wheelers would be most anxious to invite us. I cannot understand it. I wonder if the letter has got trapped behind the door? I shall send Marigold to search for it."

"Mama," Alice said, sighing, "I have already explained that my betrothal to Lord Vickery is not to be made public until he has fulfilled the terms of Lady Membury's will, so it is not surprising that the Wheelers do not know of it."

Lizzie, who was eating turtalong and seed cake with great gusto, make a sound of disgust. "And anyway, dear ma'am, Alice would not be able to attend the wedding even if you were both invited! She will be too busy at the Bedlam Hospital—" Lizzie glared at Alice at this point "—where I shall be delivering her personally for being mad enough to betroth herself to Lord Vickery!"

"Oh, Lizzie," Alice said on a sigh. "Can we not drop the subject now?" She stirred her cup of chocolate and picked at the cake very halfheartedly. She was blue-deviled that morning. Lizzie had found out about the betrothal from Lowell the previous night and had harangued her all the way home in the carriage. She had then followed Alice into her bedroom and had pestered her for a further half hour, demanding to know why Alice had accepted Miles's proposal and asking if her wits had gone abegging. She had even offered to fetch Dr. Salter to tend to her. None of Alice's feeble explanations had cut the slightest bit of ice with Lizzie, which was not surprising, Alice admitted to herself, since they were so unconvincing that she would not have believed them, either. And as soon as they had got up this morning Lizzie had started grousing again and Alice already had a headache. The breakfast room was overheated because Mrs. Lister insisted on having an enormous fire, and Alice wished she could be out in the fresh air rather than cooped up inside.

In addition she was still smarting over events of the previous night. She had only been awake a few seconds that morning when she had recalled the way in which her family had been slighted by the rest of Fortune's Folly society. She knew that it hurt her mother dreadfully and that Mrs. Lister would never understand why people were so cruel. And gradually, now that she had rejected so many suitors, the snubs had been growing more blatant and the language more crude, and people like George Wheeler and the Duke of Cole showed their absolute contempt and disrespect for her.

Worse, Miles had witnessed it all. She had seen him watching. He had stood by and done nothing, and she had been silently begging him to come across and speak to her. She realized that she had wanted him to rescue her from the slights and she had felt hurt and angry when he had simply turned and walked away. It was further proof, if proof were needed, of what he had told her. He cared for nothing but himself. She meant nothing to him other than as a means to save him from the debtor's prison. There was no kindness in him and she was foolish to expect it.

"What I simply cannot understand," Lizzie was saying, "is how you could be so *stupid,* Alice. You are not by nature a stupid person and yet here you are, throwing yourself away—"

"Please, Lizzie!" Alice said sharply. Her feelings felt raw. "You know that Mama wishes to see me settled," she added, despising herself for trying yet again to convince her friend, and yet somehow powerless to stop herself. "It is important to her to have a place in society—"

"Oh, indeed it is!" Mrs. Lister confirmed, beaming. "I am more than happy with Alice's choice!"

"My dear ma'am," Lizzie said, "I know that you will not be offended when I say that you would have been happy with any *one* of the other nineteen titled gentlemen who made Alice an offer. Any of whom," she added to Alice, glaring, "would have been preferable to Lord Vickery!"

An unhappy silence prevailed around the table, broken eventually by Marigold knocking at the door to tell Mrs. Lister that there was no wedding invitation but that some flowers had been delivered for Alice from Lord Vickery.

"Shall I bring them in here, miss?" she said. "Proper bright and cheerful they'll look on the windowsill."

"They will be roses, I suppose," Alice said with a sigh, putting her napkin aside and getting to her feet. "In a basket, with a ribbon. How unoriginal." She wished that it were not such a hollow gesture when she knew Miles cared nothing for her. Under the circumstances, Alice thought crossly, those roses could wilt amongst the potato peelings in the scullery for all she cared.

She bustled out of the breakfast room and almost collided with Marigold in the hall. The maid was carrying a beautiful glass vase with bright scarlet flowers that seemed to glow in the pale February morning light. Alice could see tiny pips like rubies at their centre. She caught her breath.

"Pomegranate flowers," Mrs. Lister said, coming out of the breakfast room behind her. "How charming and unusual they look. Lord Vickery must have hothouses at Drummond Castle."

Alice touched the petals lightly. They felt rich and smooth beneath her touch. "They are very pretty," she conceded.

"In the language of flowers the pomegranate means unspoken desire," Mrs. Lister said. "How very subtle of Lord Vickery."

"There is nothing remotely subtle about Lord Vickery's desires, Mama," Alice said, "nor are they unspoken."

"Really, Alice, sometimes you can be quite coarse for a lady," Mrs. Lister reproved. "At least he did not send anthurium. You know the ones—spread orange leaves with a pointed, fleshy spike standing straight up in the middle. It always reminds me of a—"

"Of a tongue. Yes, thank you, Mama," Alice said hastily, catching Marigold's wide-eyed look. "I agree it is a blessing that Lord Vickery was more subtle than that."

"Sending an anthurium is a token of a man's intense attraction," Mrs. Lister said.

"It could certainly be seen as a token of his eagerness," Alice murmured. The scent of pomegranate filled her senses, heady, fresh and sweet but with the faintest of sharp undertones.

"Was there a note?" she asked.

"No, miss," Marigold said. "His lordship delivered them himself, though. He said he would call later."

"I shall not be at home," Alice said decisively. The flowers were pretty and a far more clever choice than she would have expected, but her feelings still smarted from Miles's behavior the previous night. "His lordship is presumptuous."

"Yes, miss," Marigold said, "but he is very handsome, isn't he?"

"Which is nothing to the purpose," Alice said.

"No, miss," Marigold said, "but you like him, don't you, miss?"

"I do not," Alice snapped.

"Disappointing," an amused masculine voice drawled behind her. "I was hoping that my flowers might procure a better response than that."

"Lord Vickery!" Alice spun around, furious that she had been overheard. Miles was standing a few feet away, watching her with that lazy masculine appraisal that always made her feel hot and shivery at the same time. "I had not realized that when you said you would call later you meant later by five minutes," she said.

Miles strolled forward. He looked completely unabashed. "Forgive me," he murmured, "but when I returned to the carriage, my mama reminded me that

I was supposed to ask Mrs. Lister—" he bowed to Alice's mama "—whether she would care to join her for morning tea at the circulating library. I did knock," he added with a look that to Alice's critical eye seemed completely unapologetic, "but no one answered so when I saw that the door was ajar…"

"We must get the catch fixed, Mama," Alice said crossly. "All manner of riffraff are able to walk in off the streets."

"I should be delighted to join Lady Vickery," Mrs. Lister trilled, ignoring Alice's comment as she flitted back and forth across the hall to collect her cloak and gloves and reticule. "I will come at once. Such a pleasure!"

Alice made a sound of exasperation. All her mama's disappointment had vanished now and she was in a state of high excitement to have been remembered by her new friend.

Lizzie wandered out of the breakfast room, a piece of toast still clasped in one hand.

"Good morning, Lord Vickery," she said. "The early fortune hunter catches the heiress, eh?"

"I accept your congratulations with pleasure, Lady Elizabeth," Miles said. "It is pleasing to know that Miss Lister has now confided about our betrothal in her friends and family."

"Pray do not be too pleased," Lizzie said, "for I am doing my best to dissuade her." She looked at Alice. "I am afraid that my friend has taken leave of her senses but I hope that the real Alice Lister will return before long." She nodded to Alice. "I am taking a tray up to Lydia this morning. We shall see what *she* thinks of your betrothal, Alice."

"Lady Elizabeth has not taken the news well, then," Miles observed, as Lizzie trotted away.

"As you see," Alice snapped.

Miles touched the petals of the pomegranate flowers that Alice was still holding. "They reminded me of you," he said in a low voice, for her ears only. "Beautiful but with tartness beneath the sweetness." His lips curved into a rueful smile. "Do you know, when I first thought to marry you I believed you would be quite biddable? It seems I did not know you very well."

"I am not in the least sorry to disappoint you," Alice said. She looked him in the eye. "It does not surprise me that you misjudged my character so, my lord. The only thing that you were interested in was that I was rich."

"Not the only thing," Miles corrected gently. He touched the flowers again. "The fruit tastes very sweet, too," he whispered to her.

Alice felt the heat blossom through her. She blushed vividly and was annoyed with herself for doing so. "Marigold," she said, proffering the vase to the maid, "pray would you put these in the breakfast room?" She turned to Miles as Mrs. Lister swept out the front door in a flurry of excitement and farewells. "Should you not accompany the ladies, Lord Vickery?"

"They can manage very well without me," Miles said, "and I prefer to speak with you." He looked at her. "In private, if you please."

His hand closed about her wrist and he drew her into the parlor and closed the door behind them, blocking out the sight of Marigold's fascinated face.

"Well?" he said, leaning his shoulders back against the door panels. "You seem out of charity with me this morning, Miss Lister. I expected better—"

"And I expected better of you last night!" Alice flashed, her indignation and anger catching alight. "Why, you could not even bring yourself to come across to speak with us when everyone else shunned our company and slighted us! I will not wed a man who is ashamed to call me his wife, Lord Vickery. What would you do with me—lock me up in Drum Castle because I am not fit for polite society?" She stalked away from him. "You could have helped us last night but instead you merely stood watching the others insult us! And I do not know why I expected any differently of you for I know you care nothing for me— you could not have proved it more eloquently!"

Miles walked across to the window, then turned to face her. His expression was impassive. "It is true that I could have come across to speak with you," he said.

"So why did you not?" Alice demanded. She felt angry, hurt and upset, and unsure why it mattered to her so much.

"Unless you permit a formal betrothal between us," Miles said, "I cannot help you."

"You mean that you *will* not!" Alice said. Once again his callousness shocked her.

Miles shrugged. "There is a price to be paid for everything, Miss Lister," he said. "I want to give you the protection of my name and I want to have the right to defend you against the sort of slights you experienced last night, but unless we announce our betrothal officially there is nothing I can do."

Alice tilted her head to one side to look up at him. "Why would you want to defend me?" she asked. "It is not as though you give a rush."

"Because it is not appropriate that my future wife—

and her family—should suffer such snubs," Miles said, "and if it were known that you are the future Marchioness of Drummond you would not experience such insults."

Alice looked at him. His expression was hard, unemotional. "So this is about your pride?" Alice said.

"It is about possession," Miles said. He came across to her and took her lightly by the wrists and as always when he touched her, her heart pounded. "I want you as my wife, Alice," he said. "You *will* be Marchioness of Drummond. Agree to a formal betrothal. It will give us both what we want."

Alice tried to think. It was almost impossible with his hands on her and the blood beating so hard and fast in her veins. She could see how cleverly Miles had taken her insecurities and used them for his purposes, to push for an official engagement. She had wanted to avoid it until he had fulfilled the terms of Lady Membury's will but she could see that if they announced their betrothal now, no one would cut her dead to her face, not even the Duchess of Cole herself. The Duke of Cole would not make coarse comments about her. And her mother would never again wear that look of bruised incomprehension to be rebuffed by the matrons of Yorkshire society.

Alice wished it did not matter so much to her. But it did. She was so weary of being treated shabbily and the thought of Miles's protection was treacherously attractive. *Agree to a formal betrothal. It will give us both what we want...*

"You seek to use my weakness to get what you want." She whispered, "You are ruthless."

Miles shrugged. "I am a negotiator, Miss Lister.

That is my job. If there is something that we both want it makes sense to discuss it."

"You go too fast," Alice whispered.

Miles bent his lips to the tender skin of her neck, planting tiny kisses against the curve of her throat. The shivers of desire ran through her, making her catch her breath. "Not fast enough for me," he said.

Alice tried to keep a clear head even as her treacherous pulse raced beneath his fingers. "If I agree to a formal engagement…"

He paused. "Yes?"

"You still have to fulfill the terms of the will," Alice said. "If you do not I will break the engagement. If you do not keep to our terms of total honesty then you lose."

She felt Miles smile against her skin and it made her shiver. "You drive almost as hard a bargain as I do, Miss Lister."

"There is no way around the terms of the will," Alice whispered.

"You could elope with me and damn the lawyers," Miles said.

Alice turned her head slightly and his lips brushed the curve of her cheek. His physical presence was so powerful it made her head spin. "If I did," she said, trying to concentrate, "we would both lose the money and then you would not want me."

"Oh, I would still want you," Miles said. "I will always want you." His tone had roughened. "I shall arrange for the announcement of our engagement to be put in the papers."

Alice shivered. Her previous refusal to accept a formal engagement had been more than simply an attempt to preserve her good reputation by keeping their scandalous betrothal quiet; she had used it to keep Miles at arm's length, hoping against hope that he would fail to meet Lady Membury's terms and she would be free. Now, although the conditions of their bargain had not changed, it felt as though the bonds were tightening all the time.

"And since we are doing things properly," Miles continued, "I think that I should kiss you to seal the betrothal."

"Kiss me?" Alice said. Her mind seemed to have ceased working properly. His nearness, the warmth of his hands on her, the scent of his skin were utterly destroying her composure.

"I believe that it is conventional," Miles murmured, "when one becomes engaged."

"A decorous kiss," Alice said, "is what is conventional."

Miles smiled at her. "I am not certain that decorous is where my expertise lies."

"And I am not certain," Alice said truthfully, "that I am quite ready to be subjected to your expertise, my lord."

Miles put a gentle hand under her chin and tilted her face up to his. "You're shy," he said. There was surprise and something else in his voice.

Alice tried to turn her face away, annoyed that he had realized this. "I am not…experienced, my lord."

She saw the corner of his mouth lift in a smile. "I remember," he said. "I promise not to frighten you. Decorous it is."

Alice closed her eyes as his lips touched hers lightly and lingered with the most gentle of caresses. It was very nice, she thought hazily, as her senses started to swirl. She might have known that whatever he said, Miles would be as good at kissing decorously as he would be at kissing indecorously.

The thought of kissing Miles indecorously acted like a flare of fire and made her heart thud and the heat race through her. She must have made some small sound in her throat, for Miles eased back a little and let her go. Their lips clung and then parted; hers felt full and moist, her whole body ripe and heavy with a sudden wanting. The keenest disappointment slammed through her that the kiss was over before it had barely begun.

"I hope," Miles said, "that was what you wanted." He was breathing slightly fast, his eyes dark.

Alice licked her lips and watched, fascinated, as his gaze followed the movement of her tongue and his hazel eyes darkened still further.

"Alice?" There was a question in his voice, and the slightest hint of a rough undertone.

"I…" Alice cleared her throat. She felt a flutter of nerves and, at the same time, a stab of wicked excitement. She wanted more. And even as she acknowledged the thought, Miles read the truth in her eyes. His arms were about her before she could say another word, claiming her and drawing her close. Her hands came up against his chest and she felt the smooth material of his coat beneath her palms and underneath that the hard, unyielding muscle. Gently but inevitably Miles pressed her back against the paneled wall of the room until the sharp edges of the wood dug into her shoulders and thighs. Alice could feel the pressure of them keenly; all her senses seemed heightened all of a sudden. She could hear the quickness of her breathing and feel the slam of her pulse as she waited for

Miles to kiss her again. The moment seemed to spin out forever. Her legs trembled. Her entire body trembled. There was ample time for her to regret her impulse. She wavered on the verge of panic.

And then Miles's mouth took hers, deftly, demandingly, with no hesitation or gentleness, and she felt weak with relief and swamped by fierce desire.

She knew from the first second that she was way out of her depth. Her lips parted beneath the firm pressure of his, and his tongue touched hers and the taste of him was familiar and yet so raw and shocking and new that she gasped. Memories flooded her of the kiss they had shared the previous autumn. He had been restrained then, showing her only the tiniest hint of passion, holding himself under control. Now there was a ragged edge to that control as though he was warning her of the possession that was to come. Her agreement to their betrothal had sealed it. She would be his.

His tongue tangled with hers, seeking and commanding a response that Alice was helpless to refuse, did not want to refuse. His hand came up to cup her breast. The warmth of his palm seared her. Suddenly the sensible winter wool of her gown seemed as flimsy as muslin and as insubstantial in its protection. His thumb grazed her nipple and she moaned beneath his lips as cool shivers of desire set her shaking. This was so much more potent than before. She was so close to relinquishing all sense and all modesty. Miles could seduce her with her blessing. In truth she would connive at her own seduction. In fact if he did *not* seduce her, very likely *she* would seduce *him* out of sheer desperation and need.

Miles released her for a moment, his lips a hair's

breadth from hers, his breath caressing her face even as his fingers continued their torment of her breast. She was trapped between the paneled wall and Miles's body, unable to escape the delicious stroke of his palm against the curve of her breast and the rub of his fingers over her nipple. Alice's entire body tingled from that point of contact, begging for release from something she barely understood and yet knew with the deepest of instincts that she needed. Head back, she writhed against the wall, her fingers pressed hard against the panels, small cries of need and frustration forced from her.

"Hush, sweetheart...." Miles's voice was low and harsh but with an undertone of amusement. The roughness of his stubble brushed the smoothness of her cheek and made her squirm. "The door is not locked and I am certain you would not wish your maid to learn yet more of what goes on in a genteel household. The scandal of it..."

The thought of Marigold or Lizzie or Lydia opening the door and finding them there made Alice feel weak yet somehow excited almost beyond bearing. She gave a small whimper of supplication and Miles laughed.

"So the idea pleases you?"

"No!" Alice said. She was shocked, horrified at her own responses and yet somehow entrapped in the dark web of passion he was weaving.

"I think that it does," Miles said. "In your dreams at least..."

His lips brushed the corners of her mouth and returned to fully claim hers in a kiss that was deep, intimate and elemental. It was pure, primitive possession. He did not break the kiss once but she felt his fingers on the buttons on the bodice of her gown and her mind tripped over itself as it absorbed the shock of his actions.

He was undressing her in the parlor in broad daylight.

A protest formed in her mind but it was lost beneath the onslaught of her feelings. She felt the material ease a little and then Miles's fingers slipped beneath the stiff lawn of her bodice and his touch against her naked breast smashed through her mind and made her senses reel. She sagged against the wall with only the pressure of his body against hers holding her upright.

With a muttered exclamation he picked her up in his arms and placed her on the sofa. She was held upright, supported by the softer cushions against her back and the seat firm beneath her thighs. The design of the sofa made her sit up straight, like a prim debutante paying a morning visit, but there was nothing prim about either her state of undress or the wicked and abandoned sensations that were flooding her body. A burning ache was building at her very core. She felt boneless with sensual heat. She wanted to lie down. And preferably she wanted Miles to lie with her. She wanted to feel his mouth against her naked breast. As each new, outrageous thought invaded her mind, so her sense of shock grew and at the same time so did the ravenous fire within her.

She opened her eyes to see Miles kneeling in front of her on the rug. He looked up at her, his eyes blazing with a lust that stole her breath. He slid the gown and shift from her shoulders in one movement so that she was bared to the waist and then he leaned in to take her breast in his mouth. Alice gave a little keening cry as his lips brushed the tight peak of her nipple, as he circled it with his tongue. His teeth closed about the tip and bit down gently, and the hunger rolled low in her belly and she wanted to cry out again with frustration and sheer desperation. Miles's hands were firm on her bare waist now, holding her up against the rough velvet caress of the seat. She felt it rub her naked back with a sensuous but unyielding touch. She wanted to fall, to tumble down into this pit of dark desire and lose herself in it, but Miles refused to allow her to let go. The hard, deliberate grasp of his hands about her waist forced her vertical even as his lips, tongue and teeth ruthlessly plundered the delicate bounty of her breasts.

The contrast between her respectable pose on the sofa and the deeply unrespectable things that Miles was doing to her made Alice feel faint with awareness and yet she could not close her eyes and escape the consciousness of what was happening. She looked down on Miles as he bent his head to lick and suck at her breasts, now taking her fully into his mouth, now nipping at the hard tips of her nipples. His hair brushed her sensitized skin and made her squirm. Her whole body was molten with need. Her palms were pressed to the velvet of the seat and she dug her fingers into the material to keep from crying out, arching her neck back to allow him to take at will.

Where it might have ended she knew all too well, but suddenly there was a clatter in the hall, dangerously close to the door, and the sound of a knock at the front door and Marigold's voice raised as she greeted whoever was on the step. Reality intruded. Alice gave a gasp and drew back, clasping her chemise and the bodice of her gown to her with fingers that shook, and desperately tried to return her clothing to something resembling normality. Her feelings, she thought, would take a little longer to repair. She had been washed far beyond the shores of all that was familiar and safe.

There was a taut, burning look in Miles's eyes that sent another echo of desire tumbling through her and then he was standing and had drawn her to her feet, as well.

"Let me help you—"

Somehow his tenderness shook Alice even more than his passion had done. She had never expected this gentleness from him.

"I…I must…" Alice's fingers slipped on the buttons and Miles carefully put her hands aside, finishing the task himself. Her breasts still felt tender and swollen rubbing against the material of her shift, and her whole body was aroused to fever pitch. Alice raised a hand to her hair and realized the extent of the damage. "Excuse me," she said rapidly, "I really must go and tidy my clothes—"

She pulled back from him and his hands fell to his sides. She thought that she would make it to the door unscathed but even as her shaking hand slipped against the handle, Miles caught her by the wrist and jerked her back against his body. She could feel his erection hard and strong against her thigh and she shivered again.

"Don't forget that we have a bargain, Alice," he said softly. "Don't ever forget it." There was a bright, hard look in his hazel eyes. He ran his thumb over her lower lip and Alice shuddered.

"I won't," she whispered. She raised her chin, a flicker of spirit asserting itself in her. "You will be the one who breaks his word and loses."

Miles laughed and released her. "No, I will not. Now that I have had a taste of what is waiting for me at the end of it I have every incentive to keep to the terms." He bowed to her. "I will go now to place the announcement of our betrothal in the papers. I will see you at the subscription concert tonight."

Alice backed out of the parlor. Her legs shook as she climbed the stairs, but she made it to her room and slammed the door behind her, collapsing on her bed. Her body still hummed with arousal and thwarted desire. Her mind still reeled from all she had learned and experienced and the fact that she wanted much, much more. There was no denying that she was in deep, over her head.

She rolled over on her bed and stared at the drapes above her. She had learned that whatever physical demand Miles made of her she would match. Even in her innocence she had known that she wanted all he could give her. She shivered once again with awareness and unsatisfied need. Miles had shown her the sensual depths of her own nature. He had made her forget that he had forced this betrothal on her and had shown her that no matter how much she hated his coercion, she did not hate him. That shocked her deeply, for she wanted so much to despise him for representing everything that she rejected, for being like every other callous, arrogant nobleman who had ever looked on a maidservant with nothing but lust.

She could not simply blame her traitorous body that even now craved the satisfaction that only Miles could give. That would have been bad enough, she thought. But the feelings within her went deeper than that. Her instinct cried out that she knew Miles, deep in her heart, in her soul. But that affinity had to be false. It absolutely had to be.

Alice got up slowly and reached for the ewer of

water on the dresser, splashing the cool, fresh liquid onto her face in the hope that it would help clear her head. There was nothing other than blackmail that bound her to Miles Vickery. That was the stark truth and she had to remember it.

CHAPTER TEN

MILES STOOD IN THE DOORWAY of the great hall of Drummond Castle and watched whilst they sold Drum from under him. With each fall of the auctioneer's gavel another part of his inheritance was traded away. The wooden globe from the nursery his cousins had shared had gone for no more than a bare few shillings. The battered box of tin soldiers that he had fought over with his cousin Anthony during their school holidays had barely raised a single bid. It was fortunate, Miles thought, that none of the previous marquises of Drummond were alive to see how low the family had fallen. They would be spinning in their graves as it was. Barlow and Richardson, estate agents and auctioneers of fine quality property, had been trumpeting the sale for the past week:

A once-in-a-lifetime opportunity to purchase a part of the ancestral manor and possessions of the marquises of Drummond, including all lands and properties not entailed on the estate and all contents of Drum Castle, from the fine chandeliers and silver cutlery to the chamber pots and kitchen pans!

Miles shifted his broad shoulders against the hard stone of the doorway. Someone at the auctioneering house evidently had a good turn of phrase and an eye for advertising, for the sale had attracted crowds of people from Harrogate, Ripon and the surrounding villages. The great hall was packed. Barlow and Richardson would make a tidy profit from the three-day sale and the money would go some way toward paying off the hideous pile of debt that Miles had inherited along with the Drummond marquisate.

Miles's glance rested for a moment on the figure of his mother as she sat very still and very upright in the back row of seats, flanked by Philip on one side and Celia on the other. Frank Gaines, he was interested to see, was sitting on Celia's other side. The Dowager Lady Vickery had shuddered at the vulgarity of the whole commercial process but had insisted on being there to support her elder son through what she referred to as his ordeal. Miles wished that she had not. Whilst the sale of Drum was not as personally painful for his mama as the sale of Vickery Hall had been, it was still unpleasant. Miles's pride was in the dust and his family name with it. Seeing Lady Vickery's pain reminded him all too vividly of her distress and grief when his father had banished him. The anger stirred in him and for a second it blotted out all else before he suborned it ruthlessly to his will.

In the front row of seats sat the Duke and Duchess of Cole, bidding vigorously on various items like a pair of horse traders. Faye Cole had sympathized with Miles in a transparently insincere manner that had set his teeth on edge:

"My dear Lord Vickery, such a dreadful business! I am so sorry to see your family brought so low...."

"My dear Duchess," Miles had said pleasantly, "I am afraid that I do not give a damn for either my family or your pity." He had left her with her mouth hanging open.

Remembering Alice's strictures on honesty, Miles had assured himself that it was true. He did not care for Drum Castle and he did not care what people thought about him selling off his heritage piece by piece.

A couple of rows behind the Coles sat Lady Elizabeth Scarlet with John Jerrold dancing attendance on her. Alice Lister and her mother were with Lady Elizabeth. It had not occurred to Miles that Alice would attend the sale, and he felt a bitter twist of the knife within to think that she had come to witness his downfall. In an odd way it felt like some sort of betrayal. The cynic in him said it was no more than he deserved since he had obliged her to accept his proposal of marriage because he was ruthlessly materialistic in his pursuit of her fortune. Yet he found he was still angered that she had chosen to attend.

The announcement of his engagement to Alice had caused less of a stir in Fortune's Folly than might have been imagined. Everyone knew that he had courted Alice for her money the previous year and the *on dit* was that she had simply gained a better bargain now that he was a marquis, even an impoverished one. No one was surprised at the apparent trade of money and title. It was the way of the world. Only Lowell Lister and Lizzie Scarlet had expressed any public doubts or disapproval.

In the week since the engagement was announced Miles had escorted Alice and her mother, in the role of overexcited chaperone, to the spa and to the circulating library, to concerts and breakfasts. They had danced together. He had even dined at Spring House. The food had been excellent. Alice had been reserved and quiet, holding herself back and making it quite clear that she was acting the part of his fiancée under sufferance. She also gave him absolutely no opportunity to be alone with her again, and for the present Miles was prepared to indulge her in her attempts to keep him at arm's length. For the present only, and only because he knew that denial usually strengthened desire.

Miles had been interested to see how far Alice would let him go that day in the parlor at Spring House. He had recognized the sensuality in her from the very start, realizing that underneath her cool exterior was banked a fire that could brand a man to the heart. What he had not expected, in his experience and cynicism, was that her open and artless response to his lovemaking would be enough to push him to the very edge of control. It was a surprise to him but not, he told himself, a problem, other than that he was not accustomed to denying himself sexual satisfaction. He was certain that once he had made love to Alice his attraction to her—his obsession with her—would diminish. It had to do. Nevertheless, three months still seemed like an unacceptably long time to have to court her.

He looked at Alice as she sat so prim and neat between Lizzie and her mother. Just the sight of her seemed to make the lust within him tighten to almost unendurable levels. That really should not happen to a rake. It might be acceptable for a boy in his salad days, perhaps, but not to a man of experience. Miles disliked being at the mercy of his physical needs. He had seriously toyed with the idea of quenching his lust in dalliance with Ethel, the chambermaid at the Morris

Clown Inn, who had made him so very welcome the previous year. He had even gone to the inn a few days before, with the intention of seeking Ethel out and paying not only for her body but also for her silence in order to ensure that Alice's lawyers did not hear of it. Yet when he had gone into the taproom Ethel's ample charms, so proudly displayed by her low-cut blouse, had failed to move him in any way at all. Instead of purchasing her he had bought a pint of ale and sat in a corner thinking about Alice and the cool silk of her skin beneath his hands and the eagerness of her response and the soft sounds she had made as he had caressed her. He had grown hard at the thought and had slammed the half-drunk pint down on the table and gone out to stand beneath the pump, which had eased his bodily torment, at least temporarily. Fidelity was another quality he had never practiced, and to find that he was obsessed with a virgin to the point where he wanted no other woman baffled and annoyed him. But there was no fighting it. He was a realist and he knew when he was beaten. It had not helped that as he had walked out of the inn yard, dripping wet, angry and frustrated, he had met Frank Gaines casually strolling the other way and the lawyer had given him a look of complete understanding that had made Miles want to punch him.

Now he stood watching Alice for a few moments. Her head was turned away so that all he could see was her charming profile beneath the hood of her cloak, but there was some tension in the way she was sitting. Mrs. Lister turned around to hail the Dowager Lady Vickery as though they were at a garden party rather than the auction of all Miles's worldly goods, and for a moment Miles caught sight of Alice's expression.

Where Lizzie Scarlet was looking excited, Alice was looking deeply unhappy.

Miles wrenched his gaze away. Seeing Alice's compassion for his situation aroused emotions he did not want to feel. He was comfortable feeling lust for her—actually it was not comfortable but it was just about tolerable—but this complicated mixture of need and desire went deeper than the physical and he did not want it.

"How much am I bid for this fine Breguet watch?" the auctioneer demanded. "A genuine Breguet, ladies and gentlemen, from Paris, signed on the dial…"

Miles turned away. His father had given him the watch for his sixteenth birthday. When they had sold off the contents of Vickery Hall a few years before he had resisted selling too many of his personal possessions, not because of any sentimental connotations but because he had wanted to keep something back. Now, though, his finances were so dire that he could no longer afford the luxury of personal items.

"Take care of it," he remembered the late Lord Vickery telling him when he had stood before him on the worn Axminster carpet in the study at Vickery Hall. "It is very valuable."

It had been doubly precious to Miles, who had kept the gift safe right up until this moment. Even when he had left Vickery in anger and disillusionment he had held on to the watch, his father's present to him, as though it had been some sort of talisman.

And then he saw that Alice was bidding on the watch. He felt sick. Clearly he had misjudged her earlier. She had come to the Sale of Drum to crow over his plight and in his heart of hearts he knew he could not blame her, for he was the one who had forced her into this situation. He told himself that he was not disappointed in her. He did not care what Alice did; she could be as venal as he was for all he cared. Which did not really account for why he found he wanted to smash his fist through the twelfth-century paneling.

The bidding rose higher and higher. There was a strange, hollow feeling beneath Miles's breastbone. He could not place the sensation but it made him feel blue-deviled. He turned away from the auction and made his way through the stone-flagged hallway toward the study. He needed a drink but he had sold the contents of the wine cellar and the crystal glasses. He needed a bit of peace but all the rooms in the castle had been thrown open to the public so that they could view the sale items, so there was no privacy anywhere. Miles walked over to the window embrasure and stood looking out over the moors. It was a raw February day with lowering clouds and a misty sleet shrouding the rocky outcrops. The view suited his mood.

He heard the gavel come down on the watch and the auctioneer's delighted cry and the ripple of applause that meant that it had sold for some astronomical sum. Something snapped within him. Marching back into the great hall, Miles strode up to the place where Alice was sitting. She was looking flushed and triumphant. It was obvious that hers was the winning bid. Miles grabbed her wrist and dragged her to her feet in full view of the crowds. He saw Mrs. Lister's shocked face and heard his mother's horrified gasp. He ignored them. Dragging Alice behind him, oblivious to the shocked whispers that rustled through the throng, he hurried her out of the door and into his study, slamming the door behind them.

"What the devil do you think you are doing?" Miles's voice was harsh. "When we agreed to the terms of our engagement they did not include you coming to the sale here and making it plain to everyone that you were taking pleasure in buying me up twelve times over!" He realized that he was shaking with anger but seemed powerless to regain control. "I thought that I had made myself clear," he continued. "If you cannot summon up any enthusiasm for our betrothal you will at least show me a modicum of respect in public or everyone will suspect there is something suspicious about our arrangement."

Alice drew herself up. She was very pale. Her cloak was awry, her fair hair ruffled, but instead of the anger he expected to see in her eyes there was nothing but distress.

"The watch was for you," she said, with an honesty that devastated him. Her face was set and white but she continued doggedly. "Your mama told me that it was very precious to you and I did not want anyone else to have it."

Miles swore. He felt sick. "I don't want it," he started to say, instinctively rejecting both Alice and the dangerous intimacy of her gesture, but she held his gaze and continued to speak.

"It's true that I came here intending to embarrass you," she said. "I meant to spend lots of money and show you up, but—" she shrugged her shoulders beneath the crimson cloak "—I find it's not my way to take revenge like that. Perhaps I am too generous. Lizzie says I am softhearted, but—" her tone hardened "—I will not change the way that *I* am, I will not let myself become twisted out of shape because of the way that *you* have behaved to me."

Miles swallowed hard. He did not understand why her words were as painful as the sympathy in her eyes.

The last thing he wanted—the last thing he could bear—was her pity.

He could hear the echo of the auctioneer's voice rising and falling as he sold the next item, and winced as he tried to block out the sound. Alice came across to him and laid a hand on his arm.

"I am sorry," she said. "I am so sorry, Miles. It must be very difficult for you to have to do this."

Miles closed his eyes for a moment. He remembered the compassion in Alice's face ten days before when they had been at the Granby Ball and she had pressed him on his feelings for his family. He had not wanted her kindness then, or her sympathy. He did not want it now. He absolutely could *not* admit that this ghastly parade of his possessions mattered in any way at all. It did not. It could not.

He tried to find some casual words to dismiss Alice's concerns but they seemed to stick in his throat. He wanted to back away from this unexpected emotion, to dismiss it out of hand. He grasped after his customary cool cynicism. "It is of no consequence, Miss Lister. Why, when everything is sold there may even be some profit for me to gamble away...."

He told himself that it was the truth, but the words would not come.

And suddenly, with a blinding shock that shook him to his soul, he realized that he was bitter and furious that he should be the one forced to sell Vickery and Drum, to be the man who had humbled the family pride, when it was his father with his irresponsible profligate ways who had done the real damage years before. He felt sick and angry that the late Lord Vickery had once more abrogated his responsibility by dying before he had had to sell up, leaving Miles to bear the burden of all that ignominy and to sell his honor along with his possessions. His father, whom he had idolized before their terrible quarrel and cold estrangement… He could see at last that he had kept the Breguet watch for sentimental reasons hoping, perhaps, to keep faith with his father even though at times they had been so bitterly divided. And now at last he saw that everything had gone. He had lost everything and it hurt damnably.

He found that instead of dismissing Alice as he wanted to, he had put his hand over hers as it lay on his arm. Her face was tilted toward him and her lips were parted, pale pink, soft and sweet. In her eyes was something that looked like genuine pain and concern. Miles felt something shift deep within him.

He pulled her to him and kissed her with all the pent-up rage and violence that was in him, pushing the hood of her cloak back so he could tangle a hand in her bright hair and tilt her head to bring her mouth up even more ruthlessly to meet his. He felt her gasp against his lips and then she yielded to him instantly and absolutely, and her surrender lit something wild and primitive in him, and he was aware of nothing other than the unconditional need he had for her and the whirling, painful spiral of their desire. He felt shaken to the depths of his soul and yet somewhere in that raging darkness he felt a core of peace he had not known in a very long time, a peace that only Alice could give him.

He thought nothing of her youth and her inexperience. When he had kissed her in the parlor at Spring House he had been in control, dictating the encounter, planning a calculated seduction and showing her the extent of his mastery. He had had some restraint then, but there was nothing restrained about either of them now as he drew her ever closer and Alice responded, sliding her hands across his back to hold him hard against her. He felt her tug his shirt loose, and then she was running her fingers over his bare chest and shoulders, and the sensation wrenched a groan from his lips. He angled her head to take his kiss more deeply still and felt as though he was falling into a place of mystery, heat and shadows, somewhere he had never been before, somewhere that terrified him and yet offered the most tempting peace and absolute bliss that he could ever wish for, where he did not have to fight for what he wanted because his heart's desire was freely given and his for the taking....

"Alice!" Lizzie was calling for her from the hall. "Alice, are you all right? Where are you?"

For a moment the words barely penetrated Miles's brain, for he was so wrapped up in the taste and feel of Alice in his arms. Then he heard the sharp tap of footsteps on the stone floor, and sanity flooded his mind with cold clarity. He let Alice go so abruptly that he had to catch her arm to prevent her from falling. One look at her face told him she was completely stunned. Her hair was disheveled, her eyes were wide and dark with a mixture of shock and the remnants of heated passion and she was pressing her fingers against her lips in a gesture of bewilderment that sent a sharp, unexpected surge of tenderness through him.

Miles's breathing slowed and the fever in his blood

abated. He felt cold and shocked and disturbed in a manner that he could not quite analyze. A part of him was cursing the interruption, for surely he could have seduced Alice there and then, taken advantage of her honest response to him in order to oblige her to marry him at once and damn the lawyers and their conditions. But another, deeper part of him was so troubled he could not bear to think about it.

"Alice!" Lizzie was practically upon them.

Miles wrapped the cloak about Alice, pulling up the hood and dropping a brief, hard kiss on her lips.

"Lady Elizabeth is here," he whispered, and to his relief she blinked and lost the look of shock and wonderment that had held her still as a sleeping princess in a fairy tale. She spun around just as Lizzie shot through the study door. Miles took strategic cover behind his desk. He had no wish to display his current physical state to all and sundry and in doing so put Alice in an impossibly embarrassing situation.

"There you are, Alice!" Lizzie exclaimed. "We all thought that Lord Vickery must have carried you off and ravished you by now! I was the only one brave enough to come to your rescue and I am relieved to find you unharmed." She looked at Miles, making no attempt to offer him false sympathy on his losses.

Miles held Alice's gaze for a long moment. There was a reflection of his dark desire in her eyes alongside shock and some wariness, but when she spoke she sounded quite collected and a great deal less shaken than Miles felt.

"I am perfectly well, Lizzie, I thank you," she said. "Lord Vickery—" the tremor in her voice was almost undetectable "—I'll bid you good day."

"At your service, Miss Lister," Miles said. "I will call on you tomorrow."

Her gaze flickered to meet his. "Will you?"

"You may be certain of it."

Lizzie grabbed her arm. "Come along, Alice! I want to show you my latest purchase! I have bought the prettiest set of china ladies...."

They went out into the hall, Lizzie chattering like a magpie. Alice did not look back. Miles heard her footsteps fade away and then she had gone.

Miles shook himself, trying to dispel the disturbing sensation that something profound had occurred between him and Alice. It was no more than lust, pure and simple. The flare of intimacy between them when she had reached out to him counted for nothing in any emotional sense. He did not wish to have any deep connection to Alice. He only wanted to sleep with her—and to have her money. He had been bored and blue-deviled by the sale, momentarily angered to think of his father's profligacy. Alice had wanted to offer comfort and so he had taken it from her physically. He was still hard to think of her. He should have seduced her on the desk and thus compromised her so thoroughly that the lawyers would have had to retire in scandalized defeat, Lady Membury's conditions were laid waste and a priest would have been sent for immediately.

Once again the image of Alice came into his mind, but it was not the fantasy of Alice lying in wanton submission beneath him but of her reaching out to comfort him in his loss, her pity and concern somehow touching his soul. Miles swore violently. His mind was being turned by this fever he had for her. That was the only explanation. And there was only one cure.

Three months be damned. Lady Membury's conditions be damned. He would have Alice and he would have her money, too. She would surrender to their mutual desire. He would see to it that she did. And next time he would not behave like a gentleman. He would lock the door, ignore all interruptions and seduce her with the ruthlessness of the true rake.

CHAPTER ELEVEN

IT WAS SNOWING the following morning. Pushing aside the heavy drapes that kept out both the light and the drafts from her bedroom, Alice saw that the sky looked like a fat white eiderdown that was spilling flakes like feathers in thick, whirling clouds. She pulled the curtain back as Marigold knocked on the door and came in, bearing a tray with a cup of hot chocolate and a plate of toast upon it.

"Get back into bed, miss," Marigold scolded. "You will take a chill standing there in your nightgown!" She put the tray down on the nightstand and knelt to light the fire in the grate.

Alice watched, remembering the long, cold winter days when she had risen in the dark to start her household duties, breaking the ice on the water in the kitchen before she could heat it, aching as she carried her housemaid's box from floor to floor, sweeping the grates, lighting the fires, running back and forth with endless tasks until she was numb with cold and exhaustion. She knew that her mother considered her hopelessly kind to the servants—to Marigold and to Della the underhousemaid and to Cook and to Jim the footman and Jed the coachman—but Alice knew she would never forget how harsh was a servant's lot and she did all she could to soften it. They were warm and well fed, the best-paid servants in the Yorkshire Dales, granted days off from their work to visit their families, a doctor brought in for them if they were sick, their workload as light as Alice could make it.

"A lack of occupation is both a virtue and a necessity for a gentlewoman," Mrs. Lister had told Alice importantly, when Alice had insisted on showing an interest in the work of the kitchen and the stillroom. "Our idleness is a reflection of our wealth now." Alice, who hated to be idle, had not contradicted her mother but had then gone directly to the kitchens and helped Cook pickle some pears.

"I suppose that Mama will not stir from her room, as she knows it is snowing," she said now, as Marigold stood up, dusting her hands, and the fire leaped into life.

Marigold smiled. "Mrs. Lister has already taken her morning tea, has read the leaves and is now settling down with Mrs. Porter's novel *The Hungarian Brothers*. They are most dashing, so she tells me."

Alice sighed, not over her mother's choice of reading matter, but because she knew that all her plans for the day would now be canceled. Since becoming a lady of leisure, Mrs. Lister considered herself too delicate to go out in the cold winter air, a ridiculous affectation, Alice thought, for a woman who was as tough as Yorkshire grit. Still, she supposed that her mother had earned the right to be a little lazy if she chose. It was merely a shame that her own plans had to suffer as a result, for now she would not be able to go out to the shops or the spa and gain a little fresh air and company, since her chaperone was supposedly indisposed.

Looking at the swirling snowflakes that were

sweeping past the window on a stiff breeze, she thought it unlikely that there would be much company in the village, anyway. Miles Vickery, for instance, would be unlikely to come over the hills from Drum in such inclement weather, especially as it was the second day of the sale of Drum Castle and its contents. She knew that Lowell was hoping to purchase some of the farm machinery and would no doubt take pleasure in the financial ruin of a man he so richly detested.

Alice put her teacup down slowly as she thought about Miles. By her calculations it was all of a minute since she had last thought about him. Their kiss was the last thing she had thought about before she had fallen asleep the previous night. He had stalked her dreams. She had woken that morning soft and warm and entangled in her blankets as though in a lover's embrace, and Miles was the first thing she had thought about. She seemed utterly powerless to think of anything else.

After her agreement to their formal betrothal she had tried to be sensible and keep Miles at arm's length. It had not been difficult. All she had had to do was remind herself of his ruthless coercion, and she had felt angry and used and belittled. But then she had accompanied Lizzie and her mother to Drum Castle for the sale. She had seen the full extent of Miles's penury, she had witnessed the humiliation he was facing, she had met his younger brother and had seen Lady Vickery's and Celia's outward stoicism and glimpsed their inward despair. She had not expected to like Miles's family, and it had somehow made things much harder for her that she did. Celia had told her about the loss of the Vickery estates and, when her mother's back was turned, she had whispered how the late Bishop Vickery had been a terrible spendthrift who had burdened Miles with appalling debt. Alice had understood then why Miles had needed to marry an heiress and why he had pursued her with such single-minded intent. It did not excuse his blackmail of her. It could not, but she was beginning to understand Miles's cold outward shell and the reason she felt this strange affinity with him. Like her, Miles had learned early on that life was not fair. She had worked for a living and had struggled and toiled simply to survive. Miles had been burdened with a responsibility that was not his own.

They were more alike than she had realized.

It was instinct and an awareness of that affinity between them that had led her to offer Miles her sympathy and comfort, seeing in the grim and unhappy man before her someone so different from the urbane and confident Miles Vickery that she thought she knew. She had expected him to reject her. Cynical, sardonic Miles would have no time for her words of consolation, she was sure. And he *had* rejected her words and had sought comfort from her body instead.

A ripple of sensual awareness spread through Alice's body at the thought of Miles's kiss, turning her insides molten hot. Had Lizzie not interrupted them he would surely have seduced her on the desk and she would have been swept away by her desire for him, dead to any sense of propriety. This heated, feverish need that there was between them was dangerous because Miles was so experienced and she so ill-equipped to resist him. In truth she did not even *want* to resist the pleasure his touch gave her. Thinking of it now made the goose bumps rise along her skin and her whole body tremble.

I am no lady, Alice thought wryly, reflecting on the money and the time and the effort spent on expensive elocution tutors and etiquette lessons and dancing masters. *It takes more than town bronze to make a lady. I suffer from what the Duchess of Cole would no doubt refer to as immodest impulses.*

"Miss?" Marigold said, and Alice realized that the maid had asked her a question and it had gone straight over her head.

"I beg your pardon, Marigold," she said.

"I wondered if you wished for the promenade dress to be laid out," Marigold said. "Will you be going out with your handsome lord, miss?"

"No, I don't think I shall," Alice said, surprised by a catch of pain in her chest at the thought that Miles was only her handsome lord because of her fortune. "I doubt very much that Lord Vickery will be calling today," she said. "I shall wear my old blue lavender and help Cook bottle some of the plums or make a cake."

Sighing, she pulled the faded gown from the wardrobe and dressed slowly. She knew that Miles was an experienced rake and she would be the greatest fool in the world to imagine that there was anything more than lust and money between them. For a moment yesterday, at Drum Castle, she had thought there had been something more profound, something deep and sweet and emotional. She had hoped so, her foolish heart as susceptible as ever. Had there been any true emotion, then her feelings of wicked desire for Miles would have been no sin, no matter how unlady-like they were. But without love and respect, they could count for nothing, and where there was black-mail and coercion there could be no love and respect…

With another sigh Alice headed downstairs to the comfort of her cooking.

It was some two hours later that Alice emerged from the kitchens to answer the front doorbell. Jim the footman was fetching some hot water for Lydia, who had seemed more animated in the last week and was even talking of going for a walk by the river. Marigold was upstairs taking Mrs. Lister some hot buttered tea cakes, so there was no one else to do the servants' work. Alice opened the door and Miles Vickery stepped over the threshold, shaking the snow from his hat. There were flakes of it dusting the broad shoulders of his caped driving coat, and his boots were soaked.

"Thank you," he said. "It is an inclement day—" Then, as he recognized her, his tone changed. "Miss Lister! I did not expect—" He stopped. Alice knew exactly what he meant. She had heard it so many times before, most recently at one of the Fortune's Folly assemblies when she had overheard Mrs. Minchin confiding in the Duchess of Cole, "And my dear Duchess, do you know, she actually opened the door of the house herself! So dreadfully inappropriate! But then, once a servant, always a servant, I say…"

"I am perfectly capable of opening the front door for visitors," Alice said, feeling self-conscious. "It is simple—one turns the handle and pulls. Perhaps you could try it for yourself one day, my lord."

She waited for Miles to make some stuffy remark about how that would not be suitable, but he just laughed. "Do you know—I might try that. If you promise to be my mentor, of course, Miss Lister." His gaze swept over her appraisingly, from the hair escaping her hastily contrived chignon to the purple plum stains on her fingers. It felt like a physical touch. Alice started to feel very hot. "I called to ask if you would care to go driving on Fortune's Row with me, Miss Lister," Miles said, "but I see that you were not expecting visitors. Not that you do not look charming…"

"I did not expect to see you this morning," Alice said, acutely aware that her ancient lavender gown and apron were more suited to a farmer's daughter than a leisured heiress. "I know you mentioned that you would call, but the weather is so bad I assumed you would not come."

Miles laughed. "You must think me a poor fellow to be put off by a bit of snow when you are at the end of the journey, Miss Lister," he said. "After our encounter yesterday I was anxious to see you again."

Alice bit her lip. She did not want to start thinking about that encounter again. She had only just *stopped* thinking about it.

"I fear that we are not receiving visitors as Mama is indisposed," she began, stopping as she caught sight of her reflection in the hall mirror. There was a large smear of flour on her cheek. She gasped, her fingers flying to cover it even as she saw Miles laughing at her.

"It becomes you vastly," he said, but there was an intent look in his eyes that brought the color flaming into Alice's cheeks.

"I was making a plum pie," she said. "If you will excuse me, my lord, I think it best for you to leave for now. Perhaps we might meet this evening, in company—"

"I am sorry to hear of your mother's indisposition," Miles said, ignoring her blatant attempts to get rid of him, "but perhaps she might agree to your joining me for a short drive? The snow has stopped and the Row looks very pretty. I would ensure you were wrapped up against the cold," he added. "You would take no chill, I promise you."

Alice felt even more flustered now. There was something ridiculously seductive about Miles offering to wrap her up and take care of her. She wiped the palms of her hands down her apron.

"I don't think—" she began, but stopped as Miles laid one palm against her cheek where the flour still dusted her skin.

"Don't think," he said softly. "Come with me."

Alice closed her eyes. Her skin tingled beneath his fingers.

Come with me...

How easily he could make her forget that he was an unprincipled scoundrel. This unexpected sweetness between them felt like a true courtship rather than the coercion it was.

"I know you do not have to ask—you have the means to command what you are requesting," she said, angry that with no more than a smile and a touch, Miles could seduce her into liking him.

Her words were sharp and she saw the smiling light die in Miles's hazel eyes and the coldness return in its place.

"Then you had best go and fetch your cloak and not oppose me," he said, harshly now. Their gazes clashed and Miles raised his brows. "Why do you wait? As you have reminded me, I can demand whatever I want of you, Miss Lister."

Feeling a little sick, Alice hurried up the stairs well aware that Miles's gaze followed her. She felt tense and tired all of a sudden. Just for a moment it had felt as though there was something so tender between them that it had made her tremble, but it had been just another illusion.

Slipping into her mother's room, she found Mrs. Lister propped against her pillows and deeply engrossed in her book with her lapdog, Bertie, curled up beside her in his knitted jacket that bore the Lister coat of arms.

"Mama, Lord Vickery is here," she began. "He asks permission to take me for a short drive on Fortune's Row. The snow has ceased now but I am not sure that it is a very good idea to go with him."

Mrs. Lister looked startled. "Lord Vickery has come all this way from Drum in the *snow* to see you, Alice?" Her face broke into a smile. "What devotion!"

"To my money," Alice murmured, determined to remind her mama that Miles's reasons for seeking her out were scarcely disinterested.

"Hmm," Mrs. Lister said. She reached for her empty teacup. "The leaves show me an anchor, which means constancy. Yes, by all means go, my love."

"Constancy indeed," Alice said. "A constant interest in saving his own skin. Are you sure I should go, Mama? You are my chaperone and as you are indisposed I would be alone with Lord Vickery, which is most improper—"

"Lord Vickery does not want me there, Alice," her mother said in tones of one addressing a small, stupid child. "Really, my love, have some sense! It would be the greatest drawback to Lord Vickery's courtship if *I* were to accompany you." She looked at Alice over the top of her book. "You might think about showing him some kindness, too, Alice, whilst we are on the subject."

"Kindness?" Alice said. "Whatever do you mean, Mama?"

A flicker of irritation crossed Mrs. Lister's face at having to spell matters out further. "Lord Vickery is a man of somewhat…ardent…emotions," she said. "He will probably find it difficult to wait the three months or more until you are wed, my dear. That is what I mean by kindness. If you are discreet…" She let the sentence hang suggestively and looked at Alice, her eyes bright, brows arched.

"You mean that he is a rake," Alice said, sitting down heavily on the edge of her mother's bed and feeling quite scandalized at what Mrs. Lister was advocating, "and you think he will stray if I do not allow him to sleep with me."

Mrs. Lister gave a little shriek. "You can be so distressingly blunt, my love! What I meant was—"

"That he is a rake and that he will stray if I do not sleep with him," Alice repeated. "But if he does stray then he will forfeit my fortune under the terms of Lady Membury's will, won't he, Mama?" She traced a pattern on the bedspread with her fingertips. "Lord Vickery is trapped. He will have to try to exercise some restraint in his intimate affairs—for a change."

As she slipped on the promenade gown that Marigold had wanted to lay out for her earlier, Alice reflected that it would probably be too much to expect her mama to behave as a chaperone ought, for Mrs. Lister was so desperate to see the match made and her daughter a marchioness that if Miles suggested an elopement she would probably pack Alice's bag herself. Shaking her head in resignation, Alice tied her hair back with a ribbon and bundled it up under her

bonnet, grabbed a thick pelisse and put on her sturdi-
est boots. She hoped Miles's horses had not taken cold
standing out in the snow. Actually when she came to
think of it she was surprised that he *had* any horses,
and when she saw the curricle, all gleaming silver and
green with fine chestnuts at the head, she was more
surprised still.

"Mr. Haven at the livery stables has loaned it to me
against my expectations," Miles said, handing her up
into the carriage, "so I have you to thank for this, Miss
Lister." He gave her a mocking look. "You see how my
betrothal to you materially benefits me."

The groom came forward with a hot brick for Alice's
feet, and Miles wrapped a warm woolen blanket about
her. Alice was relieved to see that there *was* a groom
to chaperone them—until Miles dismissed him a
second later.

"Thank you, Chester," he said. "You may go into the
village for an hour or so if you wish."

"My lord," the groom said, raising a hand in salute
and whistling as he strode away down the drive.

"So you are already borrowing against my fortune,"
Alice said coolly, as Miles swung himself up beside
her and took the reins.

Miles shot her a smile. "That's right, Miss Lister,"
he said. "I am."

Hmm, Alice thought. Miles did not appear to be
having much trouble with telling the unvarnished truth.
Perhaps it sprang from having no shame.

"I thought," she said, "that the idea was to use my
money to pay off your debts rather than use the
promise of it to incur more."

"Not at all," Miles said. "The skill is in managing

one's credit." He looked at her. "I shall always be living on tick, Miss Lister. Not even eighty thousand pounds will see me clear of debt."

It was unwelcome news to Alice. If Miles succeeded in meeting the terms of the will and she was obliged to marry him, they would be forever living in debt. She had never been in such a situation even when she had only her servant's wages to manage upon, and she did not care for it at all. The imprudent, extravagant style of the aristocracy was totally deplorable to her.

She sighed, pressing her gloved hands together within the thick fur of her muff. The snow had stopped and a pale sun was peeping through the clouds but the air was still cold and heavy. The curricle had turned out onto the lane and was rolling gently along toward the center of the village. The road had been swept clear of snow, and as they reached the main square, Miles turned the curricle onto Fortune Row. This was a miniature version of Rotten Row, and Alice and Lizzie had often laughed at Sir Montague Fortune's delusions of grandeur that had led him to create a small park with a circular drive. Now, though, she was obliged to admit that it looked very pretty with the snow glittering all around them as the sun picked out the tiny sparkling crystals. Only one other rider had ventured out that morning, a gentleman on a raking black who was galloping across the distant green between the Granby Hotel and the river.

"It is nice to be out of the house," Alice conceded, turning her face up to the pale sun. Even though Miles had forced her hand, she was obliged to admit that being out, even with him, was better than sitting around indoors.

"Yes," Miles said. "Do you ride, Miss Lister?"

"I do, but without any degree of style or finesse," Alice said with a smile. "No doubt my technique would be denounced were I to appear before the fashionable set on horseback. But I learned on a farm, you see."

"You do not keep a horse at present? Does your brother stable one for you?"

"No, I, too, hire from Mr. Haven on the rare occasions I ride out," Alice said. "Actually I prefer to walk by the river or up onto the hills, which is another activity so often frowned upon in a lady." She shook her head. "It seems that I am too active to be genteel. One benefit of being a servant was that no one cared whether I behaved in a ladylike fashion or not. It was completely irrelevant. These days, though, I am forever being tripped up by rules and regulations."

Miles turned his head and smiled at her. "I can imagine that must be trying," he said. "You do not strike me as the sort of woman who would enjoy sitting sewing before the fire for hours on end just because it is in accordance with society's dictates."

"My sewing is accounted very neat," Alice said, "but I do confess to finding it a little boring after a while." She frowned, remembering a conversation she had had with Lydia the previous night when they had been sitting together, embroidering little shirts for Lydia's baby. "May I ask you something, Lord Vickery?"

Miles smiled at her again, a rueful, boyish smile that somehow made her heart give a giddy skip and reminded her once again of how sweet things might have been between them if the circumstances had been different.

"Of course, Miss Lister," he said.

Alice squeezed her gloved hands together a little

tighter. Suddenly she felt nervous but she was not quite sure why.

"Has Tom Fortune escaped from jail?" she asked.

She saw the flare of surprise in Miles's eyes. Whatever he had imagined she had been going to ask, this was not it. The smile faded from his lips and a steely expression came into his eyes, sharp, intense, intimidating and so different from his habitual lazy demeanor that Alice felt chilled to see it and almost shivered. He slowed the horses right down to a walk and turned so that his full attention was on her.

"Why do you ask?" His voice was very quiet.

Alice held his gaze. "Can you give me an honest answer first?"

Miles inclined his head slightly. "Yes, I can give you an honest answer," he said. "Yes, Tom Fortune has escaped from jail."

Alice's breath caught in her throat. "Is Lydia in danger?"

"She might be." Miles's gaze narrowed on her. "You might all be. What prompted you to ask, Miss Lister?"

"It was something that you said to me the other day," Alice said. She fidgeted with the edge of the rug. "You asked after Lydia, and I thought it was nothing but politeness, but then Lizzie said that Lord Waterhouse had asked if Lydia received any letters, and why would he want to know that?" She raised her puzzled blue gaze to Miles's impassive face. The carriage had almost come to a standstill now beneath the laden boughs of the trees. The snow muffled all sound from the horses' hooves. "And then last night Lydia asked me—" She stopped abruptly, realizing too late that she might be about to betray Lydia's confidence with her unwary comments.

The intent, concentrated look in Miles's eyes did not waver. "What did she ask you?" he said.

"Oh, nothing…" Alice grimaced, desperately trying to think of a way to avoid betraying Lydia any further. She was a very poor liar and could not even think of a convincing remark that Lydia *might* have made. And she knew instinctively that Miles would not believe her evasion anyway. His perceptive hazel gaze was too searching for that.

"Well, Miss Lister?" he prompted softly. "What did Miss Cole ask you? Pray do not waste your time trying to think something up. I would know it for the fiction it was."

Alice jumped to have her thoughts echoed so precisely. "Since when did you become the expert on telling the truth?" she snapped.

"Since my courtship of you obliged me to be honest all the time," Miles said dryly. "So?"

"Lydia said that if Tom Fortune had *not* murdered Sir William Crosby or Warren Sampson, who did I think the perpetrator might be?" Alice said, capitulating in a rush. "But I am sure it was no more than idle speculation on her part! If she is still in love with Tom it is natural that she would want to exonerate him of blame."

Miles's eyes were narrowed thoughtfully. "That's true. Or it may be that Tom Fortune has contacted Miss Cole, persuaded her of his innocence and asked for her help. Do you know if that is the case, Miss Lister?"

"No, I do not," Alice said, blushing, and angry because of it, for she knew it made her seem the picture of guilt. "She has confided nothing like that in me. That was all she said."

"I see," Miles said, his tone revealing nothing of

whether he believed her—or not. "And Miss Cole has definitely received no letters?"

"Not to my knowledge." Alice frowned. "I only asked you about Tom because I was afraid that Lydia might be in danger. Now that you are interrogating me I begin to wish that I had kept silent."

"It would be useful if you could keep an eye on Miss Cole," Miles said, "and let us know if anything suspicious happens."

"I won't spy on Lydia!" Alice said, firing up. She already felt monstrously guilty for raising Miles's suspicions and could have kicked herself for her clumsiness. "You are trying to use me," she added bitterly. "Again. Will I never learn? I spoke up out of concern for Lydia, but you—" she shook her head "—for all your purported desire to protect us from Tom Fortune, the only thing that you care about is recapturing him. Lydia was right!"

"So she did say something else about the case," Miles observed calmly. "I thought so."

"Yes, she did!" Alice said, even more annoyed that she had been caught out in the only lie she had ever knowingly told him. "She said that the authorities should look no further than you for an alternative culprit to Tom, for you had the necessary ruthlessness and the skill to be the murderer!"

She heard Miles swear under his breath. He brought the carriage to a halt so quickly that the horses jibbed, and then he swung around in his seat to face her. His physical presence was so intimidating and the anger she sensed in him so powerful that Alice instinctively drew back, only to feel the corner of the seat dig painfully into the small of her back.

"And did you believe that of me?" Miles's voice was still quiet but there was an undertone in it now that made Alice shiver. His gloved fingers were hard against her cold cheek as he turned her face to his and forced her to meet his eyes. "Did you believe it, Alice?" he repeated softly. "Do you think me a murderer?"

"I do not know!" Alice burst out. "It is true you have the necessary ruthlessness! How could I think otherwise when you are forcing me into marriage? And Lydia was right that there must be a dozen things in your past that would make you the perfect candidate for blackmail by a criminal like Warren Sampson—"

She broke off as Miles swore again, viciously and fluently. "So you have worked out my motive, too?"

"Of course not!" Alice said. She was starting to feel a little scared of the violence she could see in his eyes. "I am not saying that you *did* murder Sampson—"

"No, you have merely demonstrated your complete lack of trust in me," Miles said.

Alice saw red. "I was not aware that you wanted trust from me," she said. "You want me in order to have my money to pay off your debts, that is all!"

"And to have you in my bed, Miss Lister," Miles said silkily. "Do not forget that."

"None of which requires trust or even liking," Alice said, "or so you told me."

"So I did," Miles said, still in the same dangerous tone.

"You are angry," Alice observed. "You cannot be angry with me if you do not care about my opinion."

"Your logic slays me, Miss Lister," Miles snapped. His expression was grim and furious. It made Alice quail, but at the same time she was puzzled that her good opinion seemed to matter so much to him. She put out a hand toward him, but before she could speak again there was a sudden crack like the sound of a branch snapping under the weight of snow and then Alice felt a sharp pain in her arm like a burning brand raked across her skin. The carriage horses shied, throwing her off balance, and in the same instant Miles grabbed her with lightning reflexes and lifted her clean out of her seat, jumping down into the snow with her in his arms.

They hit the ground and rolled over, and all the air was knocked from Alice's body and she lay still, winded, with Miles's arms still wrapped close about her. Her body was sheltered beneath his and her face pressed against his coat. She could feel the hardness of his hands as he held her brutally tight. Every muscle in his body was tensed and waiting.

Alice threw back her head and drew in a deep, steadying breath.

"What on earth—"

"Keep still!"

Miles's face, so close to hers, was dark and set. His eyes were blazing. Still half crouching, he drew her into the shelter of the carriage. The horses were spooked, stamping and blowing, but fortunately they seemed disinclined to panic.

"Don't move!"

Miles let go of her briefly to peer around the side of the carriage and immediately there was another crack and a chip of paint flew off Mr. Haven's beautiful livery. The bullet passed so close that Alice felt the air move with it. This time the horses whinnied and shied and the carriage creaked forward a few agonizing feet, exposing Alice to the gunman's line of sight.

Another bullet followed swiftly, digging up the snow with a white puff, even as Miles caught her arm in a vicious grip and dragged her back behind cover, drawing her close once again to the shelter of his body.

"Damnation," he muttered. "We are sitting ducks here."

"Why is someone shooting at us?" Alice demanded. Her voice sounded high and thin. She was shaking uncontrollably. Everything had happened so fast that it seemed utterly unreal. Only the calmness of Miles's reactions, the absolute steadiness she sensed in him, kept her from utter panic.

His arms were about her, immeasurably comforting. Extraordinarily, under the circumstances, she felt safe.

"I don't think we have time to discuss that properly now," Miles said, a thread of amusement in his tone. He pressed his lips to her hair and she felt the conflict in him—the need to take action versus the desperate desire to offer her protection. She remembered then his army training; his first instinct must surely be to give chase to the enemy and yet he had held back to defend her.

"I do not want to leave you, Alice," Miles said, "but I need to try and work my way around to where he is shooting from or we have no chance of stopping him—"

"Go," Alice said. Her voice came out as a thread of sound. She was trembling now with shock and cold and reaction, the snow clinging to her clothes, her bonnet squashed beyond recognition. She could see a smear of blood on the snow where her arm had rested. Her gloves were stained with it, too, and she put up her hand to her sleeve and felt the ragged edges of material around the bullet hole.

"You're injured." Miles's voice sharpened and there was a note in it she had never heard before. "Alice—"

"It's nothing," Alice said, teeth chattering. "It barely grazed me. Go! Better to stop him than sit here like a couple of prizes in the shooting gallery. But for pity's sake, take care—"

Their eyes met. Miles looked torn. They both knew that if the carriage horses were panicked and took flight before he had disarmed the marksman, Alice would be defenseless. Her fingers clung to his for a long moment and then she deliberately freed herself.

"Go," she said for a third time.

"Vickery!" The shout came from behind them and they both spun around. Nat Waterhouse was galloping up on a bay stallion. He leaped down and grabbed the carriage horses, soothing the panicked animals until they quietened.

"I heard a shot," he said tersely, over his shoulder. "What the hell is going on, Miles?"

"Someone has been using us for target practice," Miles said, getting to his feet. "Thank God you're here. At least that will have scared him off. I must get Miss Lister back to Spring House and call for the doctor before we can try to discover who has been shooting at us."

"I am perfectly fine," Alice said, scrambling to her feet and shaking the snow off her skirts with hands that still trembled a little. "I can walk back. You two must go and do…whatever it is you have to do. If you leave it too long he will have got away and no one will remember seeing anything."

"I'm not leaving you," Miles said. "What if some-one tries to shoot at you again? You would be totally unprotected."

"They won't," Alice said. Suddenly she felt exhausted and all she wanted was to be at home, to take refuge deep in her feather bed and sleep until she felt better. "I doubt I was the target," she added. "Why would anyone shoot at me? I do not have a family curse hanging over my head."

Miles and Nat exchanged a look.

"Miss Lister has a point," Nat said. "Perhaps you were the intended victim, Miles."

Miles shook his head. "He was not aiming at me," he said. "Miss Lister—" there was unflinching determination in his tone "—I'm not leaving you to travel back alone. The idea is absurd." His tone brooked no refusal.

"I'll check out the tree cover to the south and see from where he was shooting," Nat said. "I'll send word to Dexter, too. Join us at the Granby once you have seen Miss Lister safely attended to." He nodded to Alice, a smile in his eyes. "Your servant, Miss Lister. You are most indomitable, you know. Nine women out of ten would be having the vapors by now." He raised a hand in salute, jumped up into the saddle and turned his horse to the south.

Miles scooped Alice up in his arms without another word and placed her in the carriage, arranging the rug about her as carefully as though she were made of spun glass. She watched him as, grim-faced and silent, he steered the chilled and skittish horses back into the town. Her arm had stopped bleeding now but it throbbed painfully in a way that set her teeth on edge. Miles insisted on carrying her into the house even though she told him quite firmly that she could walk. In the hallway, though, a diversion was created when Mrs. Lister heard the news and promptly fell into a swoon.

"A shame she did not see this in her tea leaves," Alice said sotto voce to Miles. "She would have been better prepared."

She saw him smile a little but the deep lines around his eyes did not ease and he seemed uncharacteristically stern. Whilst Marigold ran for the smelling salts and everyone fussed around Mrs. Lister, he drew Alice gently aside.

"You are sure you do not require a doctor, Miss Lister?" he asked.

"Good gracious, no!" Alice said, determined to remain strong. "Hot water and some clean linen to bind the cut and a glass of brandy will suffice."

"You seem to be made of stern stuff," Miles observed.

"It comes from being in service," Alice said briskly. "I can deal with most emergencies." She lowered her voice. "You do not think it could have been an accident, Lord Vickery? Someone out shooting at rabbits, perhaps?" She stopped as Miles shook his head. "No, I see you do not."

"They would have to have been a lamentably bad shot," Miles said. "We were several feet off the ground in that curricle and who ever saw a rabbit in midair?"

Alice sighed. "Then someone was attempting to kill either you or me, but that makes no sense at all. Who would do such a thing—and why?"

"I will come back and talk to you about it later," Miles said. "I must rejoin Waterhouse and see what he has been able to discover." He looked at her. "You are very valiant, Miss Lister, but you look exhausted, you know. You should rest."

Alice *felt* exhausted though it was not particularly flattering to know that she looked it, too. The babble of voices in the hall made her head pound. The graze on her arm throbbed painfully. Her soaked and freezing clothes clung to her, making her shiver convulsively. She felt a strong and most uncharacteristic desire to cry.

She put a hand on Miles's arm. "Thank you for saving my life," she said. "If you had not pulled me from the carriage so quickly—" Another convulsive shiver shook her. She looked at his face. He was watching her with a dark and unreadable expression, and suddenly the reaction and misery hit her at the same time. Of course Miles would want to save her life. She was worth a great deal of money to him. There could be no reason why he would protect her other than for his own gain. She was naive in the extreme to think that he had done it because he cared about her rather than her fortune.

"I suppose," she added bitterly, into the silence, "that it was in your interests to save me. You have invested a lot of time and effort in claiming me."

Miles's gaze, hard and implacable, held hers for a long moment. "I have," he said. His voice was rough. He pulled her to him and gave her a brief, hard kiss. There was anger in it and a savage desire, and for a moment Alice yielded helplessly before he let her go.

"Go to bed," he said. "Tell your servants to open the door to no one you do not trust. I shall be back soon."

Alice watched as he paused before the door, instructing the footman to carry Mrs. Lister into the parlor and Marigold to fetch hot water for Alice, and then he had raised a hand in farewell and was gone, and Alice climbed the stairs laboriously and slipped off her wet clothes. She bandaged her own arm because

Marigold was so upset that her hands shook too much, and Lizzie was so clumsy that when she tried, she tied the linen so tight that Alice lost the sensation in her arm altogether. Lizzie chattered and speculated about the shooting, and Marigold looked pale and anxious. Mrs. Lister demanded hot tea and as much seed cake as cook could provide in order to ward off the shock.

And all the while Alice thought of the tenderness that she had glimpsed for that split second in Miles's eyes, and thought of the seductive attraction of his strength and protection. She remembered the steadiness of his arms as he had held her and the utter confidence she had had in his power to keep her safe. He had saved her life. He had risked his own life to protect her. If only he had offered everything to her freely. But she knew that she was in danger of seeing Miles with the same illusions that had been her downfall the previous year. His motives were not pure. Not in the least. He was driven by no more than self-interest, lust and greed. She must remember that before she wove the same dreams around him as she had done before and ended up even more hurt and betrayed than she had then. She had to remember that to Miles Vickery she was no more than the means to save himself from debt and disgrace.

CHAPTER TWELVE

IT WAS SNOWING AGAIN by the time that Miles reached the Granby—big white flakes this time that obscured the view and would, he knew, already have covered over any evidence of footprints on Fortune Row. In the private parlor he found Nat Waterhouse and Dexter Anstruther encamped before a roaring fire.

"Not looking quite your usual immaculate self, old chap," Dexter said by way of greeting. "Nat's filled me in on what has happened. You're unhurt?"

"Completely," Miles said. He stripped off his gloves and crossed to the fire to warm his hands.

"And Miss Lister?" Nat asked. "That looked like a nasty scratch on her arm."

"She was cold and shaken but she refused to see a doctor," Miles said. "She's a most remarkable woman." He saw Nat and Dexter exchange a glance. "What?" he demanded testily.

"Nothing at all," Dexter said smoothly. "Do you need a drink?"

"Just coffee," Miles said. "Strong."

He took a cup and sank into one of the armchairs with a deep sigh. He had faced many situations in his career that were far more dangerous than the one that he and Alice had been in and yet in some obscure way the incident had shaken him far more than it ought to have done. Alice's tense white face was before his eyes; he could see the blood seeping from between her gloved fingers as she had tried to stem the flow from the bullet wound. She had been terrified and yet so calm, when many women would have succumbed to the vapors or worse. He had been right in thinking her valiant.

Would I had the right to protect her....

When he had seen that she had been shot, terror had grabbed him by the throat in a way he had never experienced before. He had known fear many times in his life. Only a fool or a madman would deny that they were afraid in battle or when they were on the wrong end of a gun. But the fear he had felt for Alice had been different. It had been a dread of losing something he had barely found, a horror that something immeasurably important was about to be snatched from him before he had even had chance to grasp it properly. It was probably a dread of losing Alice's money, he told himself, but nevertheless a feeling stirred within him that was strange and unfamiliar. He cleared his throat abruptly and put down his cup with a sharp snap.

"Did you have a chance to discover any evidence on the Row before the snow came down again?" he asked Nat.

Nat nodded. "There were footprints in the snow around Seven Acre Covert. I took some measurements. He was a big man with a firm tread. There had been a horse there, as well. The distance from where your carriage was situated was about two hundred yards."

"No great distance for an accurate marksman," Dexter observed.

"He wasn't very accurate," Miles said. "He missed

three times." He turned to Nat. "Would you have missed at that distance?"

Nat shook his head slowly. "No. Most trained riflemen would hit the target at that range."

"As would plenty of countrymen accustomed to shooting game," Miles said. "A farmer, say."

Dexter's blue eyes narrowed. "What are you suggesting?" he said softly.

"I'm thinking of Lowell Lister," Miles said. "Whoever our assailant was, he was aiming at Miss Lister, not at me. I am sure of it. Who would inherit her fortune if she died?"

"Her mother, I imagine," Nat said. "But surely you cannot imagine Mrs. Lister running around on Fortune Row with a rifle?"

Miles shrugged. "One forgets that Mrs. Lister was once a farmer's wife. She can probably shoot." He eased his shoulders back in the chair. "But no, I do not think she would be taking potshots at her daughter. But Lowell…" He sighed. "He stands to gain if Alice dies and Mrs. Lister inherits, and he does not want Alice to marry me…."

There was a short silence. "Lowell Lister always seems very fond of his sister," Nat ventured. "Not that that proves anything, but—" he frowned "—you are *certain* the marksman was aiming at Miss Lister, Miles?"

"Well," Miles said dryly, "he did wound her even if it was not fatally. That suggests she was his target."

"How close were you to her at the time?" Dexter questioned.

"A proper distance." Miles gave him an old-fashioned look. "What are you suggesting, Dexter?"

"Merely that if Miss Lister was in your arms it

might have been easier to confuse the two targets," Dexter said smoothly.

"Well, she was not," Miles said, with a ferocious glare. He remembered the shaking in Alice's body as she lay beneath him in the snow and the momentary flash of terror in her eyes. The thought of someone threatening her life made the anger seethe within him.

"Entertain for a moment the idea that you were the target instead," Nat said.

Miles shrugged again, a little irritably. "I've already thought about it and it makes no sense. None of my family want me dead. On the contrary they all want me to stay alive so that the Curse of Drum does not fall on Philip. As for the curse itself—" he paused, reaching for the coffeepot "—well, you know that I give that no credence."

"Tom Fortune?" Nat suggested.

Miles shook his head. "Why kill me? Why kill any of the Guardians? He knows that if he removes all three of us the Home Secretary will only send someone else to recapture him." His eyes narrowed thoughtfully over the rim of his cup. "It makes more sense, in fact—if it is Fortune—that it should be Miss Lister he was shooting at."

"Because?" Dexter prompted.

"Because Miss Lister and Lady Elizabeth—" Miles glanced at Nat "—have worked out that Tom has escaped. Miss Lister asked me about it this morning. I suspect that Tom has contacted Miss Cole and if he thought that Miss Lister was telling me about it…" He spread his hands wide. "Well, you have a possible motive, I suppose."

"No one saw a man fitting Tom Fortune's description in the vicinity of the village this morning," Nat said.

"I doubt anyone saw anything," Miles countered. "Few people were out in the snow."

"Lady Elizabeth and I saw no one," Nat agreed.

Dexter swung around to look at him. "You were out riding with Lady Elizabeth Scarlet when this happened?"

"I was on my way back from escorting her to Spring House when I saw Miles and Miss Lister," Nat said. "Miss Minchin does not ride," he added, a shade of defensiveness in his tone as he caught the look Dexter gave Miles.

"Then she must be relieved that you have Lady Elizabeth to accompany you on your outings instead," Miles drawled, taking pleasure from his friend's obvious discomfiture.

"Leave it, Miles," Nat snapped, "before I dissect your feelings for Miss Lister, which are nowhere near as straightforward as you appear to think."

"Gentlemen," Dexter said, a smile lurking in his eyes, "before you come to blows, did either of you see anyone else out riding this morning?"

"Miss Lister and I saw one other horseman," Miles said. "A gentleman riding a black hunter."

"Not exactly a detailed description," Nat said. "There are half a dozen of those in Fortune's Folly and Dexter is one of them."

"I had Miss Lister in the carriage with me," Miles said, glaring at him. "Do you think I was concentrating on anyone else?" He turned to Dexter. "I sent Chester to the livery stables to inquire if anyone had hired a hack like that this morning."

"Good," Dexter said. He seemed to be trying hard not to laugh at the overt aggression between his colleagues. "I think we need to interview Miss Cole and

see if it is true Tom Fortune has tried to contact her."
He rubbed a hand over his brow. "I know she will be
reluctant but perhaps she can be persuaded to speak to
Laura. They are cousins, after all, and Laura has
always had a kindness for her."

Nat nodded. "A good idea, Dexter."

"Meanwhile you need to discuss with Miss Lister
who would benefit from her death," Dexter said to
Miles, "and see if there is any other reason why anyone
might try to kill her."

Miles stood up, driving his hands into his pockets.
"I don't care for this," he said. "If it is Tom Fortune
who is behind this then all those women are in
danger—Miss Lister, Miss Cole and Lady Elizabeth.
There is no one with them at Spring House other than
servants. One of us should be there to protect them."

"You think that one of us should move in there?"
Dexter raised his brows. "That would be highly irregular."

"This is a highly irregular situation," Miles pointed
out.

"It would be better to move them all to a place of
safety," Nat said, "if we can get them to agree." He
looked at Dexter. "Could they stay with you and Laura
at the Old Palace?"

"They could," Dexter said. "There certainly is room,
but I suspect you would have the devil of a job persuading Miss Lister of the need for it, and it's hardly a place
of safety. Spring House is more secure." He turned to
Miles. "I agree that it would be better if you can
persuade Miss Lister to allow you to stay there, I think."

"Oh, I will persuade her," Miles said. He felt a little
easier to think that he would be on hand to protect

Alice if anything happened. He turned to Dexter, slight color creeping up under his skin.

"I never thanked you and Laura for giving Mama and Celia and Philip refuge at the Old Palace," he said gruffly. "Truth is that I never wanted them to stay but I am glad now that they are not out at Drum."

"Don't give it another thought, old fellow," Dexter said, slapping him on the shoulder. "Laura's blue-deviled that she is currently too sick with her pregnancy to go out much. She is enjoying the company."

"The story of the shooting is bound to have traveled around the village by now," Nat said thoughtfully. "How do we play it? As a bit of wayward target practice by some of the local youths?"

"That sounds ideal," Miles said. "Let us dampen down the speculation. Now all I have to do is persuade Miss Lister of the opposite and that her life is in danger." He saw Nat and Dexter exchange a look and raised his brows sharply. "What is it that you aren't saying to me?"

"We did wonder," Dexter said after a moment, "whether there was one other possibility that we have not already discussed."

"Well?" Miles said interrogatively.

"You told me a while ago that you are blackmailing Miss Lister into marriage, Miles," Nat said slowly. "People are notoriously dangerous when put under pressure in that way. You don't need me to tell you that. Would Miss Lister dislike you enough and resent your hold over her sufficiently to kill you?"

"No." Miles was shocked at how deeply and instinctively he repudiated the suggestion. He took a careful breath and tried to think dispassionately. "I suppose that she has good enough reason," he admitted. He ran a hand over his hair. "I cannot imagine that she would do it," he said. "She is too good a person—"

"Are you sure?" Dexter probed. "If you are pushing her too hard…"

"No," Miles said again. Agitated, he stood up abruptly and paced across the room. The thought of Alice betraying him in such a sickening way appalled him. "No," he repeated. "God knows, I deserve it, but I still maintain that Miss Lister herself is the target, not I."

"She could have paid someone else," Nat pointed out. "Or it could be the work of Miss Lister and her brother together, perhaps."

"No!" Miles almost shouted. He grabbed his coat, which was steaming gently by the fire, and shrugged it on. "I am going back to Spring House," he said abruptly. "I will see you both later."

There was a short silence after he had gone out. Then Dexter raised his brows at Nat Waterhouse and Nat smiled.

"I saw his face when he realized that Miss Lister was injured," Nat said. "He's in a devil of a mess."

"He certainly is," Dexter agreed, pouring more coffee.

CELIA VICKERY WAS TAKEN aback to recognize the gentleman who held open the door of the Fortune's Folly Post Office for her with such exemplary courtesy.

"Mr. Gaines," she said, "I did not expect to see you this morning. So few people venture out when it is snowing. Silly of them, of course, for what harm can a few flakes do, but even so…"

She was chattering. She was aware of it. She,

who was known for a glacial *froideur* when confronting the opposite sex, she who could reduce young men to stammers and then pitiful silence, was stuttering herself. Remembering the ball the previous night and the way in which she had importuned Frank Gaines for four dances, she felt an uncharacteristic mortification wash over her. He must imagine that she had taken too much rum punch— or that she was so desperate to engage the interest of a man that she would throw herself at his head. And now for him to find her here! Had he arrived a minute sooner she would still have been in the process of dispatching her parcel and *that* would have been very hard to explain. Had he seen the address, he might guess…

"Lady Celia." Gaines bowed. "May I escort you anywhere? The Pump Rooms, perhaps?"

"Gracious, no!" Celia exclaimed. "I am not so feeble as to require spa water to bolster my constitution."

"I am sure you are not," Frank Gaines said, falling into step beside her. She became aware once again of how very tall and powerfully built he was. His broad shoulders practically blocked out the light. "In that case," he said, "I wonder whether I might beg a word with you, Lady Celia? In private?"

Celia looked at him. He looked directly back. Her heart missed a beat. The trouble with lawyers like Frank Gaines, she thought, was that they were very shrewd. Gaines would, she was sure, have been digging into Miles's past to discover anything that might be to his discredit and might ruin the match with Alice Lister. It was his job, after all. But the danger was that in the process he would discover other secrets…

"Of course," she murmured, "although I am not sure what you could possibly wish to say to me."

"We shall leave that for a moment, if we may," Frank Gaines said blandly. His bright, perceptive gaze seemed to see through her and see all the things she was hiding.

Oh dear, Celia thought helplessly. *He knows.*

"It is too inclement to sit outside today," Gaines continued. "Would you be so good as to join me in a cup of tea at the spa?"

"Very well," Celia said, bowing to the inevitable.

In very short order she found herself installed on a charming wrought-iron bench in the tiled tearooms. Gaines seated himself beside her and summoned a maid with no more than a slight inclination of his head. When the girl had taken their order he turned to Celia, a thoughtful look in his eyes. She was very aware of the way in which his hand rested along the back of the seat, almost, but not quite, touching her shoulder.

"You *know,* don't you!" she burst out, wishing that she did not sound quite so gauche but somehow feeling that fifteen years of town bronze had deserted her in an instant.

"Yes," Gaines said slowly. "I do."

"I had to do it." Celia met his eyes. "We need the money and Mama has no idea how to economize. Not really. Oh, she thinks she is frightfully good at saving a little here and there but there is never enough to meet the bills and so…" Her voice trailed away. "I know no one could possibly approve—"

"Approve?" Gaines said. There was a spark of laughter deep in his gray eyes. "I should rather think not, Lady Celia. You are a bishop's daughter."

Celia spread her hands appealingly. "But don't you see that I had no choice? I had to think of something for which I had a talent—"

"And you came up with this?" There was unflattering surprise in Frank Gaines's tone and it stiffened Celia's spine.

"Yes," she snapped. "I did. You may think it surprising, Mr. Gaines, but I assure you I am *very* good at it!"

"I do not doubt that." Frank Gaines sounded unruffled. "My inquiries show me that you make a good income, but what puzzles me…" He paused, a slight frown on his brow as he looked at her. Celia's heart was beating very fast. She did not quite understand why it was important to have this man's respect, and yet it had been from the first. She had met so many men over the long years of the London Season. She was not a heiress, nor was she especially good-looking, and she had always had decided opinions, so she had never found a particular gentleman who was her match, and perversely it would *have* to be Frank Gaines who had engaged her regard. She sighed in exasperation. She and her brother Miles, both so determined not to love…They had more in common than Miles had ever realized.

"What puzzles you…" she prompted, as Frank Gaines seemed in no hurry to expand on his thoughts but merely sat pinning her in that observant gray gaze, like a butterfly spread wide beneath his inquiring eyes.

"Is where you get your ideas from," Gaines said. "I have read some of your work, Lady Celia. Indeed, I went specially to purchase your books when I discovered your secret. They were very—" a smile curved his lips "—very engrossing indeed."

"I have some experience," Celia snapped, blushing, "and I have observation and imagination."

"Indeed, you must have."

The tea arrived. Neither of them seemed inclined to drink any of it. There was a silence between them. Celia fidgeted with her spoon and with her gloves and with the edge of her cloak. Eventually she looked up to see that Gaines was still watching her with that unfathomable look. He seemed to have moved infinitesimally closer to her along the bench. His hand was touching her shoulder now in the lightest and most casual of gestures.

"Oh, for goodness' sake," she snapped, "I need to know if you are going to tell anyone!"

Gaines stretched a little. He looked like a lazy cat, all sleek muscle and with a predatory gleam in his eyes.

"I see no reason why I should," he said slowly. "After all, it is not relevant to the inquiries I am making on behalf of Miss Lister."

Celia felt weak with relief. "Thank you," she murmured.

"But," Gaines continued, "I confess I would like something in return."

Celia's gaze snapped up to his and saw the amusement in his face. Her heart started to thud again, long slow beats that made her whole body quiver.

"Are you seeking to *blackmail* me?" she demanded.

"Of course not." His voice was soothing. "Nothing could be further from my mind. I merely thought that I might…help you? Provide some inspiration, perhaps?"

Celia swallowed convulsively. "I do not believe I need to trouble you on that."

His hand brushed her sleeve. Celia shivered. "It would be no trouble."

Celia sat there, frozen, her tea cooling on the table in front of her. Could she do it? She was astonished to realize quite how tempted she was. To learn, to explore… She bit her lip. Frank Gaines said nothing to either persuade her or hurry her, but there was something in his bright gaze that captured her and made her heart race.

"Very well," she whispered, feeling the excitement make her blood sing even as she marveled at her own audacity, "but where can we do it? No one must guess…."

He shifted a little. "Trust me. I know somewhere." He rose to his feet and proffered her his arm. "Shall we go?"

Celia stared at him. "Now?"

"Why not?" He smiled at her. "You did not want that tea, did you?"

"No, I…" Celia paused, light-headed at the speed at which everything had happened. "Very well," she repeated. She took his arm. Her fingers shook slightly as they rested on his sleeve. He covered them with his hand in a gesture that half reassured, half disturbed her.

"You are nervous?"

"Of course."

He laughed. "Surely you need not be. As you have said, you have some experience and I hope to add greatly to your store." He raised her hand to his lips. "My very dear Lady Celia… Or perhaps I should call you Celia, since we are to become so much better acquainted?"

She did not correct him. They went out into the snow and soon the whirling flakes had covered their tracks.

CHAPTER THIRTEEN

Miles was in a thoroughly bad mood by the time he returned to Spring House that evening. When he had called earlier in the day it was to be told that Alice was sleeping and so he had had several hours in which to cool his heels and mull over whether or not Nat and Dexter could possibly be right in their suggestion that Alice herself had procured a marksman to kill him. He knew that no one had a better motive. He knew that he should probably confront Alice about it. He knew he did not want to believe it. The thought pained him so much that he could hardly bear it and he did not understand why.

He knew he deserved it.

He had seen plenty of blackmailers come to an unpleasant end as a result of their crimes, and he had never had an ounce of sympathy for them.

He knocked impatiently on the door of Spring House just as dusk was falling. The snow clouds had gone and the night was crisp and cold, with a sickle moon rising in the deep blue of the evening sky. When Marigold answered the door he hurried inside.

"Is Miss Lister awake?" he demanded.

The maid bobbed an awkward curtsy. "Miss Lister is not in the house, my lord. She said that she needed fresh air and would take a turn in the gardens—"

"What?" Miles had been in the act of divesting himself of his coat but now he froze. Surely Alice could not have been foolish enough to go out alone?

Or confident enough that she was safe, a voice whispered in his mind, *because she knew she was not the murderer's target....*

Swearing, Miles dragged his coat on again, ran out the door and down the front steps two at a time. In the gardens, Marigold had said. And darkness was falling, which would provide perfect cover for an assassin...

The old walled garden was empty. So was the parterre, its neat box hedges swathed in a blanket of pristine snow. A blackbird sped from his path with a startled squawk. He scanned the lawns but they were empty, too, turning misty in the twilight. And then he saw a figure walking under the gnarled branches of the orchard and let his breath out on a sigh that was half relief, half fury. He ran.

"What the *hell* are you doing out here on your own?"

Alice turned toward him and Miles felt fierce emotion slam through his gut. He looked at her. Her face was white and set, the rich gold of her hair seeming to accentuate her pallor. Everything that she had been through that day had evidently exhausted her, for her blue eyes looked so tired and strained that he had a sudden, violent urge to wrap her up and hold her close to give her a comfort that was for once entirely unselfish and not remotely sexual.

The feeling floored him. He knew he was losing his detachment and he had no idea how it could have happened. Earlier on, when he had been trying to rationalize why he had felt so disturbed when Alice was shot, he had told himself that he would dread losing her simply because she was the only one who stood between him and the debtor's prison. If something happened to Alice he could hardly wed her mother instead. Not even *he* would stoop to courting Mrs. Lister in order to marry a fortune. He had some standards. So it was, literally, a matter of survival—*his* survival—that he should protect Alice, guard her and keep her safe.

Yet such glib excuses hardly explained the depth of his feelings. Suddenly it was no longer all about *him* and what Alice could give to him but seemed to be about *her* instead. He wanted to comfort and reassure her, care for her and cherish her. And suddenly he knew with a deep conviction that Alice would never seek to hurt him. Dexter's and Nat's suggestions were completely wrong. He had no evidence to support the belief, other than his feelings, but his faith in her was absolute.

It shook him to the core.

It was inexplicable. It was alarming.

It was wrong.

He simply could not feel like this. His emotional reaction could only be a rather odd manifestation of his frustration at being denied Alice's bed. Everything came down to physical lust in the end. It had to. And he had to find a way to regain control.

"I had a headache," Alice said. "I needed some fresh air." She smiled at him. She even looked pleased to see him, which only served to irritate Miles more when he was so angry with her for putting herself at risk.

"So you thought to come out here alone when there is a madman running around with a rifle," Miles said cuttingly. "What an astoundingly bad idea, Miss Lister!"

Alice paused, one hand resting against the trunk of

one of the apple trees. A small frown dented her brow. "You are angry with me," she said.

Miles tried to get a grip on his feelings. "I am trying to protect you," he said, "and you are making it difficult for me." He took her arm in a tight grip. "I am taking you back inside."

Alice's face set in stubborn lines. "I came out here because I wished for some solitude."

"And now you are going back."

Alice gave a sharp sigh. "You are overbearing." She shot him a look of irritation. "Mama tells me that you wish to stay here at Spring House in order to protect me. I cannot allow it. It is quite unnecessary."

"To the contrary," Miles said. "It is absolutely necessary and you do not have any choice, Miss Lister."

Alice shook her head. "Always you push for more, do you not, Lord Vickery?" she said. She sounded bitter. "And always I am compelled to agree."

"It is the nature of the game between us," Miles said, unsmiling.

"It isn't a game!" Alice snapped. "And this whole thing is so foolish! I have been thinking, and there is no one who could possibly want to kill me! The only people who would benefit from my death would be Mama and Lowell, and neither of them—" She stopped abruptly, seeing the look on Miles's face. He knew she had read it, that she understood it. Her face went blank with shock. "You think that *Lowell* might want to harm me," she whispered. "You do, don't you?"

Miles sighed. "Not necessarily," he said, "but we must consider all possibilities, Miss Lister."

"No," Alice said. "No!" She stopped walking and snapped a twig from one of the trees, breaking it agitatedly between her fingers. "You have seen how protective he is of me," she said. "Mama and Lizzie said he was distraught when he first heard the news." She made a little gesture of desperation. "Surely you *cannot* believe that he would hurt me? My own brother?"

Miles said nothing. He understood how difficult it was for people to accept sometimes that those they loved could hurt them. And he did not really suspect Lowell Lister of wishing Alice dead. Lowell might want *him* dead, which was an entirely reasonable desire, he thought wryly, but he doubted Lowell would hurt Alice.

"There is another possibility," he said. "We also need to consider that it might have been Tom Fortune."

"Tom?" Alice said. She looked taken aback. "But why would he hurt *me*?"

"I don't know," Miles said. "Perhaps Miss Cole told you something significant that he was afraid you might pass on to me?"

They had reached the garden door now and Miles stood back to allow Alice to precede him into the house. She walked slowly down the corridor into the hall, drawing off her gloves as she went. Her head was bent and he could not see her expression.

"I can think of nothing else that Lydia said to me," she said, after a moment. Miles helped her off with her coat, allowing his hands to linger on her shoulders as he turned her around.

"You are sure?" he pressed, and saw the pink color stain her cheekbones. "You look very guilty," he added smoothly. "What secrets are you keeping from me?"

Alice blushed all the hotter. It made Miles want to touch her, to see if her skin felt as warm and silken as it looked.

"Nothing!" she said. "It is nothing to do with this matter—"

"Tell me," Miles said.

She shot him a look from under her lashes. "It is none of your business."

"I am your affianced husband," Miles said. "It is all my business." He took her chin in his hand and forced her to meet his gaze. "Tell me," he said again.

Alice looked cross. "Oh, very well. I suppose that if you were to fulfill Lady Membury's conditions and we actually do marry then you will surely find out the truth anyway—"

"Are you trying to tell me that you are not a virgin, Miss Lister?" Miles said. He thought of the open and artless way in which she had responded to his lovemaking. Had he been mistaken in thinking her innocent? And if she were not did he have any grounds whatsoever for objecting? He had scarcely behaved like a saint. With his reputation he would seem an utter hypocrite were he to cut up rough about his wife's lack of virtue. Except, of course, that society had the most appalling double standards on the subject, and he might be unconventional but he was not sure that he was unconventional *enough* to deal with it....

"Lord Vickery!" Alice's pale face was totally suffused with color now. "What is that to the purpose?" she inquired, sounding like an outraged archduchess. "Would it matter to you if I were not?"

"No," Miles said, still trying desperately to dispel the vision of Alice rolling in a haystack with some well-set-up young farmhand. Then he realized he was lying. "Yes, it would," he said.

"I see," Alice said frostily. "I cannot quite see how we come to be discussing this matter in public—"

Miles turned and saw that Marigold and Jim had both emerged from the servants' quarters and were tidying up their damp outdoor clothing whilst at the same time making no attempt to disguise the fact that they were eavesdropping shamelessly. He grabbed Alice's arm and hustled her through the door into the parlor.

"This was *not* what I wanted to talk about," Alice said as Miles closed the door behind them. "I was broaching a different subject entirely—"

"We'll discuss that in a moment," Miles said. "Miss Lister, I am aware that you have been in service and as such may have been unprotected and prey to the lusts of gentlemen—"

"There is nothing remotely gentlemanly about making a servant girl the object of your lust," Alice said sharply. Suddenly there was so much anger clear in her voice that Miles was shocked to hear it.

"It is quite acceptable for a man of your stamp to seduce a housemaid for sport," she said, "and yet you demand virginity from the housemaid you *blackmail* into being your wife." She gripped her hands together. "You are all the same. You are all callous and selfish and think that a woman is fair game for your seduction—"

"Wait," Miles said. He grabbed her wrists. "*Who* are all the same?" he demanded.

"You so-called gentlemen," Alice said, and Miles could see that her eyes were suddenly bright with tears as well as anger. "You, with your blackmail and your wager on my virtue, and Tom Fortune seducing Lydia and then abandoning her, and every last *despicable* nobleman who forces himself on a woman be she maidservant or debutante—" She caught her breath on a sob. "I *hate* you all for it," she finished starkly. Her frame was racked by sobs now.

Miles put his arms about her. She stood quite still within his embrace, neither accepting nor repudiating him. Her misery was locked tightly within her and her eyes were screwed up, but a tear escaped from the corner of one of them to plop onto Miles's sleeve. Miles, who normally hated women's tears, drew her closer and pressed his lips to her hair and found himself uttering some words he had thought never to say in his entire life.

"Don't cry," he said. "Alice, please… Sweetheart, tell me what this is about. Has someone hurt you?" The images were in his mind now, filling it with appalling and excruciating detail. He had never forced a woman in his life; it was not his way. But he knew there were plenty of men who behaved exactly as Alice had described. If one of them had hurt her he would have to seek him out and tear him limb from limb….

"No," Alice said. "Not me. Not like that. I am as innocent as *you* require." She sounded furious. "But I hate your compulsion of me, Miles, and I am angry for Lydia and for all the girls I knew who suffered at the whims of men." She beat her fists against Miles's chest with a small impotent gesture. "Jenny had a child and was turned off," she said. "Jane died because someone abused her—" she swallowed a sob "—and there was nothing that I could *do!*"

Miles held her until her body softened in his arms and her sobs quietened and then he drew her down to sit beside him on the sofa. Alice scrubbed the tears from her face with shaking fingers and Miles captured her hands in his and held her.

"I am sorry," he said. "I am sorry for all the things that you describe. It would be stupid and pointless of me to deny that they happen or that they are not as terrible as you say."

Alice raised her head. "I did not think you would care," she said.

"I do have some basic humanity," Miles pointed out and won a small smile from her.

"I fight against the injustice because it is so wrong, but there seems so little that I can do," Alice said. She looked up and her clear blue gaze met his. "I thought you were different," she said, with the simplicity that always stole Miles's breath. "Last year when we first met I thought that because you worked for justice and the common good…" She let the sentence fade away, shaking her head a little. There was an undertone of disappointment in her voice. "I made a mistake," she finished. "You were merciless and selfish in pursuing what you wanted, just as you are now."

"I wanted you and I wanted your money," Miles said. "I still do." He knew he could not defend himself against her accusation. It was true.

"So you seek to blackmail me into marrying you," Alice said, "which amounts to forcing me to your bed."

"I may be a fortune hunter and a rake," Miles said, "but I have never forced an unwilling woman to lie with me. I would never do that." He looked at her. There was no skepticism in her gaze and once again he was struck by how naturally open and honest she was. He had never met a woman like her.

He did not deserve a woman like her. That was the truth.

"Never?" she said.

"I am being honest," Miles said dryly. "I would never do that."

Something eased in Alice's face and she smiled a little again, and her radiance hit him like a punch.

"So you would not force me to lie with you even if we wed," she said.

Miles gave her a very straight look. "But I would not be forcing you, would I, sweetheart? You would come to me of your own free will. You know you want me as much as I want you."

"I…" Alice put her hands up to her scarlet cheeks.

Miles took one of her hands away from her face and imprisoned it in her lap. "That is the thing that troubles you," he said softly. "That you can dislike what I stand for and yet still desire me."

Alice sat looking at him, her lips parted, the troubled look still in her eyes. There was a flush on her cheekbones that was, Miles suspected, a compound of indignation and the deep desire that he knew he could arouse in her.

"I will tell you what *would* trouble me," she said. "I would hate it if we were wed and you were unfaithful to me. You are a rake, Miles. Can you be faithful, or would that be too difficult for you?"

Miles thought about it. To be true to her as long as they both lived… That was a hell of a commitment to make, forsaking all other women. But since he did not appear to have any space in his mind even to think about any other women at present, let alone any desire to make love to one, it suddenly seemed less implausible than it might have done.

"I don't know," he said slowly. "That is the truth. I have never attempted to be faithful to anyone. I think

I can say that I would try my hardest." He stopped. Once again a strange tenderness for her took him. To try his best seemed woefully inadequate and far, far less than Alice deserved. Damnation, he really was losing his grip now, striving to become a better man to please her. He had never had any urge to improve before. He was quite happy as he was. And now he found himself trying to change. He did not like it.

"I suppose I cannot fault you on your honesty," Alice said, "even when I might prefer a different answer." She spoke lightly but Miles thought he could detect a hint of some emotion beneath. She freed herself from his clasp and moved away a little along the seat. "I am not at all clear how we come to be discussing this," she said. "I was trying to tell you that I had misled you as to my fortune." She looked at him, her eyes suddenly both wary and challenging. "I am not…quite…as rich as everyone supposes."

"You have misled me as to your fortune," Miles repeated. He felt a rather chill sense of premonition as he looked at her pink, defiant face.

"Well, not precisely misled," Alice said. "The eighty thousand pounds is intact and safely invested."

Miles experienced a sinking sensation. "I sense a *but*," he said.

"But I have spent all the current interest and have borrowed against future interest, as well," Alice said, "which I am entitled to do under the terms of my inheritance." She took a deep breath. "So theoretically I am in debt."

Miles felt like putting his head in his hands. Alice was watching him and although she was trying to look nonchalant he could see that she was nervous of his reaction. *Theoretically* she was in debt? What the hell was a *theoretical* debt? He had yet to come across a debt that was not very, very real.

"Your trustees should be shot for letting you do this," Miles said. He tried to hold on to his temper. "How much?" he added softly.

"Oh, a few thousand pounds to Lowell to buy modern machinery and livestock for the farm, and sufficient invested for Mama to live out her days in comfort, and then some for the workhouse children and other charities and…" She looked sideways at Miles as though to assess his reaction. "I also invested in the windmill cooperative."

"The windmill cooperative," Miles repeated. He felt slightly dazed.

"Yes," Alice said. "A great many of us have invested as a way to encourage new businesses in the village."

A small silence fell between them.

"What else?" Miles said.

"Well," Alice excused. "There are a few other small things. Mama, for example, is very extravagant and does like the trappings of luxury. I did not like the money, anyway," she added defiantly. "It was making me unhappy."

"Lack of money has been making me unhappy for quite some time," Miles said. "Why did the possession of it have the opposite effect on you?"

"Because I had been a servant and I am accustomed to working," Alice said. "Sitting around sewing or reading or drinking tea and gossiping…" She shrugged. "Once the novelty of having leisure had worn off, it seemed like a monstrous waste of time to me. Oh, I love some of the things that money can buy," she added. "I love that I am not obliged to work until I drop with tiredness. I love buying clothes. But I was bored, I am afraid. I needed to be active." Miles saw her steal another look at him under her lashes. She looked scared and defiant. He wanted to shake her. He wanted to kiss her.

"And I have made over the house in Skipton to Miss Cole as a place where she and her baby may live in future," she finished.

Miles was shaking his head. "Alice, you really are the most infuriating woman—"

"It is *my* money," Alice argued, "and I can do with it whatever I like until I am wed." She looked at him. "You are angry."

Miles looked at her. "I would be less than human— or lying—if I denied it." He ran a hand over his hair. He was aware of feeling furious and frustrated but at the same time of a perplexing admiration for her and what she had done.

"Devil take it, Alice…" He ground out. "We shall *both* end in the Fleet at this rate."

"Well, I was not to know that you were so desperate that you would want all the eighty thousand and all the interest, as well," Alice pointed out. "Blackmailers deserve a few unpleasant surprises," she added trenchantly.

Miles reached out and pulled her angrily into his arms. "I am furious with you," he said, his cheek against hers.

She glanced up at him, and the softness of her cheek moved against the rough stubble on his skin. "You are greedy," she said huskily.

Miles shook her a little. "I want everything."

"You cannot have it." She slanted her head and gave him a look of challenge. "Are you going to jilt me now that I am not as rich as you thought?"

A wave of desire took Miles so hard it almost floored him. "No," he said. "I will have you, Alice. Perhaps you are not quite as rich as I had hoped but I will have you all the same."

She sat back, out of his arms, and gave him another look of challenge that made him burn. "You forget that there are still two months of our courtship to run," she said. "Free me from the blackmail," she added suddenly. "Let me make my own choices."

Miles thought about it. Surprisingly he found it more difficult to refuse her than he had expected. There was something about Alice's shining honesty that demanded an equal integrity in return. But the risk was too great. He could not gamble on losing Alice or her money and anyway, it was a long time since he had prided himself on his integrity.

"No," he said. "I cannot."

Her expression did not alter. She did not even look surprised, rather as though she had not expected it of him anyway. He supposed that he had not disappointed her because by now she had no illusions about him.

"I do not like to be coerced," she said evenly.

"None of us do," Miles said. He drew her close again and tilted her face up to his. She met his gaze fearlessly but he could feel the tension in her. "I am not going to risk losing my advantage," he said, against her mouth. He kissed her, parting her lips with his tongue, delving into the sweetness of her mouth, demanding a response. She was still beneath his touch as she had been before when he had comforted her, neither withdrawing nor engaging. He closed his teeth about her lower lip and bit down just hard enough to force a gasp from her.

"Respond to me," he said, taking her mouth again, his hand coming up to palm her breast. The rough silken slide of the velvet bodice skimmed under his fingers and she gasped again at the friction.

"That is one thing you cannot make me do," she whispered. Her lips were damp and parted, tempting him unbearably. He wanted to kiss her senseless. "You said earlier that I would come to you of my own free will," she said. "You were wrong. You may be able to blackmail me into marrying you, but you cannot force me to respond to you."

Miles knew it was true, but all his frustration at her damned independence and her refusal to break suddenly went into the kiss, and he pushed her down on the sofa and plundered her mouth until she was helpless and quiescent in his arms. She offered no resistance to him but neither did she return his embrace, which only angered him the more. The need to command a response from her, to make her acknowledge her desire for him, roared through him. He held her head still so he could take her mouth in kisses that were deeper still and loosed the gown from about her neck to expose her tender skin to the questing exploration of his lips and hands. The demands he made on her were merciless; the pale skin of her throat and shoulders was pink and ravished from his touch and her nipples peaked hard against the velvet of her bodice. And at last he felt the answering desire in her and the triumphant masculine possession flared in him—until he drew back, saw the look in her blue eyes and knew her spirit was far from broken. For a moment they stared at each other like gladiators, and then Miles remembered all the things Alice had said about taking by force. It was like a shower of icy water. He let her go with a savage oath, gathering her close in his arms, feeling the instinctive resistance in her and hating himself for causing it.

Gradually her tense breathing eased and she relaxed against him and he pressed his cheek against hers in apology and penance.

"I am sorry," he said. "My desire for you almost made me a liar."

She moved against him a little, her body soft and yielding against his now. "And I would be lying, too, if I pretended I did not want you," she said, "but I will not give in." She put a hand up and touched his lips gently. "Miles. I hate what you are doing to me. I cannot concede."

"I know," Miles said softly. "You cannot capitulate but neither will I."

He was wrenched with a sudden deep regret. He could not risk losing her and yet more than anything he wanted her response to be freely given. The conflict tightened deep within him.

"Do you know what happens when you deny yourself something that you want very badly?" he murmured.

Alice's eyes met his, deep lavender blue in the lamplit room. "You develop exceptionally good self-discipline?" she said.

Miles smiled. "No," he said. "You just want it all the more."

CHAPTER FOURTEEN

"WAS IT YOU?" Lydia, panting and crying, threw herself into Tom Fortune's arms. "Did you do it, Tom? Did you try to kill Alice?"

She had run all the way from Spring House across the snowy meadows to the ruins of the old priory where Tom was currently encamped. She had been waiting all day for word from him, growing steadily more anxious and upset, and now she could not seem to stop the tears or stop the shaking in her body.

Tom swung the cellar doors closed behind them and drew her into the shelter of his arms. He held her close, soothing and petting her and speaking softly to her, Lydia thought, much as he would calm a skittish horse. And surprisingly, it was comforting. The sobs that racked her body died away and she felt strangely at peace. Except that he had not answered her question.

"Well?" she demanded. She could not see his expression clearly because the wick on the candle had already burned so low, but she thought that he was smiling at her.

"Of course not," Tom said. "Why would I wish to kill Miss Lister?"

"I don't know," Lydia said, shivering, "but someone did."

Tom drew her down to sit beside him on the floor.

THE SCANDALS OF AN INNOCENT

The cellar was surprisingly warm in comparison to the frosty night outside but it was scarcely welcoming. Tom's pitifully small collection of possessions were scattered about: a bag, a cloak, a pistol. Lydia shuddered to see it.

"Whoever shot at Miss Lister had a rifle," Tom said, following her gaze. "I heard the tales in the tavern." He unstoppered a bottle and tilted it to his lips. "Elderflower champagne," he said. "Mrs. Anstruther keeps her wine down here. Would you like some?"

"I don't think you should steal it," Lydia said primly.

Tom's lips twisted. "It is only one more thing to add to the list against me. I know they will be looking for me twice as hard now they think I tried to kill again."

"It isn't safe for you here," Lydia said. "Dexter Anstruther is a bare hundred yards away in the Old Palace, and Miles Vickery is staying at Spring House."

"I know," Tom said. He leaned forward and kissed her. He tasted of champagne and smelled of musk and leather, and Lydia shivered at the memory of his skin against hers.

"I like the danger," Tom said, his words muffled against her lips. "I cannot help myself. It excites me."

"Then it is a good job that I have more sense than you," Lydia said, pushing him away, albeit reluctantly. "Now listen, Tom—" She paused, losing the thread of her thoughts as he started to nibble at the soft skin of her neck, using his teeth and lips and tongue to raise the goose bumps on her skin. "Stop!" she said. "I need to think and you are distracting me!"

"Good," Tom said, pulling the ribbon that held her cloak in place and unraveling it slowly.

"Be serious," Lydia said weakly. "Do you think that

these murders or attempted murders are all the work of one man?"

"They must be," Tom said, raising his head for a second. "I refuse to believe that there is more than one dangerous criminal on the loose in Fortune's Folly." He pushed her cloak aside and started to nuzzle at the neckline of her gown, his tongue dipping wickedly into the cleft between her breasts.

"Who," Lydia said, determinedly ignoring him even as her heart pounded like a drum, "is the least likely person to be that criminal?"

"Hmm…my brother, Monty? Your parents?" Tom really did not sound as though he cared. He popped Lydia's breast out of the rounded neckline of the gown with shocking suddenness and bent to suckle it.

"Tom!" Lydia remembered at the last moment that she was supposed to keep quiet, and her keening cry came out as a ragged whisper instead. His mouth at her breast evoked all the welter of emotion and need she had ever felt for him, dangerous feelings she had thought were buried forever.

"I am five months pregnant," she protested, even as she arched to his touch.

Tom's free hand curved over the swelling of her belly. "That just excites me the more," he said.

"That cannot possibly be true," Lydia said. She had hated the sight of her thickening body because it had seemed to mock her stupidity in giving herself to Tom in the first place.

"It is true." Tom released her breast and kissed her with all the simmering passion she remembered. "It makes you very, very desirable, Lyddy."

When they broke apart Lydia was breathing fast,

and she felt as though her entire body was lit as bright as the candle flame. She looked at Tom and his eyes were dark with all the secrets and wickedness and excitement that she remembered.

"Could we…" she began hesitantly, and saw him smile.

"If you want to."

"Oh, I *do*." Suddenly she was feverish with need. "Only, it will not hurt the baby?"

"No," Tom said. "We will be very gentle and very careful…."

"Oh, *yes,*" Lydia said, settling down into his arms with a sigh.

ALICE SAT IN FRONT of the mirror in her bedroom, brushing her hair very slowly. The fire was banked down in the grate ready for the night, and the candle stood on her nightstand ready to light her bedtime reading. The house was creaking and settling softly down to sleep.

Alice was thinking about Lydia. She had caught her friend creeping into the house very late, shaking the snow from her cloak and easing herself out of her sodden boots. Lydia had looked radiant, glowing and vibrant, as pretty as Alice had ever seen her. Her eyes were bright, her cheeks rosy. Alice had known at once that Lydia must have been with Tom Fortune.

Alice sighed now as she viewed her reflection in the glass. Lydia's situation worried her very much indeed, for her friend had looked so happy and Alice simply could not bear to think that she might get hurt again. They had had no chance to speak, for Miles had come down the stairs just after Lydia had come in, and the smile had immediately drained from Lydia's face leaving her looking pale and terrified. She had thrown Alice a pleading look, had muttered a good-night to Miles and had run away up to her room. Alice had picked up Lydia's cloak and taken it off to the kitchens to dry out, and now she felt guilty and with her loyalties painfully torn.

The hand holding the brush stilled and came to rest on the dressing tabletop. Alice sat still. What was she to do? She cared deeply what happened to Lydia but she was so afraid that Tom would betray her friend yet again. And she wanted to confide in Miles—she wanted to trust him with a strength of feeling that surprised her—and yet, she could not do so if that would cause more misery and pain for Lydia.

She got to her feet. Laura Anstruther was coming to visit in the morning. She was Lydia's cousin by marriage as well as Miles's cousin. Perhaps she might be the very person to bridge the gap between them all and persuade Lydia to talk. And in the meantime, Alice thought, the best thing that she could do would be to get a good night's sleep. Her injured arm still ached abominably and she felt tired to her bones. In the end she had given in to Miles's demands that he be permitted to stay at Spring House. Her mother had wanted it and Alice had felt too tired to continue objecting. So now Miles was sharing her roof, occupying a room across the landing from her, and she felt oddly on edge at the thought even though the house was full of other people, as well.

Perhaps it had been Miles's parting words to her in the parlor earlier that had been the problem. *You know what happens when you deny yourself something that you want very badly...You just want it all the more...*

She knew that he had been speaking for himself. Unfortunately his words applied to her, too. She *did* want him, too much to be comfortable in such proximity to him. But she could not surrender to him whilst he still refused her a free choice in her future. No matter how difficult the denial, she was determined not to give in.

There was a knock at the door.

"Come in," Alice called, thinking that Marigold had come to bring her a cup of hot milk.

The door opened and Miles walked in. He stopped when he saw her and his gaze went from the corn-colored hair loose about her shoulders to her bare feet, where they peeped from beneath the hem of her night-gown. Alice was suddenly acutely aware that she was naked beneath her night rail and robe and that Miles was still fully dressed. For some reason it felt doubly disturbing that he had all his clothes on whilst she lacked most of hers.

She could feel the pink color stinging her face. Sometimes it was a terrible curse to be so fair and blush so easily. "Lord Vickery!" Her voice was not quite steady. "I thought you were my maid. What on earth are you doing here?"

Miles's gaze came up to meet hers. "I have come to search your room and make sure that you are safe for the night," he said.

"To search my room?" Alice felt appalled. "Surely you do not suspect anyone of breaking in and conceal-ing themselves in here?"

"I don't know until I check," Miles said. He moved

across to the window, looking behind the long curtains. His gaze seemed to rest on the bed for a long time, contemplating its rumpled sheets and invitingly tumbled pillows. Alice's breath hitched as he looked back at her.

"A somewhat inflammatory choice of reading for bedtime, Miss Lister," Miles said, gesturing to the copy of *Tom Jones* that was on the nightstand.

Alice raised her chin. "It is a classic novel," she said.

"I do not dispute it," Miles agreed, "but I suspect it will cause you a restless night."

Alice doubted that a mere book could disturb her as much as Miles was doing now. He had moved across to the big rosewood wardrobe and opened the door. Alice's breath caught again. She had not imagined that he would be searching through her clothes. This felt far too intimate, though why it should disquiet her she was not sure, since he had eased her out of that very underwear only a fortnight back, so there really was no cause for false modesty. His hands moved amongst the linen and lawn of her underclothes, tanned against the pristine whiteness. It made Alice shiver as though he was touching her skin.

"There, uh, there does not appear to be anyone in here," Miles said. His tone was a little rough. His gaze, dark and intense, tangled with hers. He shut the wardrobe door carefully.

"Well, um, thank you," Alice said, feeling absurdly self-conscious. She wondered a little despairingly whether Miles's presence in the house would always make her this uncomfortable. She would have to hope that they would find the criminal soon or she might just combust.

Miles paused with his hand on the doorknob. "Do

you think that Miss Cole was with Tom Fortune tonight?" he asked suddenly, over his shoulder.

Alice jumped, taken by surprise. She realized that he had sprung the question on her deliberately, knowing she would have no time to dissemble.

"Yes, I think that she was," she said evenly.

"She did not say anything to you?"

"No, she did not," Alice said.

Miles nodded slowly. He turned fully to face her, leaning back against the door panels. "Do you think she will speak to Laura tomorrow?"

"I doubt it," Alice said. "I know that Mrs. Anstruther is her cousin but—" she shrugged helplessly "—her feelings for Tom are too strong to betray him."

"Why do you think that she trusts him?" Miles asked.

Their eyes met and held. "Because she loves him," Alice said. She sighed. "For no better reason than that."

"Do you think her instinct to trust him is correct?" Miles said.

"I doubt it," Alice said. "Tom is a scoundrel, and love is more likely to distort one's good sense than to reinforce it."

Miles smiled slightly. "You sound almost as cynical as me, Miss Lister," he said. "Lock the door behind me," he added, checking that there was a key, "and do not open it until your maid knocks in the morning. Ask her to call out to identify herself first. I will be in the room across the landing—should you need me."

He went out and Alice turned the key in the lock with fingers that shook a little. She got into bed and lay there for a moment before blowing out the candle. *Tom Jones* would have to wait for another night. She was already quite sufficiently disturbed as it was.

Perhaps it was the relentless ache in her arm, or the fear that someone might indeed attempt to break into her room, or more likely the disquieting thought of Miles Vickery across the corridor, barely feet away from her, but Alice did not sleep well that night. Miles's face seemed obstinately to appear in her broken dreams. His dark hazel eyes invaded her most private thoughts. Even after he had left her bedchamber his presence seemed to dominate the room, as though she could not escape him. She could hear the echo of his question about Lydia in her dreams and her answer: She trusts him because she loves him…

She woke shivering whilst it was still dark and burrowed under the blankets as much for comfort as warmth. Love made one do such foolish things, such as entrusting oneself to a man who might be a dangerous criminal, or indeed to one who was an accredited rake who could never be faithful or trustworthy or any of the things that a sensible woman would wish for in a husband. She opened her eyes and stared at the shadowy canopy of her bed. She could *not* be falling in love with Miles Vickery all over again, not when she could see so clearly his faults and imperfections now, not when she was supposed to have learned from her bitter lesson of the previous year. She was far too levelheaded for that, too practical, too wise. She knew that she was suffering from a bad case of thwarted lust—the sort of thing that ladies pretended never to experience, let alone speak about—but that was merely a physical problem. Anything deeper and more profound was out of the question.

She rolled over and buried her head under the pillow. She had forced Miles to honesty, and now she knew she was being most dreadfully dishonest herself. She threw the pillow aside and gave a long sigh.

She was starting to love Miles all over again, against her will, perhaps against all sense but with a helpless inevitability that she was not sure she even wanted to fight. The tenderness she had sometimes glimpsed in him and his determination to hold her safe had completely undermined her resistance even though she knew he was acting as much out of self-interest as concern for her. Now, more strongly than ever, she sensed the complex and damaged reality under Miles's cynical outward shell, and she wanted to reach him. She was a fool. There was no doubt about it. She, who prided herself on her practicality, was behaving like a silly little scatterbrain, just like Lydia. Her mind told her she was making a mistake but her heart was not listening.

A sound out on the landing caught her attention. Thinking of Lydia made her wonder whether her friend could be so imprudent as to creep out before dawn to risk another hour in her lover's arms. Alice slid softly from the bed and padded over to the door. She remembered Miles's strictures about not opening it until Marigold called her in the morning, but then she heard another soft sound and she turned the key and opened the door a crack.

There was a single lamp burning down the hall and by its light Alice could see that Miles was sleeping on a pallet outside her door. Her heart gave a huge leap of shock and something else. She stared down at him, absolutely rooted to the spot. In sleep he looked relaxed and the hard lines and planes of his face were softened. His dark eyelashes rested against the curve of his cheek. A day's stubble already darkened his jaw and

Alice suddenly felt a huge, near-ungovernable urge to fall to her knees beside him and run her fingers along his cheek to feel that skin rough beneath her hands.

She must have made some noise, or perhaps a tiny movement, because the next moment she found herself flat on her back on the pallet with Miles's body on top of hers, pinning her down. He was breathing fast, and there was a hard, dangerous light in his eyes. Alice was so shocked that for a second she could not move and barely remembered to breathe. Then she tried to struggle but it was as humiliating as when he had caught her outside the gown shop; he was too strong and she could barely do more than wriggle beneath him, a maneuver that did not seem to do anything to ease the situation, for something even more danger-ous flared in his eyes. Her hands came up against his chest and it was then that she realized he was naked, or at least partially so. The skin beneath her palms was warm, hard and smooth. Alice swallowed, her throat suddenly feeling as parched as a dry riverbed.

"You are lying outside my bedroom door and you aren't wearing any clothes!" she blurted out, realizing a second too late that she had spoken her thoughts aloud. She saw Miles's smile, and then he rolled off her and sat up.

"I still have my breeches on," he said mockingly. His tone changed. "Don't ever do that again, Miss Lister. I could have hurt you."

"I didn't do anything!" Alice protested. "I thought I heard a sound—"

"And so you came to investigate even though I had expressly told you not to do so?"

Alice sighed. "It was wrong of me," she conceded.

"It was." Miles still sounded furious.

Alice sighed again and struggled to her knees, abruptly aware that her nightgown was bunched up and revealed the backs of her thighs. She grabbed the gown and dragged it down, and in the same moment she saw Miles's gaze slide over her naked skin, and then his eyes widened and darkened with an equal mixture of shock and something Alice immediately identified as lust.

"*What,*" he said, "is that?" His voice was rough and just the tone of it sent flickers of erotic sensation through her body.

"Wh…what?" Alice asked, dragging the lawn and lace as far down as she could and gripping it tightly about her ankles.

Oh Lord, he had seen. And she could never, ever explain…

In a panic now, she tried to scramble to her feet and back away from him, but Miles put out one lazy hand, grabbed her about the ankle and she tumbled back down onto the pallet with a little shriek.

"Shh." Miles put a hand over her lips. "You'll wake everyone."

Before Alice could protest he scooped her up in his arms, strode through the door of her bedroom and deposited her on the bed. She sprawled there, out of breath and indignant, her nightgown riding up again, her face bright pink.

"Lord Vickery, *what* are you doing?" Her words came out as a strangled croak. Her body was one huge, burning blush of combined mortification and utter desire.

She tried to crawl away from him up the bed, but once again Miles was too quick for her, his hand clamping about her bare ankle again and holding her still.

"You will tell me," he said softly, "what it was that I saw just now—or I will take a look for myself. Well?"

Alice clutched the nightgown tighter about her legs. "I-it…" *It is just more proof, if that were needed, that I am not a lady.…*

Miles's bright hazel gaze pinned her against the pillows. "I thought that I knew all your secrets now, Alice, but it seems not." His glance traveled over her slowly, from flushed face and tumbled hair to bare feet. "You do realize that when we are wed," he said, "if not before, I will see you—all of you—without your nightgown?"

Alice made another choked little noise. She did not think she could feel any hotter without burning up. "Then you will just have to wait, won't you?" she whispered.

"Unfortunately, I am of an impatient disposition," Miles said. "Forgive me, but I am about to behave most improperly."

He caught both her ankles and tossed her over onto her stomach. Alice lay sprawling, tangled in her hair and the blankets, the breath knocked from her, the shock pounding through her. It was so sudden that for a moment she lay still, completely stunned, and then she felt one of Miles's hands easing the nightgown up the backs of her bare thighs. She struggled to raise her head and tried to whip herself over, but Miles's free hand was in the small of her back, holding her still, pressed down on the bed.

"No," he said. "Don't move."

"Miles," Alice wailed.

"Darling Alice," Miles said, the intimacy of his tone making her completely weak, "I *have* to see."

Alice made a sound that was mingled appeal and

surrender. She turned her head away, allowing her hair to fall forward to cloak her face. She felt hot and hopelessly aroused and at the same time breathless with nerves. Since her formal betrothal to Miles she had managed to ignore the little pinpricks of anxiety that had reminded her that she was a former servant girl and as such no suitable wife for a marquis. She had told herself she was good enough for anyone and she had almost believed it. But here was proof that she was utterly *unsuitable,* for what other marchioness in the entire country would have a *tattoo?* She could imagine the Duchess of Cole's horrified tones if ever she heard this scandalous piece of news: "My dear Miss Lister, only circus freaks and sailors have tattoos…."

She felt Miles pull up the linen of her night rail so that it skimmed the tops of her thighs and stopped just below of the curve of her buttocks. Alice's heart was almost bursting in her chest. There was a silence. She turned her head against the bedcovers and stole a look at Miles from beneath her lashes. His hand had stilled on the back of her leg and he was staring fixedly at the little flower that was pricked out in ink on the soft skin of her upper thigh.

She heard his breath catch hard and then his fingers, lighter than the graze of a butterfly's wing, brushed the curve of her leg and slid across her inner thigh. Alice's body clenched.

"A tattoo," he said, and his voice barely sounded like his own. "Well, well, Miss Lister, what a surprise you are turning out to be!"

Alice squirmed. "I only had it done as a prank," she said. "The fair was on the stray in Harrogate one summer and a number of us went from my employer's one night." She knew she was gabbling and could not seem to stop. "I thought it would be fun but I was young and foolish and didn't realize that it would not wash off. I scrubbed and scrubbed at it until my skin was sore and then I covered it up and pretended it was not really there!"

Miles laughed but the hot, heavy look in his eyes did not ease, nor did the pressure of his hand in her back, holding her still. She lay prone and unmoving, very aware of her exposure to his hungry gaze.

"Did it hurt?" he asked.

"Yes," Alice said. "The tattooist was an old woman who laughed at me when I screamed." She hesitated. "You like it, then. The old witch who did it said that my lover would like it, and I did not understand her at the time."

"And now you do," Miles said roughly. The look of concentrated desire in his eyes made her feel faint.

"I was afraid you might think it quite inappropriate for a lady," Alice said.

"Oh, it is," Miles said. He gave a ragged laugh. "That is why I like it so much." He sighed, shaking his head. "What an odd mixture of innocence and impropriety you are, sweetheart. You confound me. Fascinate me."

He touched the tattoo again, with a fingertip, in a caress that made Alice give a little sound that was halfway between a sigh and a groan.

"I am no proper lady," she whispered. "I know that. No lady would visit a tattooist's tent at a fairground."

"I do not want a proper lady in my bed," Miles said. He bent his head, and Alice felt his tongue flicker across the tiny flower, and her body caught alight and burned. She was aware of every sensitive inch of her skin against the yielding bed, of the way that the friction of the covers rubbed her nipples and pressed against her belly. She was even more acutely aware of her bare legs and the slide of her nightgown over the curve of her buttocks. The cold air ravished her naked skin and the hot flick of Miles's tongue made her squirm, and then he sucked on the tattoo, hard enough for her to feel a bite of pain that mixed exquisitely with the pleasure, and his hand slipped between her thighs and they fell apart irresistibly to allow him to touch her intimately.

His fingers were at the very core of her. Alice's mind reeled with shock and disbelief at the sensation.

"Miles, what—"

"Trust me. Do you like that?"

Did she like it? She thought she was melting into bliss, except that her belly was coiling tighter and tighter with the sweetest, most desperate ache of need.

His fingers shifted their pressure. She was moist and hopelessly aroused and it took only one sly stroke, and then another, and her body exploded in a cascade of pleasure and her mind filled with light and she would have screamed aloud except that Miles tumbled her over onto her back and covered her mouth with his, smothering her cries. He held her with her wrists bracketed above her head and kissed her. She was dizzy and panting and breathless and he sucked on her lower lip and darted his tongue into her mouth and demanded a response from her even as her mind and body still trembled with the enormity of what had happened to her. And this time she did not refuse him. She opened her lips to him so that he could do devastating things to her mouth and he plundered it without reservation, kissing her deeply and with a fierce need. Though her body still clenched with the pleasure he had given her, Alice wanted more. She knew that her nightgown was up around her waist and her legs spread and Miles was lying between them, hugely aroused, and that in a second he would take her, and she wanted to feel him inside her more than she had ever wanted anything in the entire world.

And then, unbelievably, he stopped and eased back from her. His gaze rested on the curve of her bare stomach and dropped, dark and primitive, to the juncture of her thighs. Then she felt his hand clench in the material of her nightdress and he smoothed it carefully down over her nakedness in a gesture that was so intimate and tender that she felt shaken. His expression was harsh and set, and a muscle worked in his cheek.

"Miles?" she whispered.

His eyes met hers, torment in their depths.

"If I take you now I will break every rule," he said. "I am sworn to protect you and…" He shook his head, biting off whatever it was he was about to say.

"I thought that breaking the rules was what you did," Alice said. Her voice came out as only a thread of sound. He looked angry and she felt cold and confused to see it. A moment ago he had held her with tenderness and desire. Now he was looking at her as though he did not even like her very much.

"I thought so, too," he ground out. "Unfortunately, I appear to be plagued by an honor I did not know I possessed."

Miles wrenched himself away from her. The door slammed after him and Alice was left stunned and breathless on the bed. Her body felt soft and boneless with the bliss it had already sampled and yet cheated and unsatisfied, longing for more.

What had Miles meant when he had said that he was plagued by an honor he did not know he possessed? She could only assume that he had intended to seduce her there and then—that he had planned it ruthlessly in order to circumvent the conditions of their betrothal and force her to marry him at once. She had suspected from the start that he might plan to do such a thing. But at the last moment it appeared he had not been able to go through with it. Yet he must have known that she had no will, no desire to resist. His discovery of the tattoo had aroused them both beyond bearing, and she had longed for him with a hunger that had matched his own.

Alice rolled off the bed and walked slowly over to the dresser, splashing water from the ewer into a bowl and from there onto her face. She knew that she had to take a measure of responsibility for what happened now. She was done resisting Miles. If he were to make love to her, then she would be a willing participant in her own seduction, and nothing, not even her anger and frustration at his blackmail was powerful enough to stop the desire she had for him. *Oh, she was very willing, against all sense and against all propriety....*

She shivered a little, wrapping her arms about herself. The siren voice of temptation whispered in her mind. What was to prevent them? They were betrothed, and Miles had every intention of making her his bride. She would have the protection of his name. Even if there were a child she would be safe from censure, or as safe from scandal as a housemaid turned heiress could ever be. She stared at her flushed reflection in the pier glass. She wanted Miles with the fiercest of aches, but the shreds of common sense that she still possessed told her that she *had* to be careful of herself and her reputation. There was many a slip between seduction and marriage. If Lydia's situation proved anything it was that. If the marriage between herself and Miles never happened she would be ruined. Her mother would be distraught. All the respectability they had worked so hard to achieve would be lost.

With a sigh Alice reached for her robe and tied it about her with fingers that still shook slightly. It was a little too late to be thinking of respectability. Miles had shown her precisely how unrespectable she wanted to be.

MILES SAT AT THE BREAKFAST table wondering how the hell he had got into this situation. He had never been much troubled by self-denial before. Generally if there was something he wanted he found a way to have it. He wanted Alice and he had thought it would be easy to have her, to seduce her into marrying him so that he could gain everything he wanted—her body, her money, his own financial security. He had planned to go to the lawyers and tell them openly that he had slept with Alice and to point out that Lady Membury's conditions had to be rendered null and void now or she would be ruined. Two hours before, he had had the perfect opportunity to take her. Yet he had hesitated, prevented by principles that had never before caused him a moment's trouble. He had discovered scruples he did not even realize he possessed. He had thought himself utterly devoid of conscience. It was disconcerting to discover he had one after all.

The trouble had started the previous night when he had searched Alice's room. The clothes in her cupboards had smelled as sweet as she did herself, of the same apple and lavender and rose scents, and the lust had suddenly grabbed him like a vise. The neat piles of virginal white underwear had done nothing to assuage his desire. He had found himself staring at them and imagining the cool press of the linen against Alice's naked skin, the laces and transparent lawn wrapped about her, trussing her up, and the warmth of her body beneath. Heated dreams in which he uncovered her nakedness to his lips and hands had stalked him all night.

And then there had been the shocking revelations that morning. He looked at Alice. She was sitting across the table from him and was concentrating fiercely on buttering a piece of toast. He knew that she was as intensely aware of him as he was of her. She was wearing a gown of spring yellow decorated with lace and she looked demure and fresh and pretty and Miles knew—*he knew*—that beneath the muslin skirts and the crisp petticoats was a tiny tattoo of a flower. He closed his eyes. He had not stopped thinking about that flower for a single moment since he had left Alice's bedchamber. He wanted to touch it. He wanted to kiss it again. He wanted to lick it and allow his tongue to slide down from that tempting little tattoo to the softness of her inner thigh and on until his mouth met the heated center of her being.

She had been so soft and sweet in his arms, her skin like silk beneath his fingers. Discovering her tattoo had driven him half-mad with wanting. The moist slide of her against his fingers had undone him. He had been so close to taking her. Now that he had experienced the intimacy of watching her take pleasure at his hands he knew he was never, ever going to let her go.

His body tightened unbearably at the thought of that private bliss they had shared. He had been in a state of semiarousal for several hours despite the tub of cold water he had emptied over his head, out in the frozen courtyard, after leaving Alice. He was already obsessing about her body far too much. He did not seem to be able to think about anything else. He doubted he ever would until he could actually see her completely, touch her freely, take from her and give to her in equal measure until their desires were sated. And already he had the suspicion that it would not be as easy as that to rid himself of his driving lust for her. Once he had tasted her he would want to do so again and again....

"Whiskey marmalade, Lord Vickery?"

Mrs. Lister was smiling at him and nodding to the footman to pass him the pot of preserve. Miles blinked.

"Thank you, ma'am."

"I trust that nothing disturbed your sleep?" Mrs. Lister continued.

Alice's gaze met Miles's in a brief flash of blue.

"No, thank you, ma'am," Miles said. "I was completely undisturbed."

He saw Alice raise her brows infinitesimally. A tiny smile curved her lips. Miles gritted his teeth. Minx. He wanted to kiss her. He wanted to make love to her on the breakfast table. She was learning frighteningly fast just how much power she had over him, and he was suffering every step of the way.

CHAPTER FIFTEEN

ALICE HAD FOUND IT VERY ODD and disturbing to meet Miles at the breakfast table. After what they had shared, it felt as though every nerve in her body was supremely aware of him. The low tones of his voice made her tingle. Each glance that he cast her seemed to heat her from the inside out. She felt utterly at his mercy—and the mercy of her own needs and desires.

She was sure that the others must be aware of the atmosphere that simmered between them, and yet it seemed they were not. Lizzie chattered with her usual frankness. Mrs. Lister read the tea leaves and bemoaned the fact that there were only bad signs in the cup.

"A pair of scissors!" she announced. "A quarrel or separation! Alice, dear—" her gaze traveled from Alice to Miles and back again "—I do hope you are not going to give me cause for concern."

"Of course not, Mama," Alice said. "Why would I do such a thing? Now, would you care to visit the Pump Rooms today? I understand that Lady Vickery and Mrs. Anstruther will be there."

Mrs. Lister brightened. "Oh, then I will most certainly attend! Dearest Lady Vickery and I need to discuss arrangements for the wedding." Her gaze darted from her daughter to Miles again. "I wish you would set a date, Alice dear. Now that the marquis is living in our house it is *quite* inappropriate for you to delay!"

"And even more so when I almost had you in your own bed this morning," Miles whispered in Alice's ear. "Set a date, sweetheart."

"What was that?" Mrs. Lister looked up, beaming, from the hunt for her reticule.

"Lord Vickery was adding his own words of encouragement," Alice said, glaring at Miles, "in his own inimitable style."

"Good, good," Mrs. Lister said absently. "Now, where can that have gone? There was no suggestion in the leaves that I would lose anything today!"

"Your mama truly believes in these things, does she not?" Miles commented, as they set out later to walk into the village. Lizzie and Mrs. Lister were walking ahead of them and Alice had been obliged to take Miles's arm, an irreproachably respectable maneuver that she could see amused him. She was all too conscious of the hard muscle of his arm beneath the blue superfine of his coat. She could remember the ripple and flow of that muscle beneath his skin. And she simply *had* to stop thinking about Miles without his clothes because it was doing her *no good at all.*

"Miss Lister?" Miles prompted. "I was merely making conversation about your mother's penchant for the leaves."

"Yes, I am afraid she does believe it," Alice said dolefully. "She is most shockingly superstitious. When your mother told her about the Curse of Drum I thought she would expire on the spot."

"It did not put her off the idea of your marrying me, then?" Miles inquired.

Alice laughed. "Oh, no, though it did make her even more anxious for the wedding to take place! As long as I am a marchioness before the Curse takes you, she will be quite happy!" She lowered her voice. "A little while ago Mama encouraged me to show you some kindness, my lord," she said. "She shocks me sometimes," she added.

"Some kindness," Miles said thoughtfully. "Was that what you showed me earlier, Miss Lister?"

"I permitted you far too much license earlier," Alice said.

"But you want to permit me more." Miles's voice was soft.

The cold winter air chilled Alice's hot cheeks. She fidgeted with her gloves. It was only what she had admitted to herself earlier. It was only what he already knew from her impassioned response to him, yet to confess it to *him* seemed brazen. "I admit it," she said. "I have always been honest with you—"

"You have."

"And though it is not remotely ladylike of me to confess it, you know I desire you."

"You refine too much upon being a lady," Miles said. "Women are made of flesh and blood, too."

He caught her suddenly in his arms and his lips came down on hers, cold from the March air but conjuring all the sensual passion that he could always evoke in her. Alice's head spun at the contrast of heat and chill. She closed her eyes. The pressure of his lips forced hers apart ruthlessly and then his tongue tangled with hers and suddenly she wanted him so badly that she felt as though she was falling. He let her go and the bright spring light stung her eyes and she stared in shock at the retreating figures of Lizzie and Mrs. Lister. They had not turned around. They had seen nothing.

"You take too many risks," she stammered.

"Perhaps." Miles smiled sardonically and offered her his arm again. "The worst thing that would have happened was that your mama would have turned around and seen us kissing and sent immediately for the vicar." He brushed his lips against her ear and she shivered.

"Don't keep me waiting too long," he murmured.

"To wed me?" Alice said.

Miles laughed. "Preferably. But to have you with or without the blessing of the church."

Alice's cheeks were burning as she quickened her pace after the others. "You could have had me this morning without it," she said, "and we both know it. So why did you stop?"

She sensed the change in Miles like a door slamming shut, abrupt and painful. "It seems," he said shortly, "that I could not go through with what I had planned."

The sting of his words came as a shock to Alice. Although she had suspected that Miles had had a calculated plan to seduce her, to hear him admit it hurt her. She supposed it was because her response to him had been so open and honest and yet his making love to her had been the reverse, calculated and premeditated. Once again he had shown the depths of his cynicism.

"So it is true," she whispered. "You had planned from the first to seduce me."

"I told you I would do anything to win you," Miles said. Then, as he met the look in her eyes, "Damn it, Alice, don't look so distressed! You have known all along that I am a scoundrel."

Alice bit her lip hard. She *had* known. "I keep forgetting," she said. "It is my fault. Every so often I forget and then the truth trips me up and it pains me."

She thought about his tenderness when he had saved her on Fortune Row.

I thought you had started to care for me a little...

How many times, she thought bitterly, was she going to be so foolish and be disillusioned?

She hurried after the others and Miles lengthened his stride to keep up with her and for a while there was a rather strained silence between them.

"Lord Vickery?" Alice said, after a little.

"Miss Lister?" Miles raised a brow at her formal tone.

"I wondered," Alice said, "why you felt it necessary to sleep outside my bedroom door in the first place. I assured you that there was absolutely no reason why you should."

"I was there in case you needed me," Miles said. He smiled suddenly, that flashing smile that always made her heart turn over. "My preference, as you know, would have been for sleeping *in* your bed, Miss Lister, but given that that is hardly appropriate at present, I wanted to be close by in case you cried for help."

Alice tried to banish the strange warm feeling that his words evoked. He was protecting his interests, she reminded herself. Nothing more.

"It must have been unconscionably uncomfortable sleeping on that pallet," she said.

Miles shrugged. "Not as uncomfortable as some of the places I have been obliged to sleep on campaign, I assure you."

Alice looked at him. "You never talk about your time in the Peninsular."

"War is not generally considered a topic for polite conversation."

"I suppose not," Alice said. "I would like to hear about it, though."

She realized that she genuinely wanted to know. Anything that cast light on the formation of Miles's character, on his history, fascinated her. She realized that she had absolutely no idea of the role he had had in the army, whether he had been injured and invalided out, or had resigned his commission. She tried to imagine the places he must have been and the things he must have seen. She found it impossible. In all her life she had traveled no farther than the seaside at Scarborough. Her life had been bounded first by the need to work simply to live and then by the behavior her mother had considered appropriate to a lady.

She also sensed the reluctance in Miles to talk. Once again, he was not anxious to reveal anything of himself. His mouth had set in a hard line. "I doubt that you would approve of my experiences, Miss Lister," he said. "I lived by the very things that you condemn—chicanery, compromise, negotiation. That was my job."

Alice frowned. "Whatever can you mean?"

"I was a diplomat, Miss Lister," Miles said. "Oh, not the sort of diplomat who takes tea in the palaces in the capital cities of the world, but a backstairs negotiator who makes the dirty deals that keep the peace and keep the world turning, but whom every government would deny and disown if ever they came out." There was a wealth of bitterness in his voice that Alice could not understand. "Every government connives secretly at such agreements, of course. They are all pragmatists at heart. They simply do not want to do the dirty work themselves. So that was my job and on the way I sacrificed plenty of people and my own principles along with them." He looked down into Alice's face. "If you knew even one of the deals that I had made," he said, "you would be forced to condemn me utterly."

"Tell me," Alice said. She heard the pain in his voice and reached out instinctively to him. "Tell me," she repeated, as the frown in his eyes deepened. "I cannot begin to understand if you do not explain."

Miles dropped her arm and moved a little away from her. He drove his hands into the pockets of his coat.

"Very well. I was with Wellesley at Rolica a couple of years ago," he said. "We took prisoner some local men who had been acting as guides for the French. The wife of one of them came to see me one night." He closed his eyes. "I can see her now. She was pregnant, barefoot, in rags, with a child clutching at her skirts. She told me her man had only taken the French money because the family was starving. She begged me to save him or they would all die. I promised to help her. Even as I said it I knew I lied."

Alice shook her head. "What happened?" she whispered.

"Wellesley wanted to make a bargain with the local resistance fighters," Miles said. "It was early on in our campaign and we desperately needed allies. The leader of the partisans demanded we hand over the prisoners in return for the information we needed. I knew that if we did that, the men would all be killed for collaborating with the French. Very likely they would be tortured and die horribly. But still I negotiated an agreement with the guerrillas."

Alice felt cold and sick and shocked. "You handed

the men over?" she said. Her lips felt stiff as though she could not quite form the words.

"I did," Miles said grimly. "Treaties are made in such ways, Miss Lister, for the greater good. I did it so that Wellesley had the information he needed to attack. He won the day. Those men were sacrificed so that every man, woman and child in *this* country could sleep more easily knowing that today will *not* be the day that Bonaparte invades."

Alice made a little repudiating gesture with her hands. "I had no notion," she said.

"Few people do." Miles's expression was dark. "They do not want to think about the price paid for their security."

"But does it not appall you?" Alice burst out. "It's loathsome, vile, that men will do that to their fellow men. It's hateful—I feel contaminated even knowing about it!"

Miles's expression was closed. "I have told you before, Miss Lister, that I am the most cynical of men, so no, it does not trouble me unduly. There is a price for everything and this is the price for peace. War is ugly business, which brings us rather neatly back to where we started and why this is not a fit topic of social discourse."

"I do not understand what it was that drove you to such work in the first place," Alice said. She felt frighteningly adrift, grasping after anything that might explain this terrifying coldness in Miles.

"You do not need to understand," Miles said. His tone utterly forbade any continuance of the conversation. Alice heard it, ignored it and plowed on.

"I know that something happened to cause an estrangement from your family," she said. "Was that what prompted you to join the army and take on such a role?"

"Miss Lister," Miles said in a voice with an edge that flayed, "I have no desire to pursue this discussion any further."

"No, but I do," Alice argued. "I need to understand you. I need to know what drove you from your family—"

"You need to do neither of those two things, Miss Lister," Miles said. His voice was very quiet now but absolutely icy. "I suppose you have some foolish, romantic idea that if you are able to reconcile me with my family you can heal whatever wounds you fondly believe me to be suffering. I fear that such happy endings exist only in your highly colored imagination."

They had reached the marketplace, and Lizzie and Mrs. Lister had turned to wait for them on the steps of the Pump Rooms. Alice tried to arrange her face into an expression of normality in case they guessed at the turmoil inside her. The initial shock she had felt at Miles's harshness was ebbing now but she felt a little strange. He had spared her nothing in trying to drive her away from him. He had been cruel and contemptuous. She wanted to believe that he had only done it because deep down he was angry and hurt at whatever it was that had set him on such a destructive course in the first place. She could not believe that he was truly so hard that he had no gentleness left in him. How could he make love to her with such skill and tenderness and yet rebuff all the efforts she made to be close to him? It baffled her that sometimes she could feel she was starting to understand him, that she was so drawn to him, and then he could demonstrate such indifference and remind her in the starkest possible terms that the only thing he felt for her was lust, not love.

She glanced up at his face. He looked handsome,

cool and remote, and his eyes met hers directly and
with no expression in their depths. He made no attempt
to reassure her or to apologize for upsetting her or
even to smooth matters over with light conversation.

I am the most cynical of men...

She searched his face for answers and he smiled
faintly at her though his eyes were still cold.

"Don't look so stricken, Miss Lister," he murmured.
"You knew the depths of my depravity from the start.
If you ever thought you could reform me, this should
prove to you that you cannot."

Alice caught his arm as he made to walk away from
her. "But I want to help you—"

Something raw flared in Miles's eyes. "You cannot,
nor do I wish it," he said. He grabbed her upper arms.
"You are confused," he said roughly. "You think that
because I want to make love to you that there is some
bond between us. I am sorry to disillusion you once
again but what I need from you is very simple, Miss
Lister, and it does not require emotional intimacy."

He turned away from her to hold open the doors of
the Pump Rooms for Mrs. Lister. Nothing could have
made it clearer that their conversation was at an end.

"May I fetch some spa water for you, ma'am?" he
inquired pleasantly. "They say it is most efficacious for
the health."

Alice sank down onto one of the pretty wrought-iron
seats scattered about the rotunda, and Lizzie planted
herself next to her. "Are you quite well, Alice?" she
asked. "You are looking most dreadfully pale. Lord
Vickery's wooing must lack style to leave you looking
so wan."

Alice watched Miles as he strolled over to the

counter to procure the spa water. He looked as cool and indifferent as usual, quite as though their quarrel had not occurred and he had not hurt her so deliberately or so profoundly.

"Lord Vickery was telling me about his time in the army," she said. "Oh, Lizzie, I feel so stupid and naive. I had no idea that such terrible things went on—"

"He should not have told you if it was going to upset you," Lizzie said stoutly.

"I am beginning to realize that with Miles one gets what one asks for," Alice said bitterly. "But then I asked him what had led to his estrangement from his family and he went all cold and harsh, and told me he never spoke about it and that I was not to pry."

"Men," Lizzie said, with a world-weary sigh. "You know how they can be."

"Not really," Alice said. "And neither do you," she added.

"Yes, I do!" Lizzie said defiantly. "They cannot talk about their emotions. They go all silent, and no amount of badgering will extract any information from them. It is very odd and provoking, but that is just their way and nothing can be done."

She slewed around in her seat as the rotunda door opened and Nat Waterhouse came in, escorting Flora Minchin and her mother and Mrs. Minchin's bosom friend, the Duchess of Cole. Laura Anstruther and Lady Vickery followed them in. The duchess was pointedly ignoring both Laura and Lady Vickery.

Lizzie's mouth turned down at the corners.

"Spiteful old buzzard," she muttered. "It serves Nat right that he is obliged to dance attendance on those two old witches just so that he can get his hands on

Flora's money. You know that they are to wed in two months' time, Alice?" She clenched her fists. "I cannot comprehend how Nat can be so stupid!" This final word was hissed in a whisper loud enough to echo off the domed ceiling of the rotunda and draw the attention of everyone inside.

"What else would you have him do, Lizzie?" Alice said wearily. She felt sorry for Nat. "He needs to marry for money and has never made any secret of the fact. Unless you marry him yourself—"

"I'd rather pull my own ears off!" Lizzie interrupted, turning bright red.

"Then stop complaining," Alice said, rather shortly. "If you are his friend you should be happy for him. If you have other feelings for him then you should do something about them before it is too late."

Lizzie fell silent, biting her lip, and looking at her Alice suddenly felt a strong misgiving that she had said quite the wrong thing and put some sort of idea into Lizzie's head that was going to explode in a spectacular way. She had no time to pursue the idea, though, for Laura and Lady Vickery were coming across to join them. Alice saw Miles glance over at his mother, and something changed in his face. What was it—regret, unhappiness? She sat forward urgently.

"Lizzie, do *you* know why Lord Vickery became estranged from his family?" she asked. "It is so odd— as though he resists all attempts to draw closer to them."

Lizzie shook her head. "Why do you not ask Laura? She is his cousin. She might know."

Laura eased herself into the chair beside Alice with a heartfelt sigh, for like her cousin Lydia she was in the fifth month of her pregnancy and was looking rather tired. Lady Vickery took a seat beside Mrs. Lister and they started to chatter like old friends. The Duchess of Cole and Mrs. Minchin had settled on chairs diagonally across from them in prime position to send poisonous little glances across the room.

"It seems the spa water has done nothing to improve Cousin Faye's temper," Laura said with a sigh. "We met at the library yesterday and she was monstrous rude to me. She commented that my family seemed hell-bent on marrying beneath themselves, first me, then Miles— begging your pardon, Alice, but you know what arrant nonsense Faye talks—and now Celia." She smiled. "I must admit that Celia does seem to have a partiality for Mr. Gaines. I saw them hurrying off together some- where this morning—" She broke off as Miles brought the beakers of spa water across to them. Miles gave Alice hers and then excused himself, going instead to talk to Nat Waterhouse. Laura raised her brows.

"How singular of Miles not to join us! Have you quarreled with him, Alice?"

"Yes," Alice said baldly. "I asked about his estrange- ment from his family."

Laura's face fell. "He never speaks of it." She gave a little shrug. "I was already married to Charles when the breach occurred and I do not know what happened." She gave a quick glance at Lady Vickery, who was still engrossed in her conversation with Mrs. Lister. "All I heard was that Miles had had a terrible argument with his father and went off to join the army immediately. My uncle was furious—he had wanted Miles to follow him into the church."

Lizzie gave a little giggle. "Now *that* would have been most inappropriate!"

"Dexter has taken Philip out fishing this morning," Laura went on, lowering her voice still further. "My aunt pets him as though he is still a child, but Philip is of an age where he likes to do more masculine things." She glanced over at Miles and shook her head. "I wish that Miles would take more of an interest in his younger brother. Philip worships him, yet Miles spends barely any time with him." She looked exasperated. "Miles is so good with Hattie, and she is only his goddaughter. I cannot understand it."

"Please let us talk of something else," Alice said. Her feelings were still rubbed raw by Miles's sharp rejection, and she could see that there was no explanation here for his behavior. Whatever the family secret was, it had been buried very deep.

"When does Sir Montague return from London, Lizzie?" she asked, to turn the subject.

"In a day or two, according to his last letter," Lizzie said. "I expect he has thought up some more medieval taxes to torment us with. How peaceful it has been in Fortune's Folly without him."

As they finished their spa water and prepared to leave, Miles bade farewell to Nat and came over to join them. He was not behaving much like a suitor, Alice thought, but more like a jailer.

"I will drive back to Spring House with Mrs. Anstruther," she said.

"Then I will join you," Miles said promptly. "I can scarcely protect you if we are in different places."

"I wish you would not bother," Alice said crossly,

as he handed Laura into the carriage and turned to help her. "I don't want—"

She broke off as Miles bundled her unceremoniously into the coach, jumping in after her. He grabbed her wrist and pulled her to sit beside him on the seat.

"Just for once," he said, "you will do as you are told."

"My, my," Laura said, trying not to smile as she looked from one to the other, "this is going to feel like a very long journey!"

They sat in pointed silence as the coach trundled back along the route they had walked earlier. Miles did not take his hand from Alice's wrist. She tried to free herself, furious at his restraint of her after his earlier coldness, but he held her fast.

With only that single point of contact between them, Alice soon found her skin becoming warm and tender to his touch, as though she were heating from the inside out. Her wrist tingled, incredibly sensitized. She clenched her fingers as prickles of sensation ran through her body, making her quiver. It seemed impossible that one light touch from Miles could do this to her, and yet she could concentrate on nothing else but the insistent pressure of his hand. His fingers moved, sweeping her palm in a caress that had her catching her breath. The air in the carriage grew sultry. Alice sat still, transfixed, the blood thrumming through her veins in hard, heavy strokes. The heat built in her body. She did not dare move for fear that Laura would guess her state and for fear that *Miles* would see what he was doing to her.

But then the pressure of his fingers increased infinitesimally and Alice was powerless to resist looking at him and saw in his dark, heavy-lidded gaze that he knew exactly how she felt. The knowledge made another wave of delicious sensuality roll over her leaving her languid and warm. She shifted on the seat, unable to prevent the tiny shivers of awareness that racked her body. This was almost unbearable. How could Miles do this to her when she was so angry and frustrated with him? How could her body betray her so thoroughly? And yet it seemed that that vicious frustration was part of the friction between them, for it chafed her feelings and gave her no peace, and she wanted to be free of Miles and yet she also wanted him so badly she could barely breathe.

Miles leaned forward and spoke softly in her ear. His breath tickled her neck sending more tremors of feeling along her nerves.

"You seem a little distracted, Miss Lister," he said. "Are you quite well?"

Laura looked up. "You are very flushed, Alice," she said. "Are you developing a fever?"

Alice saw a faint smile curve Miles's firm lips.

"Yes!" she said. "No. I do not know."

"You sound confused," Miles said soothingly.

"I am quite well," Alice said. With inexpressible relief she saw that they were turning into the gate at Spring House. She had spent the entire journey aware of nothing other than the touch of Miles's hand on hers. Tiny shivers still seemed to be tiptoeing over her skin as she looked at him and he returned the gaze with a very direct look of his own. She could see in his eyes how much he wanted her. She could feel the tension tight in him, held under absolute control. She thought of their quarrel and how it did not seem to make an ounce of difference as to whether she wanted him in her bed or not and she felt helpless and eager and wanton and wicked.

As soon as the carriage rolled onto the sweep there was a shout, and both Marigold and Jim the footman ran out to greet them. Alice jumped and freed herself from Miles's grip. Marigold was twisting her hands in her apron and looked as though she wanted to cry.

"Miss Alice!" She looked stricken.

"What is it, Marigold?" Alice asked. She was aware of Miles standing tense and watchful at her shoulder. "What has happened?"

"It's Miss Lydia!" Marigold wailed. "She has run away!"

CHAPTER SIXTEEN

THEY SEARCHED throughout the long, cold day, but found no trace of Lydia or Tom Fortune. As the afternoon progressed, the snow returned and the temperature fell. It was going to be a cold night. Lady Vickery huddled before the fire and declared that they would find Lydia frozen to death by the morning. Mrs. Lister made endless cups of tea and read the leaves, bemoaning the fact that all the omens were bad ones. Celia Vickery seemed to have vanished, and Philip sat moodily in a corner carving a stick and trying to look as though he was not too disappointed that his mother had banned him from accompanying the search parties.

"I blame myself," Laura said to Alice that afternoon as they worked side by side in the kitchen of the Old Palace to help the servants prepare refreshment for the search parties. "Lydia must have been afraid that I would bully her into telling the truth about Tom's whereabouts." She shook her head. "I can only hope he is looking after her. Poor Lydia—she is so alone."

"I had heard the news that the Duke and Duchess of Cole refused to spare any staff for the search," Alice said. She had been disgusted at their attitude. "They said that their servants had better things to do with their time!"

Miles came in. He was wearing a greatcoat dusted with snow and looked moody and bad-tempered. Alice had barely spoken to him since their quarrel that morning, but now, despite his impatient expression, she thought she sensed a softening in him.

"I should have predicted that this would happen," he said to her as he took the mug of hot chocolate she proffered. "Last night we both thought that Miss Cole had slipped out to meet Tom Fortune. I should have realized that her next step would be to run away to him." His gaze dwelled on Alice's face. "I was distracted," he said. "It was a great mistake to move into Spring House to keep an eye on you, Alice. It seems I can see nothing else." His lips twitched and she thought he was almost smiling. "Try not to look so pleased," he added dryly.

"I thought," Alice said, taking advantage of the fact that he appeared to be in a better mood, "that you might like to take Philip with you when you go back out to search. He is desperate to be of use and I am sure he would be able to help—"

She stopped at the sight of Miles's black frown. "Philip is more likely to be a hindrance than a help," Miles said shortly. "It would be better for him to stay here with Mama. She will only fret all the more otherwise."

Alice turned away and crashed a few pans with unnecessary force onto the stove. Some soup slopped onto the floor. Fuming silently, she reflected that Miles really was utterly impossible.

"Alice," Miles said, a tiny hint of humor in his voice.

Alice ignored him. She had heard the tone of his voice and her pulse had started to race with renewed hope, but she was not going to give Miles the satisfaction of dictating their conversation. She took the ham pie down from the larder shelf and sliced it with quick, vicious chops of the knife.

"Very wifely," Miles commented.

"I have nothing to say to you, Miles," Alice said. "You are a horrid, bad tempered, unkind and mean-spirited person and I was quite wrong in thinking that there was an *ounce* of goodness in you."

"I told you I had absolutely no saving graces," Miles said. "You should have listened to me. I never lie to you."

"Clearly," Alice said. She slapped a dish of potted venison and some butter down on the table. "Would you care for me to slice some bread for you?" she inquired coldly.

"No, thank you," Miles said. "You would probably have my hand off." He sighed heavily. "Oh, very well. Philip can come with me." He shot her a look. "I suppose you are pleased with yourself now?"

"Not at all," Alice said airily, smothering her smile. "I will go and fetch him for you."

Miles grabbed her arm. "I'll take a kiss first. It's the least you can do by way of payment."

"In front of your cousin?" Alice demanded a little breathlessly.

"She can look the other way, can't you, Laura?" Miles said. "After all, we are betrothed so I am entirely within my rights."

"*I'll* go and fetch Philip," Laura said, drying her hands on her apron. "How long do you need?"

As the door closed behind her, Miles put his hands on Alice's shoulders.

"May I?" he said softly.

He had not asked before—he had simply taken—

and somehow it seemed to make a huge difference. Alice's heart fluttered.

"You may," she whispered.

Miles smiled at her again then, and Alice felt a wash of emotion so strong that for a moment she trembled. Then he bent his head and kissed her. It was gentle and sweet, turning into a slow burning. *Different.* The trembling feeling inside her blossomed and intensified. She slid her arms about his neck and drew him closer, feeling the care with which he held her, as though she were infinitely precious.

There was a clatter as Laura made a rather ostentatious reentry into the kitchen, and they drew apart. Miles looked down at her. There was a baffled look in his eyes, as though he were trying to decipher a particularly complex conundrum. After a moment Alice saw him shake his head slightly. He shot her another look and cleared his throat.

"I know you can shoot straight, Laura," he said, "so if anyone tries to hurt Alice whilst I am away—"

"I'll take good care of her," Laura said, beaming.

Miles nodded again, unsmiling, beckoned to Philip and walked out without another word.

"That was nicely done," Laura commented when Miles and Philip had gone out and Alice, pink-faced and rather flustered, had returned to stirring the soup. "Philip is very happy. I didn't think you'd pull it off, Alice, I confess it. Although one rarely sees it, Miles can have the devil of a temper and he can be as stubborn as a mule into the bargain."

"I know," Alice said feelingly.

Laura laid down her chopping knife and came to rest against the table at Alice's side. "I admit that when he started to pay court to you last year I was afraid he would hurt you badly," she said.

"He did," Alice said briefly.

"I never thought that he would fall in love with you," Laura said. She laughed at Alice's expression of incredulity. "Don't you see it, Alice? He took Philip with him to please *you,* as much as for the boy's sake. He did it because he wants your good opinion."

Alice felt a rush of hope and tried to quell it. "Miles is not the sort of man to fall in love," she said. She wanted to believe Laura but she knew Miles too well now. It seemed impossible. "He pushes me away at every turn," she said. "He's not like Dexter," she added in a rush. "Miles doesn't want to care for anyone. He has told me that all he wants is my money."

"He might not want to care for you," Laura said dryly, "but he has no choice. Dexter struggled pretty hard," she added with a smile. "It takes them a while sometimes. But what about you?" She looked closely at her friend. "If Miles has hurt you once you might not wish to give him that chance again."

"I can't help it," Alice said simply. She put her hands up to her burning cheeks in a helpless gesture. "I can't help my feelings for him, Laura. I wish I could, but you know what I am like. I am a very simple person—"

"There is no artifice in you," Laura said, giving her a hug, "and that is a good thing."

"What did Miles mean when he said that you could shoot straight?" Alice asked curiously.

Laura sighed. "I was not always five months pregnant and as sick as a cushion." She looked at Alice. "Do you remember the tales of the Glory Girls, Alice, the band of highwaywomen who rode the dales a few years ago?"

"Of course!" Alice said, her eyes lighting up. The Glory Girls had been heroines to her and to many others of the poor and dispossessed. "They took from the rich to right the injustices of society—" Her voice dwindled as she looked at Laura. "No!" she said, her eyes widening to their furthest extent. "You could not have been!"

"I was," Laura said.

"But…" Alice's mind whirled. "You were a duchess! I mean… No, it is impossible. Does Dexter know?"

Laura smiled. "He found out last year."

"Oh," Alice said. "Oh!" she said again in a different tone, remembering Laura and Dexter's rather stormy courtship.

"Yes," Laura said, "he was not pleased."

"I imagine not," Alice said, "since he is one of the Guardians."

Laura pulled a face. "Dexter can be very stuffy."

"In a most attractive sort of way," Alice said, smiling.

"But the point," Laura said, blushing a little, "is that it was *Miles* who helped me to gain a pardon from the Home Secretary, Alice. I'll tell you all about it in a moment, but it was Miles who saved me. If it comes to that," she added with a laugh, "it was Miles who told Dexter to marry me only if he could love me with all his heart and it was Miles who brought gifts for Hattie from London even when he could not afford it, and Miles who has been so anxious to protect you and is even now taking his brother out with him because he wants, deep down, for Philip to be happy…." She stopped and looked at Alice expectantly. "Isn't it?"

Alice wiped her hands on her apron. "I do not know," she said. "I wish I could believe you, Laura. I wish I could believe that Miles cares for anyone other than himself, but the truth is that he is coercing me into marriage for my money, and unless I have a free choice I cannot love him the way that my heart demands." She saw Laura's shocked expression and said quickly, "Do not look so appalled. He has not hurt me—"

"Thank God," Laura said, recovering, "or I would have to put a bullet through him!"

"It is tempting to ask you to do so," Alice said, laughing. She sobered. "The truth is that I want Miles to care for me but I am not sure he can. Something happened to him, Laura, that drove all the tenderness and love out of him, and he will not tell me what that is."

"He will," Laura said. "He will tell you when the time is right. Have faith."

Dexter and Nat Waterhouse came into the kitchen then with Lowell and a group of his farmworkers and there was no more chance of conversation, but Alice nurtured the small spark of hope that Laura had lit inside her. Perhaps Laura was right, she thought, and Miles would tell her the whole truth in his own good time. For if he did not—and if he could not release her to make her choices freely—her love for him could come to nothing.

MILES WAS STILL WONDERING what the hell had happened as he rode out of the stable yard with his brother. He had been furious with himself for taking his eye off the wider picture and not realizing that Lydia would run to Tom. The trouble, he realized now, was that he had been utterly consumed by his anxieties for Alice. His every waking thought centered on her. He had compromised his own efficiency because he could not see beyond the need to protect her. Even now he was wishing that he were back in the house with Alice in his arms, wishing that he could lose himself in her and find that elusive peace that only she seemed able to give him. That kiss they had shared... He shifted uncomfortably. He was not at all sure what had happened. He felt as though the world had swung on its axis, which was patently absurd. It was only a kiss. It did not have to be earth-shattering. He liked kissing Alice—hell, he adored kissing Alice—but the effect it had on him was starting to disturb him.

He had been so angry with Alice earlier when she had pressed him on his quarrel with his family. She had been prying into the dark corners of his mind and the places where he dared not go. He had instinctively turned away from those old secrets and had rejected her cruelly. In the past, displaying such harshness and cynicism would not have mattered to him. He would have protected himself and that was what counted. This time, though, he had been berating himself for his brutality from the moment that the words had left his lips. He had tried to drive Alice away when in fact the last thing that he wanted was to lose her.

And then there was Philip. He looked at his brother. How had Alice managed to persuade him to take his brother with him? It had been the very last thing he had intended to do and yet somehow he had not been able to resist the entreaty in her eyes. He felt strange thinking about it now. He had wanted to please her. The sensation was alien to him. It made him feel uncomfortable, as though he were surrendering some part of himself. He shifted in the saddle again. Very well, he would admit it, if only to himself.

He was starting to care for Alice.

Damnation take it.

To distract his mind he turned to Philip. The boy rode well, he noted, and he was looking about him with a sharp eye for tracks in the snow that might lead to a hiding place. Philip turned in the saddle and gave Miles a grin that was pure, infectious excitement, and Miles felt his heart lurch. For a moment Philip had reminded him of himself, in the days before he had quarreled with their father and life had been good and uncomplicated. He felt a wave of nostalgia that almost crushed him, then a determination that for Philip, at least, the future would be different from his own. He might not be able to turn back the clock or even to escape the dark cynicism that dogged his own soul but he could at least make sure that Philip was never so disillusioned.

"I'll race you to the stand of trees by the river," he said, and saw his brother's face light up before the boy dug his heels into the horse's side and stole a head start.

CHAPTER SEVENTEEN

"IT DOES NOT FEEL RIGHT coming out to a musicale when Lydia and Tom have not been found," Lizzie said dolefully to Alice two nights later, as they sat in the Pump Rooms and waited for the orchestra to tune up. "I do not think I will dance tonight. I am far too cast down."

They were sitting in the front row, with Lady Vickery and Celia to Alice's right and Mrs. Lister and Lowell to Lizzie's left. Miles had paused on the way in to exchange a few words with Nat Waterhouse. He had kissed Alice's hand and told her he would join her shortly. Nat had pointedly made no such promise to Lizzie, who had glared at him.

"I feel monstrous sad, Alice," Lizzie was saying. "If they find Tom then he will be clapped in prison and hanged for sure this time, and if they do not we cannot be sure that Lydia is safe, and meanwhile there is some madman on the loose with a rifle who might take a potshot at us at any time." She sighed. "I think I preferred it when Monty was here inflicting his ghastly medieval taxes on us! At least that was more fun!"

"Talk of the devil," Alice said. She looked at the portly figure who was standing in the doorway to the Pump Rooms with all the preening self-importance of a cock pheasant. "I do believe your brother has returned, Lizzie. Is that not Sir Montague in the entrance, chatting to Mr. Pullen?"

Lizzie swung around in her chair. "Goodness!" she said. "So it is! He must have come back from London for Mary Wheeler's wedding. I heard he had asked Lord Armitage for a cut of her fortune because he claimed they would not have wed without the Dames' Tax, and Lord Armitage told him to go hang!" She sighed, slumping back in her chair. "Drat! I suppose Monty will be all stuffy now and demand that I return to live with him at the Hall, and it has been so much more fun with you, Alice. Good Lord!" she added, grabbing Alice's arm as her brother came into the room accompanied by a lady. "Has Monty attached himself to some female?" She screwed her face up tightly. "Surely she cannot be a…a *lightskirt?* Have you ever seen a gown like that in the Fortune's Folly Pump Rooms before, Alice?"

"Not on a lady, certainly," Alice said. She was torn between horror and amusement at the spectacle Sir Montague was making. "Gracious," she said, "I do believe the lady is about to lose the bodice altogether!"

Sir Montague Fortune's fair companion was waiting quite blatantly until everyone in the room was looking at her. Dressed—barely—in a glittering gown of dampened silver gauze, she looked exotic and disdainful. The murmur of voices in the room rose to a crescendo and then died away to a shocked whisper as the couple came forward.

"Oh, my!" Lizzie whispered irrepressibly in Alice's ear. "My brother is about to introduce me to his mistress, here in front of everyone! I always knew

Monty was a ramshackle fellow, but this! What shall I do, Alice?"

"Nothing," Alice said. "Wait. I think there may be something else going on...." She had started to feel a little anxious, for she had seen that Miles and Nat Waterhouse had also spotted Sir Montague. Nat was saying something to Miles, and a rather strained look had come over Miles's face all of a sudden. A cold premonition tiptoed down Alice's neck and a slightly sick feeling was turning her stomach.

"She does have a certain style," Lizzie was murmuring. "I wonder what she can possibly see in Monty? And what on earth possessed him to bring her here? She looks like a bird of paradise in a farmyard!"

"That is Louisa Caton," Lady Vickery whispered, waking from what seemed to be a scandalized trance. "Look away, girls! Whatever can Sir Montague be thinking to bring the most notorious courtesan in London *here?* Look away, I say," she said again, catching Alice's arm. "Really, this is most vulgar and an utter disgrace."

"That is Monty for you," Lizzie said irrepressibly. "Dear ma'am, have no fear! I do not think we shall be corrupted simply *looking* at a courtesan—" She broke off. "Oh, but...wasn't Miss Caton the one—" She stopped again, looking at Alice. "Oh dear," she said, stricken. "Oh, Alice."

"Yes," Alice said. She realized her voice was shaking. "I do believe that Miss Caton *was* the courtesan with whom Lord Vickery was involved when last he was in London."

"Alice!" Mrs. Lister snapped. "You are not supposed to know such things. And if you *do* know, you are to pretend that you do *not* know!"

"I am sorry, Mama," Alice said. "No doubt you are correct and that a lady would pretend ignorance. But you have always known that I am no lady."

Mrs. Lister made a little sound of abject misery. "Oh, what are we to do?" She turned to Lady Vickery. "In front of his mama, too!"

"In front of his betrothed," Lady Vickery said hollowly. "In front of the *lawyers!*" She glanced across at the row of chairs that contained Mr. Churchward and Mr. Gaines. Gaines had a look of extreme interest on his face as he watched Louisa Caton approach Miles. Mr. Churchward, in contrast, looked as shocked as though the courtesan had sat herself down on his lap. His face was red, his eyes as round as dinner plates behind his spectacles and his mouth was an equally round, scandalized circle of shock. Alice knew exactly how he felt.

"Whistling away an heiress—and before the knot is tied, too!" Lady Vickery wailed. "Stupid, stupid boy." She turned to Alice. "Miss Lister, I appeal to you to give Miles a chance to explain—"

"I do not think so," Alice said. "Events are rather speaking for themselves, are they not?"

She watched in fascinated horror as Sir Montague accosted Miles. It almost felt as though she was watching a play, seeing the moves, hearing the lines. In the moment she felt nothing but she knew that at any point the chill carapace that held her might crack and the pain would rush in and she was afraid she could not bear it. *This* was the gilded creature with whom Miles had had a torrid affair. This was the woman whose bed he had sought after he had jilted her the previous year. This was the salt in the wound.

She tried to tell herself that it was all a terrible co-incidence, that Miles knew nothing of this, that Sir Montague was probably Miss Caton's lover now and with his typical disregard for good taste and propriety was set on thrusting her into Fortune's Folly society. The thoughts and words and images jostled in her head, the anger and fear stung her and then she heard Sir Montague's greeting:

"Vickery! Got your letter!" Sir Montague slapped Miles on the back. His stentorian tones seemed to bounce off the ceiling of the concert room so that every person present could hear his words with excruciating clarity. "Happy to oblige, old chap, and escort this gorgeous creature to Yorkshire. A rather splendid present for you, what!"

He stood aside beaming and Miss Caton reached up and in view of the entire company kissed Miles full on the mouth.

There was a scandalized silence in the room.

Alice stood up. Her fan and reticule clattered to the floor, but she did not bother to stop and retrieve them. She was conscious of nothing other than the need to escape. Up until that moment she had been so deter-mined to believe that the whole scene had been either a mistake or a rather unpleasant coincidence. She had fiercely resisted the whispered thoughts in her own mind that said that Miles was bored of courting a virgin heiress, bored because he did not have a sophisticated woman in his bed, and so he had sent for his mistress. She had refused to accept it. She had not wanted even to think it because she had hoped against hope that Miles's outward coldness was a mask that would one day crack and she would be the one to reach the man beneath.

Now she saw her hopes for the naive dreams they were, for Miles had *always* told her the truth with the brutal honesty that the terms of her inheritance had demanded. He had wanted her for her money. She was the one to save him from the debtor's prison not the one to win his heart.

Got your letter! Happy to oblige...

Damn Sir Montague and his thoughtless masculine bonhomie! Damn him and the beautiful painted creature at his side whom Miles was even now putting away from him as he turned toward her....

"Alice," Miles said.

Alice ignored him. She started to walk, very slowly and carefully, toward the door. She could see that people were staring at her. It felt dreadful. Her confidence was suddenly wafer thin. Every last one of her insecurities rose to mock her, the scorned little housemaid turned heiress, courted for her fortune, humiliated by her fiancé and his mistress in full public view.

"Of course he has to go after her," she heard Miss Caton say with languid lack of interest. "She is very rich, after all, so I hear, and he is very poor and *I* am very expensive." And she gave a small trill of affected laughter.

Alice's face flamed with absolute fury to think that her money would be paying for Miles's pleasure in some harlot's bed. Perhaps, she thought, through the haze of anger, the aristocracy were so sophisticated, so debauched, that a wife would not even blanch at subsidizing her husband's amorous activities. It was only another entertainment, after all, like gambling or drinking. But such aristocratic cold-bloodedness was foreign to her nature. She could not be so complacent.

Every thought, every feeling, seemed to hurt. She

recognized the sensation with some shock. She had not expected to feel such pain. She might have expected anger at so public a humiliation, or embarrassment to be shown to be so painfully naive in contrast to Miss Caton's brazen worldliness. But this naked, piercing grief that seemed to skewer her heart—that was something both unexpected and deeply painful, and it could only mean that she had compounded all her other follies by falling in love with Miles all over again, far more deeply and hopelessly than she had realized.

"Alice, wait!"

She heard Miles's step behind her and then he had caught her arm and was bundling her through a doorway and into a room beyond. It was the spa baths. At this time of night they were deserted but for a servant stolidly folding towels and tidying up in preparation for the morning. A lamp glowed on a low table, its red heart a match for the embers that glowed in the wide fireplace. The steam rose from the water in the square stone bath like eerie fingers of mist. During the day the communal baths were packed with Fortune's Folly visitors. Now the cushioned benches with their pretty carvings designed to resemble Roman baths were empty and the room echoed to the soft bubble of the waters. Alice saw the warmth around her but she could not feel it in her bones. She felt chilled through and through.

Miles looked at the maid and jerked his head toward the door. "If you would be so good…" The courtesy of his tone was belied by the look in his eyes. The girl dropped a frightened curtsy and fled.

Alice heard Miles turn the key in the lock.

"You can't do that," she said, rousing herself from

her cold stupor. "It isn't proper." Then she laughed, a bitter sound to think of herself pleading for propriety when Miles's mistress had just accosted him in the concert hall in front of everyone in Fortune's Folly.

"Alice, listen." Miles ran a hand over his hair, disordering it. Alice noted with detachment that it was the first time she had seen him looking anything less than immaculate. There was strain in his face and deep lines about his eyes. His expression was pale and set.

"I suppose she is your mistress," Alice cut in, wondering even as she spoke why on earth she had to prolong this agony. She sighed. "Actually, I don't think you need to answer that, Miles. Of course she is."

"She *was* my mistress," Miles said.

Alice looked sharply at him. "Sir Montague said he had brought her as a present for you." Her face twisted. "Did you...did you send for her like he said?"

"No," Miles said. "No," he repeated more forcefully. "I had no notion Monty was bringing her. I think he probably did it on purpose to try to wreck my betrothal to you. You know he has always wanted to wed you himself or failing that to claim half of your money under the Dames' Tax."

Alice's gaze searched his face. Her heart felt sore, torn. "So you swear you did not know?" she whispered.

A rueful, boyish smile touched Miles's lips. "You have never doubted that I was telling you the truth before, Alice," he said. "Why now?"

"Because you are a rake," Alice said, "and I—" She stopped. "I am jealous," she said with some surprise. The feelings scored her again with the painful intensity of cats' claws. "Very jealous," she added. "I hate it. It feels horrible."

Miles was watching her intently. "You always knew I was a rake," he said. "I never concealed my past from you."

"No," Alice agreed, "but I had not thought it would ever matter to me. I had not thought I would care."

Miles's eyes darkened. He took a step toward her, put out a hand. "You care?" he said.

"About some lightskirt from London coming in and kissing you in front of half of Fortune's Folly?" Alice retorted. "Yes, I care about that! It hurts my pride."

"Pride," Miles said. "I see." His hand fell to his side. "There is nothing between Miss Caton and me," he said. "I care nothing for her. I never did. It was over before I came back to Yorkshire."

"Then why is she here?" Alice demanded. The pain twisted inside her, tighter than a knot. The room was hot and steamy, and her gown was sticking to her skin. No lady should perspire, of course, but Alice felt her shift and petticoats absorb the moist heat of the steam, felt her body start to heat and the sweat run. The tiny curls of hair that nestled in her neck were clinging to its nape. Her physical discomfort seemed only to mock her mental misery.

"I don't trust you," she said, and the words fell quietly into the silence of the room.

"I can see that," Miles said. She sensed the anger in him as she had done that day on Fortune Row when last she had shown how little trust she had in him. This time it felt different though. She sensed an edge of something else to Miles's fury, something that felt oddly like unhappiness.

"Why should I?" Alice demanded. "You have never done anything to earn my trust! You have tried to blackmail me into marriage—"

"Well, that is all at an end now," Miles said. "Now that my ex-mistress has kissed me in front of your trustees, thereby proving irrevocably that I am not worthy of you." He shrugged. "You are free, Alice. They will never let you wed me now." He drove his hands into his pockets. His gaze was hot and dark and angry as it rested on her. "Why don't you go?"

Alice did not know. His words—and the realization that Louisa Caton had shattered the conditions of their betrothal—broke over her with the force of a tidal wave. She felt light-headed and free and yet so dreadfully unhappy.

She could not pull away from the expression in his eyes. "It was not your fault," she whispered. "*She* kissed *you.*"

Miles's expression was contemptuous. "Do you think that will have any influence with the lawyers? Gaines has been ceaselessly searching to find a reason to reject my suit. This is a gift to him. And to you." He clenched his fists. "Go, Alice!" He sounded murderous. "Go and tell him the betrothal is at an end."

"But you will be imprisoned for debt," Alice whispered.

"So why would you care? I tried to blackmail you." Miles turned away as though he could not even bear to look at her.

Alice put her hand on his arm. He felt as tense as a strung bow. She could sense despair and violence in him and she wondered why she did not run as fast as she could, but still she did not go.

"Have you taken a mistress since our betrothal?" she whispered.

A muscle moved in Miles's jaw. "I have not."

She could read him too well by now and almost hated herself for it. "But you have thought about it?" she persisted, wondering even as she did so why she needed to know and to give herself more pain. Why could she not just run, back to the light, back to the lawyers, and tell them it was all over...

"I never sent for Louisa Caton but I did think about slaking my lust with a willing maidservant," Miles said, with a brutality that shook her. His deliberate use of the word *maidservant* flicked her on the raw and she flinched. Miles saw it and shrugged.

"I don't need to tell you the truth anymore," he continued mercilessly, "but I will. Courting a virgin was proving frustrating work and the girl at the Morris Clown offered her favors, so..."

"So you thought about accepting her offer?" Alice forced the words out past the tears blocking her throat.

"I wanted to." Miles's eyes met hers. She could see at last that the anger in him was for himself, not for her, and her heart missed a beat. "Give me no credit," he said bitterly. "I would have bedded her if I could."

The fury flicked at Alice again like a whip. "Then I cannot see why you held back."

Something flared in Miles's eyes, dark, primal and fierce. His fingers gripped her wrist. "How could I take her," he ground out, "when I burn for you?" He gave her a little shake. "It would not be wise to push me any further, Alice, unless you can take the consequences. Do you understand me? I have wanted you a long time."

Alice thought about it. She really thought about it for several moments. Sensible Alice, practical Alice would draw back, of course, play safe, preserve what was left of her innocence. She was free now. She could leave and Miles could not force her into marriage because he had been proved the unworthy man that she had always known him to be. His past had caught him out, betrayed him and delivered her. And yet she did not want to flee. Trapped there in the complicated web of anger and desire she wanted nothing but him and that was the honest truth between them.

She pressed her fingers to Miles's lips and saw him close his eyes. A muscle flickered in his cheek. She rubbed the stubble of his lean jaw with gentle, experimental fingers and slid her hand around to the back of his neck to bring his head down to hers in a kiss.

Her lips touched his, inexpert, hesitant, and suddenly Alice was afraid because for all the things she had learned from him and everything they had done, there was still an enormous leap between imagination and experience, and she felt woefully inadequate. She made to draw back, anxiety gnawing her stomach, but then Miles angled his head and took her mouth with ruthless precision, and her fear was flattened by a need so great it stifled everything else.

She could feel the anger still in him and the tension and a driving desire that burned up everything in its path. She did not understand it but she clung to him and felt the material of his jacket beneath the desperate clutch of her fingers. His arms went about her and then suddenly she was down on the stone slabs of the floor and they felt hot and slippery beneath her back, as hot as her body felt within the damp evening gown. She gasped and Miles covered her mouth with his and his tongue invaded deeply, and his hand moved to cup her breast and her senses swam.

She knew then, suddenly, that he was not going to stop. He was going to take her here, now, on the stone floor, with the steam clinging in wisps to her body and the heat of it in her blood and her clothes still on and no words spoken. The terror and the excitement made her heart pound so hard she thought the strength of it would lift her entire body from the ground. She could hear the blood drumming in her ears and feel her sweat mingle with the water vapor as she gave herself up to the seeking mouth that was demanding every last ounce of submission from her.

The command was in his hands as they moved over the bodice of her gown, skimming her breasts, stroking through the muslin that was soaking now and clinging to her like a second skin. Her nipples hardened and peaked unbearably tight and he lowered his lips to them and nipped and sucked through the muslin. Alice arched upward, obedient to that absolute demand, and felt him lick up the salty sweat that ran in the cleft between her breasts. He groaned and his mouth returned to hers, roughly now, and she responded eagerly, drinking deep of him, learning the touch and the taste of him even as the hard coiling desire within her threatened to explode. His hands moved blindly, bunching up the skirts of her gown, tugging her drawers aside, then moving to the fastening of his breeches.

The hot, moist air touched her bare thighs like a caress. She felt Miles's hand push her legs apart and they fell open to the damp kiss of the air. The tight, whirling, painful spiral of need in her stomach intensified. She was frantic, desperate for something that felt so close but yet was still so elusive. She could feel the shimmer of it just out of reach and the painful tightening of desire like a ratchet twisting so taut that it was unbearable.

"Don't stop." The words were wrenched from her. "Please don't stop now."

And then his fingers were at the very heart of her, parting her, sliding over the slick, tight core and she felt him between her legs and then he was inside her in one smooth stroke.

The pain was fleeting. She noticed it and lost the sensation almost at once as others crowded it out. Her body, rippling with pleasure, seemed to move to accommodate Miles. She felt the size of him, filling her completely, stretching her, impaling her, the feeling so strange and yet so familiar that she felt she had always known him. She was claimed, taken, all innocence stolen, and yet she felt so wicked and wanton in her newfound knowledge that she writhed beneath him instinctively and heard him groan. Her fingers were deep in his hair, pulling his mouth back down to hers as he started to move within her, the rhythm gentle at first but so relentless, so inexorable, that she felt utterly ravished. The damp material of his pantaloons slid against her bare thighs as he moved within her. The stone was hard and hot beneath her, but Miles's arm was about her, holding her up to meet the thrusts of his body and protect her from the unyielding solidity of the stone floor.

Her body grasped greedily after the pleasure he offered and sensations took hold in response to the slick thrust and slide of him within her. It built and built in shimmering bliss until the world came apart in a shocking, shattering explosion that gathered her up and utterly consumed her. She felt Miles grip her hips and bury himself so deep within her. She heard him groan and felt him shudder as the same intense force took him to tumble them both over the edge and into the whirling darkness below. And then he had gathered her close, his arms about her as though he would never let her go, and she felt completed and triumphant.

MINE. THE WORD ECHOED through Miles's head.

He gathered Alice closer to him. Her body felt soft and utterly relaxed in his arms, completely trusting and surrendered. Her eyes were closed, the moisture beaded on her lashes. Her skin was rosy and flushed. Her curls tickled his chin. She smelled faintly of flower scent but also of sweat and the salt he had tasted on her skin. The scent drove another spike of lust through him. His desire for her was not diminished. He wanted to carry her out of there to some impossibly soft and comfortable bed and make love to her for the rest of the night and probably forever after. Yet at the same time he felt enormously, powerfully protective and possessive of her. The sensation ambushed him with all the unexpectedness and force of a tidal wave, and for a moment he felt lost and adrift in uncharted waters. This was the moment when he usually made his excuses to his lovers and left. He had never had the urge to cherish them and hold them and simply look at them with this mixture of awe and triumph.

It was only because Alice had been a virgin, he told himself. It was natural that he should feel some sense of responsibility for her pleasure, even he who had never cared a rush for anyone's satisfaction but his own. He looked at Alice and felt a wash of regret. It really should not have been like this. He should have had more care for her than to have ravished her on the hard stone floor of the spa baths. Yet despite his regrets over the mode of Alice's seduction it had been the most extraordinary and perfect lovemaking that he could ever remember. Although that, too, was no doubt an illusion brought on by this strange sense of responsibility he was feeling. Or so he tried to reassure himself. He shifted a little under the unaccustomed weight of the feeling. The reaction felt strange, almost unwelcome, and yet there was something about it that also felt inevitable, as though all his certainties were shifting and dissolving away and something new was taking their place.

Fanciful stuff. The simple truth was that in his anger and his selfish desire he had taken his virginal fiancée on the floor in the spa at the Pump Rooms and everyone in the entire building would know it by now. Which actually worked in his favor, for neither Mr. Gaines nor Mr. Churchward would stand in the way of a marriage now, not with the whole village talking scandal. It did not matter now that his ex-mistress had proved him to be the unworthy and unrespectable man he knew that he was. The disgrace of Alice's ravishment was the greater dishonor and it worked to his advantage. He had Alice and he had her money, too.

He waited to feel triumph, relief and conquest. The feelings never came. He looked at Alice, and the vise of his need for her tightened impossibly. He had to marry her, not for the money but because it felt right and natural and absolutely the only thing to do.

Hell and damnation. He was losing his mind.

Alice opened her eyes. They were soft and unfocused, deep harebell blue. And then she smiled at him and the emotion thumped him in the gut and he felt as though he was falling.

"Miles."

She raised a hand to his cheek and the same wallop of emotion took him again. He was beginning to recognize it now. He was even beginning to like it, and that was even more frightening. He opened his mouth to speak, but there came a heavy knocking at the door of the spa. Miles made to get up but Alice grabbed his lapels and held him close.

"Leave it." The curve of her smile made him want to kiss her. He hesitated, but the knocking was becoming more insistent and then there was Dexter's voice.

"Miles? For God's sake, open up, man!"

Cursing under his breath, feeling a most unfamiliar sense of responsibility that he simply had to shield Alice from whatever happened next, Miles helped her to her feet. He looked at her. Her clothing was all still in place since he had not removed any of it to make love to her. On one level she looked quite respectable, though the muslin gown clung to her luscious curves, and her damp hair was starting to riot in tiny curls about her face, and she was flushed and pink. Theoretically one could not tell that she had just been tumbled on the floor by the worst rake in Fortune's Folly. Except…except that in her eyes was a mixture of slumberous satisfaction and new discovery that Miles found utterly sensual and he knew everyone else would recognize it for what it was, too.

"Miles!" Dexter's voice rose in urgency and Miles turned the key and opened the door.

"What the hell—" he began, then stopped.

What seemed to be the entire population of Fortune's

Folly was gathered on the other side of the door. As it swung wide, the deep silence was broken by a whisper of voices that grew to a torrent. He saw the expression on Alice's face shift to appalled shock at this intrusion of reality and he stepped in front of her to shield her from the prying eyes. He felt murderously angry.

"I'm sorry, Miles," Dexter was saying quickly. "I did what I could, but the magistrate is here. Someone has laid evidence against Miss Lister."

Mr. Pullen, the magistrate, pushed his way to the front of the crowd. "My lord," he said. "There has been an accusation of the utmost gravity against Miss Lister. The suggestion that she robbed Madame Claudine's gown shop of a wedding dress—"

"Outrageous!" Mrs. Lister interrupted, her feathered headdress wagging. "Madness!"

"And," Pullen continued doggedly, clearly extremely uncomfortable, "that *you* were a witness to the event, my lord." He drew a deep breath. "Can it possibly be true? Did you see Miss Lister outside the gown shop on the night of February seven, my lord?"

Miles turned and looked at Alice. Her gaze, wide with horror, clung to his. He felt a terrible stab of regret at what he was going to do and a helpless tide of tenderness for Alice even as he knew that he was going to betray her.

"Miles," she said. "Don't…"

Don't tell the truth….

But he had to. Alice had wanted him to reform, and slowly, painfully, against his will, he was becoming an honest man. He could not go back now. He could not lie when it suited him and still claim to be worthy of her. Alice deserved the best, not some scoundrel who had barely found his principles before he decided to compromise them.

"Yes, Mr. Pullen," Miles said, "I can confirm it." He turned to the magistrate, who was looking at him, his mouth open in shock.

"My lord?" Pullen stuttered.

"It is quite correct," Miles repeated. "I saw Miss Lister outside the gown shop on the night of February seven. I cannot tell a lie."

CHAPTER EIGHTEEN

ALICE SAT ON THE hard little bench in her cell and stared blindly at the damp wall opposite. The jail in Fortune's Folly was tiny—two cells only—and they usually held drunken villagers who had taken too much ale on a night out at the Morris Clown Inn. Tonight there was one such miscreant in the first cell and she was in the other. Mr. Pullen, apologizing profusely, had professed that he had no alternative other than to have her locked up due to the seriousness of the allegation against her.

The name of the person who had laid the complaint was still unknown to her, as was any information on what might happen to her next. Lowell had grabbed her hand as she was being taken away and had promised to come to get her out, but Alice had known he was as ignorant of the law as she was and had no idea what needed to be done. She could only hope that Mr. Gaines and Mr. Churchward between them would be able to help.

Even whilst Mr. Pullen was formally reading the charge against her, the crowd was shifting and talking scandal about her as though she was not there, the malicious faces of the Duchess of Cole and Mrs. Minchin and their cronies swimming before Alice's eyes like some horrible nightmare. The scent of Miles's skin was still on her, she knew she looked tumbled and taken, and she knew that everyone in Fortune's Folly knew Miles had had her like some cheap whore he had bedded at the Morris Clown Inn. She had felt utterly humiliated and did not know where to turn.

Then Lizzie had provided some much-needed distraction by emptying a bucket of spa water over Miss Caton's immaculately coiffed head and Miss Caton had screamed and sworn like a fishwife. Lowell had tried to hit Miles and had had to be restrained by Dexter Anstruther. Mrs. Lister had succumbed to hysterics and Lady Vickery had tended to her with smelling salts. Nat Waterhouse had finally managed to force the crowd to disperse. Mr. Pullen had taken Alice away and she had seen no point in making any resistance.

And through it all Miles had stood there, his expression carved from granite, as though he had not held her in his arms five minutes before and had not made love to her with such tender, driving passion and had never cared for her for a single moment. Alice had felt incredulous and confused, betrayed and bereft. She had seen Nat arguing with Miles in a furious undertone and Miles shake his head, and although she knew he was an officer of the law himself she had felt bitterly angry that he had not broken that law by lying to protect her. He had said himself that the terms of Lady Membury's will were wrecked so there was no longer any compulsion upon him to tell the truth. So why the *hell* had he not lied to save her?

Now, sitting alone in the little cell and listening to the drip of the water off the mossy walls, she felt little better. In fact, she felt worse. She knew she was guilty. She and Lizzie *had* broken into the gown shop to find

Mary's dress. She had forgotten all about it, but clearly someone else had not; they had seen her and had waited and had used the information they had to bring her to this.

None of it seemed to matter much compared with Miles's betrayal of her. Everything had happened too fast, with too little time to adjust. She shifted on the bench as the slight soreness in her body, the faint bruises on her skin, reminded her of Miles's lovemaking. She had been dazzled by the sensations he had aroused in her, feelings and emotions that were new and untried and yet somehow as old as time. She had barely started to come to terms with what had happened between them when Dexter had been hammering on the door and reality had torn apart her blissful dreams. And now she felt used and cheap and instead of bliss she felt humiliation. She could not wash Miles's scent off her skin nor seem to erase the feeling that he had imprinted himself on her body. The sense that she could never be free of him made her feel the most abject shame of all.

The slamming of the jail door made Alice jump and dragged her from her misery for a moment. She could hear her mother's voice. Evidently, Mrs. Lister had recovered from her hysterics.

"It's a scandal and an outrage. He deserves to be horsewhipped!" Alice had wondered what it would take for her mother to change her mind about Miles Vickery. Now she knew. Degrading her daughter in front of the whole village and having her locked up in jail had finally helped Mrs. Lister realize that he was nothing more than a scoundrel.

"Release my daughter at once, you poltroon!" By

the muffled thumps coming from outside, Alice thought it probable that her mother was attacking the guard with her reticule. Perhaps they would be sharing a cell shortly.

"Mama…" This was Lowell's more-measured tone. "Pray calm down. This is not helping Alice."

"I don't care!" More thumps. "Knaves and ruffians, all of them! You should be ashamed of yourself, locking up a young lady like this!"

There was the sound of a scuffle, which Alice presumed was Lowell forcibly removing Mrs. Lister from the jail before she became its next inmate. Then the door crashed again and Lizzie Scarlet's imperious voice rang out.

"Officer, I am here to confess to the theft of a wedding gown from Madame Claudine's dress shop!"

Alice pressed her ear closer to the door. Despite herself she was actually beginning to enjoy this.

"Can't take any confessions here, m'lady," the guard said calmly. "I'm not qualified for it. You need to speak to the magistrate."

"I have done," Lizzie said indignantly, "and he will not heed me. I want to explain that I am the one who stole the dress, not Alice!"

"Lizzie, be quiet." Alice could hear Nat Waterhouse now and he sounded exasperated. So Lizzie had turned to Nat in her time of need and Nat had responded. That, Alice thought, was interesting.

"You will do no good with such wild confessions," Nat continued. "I agreed to come with you to help get Miss Lister out, not to assist you in joining her. Officer—" his voice faded slightly as he had obviously turned to appeal to the guard "—there has clearly been some mistake. I am sure Miss Lister is entirely innocent of any crime."

"No mistake, my lord." The guard was at his most stolid. "Your colleague Lord Vickery identified her as the thief, and Madame Claudine is pressing charges."

Lizzie started to say something but Nat cut her off and miraculously she remained silent.

"I am sure that Lord Vickery must be mistaken," Nat said. "Miss Lister is no criminal. It can only be a case of mistaken identity."

"There's nothing I can do, my lord," the guard said, even more woodenly.

"I'll pay you to let her go!" Lizzie said suddenly. "Fifty guineas! One hundred! Whatever you want!"

"Lizzie," Nat said strongly. "You will not make matters any better by attempting to bribe an officer of the law."

"That's right, my lady," the guard said, sounding regretful.

Lizzie gave an outraged snort. "At least I am trying to do *something*," Alice heard her say. "The rest of you are imbeciles."

"Miles is trying to get Miss Lister out by the proper means," Nat said.

"Do you hear that, Alice?" Lizzie bellowed, making Alice jump. "Miles is trying to get you out. Sweet of him, when he had you arrested in the first place! I'll shoot him for this!"

There was the sound of a scuffle in the corridor outside and then Lizzie, her voice fading as she protested faintly, "Nat! Stop that—"

Once again the jail door crashed shut and the sounds died away leaving Alice in silence.

The candle burned down and the little jail started to quieten down for the night. The drunkard in the next cell must evidently have fallen asleep. The cold and the silence began to seep into Alice's bones, setting her shivering. She could not believe that her family and friends had all abandoned her to her fate and gone home to their comfortable beds whilst she lay here in the dark listening to the scuttering of the rats in the wall and the steady drip of water in the tiny closet. Would they return in the morning? Would anyone be able to get her out of this hellhole? Did Miles, whose fault it was that she was here in the first place, really care enough to have her released? The fury and misery stirred within her, a tight pain in her chest sharp with bitter loss. Twice now she had trusted Miles Vickery, twice she had loved him, and twice he had betrayed that trust. This time was even worse than before, because she had fallen in love with him with her eyes open, knowing full well what she was doing yet still wanting him and believing, oh, so foolishly, that she could make him love her in return.

She got up a little stiffly and made her way into the tiny closet. On the floor was an open bucket. Alice wrinkled up her nose. It was fortunate, she thought, that she had not been raised in any degree of luxury. Most young ladies would assuredly have passed the stage of having the vapors by now and would be insensible with outraged decency.

Having seen to her bodily needs as best she could, Alice made her way back into the cell and curled up tightly on the bench, huddling under the frowsty blanket in a vain attempt to keep warm. She must have slept a little because the next thing she remembered was the thud of the bolts being drawn back and the long, slow scrape of the door being opened. She felt stiff and cold from lying on the narrow bench, and her clothes felt dirty and slept in. The cell was in complete darkness, but as the door swung open, candlelight flooded in from the corridor outside.

Alice rubbed the back of her hand across her eyes. Miles Vickery was standing in the doorway. He looked as immaculate as though he had come to collect her for a ball. Alice, aware of the dust clinging to her skirts and her skin, felt grubby and cobwebbed.

"She's all yours, my lord," the guard said. "Glad to be rid of her. She's been no trouble but her friends and relations are a different matter...." He shook his head sorrowfully.

Shamefully Alice discovered that her first instinct was to throw herself into Miles's arms, cling to him and beg him to get her out of there. The urge to do so was so strong and overwhelming that she was shocked. And then, hot on the heels of her first instinct came fury, cleansing and strong.

"What are you doing here?"

"I'm here to get you out," Miles said.

"That's wonderful!" Alice said. "Since you were the one who put me in here in the first place!" She scrambled to her feet and stood facing him, hands on hips. "I do not want to see you, Miles, and I do not want your help. I hate you! Go away!"

Miles came into the little cell. His physical presence seemed to dominate the tiny space, almost overwhelming her. She backed away from him until she tripped over the wooden bench and he put out a casual hand to steady her, scooping her up and into his arms with almost insulting ease. Alice kicked and wriggled, inflamed with fury and with the knowledge that his hands on her body were arousing the sorts of feelings she never, ever wanted him to incite in her again.

"Put me down!" she squeaked.

"No." He was not even prepared to discuss it. He strode out into the corridor, where a cold breeze blew, setting the lamp guttering on the guard's table.

"Put me *down!*" Alice's voice rose as close to hysteria as she had ever been. "You think it is acceptable to…to make love to me and then to have me locked up in jail and then to come marching in here and carry me off as though nothing has happened!" She caught the fascinated expression on the guard's face and snapped, "Oh, do not look so surprised! I know the entire village has already heard that Lord Vickery ravished me in the spa baths before having me arrested!"

"Yes, miss," the guard said. "I had heard that."

"You see?" Alice said to Miles. "Everyone knows."

"They certainly will do if you keep shouting like that," Miles said. "Thank you, Compton."

"My lord," the guard said, shutting the door behind them with a bang. Alice heard the bolts shoot home.

"Put me down!" she said for a third time, and this time Miles complied.

Out in the street the air cut like a knife and little flakes of snow whirled past on the wind. Alice ignored Miles completely and set off along the lane toward Spring House. When Miles lengthened his stride to keep up with her she broke into a run, and he grabbed her arm to slow her down.

"Wait!" he said.

"I don't want to talk to you," Alice said. She swung

around so fast that he had to tighten his grip to steady her. Her throat felt dry as cardboard and she knew she was about to cry, and the very last thing she wanted to do was burst into tears in front of him. That she simply could not bear.

"I don't want your company," she snapped. "Leave me alone!"

"I cannot," Miles said. He sounded regretful. "I cannot allow you to walk home alone in the middle of the night. I am sworn to protect you."

"Which you did by having me thrown into jail," Alice said. "Excellent work, Lord Vickery."

Miles spread his hands wide. "What would you have me do?" he asked. "Lie to save you?"

"Yes!" Alice said. Her temper soared. "Yes!" she said again. "That is *exactly* what I wanted you to do, Lord Vickery. You were the one who told me that there were good social reasons for lying. Well, this was the best reason ever." She stopped in the middle of the road and planted her hands on her hips, glaring at him. "You did not even have the requirement of honesty placed on you anymore!" she shouted. "You had said yourself that you had broken the terms of our betrothal, so you were no longer even required to be truthful, and yet you suddenly decided that you are going to be excruciatingly honest and have me thrown in jail!"

"I had to do it, Alice," Miles said. He faced her down. "You didn't want me to be truthful just to win your hand in marriage," he said. "You didn't want me to be honest for three months and then return to my old ways. At the very beginning, when we made our bargain, you wanted me to reform." His tone roughened. "Well, you have reformed me, against my will and against my nature and tonight against my wishes. Do you think it was easy for me?"

"Yes!" Alice said. The fury was trailing little sparks of fire through her blood and it felt good. She so seldom lost her temper. "It was a damned sight easier for you than it was for me!" she said. "You suddenly feel you have to reform, and as a result *I* have been cold and hungry and tired and dirty and have had to relieve myself in a bucket! Oh, and I have been branded a criminal and a whore and my reputation is ruined. I hope you are pleased with the results of your honesty!" She tried to pull away from him but he grabbed her and held her tightly.

"Tonight I wanted more than anything to protect you," Miles said. His voice was shaking. "I am an officer of the government and I wanted to *lie* to a magistrate to save you but I could not. I wanted to be worthy, not because I had to fulfill the conditions of our betrothal but to please *you*—"

"Well, it did *not* please me for you to tell the truth," Alice snapped. "I might have known that you would discover your deeply buried honesty at this particularly inconvenient moment. Leave me alone," she added, struggling against his grip. "I am going home and I never want to see you again."

"You will be seeing me again," Miles said. "In fact, you will be marrying me as soon as I can fetch a special license."

He spun her around and into his arms. They closed like steel bands about her, holding her fast. "I have just spent the last four hours arranging your release from jail, Alice," he said, holding her still as she struggled frantically against him, "and trying to discover whom it was who informed against you in the first place. I have worked damned hard to secure your freedom."

"But you had me locked up in the first place!" Alice said, panting. "Do you expect me to be grateful?"

"If not to me then to Gaines," Miles said. "He did a sterling job for you. He argued that as you were outside the shop rather than inside there was no proof you had ever been inside."

"And the wedding gown?" Alice objected.

"He said that you had probably found it in the street, where the true thief had dropped it, and that you picked it up out of curiosity." Miles laughed. "He was very plausible."

"He's a good man in a crisis," Alice said. She sighed. "I suppose he was even able to come up with a reason as to why I was in the street at midnight in the first place?"

"Of course," Miles said. "You were there to meet me."

"I suppose you denied it?"

"No," Miles said. "No one asked me if it was true."

"So now I am supposed to have been trysting with you before we were betrothed!" Alice said wrathfully. "So much for my good reputation!"

"You have no reputation left," Miles said. "You are scandalous, Alice. Ruined."

The exasperation and anger swelled in Alice. "Mostly thanks to you! You madden me! Why did you have to decide to reform now?"

"I can't help it," Miles bit out. "Have you not heard a word I've said? Do you think I wanted to change? I was perfectly fine until I met you."

"You were ruthless and arrogant unreformed," Alice said. " I have yet to see a difference in you." The anger within her was starting to ease slightly at the sound of the irritation in Miles's voice. Clearly his reformation was not proving a comfortable experience for him. She stopped struggling and smoothed her fingers down the material of his jacket.

"I am not marrying you," she added. "I don't have to, now that you have broken the terms of our agreement."

"You *are* marrying me," Miles corrected. "You have not a shred of reputation left and if you do not wed me you will be shunned by society and incur all the scandalous gossip that your mother fears and that you have tried so hard to avoid. You know you would hate that and your mama would be distraught."

"The scandal is of *your* making, not mine!" Alice said, incensed. "You were the one who locked us in the spa baths and made love to me!"

"That is beside the point," Miles said. "And anyway—" a wicked grin tilted his lips "—I did not hear you protesting. In fact I seem to remember that you connived enthusiastically in your own seduction. You begged me not to stop."

Alice remembered. She felt a stab of anguish. No wonder Miles looked so pleased with himself. She had *pleaded* with him to make love to her. And thinking about it now, through all her fury and frustration, she felt like begging him all over again because it had been so unutterably blissful and she could not deny it.

"You are no gentleman to remind me," she said.

"I am as much a gentleman as you are a lady," Miles said. He dropped his voice. "You know that what you really want now is to return home to a hot bath and a deep feather bed and to make love with me again—and again—until we are both satiated. You know it, Alice." His lips brushed her ear, his breath warm in the cold of the night. He held her caged in his arms. "What we did was wonderful. Sinful and decadent and so very, very wicked but so delicious—"

"No!" Alice whispered. The low murmur of his words tormented her. Her pulse beat frantically in her throat. The heat pooled within her.

"I don't want to forgive you," she said truthfully, but even as she spoke she could feel herself weakening. "Damn you, Miles."

"Damn me to perdition if you wish," Miles said, "but you'll have me just the same."

Alice made an infuriated sound and grabbed him and kissed him hard. He tasted cold, tasted delicious.

"I am still very angry with you," she said as her lips left his. "I want to punish you."

"I can tell," Miles said.

He kissed her this time, a soft brushing of his lips against hers.

"Still angry with me?" Then as she made a tiny sound of assent he said, "You can settle the score when we get back to Spring House."

"I doubt it," Alice said regretfully. "Mama will be there, and Lizzie and the servants and everyone will want to know how I am—"

"No, they won't," Miles said. "Sir Montague has taken Lady Elizabeth back to Fortune Hall and your mama is staying with Laura at the Old Palace and all the servants are abed."

Alice looked at him. "Then…" *Damnation take it,* she thought. *I am no lady and we both know it but I want to make love with him again and he is right, I am going to do it.*

"What are we waiting for?" she said.

CHAPTER NINETEEN

MILES CARRIED THE FINAL pitcher of water upstairs and closed Alice's bedroom door behind him. Alice had set up the bath behind a muslin screen. The room was warm. Sweet-scented steam rose into the air, reminding him sharply of the time they had spent together in the spa baths. He could hear Alice humming softly to herself and the muted splash of the water. He rounded the screen and put the pitcher down.

Alice was sitting in the hip bath. Her blond hair was piled up on top of her head and tiny strands were escaping to curl in the steam. The hot water had stung her skin pink all over and she looked glowing and rosy, delicious enough to eat. She gave a little gasp when she saw him and made a grab for her petticoat but Miles whisked it out of her hands.

"Very virginal and modest, my love," he said, "but scarcely necessary now."

My love. The endearment had come easily to his lips, he realized. He felt a sudden uncertainty—a strange, hollow feeling inside—but he dismissed it from his mind. Later. He would think about it later. Right now he did not want to think about anything other than making love to Alice with a concentrated passion that would satisfy them both.

Alice was looking at him and her eyes were shy. He realized that despite her unrestrained response to him earlier she was still feeling diffident. This was so new to her. He felt a pang of compassion. Her gaze slid away from his. She crossed her arms over her chest.

"It's just…" Her voice was a little husky. "I know I am very plump," she said in a rush. "The ladies are always saying that I have a peasant build."

Miles felt a rush of fury. He looked at the voluptuous curves that were barely hidden. He took her wrist and gently drew her arms down. Her breasts were beautiful, lush and creamy with tight, raspberry-pink nipples. Below them the swell of her stomach and her rounded thighs looked so lavish and bountiful that he simply wanted to bury himself in her body and revel in the opulence of it.

"Sweetheart—" his voice was rough "—they are only envious of you. There is not a man on earth who would find fault with your body." He rested a hand on her shoulder, feeling the dampness and slick warmth of her skin beneath his hand. "Not," he added, "that I would wish you to put that to the test. The only man who can touch you—" he slid his hand down over her breast "—is me."

He wanted to tempt her out of her anxieties, make her forget everything but the need she had for him. At his words a smile had banished the anxiety in Alice's eyes, and Miles felt another kick of possessive tenderness. He bent his head to kiss her neck, tasting the salt on her, licking up the droplets of water that beaded the skin of her shoulders. Despite the heat in the room her nipple hardened against his palm and she sighed, leaning her head back against his shoulder to allow him greater access to her breasts. Her eyes closed slowly. As he continued to nuzzle the hot, damp skin of her neck, she gave a little moan, totally abandoned. Miles felt awed by her trust in him and more deeply, elementally possessive than he had ever felt before. Her natural sensuality delighted him. He knew and understood now the insecurity that plagued her because she had had it drummed into her so many times that she was no lady. For himself he did not care a fig about it. What mattered was that Alice was as honest in her passion as she was in everything else, and now that she had decided to give herself openly to him she held nothing back at all.

He cupped her breasts, toying with them until she was making little needful noises and arching back against him whilst his searching fingers sought her taut, pointing nipples. He squeezed the tips gently, then more firmly as she squirmed and the sounds she made became more urgent and desperate. He was hard as a rock already, but for once—was it the first time ever he had been unselfish in his lust?—he suppressed his own urges and the demands of his body. This was for Alice, the seduction he should have given her before.

He rested her carefully back against the edge of the bath so that he could lower his mouth to the place his fingers had been and could lick and pull on one tight nub and circle it with his tongue. His fingers ceaselessly rubbed back and forth across the other taut peak so that there was no escape for her from his seeking mouth and the exquisite torment of his touch. The sensation of her beneath his hands and his mouth was beautiful: hot, silken and trembling. He could sense she was wound so tightly that she wanted surcease. It was not enough. She had to be desperate for the release that only he could give her.

"Please, Miles…" She had opened her eyes and was looking at him with utter appeal.

"Do you like that?" His mouth brushed wet and hot across her breast.

"Oh yes, but—" a little frown touched her forehead "—I need to get out of this bath." The hot color deepened in her face. "I want to lie with you, to touch you."

"I want that, too," Miles said. He scooped her up out of the bath and wrapped the bath sheet about her, trailing water across the carpet toward the bed, where he laid her down gently amongst the covers. It seemed to take him an age to strip off his clothes. His hands were shaking, clumsy. He was not normally so inept. Yet the rich, slumberous blue of Alice's gaze as it rested on him seemed to make him even more ham-fisted. He felt a stab of alarm. He wanted this to be perfect for her. If he frightened her or gave her a disgust of him…

But when he came to lie beside her, all his anxieties seemed to vanish. She reached for him with the same openness and eagerness that she had before, trusting him utterly, needing him as much as he needed her. It humbled him completely. They lay skin against skin, without moving, and then she smiled, a smile that dazzled him, as she ran her hands over his body, and he felt alive beneath her touch in a way he had never experienced before.

"I had no idea," she whispered, "no thought that it could be like this…"

Neither had he.

He felt her touch him, her fingers a tentative, gentle

slide against the hardness of his erection, and he almost lost his mind.

"Yes," he said roughly. "Alice…"

He rolled her beneath him and kissed her hard, possessive in his passion, forgetting to be gentle. Her response swept him far away.

"I love you," she whispered, opening her eyes. They were a deep, drenched blue and there was so much warmth and tenderness in them that he felt a shock like a blow to the stomach. Something snapped within him then and he gathered her close, wanting to lose himself in her, knowing he could never be the same again.

She was already slick and ready for him as he slid deep inside her. He held himself still with her impaled beneath him.

"Marry me," he said.

She gasped. "That's not fair."

He moved slightly, growing hotter and harder within her. "Since when have I been fair? Marry me. Accept me freely."

Her body clenched about him and she gasped again. He thrust, unable to help himself. The tightness and the heat and the slippery sweetness of her pushed him beyond control.

Wait.

Dimly he remembered that he had wanted to wait, to spin out the experience, to give her time. He could not. The small, helpless cries of intense pleasure that Alice gave, the way that her body rippled around his as the intensity of her climax racked her, drove him on to a place he had never been, where the world dissolved into oblivion and he was free and at peace as never before.

"Yes," Alice whispered, and he found himself hoping desperately, as he had never hoped before, that she meant yes she would marry him.

He turned so that she lay in his arms, her head against his shoulder. She was already drifting into sleep, her eyes closed and a small, very self-satisfied smile on her lips. He felt her body shift and accommodate itself to the shape of his as though she had been made especially to fit there. His heart felt as though it was about to burst.

"I love you," he murmured, pressing his lips to the soft hollow beneath her ear, inhaling the sweet scent of her skin and feeling the warmth of her flood through him. The words felt strange on his lips. He felt afraid to say them in case they opened the gates to the old betrayals and he found that the past still had the power to hurt him. He would tell Alice about his father and all the secrets, he thought. Only that way would he finally be able to heal. She would be able to heal him. He knew it. She was so honest and so generous that she had already touched his soul.

"I love you," he said again. It was easier this time even though he had never, ever said those words to a woman before Alice. Perhaps, he thought wryly, he had been more honest in the past than he had given himself credit for. Not that Alice seemed moved by what he had said. She did not stir in his arms but merely shifted closer to him, soft and rounded and exquisitely perfect. Miles reflected that it was probably a good job she had not heard him. He was not very good at this business of love and when he told her next time he wanted to make sure he did it properly, when she was awake and he sounded confident of his feelings. This was all so new to him.

He wanted to make love to her again but he supposed that he should let her sleep. It would be selfish to wake her. It was his fault, one way and another, that she was so tired.

He thought about it. Could he be that unselfish? He started to kiss her gently, his hands gliding softly over the curves and hollows of Alice's body, worshipping the lovely yielding softness of her. She made a quiescent sound in her sleep and opened her lips to his and the desire flared inside him and he drew her back into his arms.

Yes, he had reformed. But not that much.

CHAPTER TWENTY

ALICE SAT TRYING TO READ the tea leaves and trying not
to feel too impatient. In the week since Miles had gone
to London to the Doctors' Commons to fetch a special
license, she had been cooped up in the house under
strict orders from him not to venture abroad unless
escorted by Nat Waterhouse or Dexter Anstruther. It had
been intolerably boring. She hated to be so constrained.

She missed Miles dreadfully. She had had no idea
that she would feel so bereft. Before he had left on the
morning after her sojourn in the Fortune's Folly jail,
he had held her tightly and told her he would be back
soon, and she felt sure that he loved her. She had felt
it in his hands as he held her and seen it in his eyes.
The lovemaking they had shared the night before had
bound them close. Dazed and dazzled by it, she had
drifted through the first few days of Miles's absence
as though in a dream, but gradually reality had intruded
and now she felt on edge and anxious. Lydia had still
not been found, Tom Fortune was still at large and
there was an air of tension about Fortune's Folly. Each
day Mrs. Lister would return from her trips into the
village, bringing the most astonishing scurrilous
gossip, and each day Alice was obliged to sit quietly
at home whilst the rain poured down outside and she

mangled another piece of embroidery and tried not to snap at the servants. In a vain effort to settle her nerves she made endless pots of jam from the stores she had laid down the previous summer. They would be eating plum conserve until Christmas at this rate.

The scandal of her seduction and subsequent night in jail had swiftly been superseded by another piece of tittle-tattle so delectable that the Fortune's Folly gossips had been overcome with excitement. Lord Armitage had jilted Mary Wheeler and her fortune of fifty thousand pounds and had disappeared off to London with Louisa Caton. Mary was said to be heartbroken. Then, before that *on dit* had been passed around the whole village, Celia Vickery had been caught with Frank Gaines in the library at Drum Castle, writing *novels*. This was a piece of news so shocking that even the most hardened scandalmongers whispered it under their breath. Lady Celia had been an author of adventure stories for boys for *several years*. Mr. Gaines had allegedly found out and had been assisting her with her plots.

The Dowager Lady Vickery had been in a terrible state for several days.

"How could Celia possibly have written such things?" she had bemoaned. "Adventure stories for boys? It is most inappropriate, especially as she is a *girl!*"

"She said that she was inspired by *Robinson Crusoe*," Alice said. Privately she thought that Lady Vickery should be grateful that her daughter had so successfully subsidized their household budget.

Lady Vickery looked scandalized. "Inspired or not, she is utterly compromised. Whatever will Miles say when he returns to discover that his sister is betrothed to Mr. Gaines?"

"I imagine that he will wish them happy," Alice said. "Dear ma'am, it might not be what you wished for your daughter, but can you not see how much pleasure they derive from each other's company? He is so very proud of her."

Lady Vickery's expression softened slightly. "I suppose he is. But adventure stories? Utterly shocking."

It was interesting, Alice thought, that Lady Vickery was conveniently able to erase the entire scandalous memory of her son's former mistress accosting him in the Pump Rooms, the subsequent seduction of her future daughter-in-law and her incarceration in jail, simply because she thought that Alice was rich and would save them from the poverty. Frank Gaines, in contrast, was considered a poor match for Celia because he was a lawyer with little money and no social standing. Alice liked Lady Vickery but she doubted that they would ever see eye to eye on such matters as rank and consequence.

The wind hurled another barrage of rain at the windows and Alice sighed. Was that a tree she could see in the tea leaves or a tower? Was it hope or disappointment? She could not be sure. Actually it looked like a large splodge of nothing in particular. She thought Mrs. Lister probably made the whole tea-leaf-reading thing up as she went along.

There was a knock at the door, and Marigold entered with a letter on a little silver tray. The silver tray had been one of Mrs. Lister's innovations. She had wanted to employ a butler to carry it, but Alice had insisted that their household was so small that they did not need one. Mrs. Lister had grumbled but complied. The tray was a compromise since Alice thought it simple enough to carry a letter in one's hand but Mrs. Lister thought it a necessary sign of rank.

"A letter for you, miss," Marigold said superfluously.

Alice took the note and unfolded it. It looked as though it had been dashed off in haste. *Alice, I need your help. Meet me at Fortune Windmill. Come quickly. Lydia.*

Alice's heart started to race. It was Nat who was acting as nursemaid for her today and just at the moment he was out at the wood pile helping Jim chop the logs. Alice did not want to deceive Nat but equally she did not want to tell him about Lydia's note. He and Dexter would go marching up to the windmill to arrest Tom, and Lydia would know that Alice had betrayed her confidence. She looked once again at the note. The writing was definitely Lydia's and the undertone of desperation was quite clear. This could be no trick. Her friend would never play her false like that.

Putting from her mind the knowledge that Miles would be absolutely furious with her when he heard that she had deliberately ignored his instructions, Alice whisked out into the hall and grabbed her coat and boots from the cupboard by the door. All was quiet, but she was shaking with nerves as she slipped out of the house and down the drive. The wet gravel slipped and slid under her hurrying feet.

Come quickly…

Was Lydia in desperate trouble? Had Tom betrayed her again? Alice lowered her head against the driving rain and quickened her pace.

Fortune Windmill stood on the hill above the village. It had only recently gone out of use, replaced by the new windmill built by the villagers a mile or so distant. Now it crouched in the rain like a great dark bird, the water dripping from its silent sails. Alice looked up at it and shivered. She wondered whether Miles and the other Guardians had already been there in their search for Tom Fortune. It seemed an obvious hiding place. The track up to it led away over the moors to Drum and beyond that to the village of Peacock Oak and eventually to Skipton. It was rutted and muddy in the spring rain. A curious, wet sheep stuck its head through a gate to look at her, but apart from that there was no one in sight.

Alice ducked in under the low lintel and stood waiting for her eyes to adjust to the interior. The air was thick and still. There was no sound but for the rain beating on the roof above.

"Lydia!" she called.

A startled bird flew out with a flap of wings. Nothing else stirred. Alice started to climb the twisting wooden stair up to the top floor.

When she got to the room at the top, Alice paused, looking about her. It was clear that someone had been there, for there was an old rug lying on the floor with a scatter of cushions and the remains of a meal. A mouse was feasting on some of the stale crumbs. Alice looked around, wondering if someone had already surprised Tom and Lydia here and if they had fled as a result. If so, they could not be far away. Perhaps she would wait. But there was something about the old windmill, crouching there like a malignant beast, creaking with the wind in the old beams, which was making her feel nervous. It was as though someone was watching—and waiting.

It was then she heard a footstep on the stair. Thinking—hoping—that Lydia might have returned, Alice went out onto the landing and peered down the stairwell. She could not make out any movement in the shadows below. The landing was quite dark, with light filtering in only from the cracks between the shutters on the platform above. Alice hesitated, aware of the silence in the building broken only by the creak and groan of the old sails in the wind. The darkness pressed in on her, and suddenly the quiet seemed so alive that it almost felt as though it was breathing.

Panic pounced on her suddenly, and Alice caught her breath, grabbed the handrail and started to descend the stairs rather more quickly than sense and caution prompted. She could not see clearly in the gloom and once or twice her foot slipped on the rotten stair. Her heart was beating in short sharp jerks and she could feel the panic rising in her throat. She wished she had not come. She had only wanted to help Lydia, but now, suddenly, it did not seem so impossible to imagine that Tom Fortune was the villain everyone believed and that Lydia had made a terrible mistake in running away to him and that she, Alice, had made an equally grave one in going to look for them.

On the first landing Alice stopped and tried to calm her breathing, telling herself that she was almost back on the ground and that soon she would be out in the daylight. She could see nothing but blackness below. The main door must have blown shut whilst she was upstairs, although she could not recall hearing the sound of it closing. She looked quickly over her shoulder, but there was nothing but darkness and silence above. She shivered, unable to shake off the feeling that there was someone watching her. Miles had warned her not to go out alone and she had done exactly as she had been told until her desire to help

Lydia had made her forget her common sense. But now, with her hand gripping the rail for dear life and the blood pounding through her veins she could feel the gooseflesh tiptoeing along her skin and for a moment felt absolutely terrified.

She began to count the steps down to the bottom.

One, two, three...

She paused and heard the echo of her steps above. But was it an echo? Or was there someone on the stairs above her, following her down into the dark?

Four, five, six...

She paused again, listening intently, every nerve and muscle strained and tense. There was silence and then the stairs creaked above her under the soft footfall of whoever was following her down.

Panic washed through her again. The footsteps had stopped when she stopped, and the building was deathly quiet, but she thought she could hear the soft breathing of whoever was above her in the dark.

Seven, eight, nine, ten...

Those quiet, furtive footsteps echoed hers, getting quicker and closer. Alice hurried down the stair, slipping, losing her footing for a moment as a tread gave way, every second expecting to feel someone reaching out for her or perhaps that push in her back that would send her sprawling down into the dark. She stumbled down onto the hard earthen floor, scrambled up and searched desperately around for the crack of light that would show where the door was. She heard someone behind her, breathing in sharp, short pants, and then her hand was slipping on the wooden latch and the door opened abruptly and she fell out into the daylight and ran.

After the darkness inside the windmill even the pale March light seemed too bright and blinded her eyes. Alice had lost the footpath and found herself stumbling across the moor, tripping in the heather and old bracken, cutting her stockings to shreds on the twisted roots and hidden rocks. She stumbled down a ravine and almost fell onto the road where she half sat, half lay winded for a moment on the verge until the rumble of approaching wheels roused her.

A carriage. Thank God. Someone would help her.

She scrambled up, waving her arms like the sails on the windmill itself, to indicate to the coachman to slow down.

The carriage passed her, then slowed to a halt, and the door opened from within.

"Miss Lister?" It was the Duchess of Cole's voice. For the first time in her life, Alice realized that she was actually pleased to see the duchess. It was an entirely new experience.

"Dear ma'am... Your Grace..." She was scrambling up into the carriage before she had been invited, before the steps were even down. "If I could beg for your assistance..."

She collapsed on one of the plush red seats, breathing hard, one hand pressed to the stitch in her side. She was vaguely aware that her mud-encrusted boots would be dropping little flakes of dirt all over the carriage, but that was probably no more than the duchess expected from one brought up on a farm. Henry Cole swung the door closed behind her and tapped sharply on the roof. The carriage set off again.

"You seem to be in some disarray, my dear." For once the duchess sounded almost benign. She was smiling at Alice. "Here, take a sip from this." She rummaged in her reticule and extracted a hip flask. "It is brandy and most restorative."

Alice accepted it gratefully and took a deep swallow. The spirit was fierce and burned her tongue but she was sure it would soon revive her. She smiled to think of the Duchess of Cole carrying a flask of spirits around with her. Wait until she told Mrs. Lister about that. Her mother would demand her own hip flask, with the family crest engraved on it of course…

"I am most dreadfully sorry to burst in upon you both like this," Alice said.

"No matter," Faye Cole said. Still there was that pleasant, almost warm, tone in her voice, which Alice had never heard from her before. "We were coming to find you anyway, my dear. There is something that we need to discuss with you."

Alice looked up. The sharp pain in her side was fading now, her breathing steadying, and now that she had time to think, she realized that there was something in the duchess's voice that sounded quite wrong, as though it had struck an odd note. Yet Faye Cole was still smiling in that gently benevolent fashion, as though Alice was the one person in the whole world that she most wanted to see, and Henry was nodding like a generous-minded godfather.

"Were you coming to see me to discuss Lydia's future, ma'am?" Alice said hesitantly. "I am sure she would be delighted to be reconciled with you both."

A pained look crossed Faye Cole's face. "Dear me, no," she said. "We want nothing further to do with *that* little strumpet. No, no." She smiled, but it was not a pleasant smile now and suddenly Alice felt a ripple of fear down her spine. Really the duchess was looking quite unhinged, sitting there like an enormous spider in her voluminous skirts, with that rictus grimace on her face.

"So unfortunate for you that Lord Vickery left you all alone for a few days," Faye Cole was saying. "But young men in love… Their judgment suffers as a result and I am sure he felt he simply *had* to get a special license after the events of last week. He has been so *very* attentive, has he not?" Her tone was indulgent. "Always at your side. Very devoted."

"Seduced you easily, I suppose," Henry Cole put in with a knowing smile. "We all know Vickery's reputation." He shifted a little closer to Alice so that their knees were brushing. "Scandalous," he added, smacking his lips, "but you are a ripe little peach for the plucking—"

"Be quiet, Henry," the duchess said as Alice recoiled. "There's no time to indulge your hobbies now. I want to talk to Miss Lister." She turned back to Alice. "Oh, I have watched and waited, Miss Lister," she said. "I knew that in the end I would have my chance. I knew that if Lydia called, you would come running."

Alice's head was spinning. She thought of the note, crumpled in the pocket of her skirt. "You mean that you *knew* Lydia was at the windmill—"

"Lydia was *never* at the windmill," Faye said sharply. "Really, Miss Lister, I thought that for all your dreadfully low antecedents you were still a clever girl! Did you not guess? The note was from me. I can do a fair copy of Lydia's hand."

Alice stared. Her heart had started to thud against her ribs. Her head was aching all of a sudden. The carriage had picked up speed without her noticing. It was ricocheting along the rutted country lane, rocking wildly from side to side. The pounding in Alice's head seemed to echo the sound of the horses' hooves. Surely one mouthful of brandy could not make her drunk, and yet the interior of the coach was now starting to spin in a manner that made her feel extremely sick. On the floor, tiny seed grains spun and danced, the same grains that had been on the dusty floor of the windmill, the same chaff that was clinging to Faye Cole's cobwebbed skirts…. Even as Alice registered surprise that the high-in-the-instep Duchess of Cole would venture abroad in dirty skirts, the significance of those grains of wheat hit her so violently that she gasped.

"It was you! You were in the windmill! You were the one who tried to push me down the stairs!"

"You have led something of a charmed life, have you not, Miss Lister?" Faye Cole said, baring her teeth in a smile that chilled. "Lord Vickery's quick reflexes saved you that day on Fortune Row, and after that he would not let you from his sight. He even managed to spring you from jail when we were so sure that we had managed to have you locked up and out of the way. And today, on the stairs, you were almost within my grasp!" Her hand moved with the swiftness of a striking snake to whip a knife from beneath her skirts and level it at Alice's throat. "Well, not anymore. Lord Vickery is not here and you are in our power now."

Alice put out a hand to grab the duchess's wrist, but even as she did the coach lurched again and her head whirled and she tumbled from the seat onto the floor. Henry Cole picked her up, his hands suddenly offensively intimate, his breath hot on her face.

"Opium," the duchess uttered. "My dear Miss Lister, you are going to sleep now."

Alice tried to wrench herself away, but she could not breathe, could barely think, and then the darkness came rushing in so quickly that it seemed all the stars went out.

CHAPTER TWENTY-ONE

LYDIA AWOKE SLOWLY. Her body felt pleasantly languid from Tom's most recent lovemaking and she was as warm and contented as was possible, given that she was curled up under a smelly old horse blanket on a prickly mattress in an old barn on the Cole Court estate. It had been Lydia's idea to take refuge at Cole because she knew every last inch of the estate, where to find food and where to hide. But time was passing and they were no closer to clearing Tom's name. In the last few days, Tom had seemed more preoccupied, barely speaking to her about his plans, though his amorous attentions to her were as ardent as ever.

Lydia stretched, relishing the echo of pleasure that rippled through her body, and reached out a hand to her lover. He was not there.

She sat up abruptly, the shreds of sleep driven from her mind by a sudden fear. Where had Tom gone? Why had he not told her he was going out? Why had he left her? *Was he safe?* Lydia's insecurities, barely hidden below the surface, rose and almost choked her. She scrambled up, tidying her clothes with trembling hands, grabbing shoes, stumbling to the door.

The cold wind hit her in the face as soon as she went outside, and the rain soaked her. She scoured the dark

moors desperately, giving a sigh of relief as she saw
Tom's figure walking down the track to the east, the
road that led down to Cole Court itself. Even now, as
a wanted man and with a price on his head, he had a
jaunty walk, a cocksure manner that Lydia had always
found so confident and appealing but that now, for
some reason, struck a chill into her heart. He looked
very purposeful. He was going somewhere—without
her. She started to stumble after him; she called out,
but the wind whipped the words from her mouth and
carried them away and Tom did not turn.

Lydia started to hurry. Perhaps, she thought, Tom
was going to Cole Court to ask her father's permission
to wed her. That was a nice idea. She had told Tom how
her family had cast her out and disowned her, how she
had lost her inheritance, and he had not seemed to care
much. He had told her that he was sure they would take
her back once his innocence was proven and their
wedding had taken place. Noble families, Tom had
said, hated scandal. Once she was finally and re-
spectably married it would all be swept under the
carpet and forgotten. Perhaps, Lydia thought, Tom was
so eager to wed her that he was going to plead her case
with her parents, proclaim his innocence and ask for
their help in clearing his name so that the marriage
could take place as soon as possible. The thought
warmed her even as the rain drenched her clothes and
made her shiver.

She had reached the edge of the deer park and was
about fifty yards from the road when she saw the Cole
carriage, driven at a breakneck pace, turn into the drive
in a spatter of mud and rather than make its way toward
the stable yard, veer off down a short track to where a

small, squat, rounded building sat on its own. Lydia knew it was the icehouse. Tom, she noted, had also seen the carriage arrive and now he moved toward it, cutting between the trees of the deer park, still ahead of her and still not looking back. Lydia opened her mouth to call out to him again, but then closed it. She was not sure what it was that prompted her to keep quiet, but a strange and unpleasant unease was creeping through her limbs now and seemed to be weighting them with lead.

The Duke and Duchess of Cole were descending the carriage, and Lydia watched as Tom sauntered across the grass toward them. She saw her mother stiffen, a horrified expression crossing her face, and her father straighten up very tall and proud as though he were about to tell the coachman to horsewhip Tom from the estate. But Tom was speaking; she crept closer to hear what he was saying, pressing herself against the stout trunk of a concealing oak, her shaking fingers digging into the rough bark. Suddenly she did not want him to know that she was there. There was something terribly wrong. She knew it. She wanted to turn and run, but hideous curiosity held her planted to the spot.

"Cole!" Tom sounded disrespectful, she thought. "I've come to talk to you about your daughter." He drove his hands into his pockets and strolled up to the duke and duchess. "I have Lydia," he said. "She is my mistress. My pregnant mistress." He gave Henry Cole an insolent look. "She must take after you, sir. She has an appetite for it."

Lydia felt suddenly faint. She wanted to put her fingers in her ears and blank out what she was hearing, to run as fast as her legs could carry her. But it was too late. Her knees were trembling and she could not run anywhere and some hateful, horrible compulsion to know the worst held her still.

"What do you want, Fortune?" The duke sounded testy but not as angry as Lydia had thought he might. There was something else in his voice that struck an odd note, something that sounded like fear.

"I want money," Tom said clearly. "I want you to make Lydia's inheritance over to me and then I will marry her and leave the country—since there is a price on my head—and we'll never trouble you again. You will be able to forget your harlot of a daughter. I'll take her off your hands so that she won't besmirch the Cole escutcheon anymore. But I'll only do it if you pay me."

"We don't want anything to do with that little trollop!" The duchess's voice rose to a screech and carried to Lydia on the wind. "Throwing herself away on you, and you barely even a gentleman. We'll not pay you a penny. Be damned to you both."

"Get out," Henry Cole said. "You heard her." He looked at his wife. "We don't give a toss whether you marry the chit or not. Get out before we call the authorities to arrest you."

Tom, Lydia thought, with a strange, cold detachment, was looking chagrined. *If only he had asked me, she thought, with the same cold clarity. If only he had told me he was going to go to my parents and ask them to pay him to take me—and my scandalous name— away. I could have told him he was wasting his time by trying to extort the money from them. Because they do not care what happens to me. And neither does he…*

Tom said something filthy and disgusting about throwing her in the gutter where she belonged with the other whores. Lydia covered her ears. The coachman really *was* going to horsewhip him now, and Tom knew he was beaten, turning away with one last lewd remark and walking off with as much dignity as he could muster. Lydia slumped against the unyielding trunk of the oak tree, the tears choking her throat, her heart pounding. She hated herself. She hated herself for being so stupid that she had trusted Tom not once, but twice, when he had never cared for her at all. Oh, he had lied and lied and told her he loved her and pretended he wished to wed her, but all the time he had been remembering that she had once been heiress to fifty thousand pounds and might be again. He was a gambler and she was his last bet....

He had lost. And so had she.

She straightened up. One day, she thought, I will tell Tom Fortune what I think of him. I will make him pay. But now she felt sick and ill and faint and all she wanted was the comfort of someone whom she knew loved her, which meant she must find her way to the village and seek out Alice or Lizzie or Laura and confess what a fool she had been again...

She was about to slip away from Cole Court and leave her parents to whatever mysterious thing they were doing at the icehouse, for really she did not give a damn about anything anymore. But then she saw that the groom had opened the door of the building and the duke and duchess were helping someone out of the carriage, supporting her between the pair of them. The woman's bonnet had come off, her head was drooping and her bright ringlets shone palely in the spring sunshine. She stumbled, dragging her feet as though she could not walk properly, and the duchess tightened her grip on her arm and said something to her.

Lydia caught her breath on a gasp. *Alice!* She started forward, but then checked herself as the duke and duchess steered Alice solicitously across the grass and into the icehouse. The iron door clanged shut behind them. The groom stood guard by the door whilst the coachman whipped the team up away toward the stables. Lydia stood staring, trying to make sense of what she had seen. Fear clawed at her. There was something very strange happening here. This must have been why the duke and duchess had seemed so ill at ease to see Tom. He had arrived most inopportunely for them, for what on earth were they doing? Alice had looked as though she was drugged. And now she was locked in the dank isolation of the icehouse and goodness only knew what the duke and duchess were planning, but whatever it was it required an armed man guarding the door...

"Lowell!" Lydia thought. His farm at High Top was no more than a quarter mile distant. If she could only reach him he would know what to do. Fear was making her legs tremble. She had never been particularly courageous, like Alice, or wild, like Lizzie. But Alice was her friend. She had taken her in when her parents had turned her from their door and left her destitute. So Lydia was not going to stand here and wait whilst Alice was in danger.

She released her comforting hold on the oak tree and slipped from its cover to the next tree and then the next, each time expecting to hear a shout from the groom when he saw her. Nothing happened. She reached the hedge and slipped through, and then she was on the muddy lane, her skirts torn and stained, her feet soaking and terror in her heart. She turned toward High Top and she ran.

ALL ALICE WANTED TO DO was sleep, but someone kept slapping her and pulling on her hair, and the sharp pain dragged her back from the darkness and forced her to open her eyes.

"Wake up, you stupid girl!" There was another sharp slap. Alice blinked, trying desperately to throw off the thick blanket that seemed to be fogging her brain. What had happened to her? There was a bitter taste in her mouth and there were images and memories at the edge of her mind, but even as she grasped after them they slid away and she groaned. She wanted to lie down but someone had forced her to sit upright, her back against a wall. It was bitterly cold. She slumped. Her head felt too heavy for her to support it so she rested it against the rough brickwork behind her.

The sharp slap came again, and Alice opened her eyes and stared into the furious face of the Duchess of Cole, so close to her own. She blinked, unable to focus as the duchess's features blurred before her eyes.

"Overdid the opium, old girl." Someone was speaking from close by. "Don't know why you had to bring her back here, anyway," the voice continued. "Damned nuisance. Should have finished her off in the carriage."

"Be quiet, Henry! I need to know if she remembers," the duchess hissed.

"Doesn't matter if she remembers or not, old girl, you've still got to get rid of her now." The duke sounded resigned. "Made a dashed mull of the whole thing, if you ask me."

"You were the one who could not hit a target directly in front of you," the duchess retorted. "If only you had shot her on Fortune Row, none of this would be necessary!"

"Remember what?" Alice said. Her throat felt rough and her tongue too big for her mouth. She did not seem to be able to form the words properly. "I remember nothing."

"You see!" the duke said triumphantly. "Waste of time. Knock her on the head now. Get rid of her like vermin!"

Alice drew back an inch against the wall. Even the tiniest effort made her feel exhausted. She was not restrained, but then she did not need to be. She could scarcely lift her head.

"Pretty little thing," the duke continued, sounding disgustingly like a boy wheedling for a treat. "Spirited little serving wench, just my type. Perhaps I could have her before we finish her off—"

His hand touched Alice's breast, stroked, and she recoiled against the rough wall, banging her head. Waves of nausea rolled through her.

"There's no time for your whoremongering ways," Faye Cole snapped. "We get her to talk and then we get rid of her."

"Pity," the duke said. There was in his voice the same geniality that had struck so oddly in his wife's tones earlier. They both appeared quite, quite mad, and equally quite unaware that they were. As her mind spun and scattered, Alice wondered if she was dreaming the entire encounter. Opium, the duchess had said. Or had she dreamed that, too?

"Talk, girl." The duchess's voice was edged with anger now. "We know you know…."

"I don't know anything…." Words were such an effort. Alice blinked to try and see through the shadows of the room. Why was it so cold? She could hear water dripping off the walls. It was like being encased in a vault of ice.

"That's it, then. Let's not waste time—"

Alice saw the duke's arm rise as though to strike her, and she turned her head blindly aside. There was no escape. She could barely even move, let alone run away. She imagined her head smashing back against the wall. It was such a ridiculous way to die, at the hands of these two. Would Miles ever know? They would probably throw her body into the millpond and no one would find her for years. No one would guess. The Duke and Duchess of Cole were above suspicion.

The duke's arm descended and Alice closed her eyes as a last defense against the blow, but Faye Cole caught him by the wrist.

"Not yet, you old fool!" She grabbed Alice, shook her. "Damn you, remember. November last year. Bonfire night."

Alice's memory lurched, taking her back to the night of the Guy Fawkes bonfire in Fortune's Folly the previous autumn. Once again she could see the terrible scene between the duchess and Lydia when Lydia had revealed that she was in love with Tom Fortune and her mother had attacked her like a fishwife on the quays. The stark horror of the duchess's denouncement of her daughter and then the discovery of Warren Sampson's body on the bonfire had made Alice forget what else she had seen that night, but now…

"I've remembered," she said.

The duchess's hands fell to her sides. The duke stepped back.

"I've remembered," Alice said again. She looked from the duchess's face to the duke's tomato-red one. "I saw you both on Guy Fawkes night, before the bonfire was lit," she said slowly. "You were struggling to lift the figure of the guy onto the top of the bonfire. I thought how odd that was, for who would imagine the Duke and Duchess of Cole helping to dress the bonfire? It is scarcely in keeping with your ducal dignity, is it?" She shook her head a little. "How stupid I was! Even when the guy fell off and Warren Sampson's body was revealed, still I did not suspect what had happened. But it was you, was it not? You killed him!"

The duchess gave a little triumphant crow, as though Alice had said something particularly clever.

"You see! She *does* remember!"

"You murdered Warren Sampson," Alice said again. "It was you, not Tom Fortune." With an enormous effort she opened her eyes to look at Faye Cole. "I suppose you killed Sir William Crosby, too," she said.

"Of course we did not, you foolish girl!" Faye snapped at her as though she was a schoolgirl having difficulty learning her spelling. "That was Sampson's work right enough. Crosby was nobility, one of us! Why should we kill him? But Sampson—" she swirled away, skirts swishing "—he was a nobody, a *beetle*. He wanted us to acknowledge him—we, the Coles of Cole Court, to invite a…a peasant turned merchant into our house? And he sought to blackmail us when we refused."

"Made me speak to him at the Fortune's Folly Ball,"

Henry Cole said, aggrieved. "Said he wanted everyone to see I had accepted him into my social circle. Damned scoundrel."

There was silence but for the monotonous drip of the water onto stone. The cold was biting into Alice's bones, but it was starting to revive her, as well, clearing the cobweb remains of the drug from her mind. She could see now that they were in the icehouse; she was sitting on blocks of ice packed in straw. They rose all around her up to the domed, thatched roof. Presumably the duke and duchess had brought her here because it was well away from the main house and the prying eyes of the servants, and it made a neat little prison with only one way in—and out. She knew she was not going to get out of there alive. She had remembered now—and in some bizarre way she had flattered Faye Cole's monstrous vanity in doing so, because clearly the duchess had wanted to boast about her crime, but now that the truth was out she would have to die.

"Sampson had a hold over you," Alice said.

"He threatened to have me tried over the death of some maidservant," Henry said. He sounded even more aggrieved now. "They found her in a ditch near here. Don't know what the fuss was all about. She was willing enough...."

The bile rose in Alice's throat. She remembered the girl that she and Lowell had found, the girl whose name Henry Cole had probably not even known before he raped her and left her in a ditch. She could not bear to think of it. Her mind reeled with horror, for Henry was coming closer now, his hot, rank breath on her face, his hands pawing at her again, excited by the thought of violence....

"How did you kill Sampson?" she asked quickly, desperately. Her voice was still croaky, her body felt bruised and aching, but her mind was sharp now.

Keep the duchess talking.... Don't let the duke touch you.... Use her against him....

Henry paused in his fumbling as Faye slapped his hands aside and came to squat at Alice's side.

"It was easy." Faye sounded excited, pleased to have been asked. "We invited him to visit us here. He never suspected a thing. An invitation to Cole Court! It was the height of his ambitions. I drugged his wine. And then—" she made a grotesque little twisting gesture with her hands "—we broke his neck."

The sickness rose in Alice's chest. She forced it down. "You hid Sampson's body, I suppose, and then decided to disguise it and dispose of it on the bonfire," she said.

"That's right!" The duchess sounded very proud of herself. "Such a cunning plan. Or it would have been had you not seen us."

"No wonder it was taking you such a great effort to haul the body up onto the top of the bonfire," Alice said. "If only I had realized!" She gave a bitter little laugh, angry at her own stupidity. "And to think I thought you were contributing to the celebrations out of kindness—providing the figure of the guy and even placing it on the fire yourself!"

"Of course, the problem was that Sampson was too heavy," Faye Cole said, in the sort of tone that made it sound as though she was discussing a difficult household dilemma. "We only realized that when the fire started to burn and settle, and the weight of the body made it roll off. No one would have known otherwise. He would have burned to a cinder and no one any the wiser."

"But it all turned out so well for you when Tom Fortune was suspected of the crime because of the ring he had given Lydia," Alice said. "You must have thought that you were safe."

"Oh, we did," Faye said. "Safe enough not to worry that *you* would remember anything dangerous. But then those incompetents allowed Fortune to escape from jail and we heard he had come back and we were afraid that it would jog your memories of that night, Miss Lister, and so—" she made a helpless, shrugging gesture "—you had to go."

"I missed you on Fortune Row," Henry said, sounding hard done by. "Used to be a good shot, damn it. Had plenty of practice with rabbits. Vickery was too quick and got you away. Damned nuisance."

"And then you had me thrown in jail," Alice said. "If you could not get rid of me one way, you tried another."

"Henry saw you and Lady Elizabeth that night," Faye said. "We were appalled—the daughter of the Earl of Scarlet behaving like a hoyden! We paid that modiste to lay charges and to say that she was the one who saw you, but Vickery got you out again with the help of that damned lawyer."

"Vickery isn't here to save you now, though, is he," Henry said. He put a hand on the neck of Alice's gown and ripped it away. "Perhaps I'll throw you in a ditch afterward, as well—"

"On the contrary, sir," a cold voice said. "I am here and *you* are under arrest." There was a scrape of stone and a shaft of light and then Miles dropped neatly through a gap in the thatch, landed like a cat and straightening, hit Henry Cole once, cleanly, on the jaw. The duke toppled over.

"Get up," Miles said. His face was white with fury. "Get up so I can hit you again."

The iron door swung inward, and Lowell ran in, closely followed by Nat Waterhouse and Dexter Anstruther. The duke tried to stumble to his feet and Miles felled him with another blow of such controlled and concentrated force that Alice winced.

"That," Miles said to Henry Cole, "is for Alice." He caught her in his arms. She felt the taut anger in him and the fear and the relief and the love. It was in the touch of his hands on her and the press of his body against hers and in his voice.

"Alice," he said. "Alice." That was all, but it was enough. His eyes were blazing. He bent his head to press his lips to her hair, and Alice felt so safe and so relieved that her knees buckled.

The duchess was wailing and crying as though her heart would break. Miles loosed Alice reluctantly and moved toward her, and at the last moment Alice saw the glint of a blade in her sleeve and Faye Cole's hand moved swiftly to strike, just as it had done in the carriage.

"Miles, she has a knife!" Alice called and, seizing one of the blocks of ice from the pile beside her, she swept it around in a low arc, hitting the duchess just behind the knees and taking her legs from under her. The duchess collapsed like a deflating marquee, the knife skittering away across the floor. The duke made a lunge for it and came up, snarling, the blade pointing at Miles's heart, but Lowell brought his hand down in a chopping motion across the duke's wrist and the knife spun away and the duke sank back down, groaning.

"My thanks, Lister," Miles said, hauling the duchess unceremoniously to her feet and handing her over to Dexter Anstruther.

"A pleasure," Lowell said. He grinned. "Fitting somehow that the Duchess of Cole is felled by a former servant girl and the duke disarmed by a farm boy."

"Alice, you were magnificent," Miles said, but then, seeing her sway, he grabbed her by the upper arms to steady her. His face was a white mask and suddenly there was so much urgency and fear in his voice that her heart turned over to hear it.

"Alice! I didn't realize... Did they hurt you?"

"No," Alice said. "I'm just a little dizzy. They gave me opium—"

The fury flared again in Miles's eyes. He looked at Henry Cole. "If that damned scoundrel wasn't already down—"

"I think you've hit him enough," Alice said, teeth chattering. "Besides, it was the duchess who gave me the opium. She is the one who planned it all, Miles." She shivered. "There is something...monstrous...about her."

"You can't arrest me!" Faye was blustering even as Nat and Dexter led her away. "Don't you know who I am? I'm the Duchess of Cole!"

"I must get you out of here, sweetheart," Miles said to Alice. "It's getting more crowded than a garden party, and you are almost frozen to death." He looked at her and although his voice was gentle, once again there was something primitive in his face. Alice thought that she would never forget the moment that

Miles had knocked Henry Cole down and she had thought for a moment that he would kill him.

"Can you walk," he asked, "or are you too light-headed?"

"I can manage," Alice said, clinging to his arm for support as he steered her toward the door. Her legs felt like jelly.

"Did you have to bring all of Fortune's Folly with you?" she joked weakly as she saw some of Lowell's farmworkers marching the groom away. "I am only surprised that you were able to persuade Mama to stay behind. I imagine she would have loved the chance to hit the duchess over the head with her reticule!"

"As it is you did the job for her," Miles said. "Nice work. Another of the maneuvers you learned to escape the attention of lecherous gentlemen?"

"Something of the sort," Alice said with a shudder. "Miles, how did Lowell come to be here?"

"Lowell was the one who sent for us," Miles said. "Lydia saw her parents bring you here and went to Lowell's farm for help. Lowell sent a man down into the village to fetch us whilst he came up here and dispatched the man guarding the door."

Lowell came across at that moment and shook Miles by the hand.

"So you two are friends, are you now?" Alice said, from the circle of Miles's arms.

Miles and Lowell exchanged a look.

"He'll look after you," Lowell said gruffly.

"I think that counts as approval from a Yorkshire man," Alice said, as her brother kissed her cheek and walked away. "I didn't think you would be back yet," she added. "If I had known…"

"If you had known perhaps you wouldn't have done anything quite so foolish as going to look for Lydia on your own," Miles said. "I'd just returned and was at the Old Palace looking for you when your brother burst in."

"You said that it was Lydia who raised the alarm," Alice said, remembering. "What was she doing here?"

A shadow touched Miles's face. "I will tell you all about it later," he said. His voice changed. "Fortune has betrayed her again, Alice. She is in a bad way."

"No!" Alice thought her heart would break for Lydia this time. "How could he?"

Miles drew her closer into his arms and held her so tightly she was afraid she would not be able to breathe for some considerable time. There was comfort in his touch, and sympathy for her anguish for Lydia as well as love for her.

"Tom is a free man now, I suppose," Alice said, sighing. "I hope he does not show his face around here though."

"Fortune is an out-and-out bastard," Miles said, under his breath. "He will get his just deserts in the end." He held her a little way away from him, his gaze moving slowly over her face, his expression hardening as he took in her ripped bodice and filthy skirts. "You gave me a hell of a fright, Alice," he said. "Next time I tell you not to venture out alone when I am away, will you obey me?"

"I hope," Alice said, "that the situation will not arise."

Miles laughed. "Now I have the special license, you will be marrying me very shortly. And then you *wil* be promising to obey me."

"Fortunate then that you saved me before Henry Cole knocked me on the head like a dying rabbit,"

Alice said. "Thank you for saving my life again." She smiled. "You would not want to see your heiress whipped from under your nose before you had a chance to save yourself from the debtor's prison."

"That," Miles said, kissing her gently, "was the least of my concerns." He released her. "Let's go home," he said. He laughed. "Let's go and get married."

CHAPTER TWENTY-TWO

THEY WERE MARRIED three days later in the little church at Fortune's Folly. Lizzie Scarlet was bridesmaid and caught Alice's bouquet. Miles had asked Philip to be his groomsman, alongside Dexter and Nat. Philip had been puffed up with pride at the honor and Lady Vickery had cried with joy. Lydia had been there, too, a silent, pale Lydia whose eyes were red from crying but who had come to see her friend wed because, as she had whispered to Alice when she had kissed her in congratulation, one of them deserved to have found a rake who had put aside his past for the love of a good woman. Alice's heart had bled for Lydia but later she had seen her friend walk away to sit quietly by the river and had seen Lowell follow her to talk to her, and she had wondered a very little. It would take a great deal for Lydia ever to trust any man again but perhaps one day...

The only sour note in the day was struck when Sir Montague Fortune announced that he was reviving the medieval Marriage Tax, which was to be levied on all couples tying the knot. Dexter and Nat had thrown him in the River Tune before returning to toast the health of the bride and groom.

"A circle with a dot in the center!" Mrs. Lister said triumphantly, looking into her teacup as she and Alice sat in the parlor at Spring House partaking of a quiet cup of tea together at the end of the wedding breakfast. "That means a baby, Alice! A honeymoon child!"

"Mama," Alice said, "that splodge in your cup looks more like a fish than a circle—"

"A fish means good news," Mrs. Lister crowed, peering closer. "Though perhaps it might be a heart or a horn…"

"It can be whatever you wish it to be," Alice said, taking her mother's hand in hers. She felt so happy that she was not sure she cared what swam out of the cup.

There was a knock at the door and Frank Gaines stuck his head around. He had been at the wedding breakfast earlier with Celia, but then a messenger had arrived for him from Harrogate and Alice had seen him speaking with Celia again afterward. It had appeared that hot words were being exchanged and Alice had wondered at it, especially when Celia had walked off, head held high, and had ignored Gaines for the whole of the rest of the afternoon. Now, she thought, he looked grim and tired.

"If I might trouble you for a moment of your time, Lady Vickery," Gaines said. He took the chair that Alice offered and sat down slowly. There was an odd expression on his face, a compound of pity and embarrassment. Even Mrs. Lister had noticed it, for she dropped her teacup back into the saucer with a clatter.

"A raven," she whispered. "Bad news."

"Mama," Alice said sharply. A strange, hard knot had formed in her throat. "What is it?" she said to Frank Gaines.

Gaines shook his head. "Mr. Churchward and I have been making the arrangements for the transfer of funds to clear Lord Vickery's debts, my lady," he said. "In the course of our discussions—" he cleared his throat "—it became apparent that there was an ongoing charge on the Vickery estate which must be honored." He stopped again.

"Please, Mr. Gaines," Alice said, trying not to sound impatient at the interminable legal language.

Frank Gaines gave a slight shrug. "In truth," he said, "it is none of my business but...Churchward and I disgreed... I said that the money was yours before it was given to your husband and so you had a right to know. I am your trustee and as such I could not do less than my duty though it pains me. I feel—" he cleared his throat and tried to loosen his neck cloth "—though it is not a fashionable view...that an intimate relationship can only succeed if based on honesty, my lady."

"I agree," Alice said, "but I am afraid that I still do not quite see—"

"None of my business," Frank Gaines said again, "but I would rather that you knew—"

"Is there a list of Lord Vickery's ex-mistresses who have all been pensioned off?" Alice inquired. She tried to keep her voice steady. She would have to be very mature about this, she thought. It might be difficult to swallow the fact that she was in effect paying off Miles's past lovers. But that was all over and done with now. He loved her now. She knew it.

"No, madam," Gaines said. "Not exactly." He took a deep breath. "Lord Vickery has in his keeping a woman named Susan Gregory who was once a maid servant in his father's house. Her rent and keep is paid from the estate on an ongoing basis, madam, and has been for eleven years." He hesitated. "She has a child madam, a little girl. She is said to be of Lord Vickery's fathering. She is just over ten years old. He visits them sometimes."

There was a long, long silence. Alice stood up abruptly, knocking over her empty teacup. Her mind was spinning.

Miles had a woman in his keeping. A maidservant. There was a child.

He had not told her. Even though he had professed to utter honesty, he had kept this secret from her.

The words repeated over and over in her head.

A maidservant. A child. He had not told her.

She grasped after something to steady herself and felt the back of her chair hard beneath her fingers. She gripped it tightly. Eleven years took them back to the time that Miles had quarreled with his father so badly that he had been banished. Eleven years before, Miles had walked out on his family, joined the army and become the hard, embittered man whom she had thought she had finally, finally reached out to touch and bring back into the light. But it seemed she had been wrong, for Miles had kept from her the most important secret of all, that of his daughter.

Mrs. Lister made a tiny noise. She seemed to have shrunk in her seat, dwindling under Alice's gaze. She spun around accusingly on Gaines.

"You should not have told her. She did not need to know!"

"Mama," Alice said, "Mr. Gaines was my trustee and he has my best interests at heart."

Mrs. Lister's face crumpled. "I saw it in the leaves," she said. "A lamp for secrets that would be revealed. Well, you are a marchioness now, Alice." Her voice broke. "Four strawberry leaves… You will just have to close your eyes and pretend that you do not know."

"I am sorry, my lady," Gaines said. "I only discovered today. Too late."

"Too late to tell me before the wedding," Alice whispered. She looked at him. "You told Celia that you were going to tell me," she said, understanding at last what it was she had seen between them. "She was upset. She knew about the mistress and the child."

"I am sorry, my lady," Gaines said again, and Alice's heart sank like a stone that he did not contradict her.

Celia had known. Lady Vickery must know, too. They all knew that when he was eighteen Miles had seduced a maidservant and the woman had given birth to his daughter. They must know that he was still paying for the upkeep of mother and child, but they all ignored it with the aristocratic disdain of their kind, pretending that it did not matter.

But it mattered to Alice because she had trusted Miles and thought that she knew him. It mattered because she loved him and thought that he loved her. It mattered because he had sworn himself honest and yet he had not told her.

"I need to think," she said. "Excuse me.…"

She went out into the gardens. The day was fine and the early spring buds were starting to show on the trees, new leaves unfurling bright green. The cool air kissed her face. A bird sang in the hawthorn.

A maidservant, Alice thought. *That could have been me.*

Miles had once told her that there would have been desire between them whether she was an heiress or a servant and it was true. Was that what had happened with Susan Gregory, the maid in his father's house? Perhaps they had been drawn to each other in mutual desire, for despite this betrayal, Alice still believed stubbornly that Miles was not the man to force an unwilling woman.

That could have been me, she thought again, *except that I am rich and so I am Marchioness of Drummond, and Susan Gregory and her bastard child have nothing but a cottage to live in and their upkeep paid quarterly.* It was something, she thought. At least Miles had not abandoned them as Tom Fortune had abandoned Lydia.

She found she was in the walled garden. She sat down on the bench close to where she had walked with Miles only a few weeks before.

Her heart was so sore she wanted to cry. He had not lied to her, she thought. He had simply omitted to tell her the truth. *You know that I have been a rake. I have never concealed my past from you....*

But neither had he exposed it. He had kept an enormous secret from her. It was no wonder that he had never wanted to tell her the truth of his quarrel with his father.

"Alice?"

She turned. Miles had come into the walled garden and was standing a few feet away, looking at her. For a moment his face seemed so dear and familiar to her that Alice wanted to throw herself into his arms and forget all she knew. She wanted to forge a future that was untroubled by the past. But even as she grasped after it she knew that it would be a fraud, based on lies and deception and pretence. She could not close her eyes, as her mother had suggested, and pretend that she did not know. Perhaps others would do that in her place. She could not.

"What is it?" Miles said. He came to sit beside her and took her hand. "Your mother said that Frank Gaines had said something to upset you." He was frowning. Alice wanted to reach up and smooth the lines from his brow, as though touching him would reassure her that he was hers and hers alone. Except that he was not because there was a woman and child who had a claim on him.

"Mr. Gaines—" Her voice was so faint she had to clear her throat and start again. "Mr. Gaines told me about Susan Gregory and her child," she said. "Why did you not tell me, Miles?" She looked up from their entwined hands to his face. He had turned chalk pale beneath his tan. "Why did you not tell me?" she said again. Her heart was breaking. "Why did you not tell me about your mistress and your child?"

"She wasn't my mistress. Clara isn't my child."

Even as he spoke Miles knew, with a feeling of utter desperation, that there was absolutely no way in which he could prove to Alice that he was telling the truth. If she chose not to believe him—and his failure to confide in her, his failure to open up and trust her, condemned him louder than any words—then there was nothing he could do except, perhaps, to break his word and force his father's former mistress out of her retirement and into the light. The damage that such a course of action would cause would surely expose all the secrets that he had striven to hide for the past eleven years.

Alice was watching him and he could read nothing in her face other than blankness and pain. She had not really heard him. She was hurting too much. His love for her stole his breath. From the very beginning he had been afraid to lose Alice and he had told himself it was because of the money, but now he knew the thing that he could not bear would be to lose Alice herself. The money was nothing in comparison. It was Alice's warmth and generosity of spirit and love that he craved. He was terrified of being left in the cold again.

The thing that he feared the most was about to come true.

"I should have told you," he said. "I should have told you about my father and our quarrel and why I have been estranged from my family for so long. Susan was my father's mistress. Clara is his child."

Some shade of expression came back into Alice's eyes and a little color into her face. "Your father's mistress," she repeated.

"I cannot prove it," Miles said rapidly. "I cannot prove to you that I am telling the truth, Alice. My name is on all the documents." He felt wretched. His future hung on the slenderest thread, that of Alice's trust, and what was so appalling to him was that he knew he did not deserve to keep her because he had not trusted her with the truth. He had never even told her that he loved her. He had meant to do it. Each day he had tried out his feelings a little further, testing his love for her and his ability to feel it, letting go of the dark past. But now the past had caught up with him and it had happened too soon because he had not told Alice the one thing that she needed to know.

"Tell me," she said, and he could not judge from her voice whether he had a chance or not.

"I was almost eighteen," Miles said. "I had finished at Eton and there was talk of me going to Oxford in the autumn to study theology." He grimaced. "Not a natural choice for me, but my papa wished me to follow him into the church." He shrugged. "Truth to tell, I was enjoying London too much to care much either way. I was young and I had a little money and…" He looked at Alice and shook his head. "Well, even then I was no saint."

He had not been. There had been women and drinking and gambling, all the temptations of town so new and so exciting for a youth who thought that he knew everything and in truth was young and naive and knew nothing at all.

"I arrived home early after a long night at the gaming tables," Miles said. "I had not lost too heavily, I hadn't even tumbled a lightskirt that night. Life was good—simple, easy. I wanted my bed, but as I walked in I heard a sound in my father's study and I thought someone might have broken into the house, so I went over to investigate. I wish…I had not." He looked up and met her eyes. "I had to break the door open," he said. "The noise roused half the household."

"Who was in there?" Alice said. "Your father?"

"My father," Miles said. His tone was harsh. "His sanctimonious Lordship, the Bishop Vickery. The man I had admired and respected, the man who preached against sin, was fornicating with a maidservant on the study desk. You can imagine what I thought when I saw him. For all my supposed sophistication I was an eighteen-year-old boy and I could scarce believe my eyes." He stopped. "It was a disaster," he said, after a moment. "People were coming running, alerted by the noise I had made breaking the door down. My mother, my sister…" He swallowed hard. "My father assessed the situation very quickly for a man in the throes of passion. He reacted far more quickly than I. He saw that we had an audience and promptly denounced me for *my* debauchery. He claimed to have been roused from his bed by the sounds of my fornication and to have come down to put a stop to his son's wanton licentiousness."

"But the girl," Alice whispered. "The servant girl. Did she say nothing?"

"She was afraid of him," Miles said. "I could see her fear. She did not say a word."

He saw Alice close her eyes for a moment as though to ward off the image, and he knew she was imagining Susan Gregory's terror and misery because it could have been her.

"What did you do?" she said. "What did you say?"

"I said nothing to contradict him," Miles said. "At first it was because I could not quite believe what my father was doing. I thought I had misunderstood him, that it was all some terrible mistake. I waited for him to tell the truth, but instead he railed at me for my depravity and shameless lust. It was quite a sermon."

Alice was staring at him and he was afraid that it was disbelief he could read in her eyes. "But surely," she said. "He was your father. Why would he do such a thing?"

Miles's lips twisted bitterly. "He was a bishop. He had his position to consider. Think of the scandal. There was my mother to think of, as well. Her family were most influential in the church." He looked down at their joined hands and suddenly he realized that he had been gripping Alice so tightly that it must have hurt her. He tried to ease his hold but as soon as he let go of her he felt bereft.

"I am sorry," he said, "I hurt you." And the words fell between them awkwardly.

He hurried on, wanting to end it now so that Alice could go if she wished.

"He sent the girl away," he said. "Later I heard that she was pregnant and had borne a child. My father made a great show of providing for them both, to atone for my sins, so he said, whilst broadcasting those apparent sins as loudly as he could. But by then we had quarreled and I had gone abroad. I never saw him again."

He stopped. He waited for Alice to say that it was the most unconvincing excuse that she had ever heard, that he had never once been honest in his life, that she did not believe a word of it. He waited for her to leave him. The silence seemed to last forever.

"You did it for your mother, didn't you?" Alice said softly. "You did it for her because you love her and you could not bear to see her hurt and you wanted to protect her. You were eighteen years old and you were betrayed by your father, yet you kept your silence for your mother's sake, and that is why you have never spoken of it since and why you push away the love she has for you—"

Miles looked up and she was watching him with understanding and compassion in her eyes and something split apart inside him and he grabbed her and held her in his arms and felt her hot tears soaking his coat and he buried his face in her neck and would not let her go.

"I wondered," Alice said breathlessly. "I wondered why you kept pushing them all away—Celia and Philip and your mother most of all. I wondered why it hurt you so much to speak of it and why you rejected me too, when I asked you."

"She adored him," Miles said roughly. "She stil

does. I could not take that from her. Not then. Not ever." He closed his eyes and unfurled his fingers against the curve of Alice's cheek. "He is dead now. The injustice of it should not matter to me anymore."

"But it does matter," Alice said. "You have kept the secret for all these years and taken the blame for a man whose duty it was to protect you. You were a child—his child! He forced you to take the responsibility and then he forced you to carry the secret forever."

"I could not live with the hypocrisy," Miles said. "That was why we quarreled. He argued that it mattered nothing because it *could* have been me, and he was right." He sighed. "As I said, I was no angel, even at eighteen years of age. I could have seduced a maidservant and made her pregnant and been as careless and as callous as you once accused me."

"But it *wasn't* you," Alice argued. She leaned forward and kissed him. "Miles," she said, "look at me. Listen to me." She cupped his face in her hands. "It was never your fault," she said. "Your father was the one who was weak. He was the one who failed you. You might have been wild but you were never cruel like he was."

Miles looked at her. "I should have told you," he said again. "I should have trusted you with the secret, but the truth was that I was afraid, Alice. I was afraid of loving and trusting ever again because I had taken my family's love for granted and suddenly it was smashed and gone and I could not bear for that to happen to me ever again."

"It will not," Alice said fiercely. She drew him back into her arms. "And the rest—all the things that followed," she said. "Your army career…"

"I joined the army because I had to get away," Miles

said. "I was angry and disillusioned, even more so when my father died and I realized how appallingly extravagant he had been as well as hypocritical. I suppose in some strange way I became the person he had branded me. I swore not to care anymore and so I took on the role I told you about, and with each step I became more hardened and cynical."

"You are lying," Alice said softly, smiling at him. "You have been caring for people since the very first, Miles, protecting your family, keeping your mother safe from the disillusionment of the truth. And Laura told me how much you did to help her, and how much you love Hattie. You even visited your father's mistress to make sure that she and the child were safe and well. Mr. Gaines told me."

"And you thought that I was visiting *my* mistress and child," Miles said.

"I did at first," Alice admitted. "What else was I to think when the evidence seemed so strong against you? But when you told me the truth I did not doubt you for a moment."

"That is the miracle," Miles said. He smoothed his hands over her, stroking gently. "How could you trust me, Alice? After all I have done?"

"I think it is because I love you," Alice said. A dimple dented her cheek as she smiled. "And, after all, you have reformed. You have become an honest man." She raised her hand to his cheek. "I love you, Miles, and I shall never stop."

"I love you, too," Miles said. He stumbled over the words a little. They still felt strange but they also felt right, a blessing and a promise. Alice looked up into his face and then he was kissing her with joy and gentleness, and she cried tears of what Miles hoped were happiness this time, and he kissed them from her cheeks and tasted them salty on his tongue.

"You *love* me," Alice said, breathless and rosy and glowing, when he finally let her go. "You love me!"

Miles started to laugh. "Why the surprise, sweetheart? Surely you must have known."

"I hoped," Alice said. "But I did not know."

"Well, now you will always know because I intend to tell you several times every day," Miles said. He scooped her up in his arms. "And to prove it to you."

He strode toward the house, in the door and up the stairs, past the scandalized faces of the wedding guests, brushing aside Mrs. Lister's anxious inquiries, taking the steps two at a time.

"What are you doing?" Alice demanded as he flung open her bedroom door and placed her gently on the bed.

"I am consummating our marriage," Miles said. He ripped open his cravat and shrugged off his jacket. "I need to prove my love to you as soon as possible."

"But, Miles," Alice said, "our guests are still downstairs. They will be wondering what on earth is happening. We cannot simply abandon them like this!"

Miles joined her on the bed and started to unbutton the tiny pearl fastenings of her wedding gown. "Of course we can abandon them," he said. He gave her a wicked smile. "And I do not think they will be in any doubt as to why we have done so."

He kissed her with hunger and passion and love.

"Oh!" Alice said, emerging from the embrace as starry-eyed as he could ever have wished.

"Yes," Miles said. "Now help me get you out of that dress. We have a marriage to celebrate."

IT WAS SOME CONSIDERABLE time later that Alice lay in her husband's arms and dreamily watched the spring breeze stir the drapes about the bed.

"How do you feel now?" she whispered against Miles's lips as he leaned over to kiss her.

"Very good," Miles said. He drew her down to lie against him. "I cannot quite believe that you trusted me," he added. "I was sure that you would leave because I was so slow to tell you the truth—and to tell you that I loved you."

"I had faith in you," Alice said, snuggling up to him and turning her face up for another kiss.

"I still do not think that I am a worthy enough man for you, Alice," Miles said a little later, "but perhaps under your influence I may reform further."

"I do not want you to be too good," Alice said, sliding a hand down his chest and lower to the taut planes of his stomach. "In fact, sometimes I rather like it when you are bad...." she added, her questing fingers seeking and finding his erection, which she was pleased to discover was already hard again. His shaft was huge and hard but as soft as velvet, silken and smooth. Alice let out a sigh of awe and pleasure. Gently she stroked, learning him, feeling so feminine and so powerful that a little smile curved her lips.

Miles gave a soft groan and kissed her again, deep and certain, and Alice felt her heart unfurl and her love for him stretch and expand like a butterfly in the sun. He had trusted her and told her the truth, she thought, as she slipped deeper into the cocoon of their bed and the warmth of his lovemaking, and had bound them all the closer for it. Maybe in time he would finally heal, too. For now all she wanted to do was pour out the love that she felt for him and hope that it could touch his soul. She stretched luxuriously as his caresses became more urgent. His lips found her breast and her thoughts fragmented. She was aware of nothing now but the hot tug as he sucked her into his mouth. The pleasure pain of it was exquisite, curling through her body, rippling deep inside her.

She met his gaze and it was dark with desire now. Slowly he moved over her body, his head dipping to lick and kiss each curve and hollow, lower and lower.

"Miles," she said, her body feeling as soft as molten honey, "what are you—" Her voice broke as he slid his hands under her bottom and raised her up. His hair tickled the smoothness of her inner thigh.

"I want to kiss you," Miles said, "just here."

He put his mouth to her and she cried out as the dazzling sensations took her. He thrust inside her, wicked flicks of his tongue that matched the rhythm his body had made when he had taken her before. Alice felt her body stretch and spiral unbearably tight as the feelings built relentlessly, and then one last wanton slide of his tongue sent her over the edge into the pool of pure pleasure below.

She was still gasping at the intensity of her climax as Miles rolled over, pulling her on top of him and then she was straddling him and sliding down and he filled her, grabbing her hips, greedy and desperate now. She bent to kiss him and their tongues tangled and he drove up into her, fierce and inexorable. His hands were in her hair and he cupped her face to kiss her more deeply and she met his heated climax and felt her own body convulse again as she poured out her love in return.

"I protest," she said drowsily, when she had finally

regained her breath. "Being Marchioness of Drummond is an arduous business."

Miles shifted beside her. "On that subject…" There was some tone in his voice that pulled her out of the sleep that threatened to claim her. She rolled over and opened her eyes.

"Miles?" she said.

Her husband, she thought, was looking somewhat nervous. "I have something to tell you," he said. He must have seen the expression on her face, for his own changed and he put out a hand toward her. "No more secrets, sweetheart. I swear it."

Alice relaxed again. "What is it, then?" she asked.

"There was a letter delivered," Miles said. "I received it just before I came to find you. I was going to tell you its contents earlier but what with our discussions, I forgot."

"Is it bad news?" Alice asked. She was starting to feel nervous now, too.

"Good news and bad news," Miles said, smiling a little. He drew her into his arms and pressed his face against the warm curve of her neck, and Alice breathed in the scent of him and felt dizzy with love and a sense of rightness.

"The bad news first," she murmured. "I feel strong enough to face it."

"I fear that your mama will not be able to bear it," Miles said, "but you are no true marchioness."

Alice drew back a little and stared at him, perplexity in her blue eyes. "Whatever can you mean, Miles?"

Miles laughed. "My esteemed cousin Freddie, the sixteenth Marquis of Drummond, is currently alive and well and sailing for an island in the East Indies. In his letter he told me that he had falsified his own death to escape his debts, has married his mistress and she is *enceinte* with what might well turn out to be the next Drummond heir."

Alice sat bolt upright, heedless of the bedcovers falling around her. "How dare he!" she said wrathfully. "The deceitful, irresponsible scoundrel! I would like to give him a piece of my mind! *He* wished to wriggle out of his obligations and so *you* were compelled to pay his debts instead. That is monstrous unfair! I hope you renounce his title and his debts at the same time, Miles, and send the creditors to hound him in the Indies!"

Miles drew her back down to his side. The warmth of his body helped soothe some of the quivering indignation and anger within her.

"That is the good news," he said. "We are not as debt-ridden as I had thought. Nor do I have the Curse of Drum hanging over my head anymore so we shall be spared the superstitious dread of our respective mothers."

He rubbed his cheek gently against Alice's and she felt herself relax further, sliding down in his arms. "For one thing only I am grateful to Freddie," Miles said, "for if I had not believed myself to be Marquis of Drummond and so desperately in debt that I was about to be thrown in the Fleet, then I would not have sought to marry you, Alice, and found myself the happiest of men against all expectation or merit."

Alice smiled reluctantly. It was difficult to resist his words. They made her feel very warm inside. "Hmm, you have a point."

"I hope," Miles said, "that now you find you are not a marchioness after all but merely the wife of a lowly baron you will still wish to be wed to me." He lowered his head to hers. "Can you bear it?"

Alice put her arms about his neck and drew him closer. "I think I will have to endure it," she whispered against his lips, "even if I am not entitled to any strawberry leaves at all now."

"Then I think you must love me very much," Miles said, "and there is something I want you to know." He frowned a little, as though he had something difficult to say, and suddenly she felt a little afraid, as though she was not sure she wanted to hear it.

"What is it?" she said. She knew Miles must be able to feel her heart pounding since she was held so close against him. He pressed a kiss against her brow, smoothing back her hair so that he could cup her cheek in one tender hand. Alice shook to feel the strength of the love in him, the love that she knew at last was utterly and completely hers.

"You may remember that before we were wed you asked me if I would be able to be faithful to you and I said that I did not know," Miles said. There was a smile in his hazel eyes now and they were so warm with love that Alice could feel herself melting inside. "That was never good enough for you. So now—" he held her in a tight grip "—I give you my answer. Alice Vickery, I will love you and only you until the day I die. I pretended to myself that it was your money that I needed, but that was a lie. It was you, Alice, that I could not bear to lose. I want no one else and I never shall."

"I think you have persuaded me, my love," Alice

whispered as her lips met his. "You speak very well for a mere baron. And after all—" she smiled "—I am only a housemaid turned heiress myself. I told you I was no lady."

"And I told you I never wanted one," Miles said as he kissed her again.

* * * * *

All's fair in love and matrimony in the next
installment of Nicola Cornick's
THE BRIDES OF FORTUNE.

Out soon
THE UNDOING OF A LADY
Scarlet by name…scandalous by nature…is
anyone man enough to take on Lizzie?

The Folly, Fortune Hall, Yorkshire—June 1810
A little before midnight

IT WAS A BEAUTIFUL night for an abduction.

The moon sailed high and bright in a starlit sky. The warm breeze sighed in the treetops, stirring the scents of pine and hot grass. Deep in the heart of the wood an owl called, a long, throaty hoot that hung on the night air.

Lady Elizabeth Scarlet sat by the window watching for the shadow, waiting to hear the step on the path outside. She knew Nat Waterhouse would come. He always came when she called. He would be annoyed, of course—what man would not be irritated to be called away from his carousing on the night before his wedding—but he would still be there. He was so responsible; he would not ignore her cry for help. She knew exactly how he would respond. She knew him so well.

Her fingertips beat an impatient tattoo on the stone window ledge. She checked the watch she had purloined earlier from her brother. It felt as though she had been waiting for hours but she was surprised to see that it was only eight minutes since she had last looked. She felt nervous, which surprised her. She knew Nat would be angry, but she was acting for his own good. The wedding had to be stopped. He would thank her for it one day.

From across the fields came the faint chime of the church bell. Midnight. There was the crunch of foot steps on the path. He was precisely on time. Of course he would be.

She sat still as a mouse as he opened the door of the folly. She had left the hallway in darkness, but there was a candle burning in the room above. If she had cal culated correctly he would go up the spiral stair and into the chamber, giving her time to lock the outer door behind him and hide the key. There was no other way out. Her half brother, Sir Montague Fortune, had had the folly built to the design of a miniature fort with arrow slits and windows too small to allow a man to pass. He had thought it a great joke to build a folly in a village called Fortune's Folly. That, Lizzie though was Monty's idea of amusement, that and dreaming u new taxes with which to torment the populace.

"Lizzie!"

She jumped. Nat was right outside the door of the guardroom. He sounded impatient. She held her breath

"Lizzie? Where are you?"

He took the spiral stair two steps at a time and sh slid like a wraith out of the tiny guardroom to turn th key in the heavy oaken door. Her fingers were shakin and slipped on the cold iron. She knew what her frien Alice Vickery would say if she were here now.

Not another of your harebrained schemes, Lizzie Stop now, before it is too late!

But it was already too late. She could not allc herself time to think about this or she would lose h nerve. She ran back into the guardroom and stole hand through one of the arrow slits. There was a nail on the wall outside. The key clinked softly against the stone. There. Nat could not escape until she willed it. She smiled to herself, well pleased. She had known there was no need to involve anyone else in the plan. She could handle an abduction unaided. It was easy.

She went out into the hall. Nat was standing at the top of the stairs, the candle in his hand. The flickering light threw a tall shadow. He looked huge, menacing and angry.

Actually, Lizzie thought, he was huge, menacing and angry, but he would never hurt her. Nat would never, ever hurt her. She knew exactly how he would behave. She knew him like a brother.

"Lizzie? What the hell's going on?"

He was drunk, as well, Lizzie thought. Not drunk enough to be even remotely incapacitated, but enough to swear in front of a lady, which was something that Nat would normally never do. But then, if she were marrying Miss Flora Minchin the next morning, she would be swearing, too. And she would have drunk herself into a stupor. Which brought her back to the point. For Nat would not be marrying Miss Minchin. Not in the morning. Not ever. She was here to make sure of it. She was here to save him.

"Good evening, Nat," Lizzie said brightly, and saw him scowl. "I trust you have had an enjoyable time on your last night of freedom?"

"Cut the pleasantries, Lizzie," Nat said. "I'm not in the mood." He held the candle a little higher so that the light fell on her face. His eyes were black, narrowed and hard. "What could possibly be so urgent that you had to talk to me in secret on the night before my wedding?"

Lizzie did not answer immediately. She caught the hem of her gown up in one hand and made her careful way up the stone stair. She felt Nat's gaze on her face every moment even though she did not look at him. He stood aside to allow her to enter the chamber at the top. It was tiny, furnished only with a table, a chair and a couch. Monty Fortune, having created his miniature fort, had not really known what to do with it.

When she was standing on the rug in the center of the little round turret room Lizzie turned to face Nat. Now that she could see him properly she could see that his black hair was tousled and his elegant clothes looked slightly less than pristine. His jacket hung open and his cravat was undone. Stubble darkened his lean cheek and the hard line of his jaw. There was a smoky air of the alehouse about him. His eyes glittered with impatience and irritation.

"I'm waiting," he said.

Lizzie spread her hands wide in an innocent gesture. "I asked you here to try to persuade you not to go through with the wedding," she said. She looked at him in appeal. "You know she will bore you within five minutes, Nat. No," she corrected herself. "You are already bored with her, aren't you, and you are not even wed yet. And you don't give a rush for her, either. You are making a terrible mistake."

Lizzie's heart hammered in her throat. "Which is why I had to do this, Nat. It's for your own good."

Fury was fast replacing the irritation in his eyes. "Do what?" he said. Then, as she did not reply, "Do what, Lizzie?"

"I've locked you in," Lizzie said rapidly. "I promise that I will release you tomorrow—when the hour of the wedding is past. I doubt that Flora or her parents will forgive you the slight of standing her up at the altar."

Nat's gaze stripped her, suddenly shockingly insolent. "Give me the key. I suppose you have hidden it about your person."

"No, I have not!" Lizzie was taken aback both by his tone and the look in his eyes. He had never looked at her like that before, as though she was some Covent Garden whore displaying her wares for the purchase. She felt humiliated; she told herself she was livid. Yet something in her, something shocking and primitive, liked it well enough. The blood warmed beneath her skin, the heat rolling through her body from her cheeks down to her toes and back up again, setting her afire.

Nat grabbed her so quickly she did not even see him move. His hands passed over her body—intimate, knowing hands, seeking and searching. The goose bumps rose all over her skin, following the path of his touch. The heat intensified inside her, burning hotter than a furnace. She squirmed within his grip, protesting against the humiliation of his restraint and her body's response to it.

"Give me the key and we'll forget this ever happened," he said.

It was too late for that, and they both knew it.

REQUEST YOUR FREE BOOKS!

2 FREE NOVELS
FROM THE ROMANCE/SUSPENSE
COLLECTION PLUS 2 FREE GIFTS!

YES! Please send me 2 FREE novels from the Romance/Suspense Collectic and my 2 FREE gifts (gifts are worth about $10). After receiving them, if I don't wis to receive any more books, I can return the shipping statement marked "cancel." If don't cancel, I will receive 4 brand-new novels every month and be billed just $5.7 per book in the U.S. or $6.24 per book in Canada. That's a savings of at least 28° off the cover price. It's quite a bargain! Shipping and handling is just 50¢ per book I understand that accepting the 2 free books and gifts places me under no obligatio to buy anything. I can always return a shipment and cancel at any time. Even if never buy another book from the Reader Service, the two free books and gifts ar mine to keep forever.   185 MDN EYNQ   385 MDN EYN

Name	(PLEASE PRINT)
Address	Apt. #
City	State/Prov.	Zip/Postal Code

Signature (if under 18, a parent or guardian must sign)

Mail to **The Reader Service:**
IN U.S.A.: P.O. Box 1867, Buffalo, NY 14240-1867
IN CANADA: P.O. Box 609, Fort Erie, Ontario L2A 5X3

Not valid to current subscribers of the Romance Collection,
the Suspense Collection or the Romance/Suspense Collection.

Want to try two free books from another line?
Call 1-800-873-8635 or visit www.morefreebooks.com.

* Terms and prices subject to change without notice. Prices do not include applicable taxes. Sale tax applicable in N.Y. Canadian residents will be charged applicable provincial taxes and GS Offer not valid in Quebec. This offer is limited to one order per household. All orders subje to approval. Credit or debit balances in a customer's account(s) may be offset by any oth outstanding balance owed by or to the customer. Please allow 4 to 6 weeks for delivery. Off available while quantities last.

Your Privacy: Harlequin is committed to protecting your privacy. Our Privac Policy is available online at www.eHarlequin.com or upon request from the Reade Service. From time to time we make our lists of customers available to reputab third parties who may have a product or service of interest to you. If you would prefer we not share your name and address, please check here. ☐

NICOLA CORNICK

77377	THE CONFESSIONS OF A DUCHESS	___ $7.99 U.S.	___ $8.99 CAN
77303	UNMASKED	___ $6.99 U.S.	___ $6.99 CAN
77211	LORD OF SCANDAL	___ $6.99 U.S.	___ $8.50 CAN

(limited quantities available)

TOTAL AMOUNT	$ _____
POSTAGE & HANDLING	$ _____
($1.00 FOR 1 BOOK, 50¢ for each additional)	
APPLICABLE TAXES*	$ _____
TOTAL PAYABLE	$ _____

(check or money order—please do not send cash)

To order, complete this form and send it, along with a check or money order for the total above, payable to HQN Books, to: **In the U.S.** 3010 Walden Avenue, P.O. Box 9077, Buffalo, NY 14269-9077, **In Canada:** P.O. Box 636, Fort Erie, Ontario, L2A 5X3.

Name: _____
Address: _____ City: _____
State/Prov.: _____ Zip/Postal Code: _____
Account Number (if applicable): _____

075 CSAS

*New York residents remit applicable sales taxes.
*Canadian residents remit applicable GST and provincial taxes.

HQN™

We *are* romance™

www.HQNBooks.com